"T. I. Lowe mixes serious issues with her own unique sense of humor and style, and her Sonny Bates is a force to reckon with. . . . A terrific read!"

FRANCINE RIVERS, *New York Times* bestselling author of *Redeeming Love* and *The Lady's Mine*, on *Indigo Isle*

"Lowe delivers a powerful coming-of-age story set on a Magnolia, S.C., tobacco farm in the 1980s. . . . The many colorful Magnolia characters, particularly the eccentrics of First Riffraff, rise to support Austin and nicely round out the slow-burning romance. Lowe's fans will be thrilled."

PUBLISHERS WEEKLY on *Under the Magnolias*

"*Under the Magnolias* is a beautifully told tale about loss, mental illness, connection, and finding both yourself and your capacity to heal."

GRAND STRAND MAGAZINE

"A family's collapse under the weight of dysfunction and mental illness becomes a luminous testimony to the power of neighbors and the ability of a community's love and faith to shelter its most vulnerable residents. Readers will close the cover with a smile and a long, satisfied sigh."

LISA WINGATE, #1 *New York Times* bestselling author of *Before We Were Yours* and *The Book of Lost Friends*, on *Under the Magnolias*

"With lyrical prose and vivid description, T. I. Lowe masterfully weaves the story of a teenage girl's quest to protect the ones she loves most in the wake of unthinkable tragedy. *Under the Magnolias* is a moving portrayal of the power of family—the one we're born into and the one we create—and the resilience of the human spirit. In this memorable and moving story, T. I. Lowe has hit her stride."

KRISTY WOODSON HARVEY, *USA Today* bestselling author of *Feels Like Falling*

"T. I. Lowe has done it again! I loved *Lulu's Café*, but I love *Under the Magnolias* even more. There is so much to admire about this book. T. I. writes with amazing grace and beautifully depicts the cost of keeping secrets when help might be available. This story is filled with rich, lovable characters, each rendered with profound compassion. Austin is an admirable young woman—flawed, but faithful to her family—and Vance Cumberland is another Michael Hosea, offering unconditional, lifelong love. *Under the Magnolias* is sure to delight and inspire."

FRANCINE RIVERS, *New York Times* bestselling author

"On a tobacco farm in 1980s South Carolina, we meet smart and spunky Austin as she struggles to keep the family farm together and raise her six siblings and mentally ill father. With a wide cast of fun, offbeat characters, a mix of heartbreak and humor, and a heaping handful of grit, *Under the Magnolias* will delight Lowe's legion of fans!"

LAUREN K. DENTON, *USA Today* bestselling author of *The Summer House*

"What a voice! If you're looking for your next Southern fiction fix, T. I. Lowe delivers. Readers of all ages will adore the spunky survivor Austin Foster, whose journey delivers both laughter and tears. Set smack-dab in the middle of South Carolina, this story will break your heart and put it back together again. A must-read."

JULIE CANTRELL, *New York Times* and *USA Today* bestselling author of *Perennials,* on *Under the Magnolias*

"Plain-speaking and gut-wrenching, T. I. Lowe leaves no detail unturned to deliver a powerful story about a family's need for healing and their lifelong efforts to run from it. This is no 'will they or won't they' romance. Rather, it's a thorough exploration of the hidden depths of the heart."

ROBIN W. PEARSON, Christy Award–winning author of *A Long Time Comin'* and *'Til I Want No More,* on *Under the Magnolias*

"I loved *Under the Magnolias!* . . . Austin Foster is one of the most memorable characters I have ever read."

SESSALEE HENSLEY, Barnes & Noble fiction buyer, retired

INDIGO ISLE

T. I. LOWE

INDIGO ISLE

a novel

Tyndale House Publishers
Carol Stream, Illinois

Visit Tyndale online at tyndale.com.

Visit T. I. Lowe's website at tilowe.com.

Tyndale and Tyndale's quill logo are registered trademarks of Tyndale House Ministries.

Indigo Isle

Designed by Lindsey Bergsma

Edited by Kathryn S. Olson

Published in association with the literary agency of Browne & Miller Literary Associates, LLC, 52 Village Place, Hinsdale, IL 60521

For information about special discounts for bulk purchases, please contact Tyndale House Publishers at csresponse@tyndale.com, or call 1-855-277-9400.

Library of Congress Cataloging-in-Publication Data

A catalog record for this book is available from the Library of Congress.

ISBN 978-1-4964-6559-7 (HC)
ISBN 978-1-4964-6560-3 (SC)

Printed in the United States of America

29	28	27	26	25	24	23
7	6	5	4	3	2	1

To Vicki Baty
Thank you for going on this Indigo Adventure
with me, my friend.

I will search for my lost ones who have strayed away,

and I will bring them safely home again.

EZEKIEL 34:16

CHAPTER ONE

So this is how it feels to be near death and utterly alone.

I turned this idea around in my head while sequestered inside the cavernous space. The cold cement slab underneath my limp body held a cool comfort compared to the sultry heat seeping through the opening in thick vapors. A heat unique to the Lowcountry, disguising itself as a body of water without having enough clout to pull it off. Oh, but it had no problem pulling off misery.

A haughty huff interrupted my train of thought. "Come on, Sonny. How much longer do you plan on lying in that crypt?"

I peeped an eye open and addressed the mermaid mane flaring out from behind my Canon EOS camera. "This isn't a crypt. It's a receiving tomb."

The camera inched down, revealing a pouty, confused face. "A what?"

"It's where undertakers used to place a corpse until the grave or mausoleum was complete. I believe this one held up to four bodies at once. Sometimes they would have to lie up in here for months if the ground was frozen in the winter. Can you imagine?"

"You're, like, lying where dead bodies have been." Lyrica's tattooed shoulders shuddered.

"They aren't here anymore." I crossed my arms over my chest, striking another deathly pose. "Get a few more photos of me."

Lyrica sucked her teeth, sounding more like a sulky teen instead of a grown woman in her midtwenties, and waved a glittery clawed hand in my direction. "This is seriously creepy. I'm ready to go."

"Then capture an Instagram-worthy shot and we'll be done." My eyes drifted shut and I went slack-jawed.

She bellyached about this *so not being her life*, but then the clicking sound of the camera went off several times in quick succession. "Doesn't it stink in there?"

"Not too bad, really." I pulled in a deep sniff, trying to detect exactly what the odd scent held. "The smell kinda reminds me of a damp fall day. Ya know? Decaying leaves and ammonia maybe . . ."

"Eww." Lyrica made a gagging sound. "I'm so over this already. And I'm melting in this heat."

I slid over and patted the cement shelf. "It's cooler in here. Want to join me?"

Lyrica rolled her fake-blue eyes that were the same shade as one of the teal streaks in her hair, letting me know she wasn't into my brand of humor. "I want air-conditioning. And a fruity cocktail on one of those islands we're supposed to be scouting. Not hanging out in a freaking cemetery. Daddy promised islands."

Watching her tug on the hem of her too-short shorts, I could almost hear my mom say, *"If you have to tug, it's too tiny."* I wondered if there was anything potentially pleasant underneath all the hair dye, makeup, and attitude. The five-hour flight from

California to South Carolina only revealed a spoiled brat thinking she wanted to give location scouting a whirl. Of course, Famous Director Daddy made that happen for his Technicolor princess. We'd only landed in Charleston less than two hours ago and I was ready to haul her back to the airport. About as round as she was tall, Lyrica was loud and refused to be ignored. I planned to make it my mission in life to ignore her theatrics as much as possible during this project.

Giving up on the idea of capturing the perfect picture, I scooted off the shelf and exited the tomb. Lyrica handed me the camera as we walked up the dirt path, dodging fresh mudholes from a recent rain shower. I paused underneath a lemony fragrant magnolia tree and took a picture of myself with my phone.

"Selfie much?" Lyrica sassed, fanning herself with a flyer she'd grabbed at the front gate that advertised a nighttime grave tour.

"Gotta keep my followers engaged," I mumbled while applying a filter and captioning it with #underthemagnolias. I added Magnolia Cemetery's location and sent it off into the social media universe before we moved along. "Let's take a few more pictures of that mausoleum shaped like a pyramid before heading to the islands."

Lyrica swatted at a fly, walking heavy footed beside me. "I don't recall a cemetery scene in *Beyond the Waves*."

"There isn't. This is some preliminary work for my next project." The very project that got pushed back by the king of movie production Whit Kessler, who made sure it fell on me to step in and clean up the mess made by his latest dalliance. The former teenage heartthrob–turned–producer couldn't keep it in his pants for the life of him.

"Aren't all cemeteries the same?" Lyrica scrunched her nose, looking unimpressed and perhaps offended by the low tide stench surrounding us.

"No. The script calls for a vastly large cemetery with deep Southern elements, such as the salt marsh and moss-draped oak trees." I waved a hand toward the graves stretching out well past what the eye could see while explaining the concept for a kidnapping scene in the psychological thriller.

Lyrica yawned. "Can we move this along? I'm so thirsty."

Trying to smother my snide retort was about as easy as smothering a biscuit with congealed gravy, but I somehow managed it by focusing on something more pleasant than my current work predicament. The dead.

After getting a few more angles of the pyramid tomb, we retraced our steps through one of the largest cemeteries in South Carolina, pausing at the entrance so I could drop a fifty in the donation box.

We walked across the street and loaded up in the rental car, a white Chevrolet Impala. Most things from my past were kept firmly in the past, but my dad's loyalty to Chevrolet stayed with me.

Not wanting to get tangled in the memory of my dad that always led to ruminating on the crime I committed against him, I cranked the air conditioner control to arctic at Lyrica's whiny demand. While she moaned as if she were dying, I made quick work of loading the photos to my laptop and then sending them to the production team.

With the graveyard research marked off the list, I switched film gears and put the car in gear as well to begin the short trek across the Ravenel Bridge, which straddled the Cooper River and connected downtown Charleston with Mount Pleasant.

"I've chartered a boat to take us out and around the barrier islands. Also . . ." I started to launch into a list of must-haves I had jotted down on the plane while reading through the script for the first time, but Lyrica turned the radio up and started belting out a Chris Stapleton song. Her voice was a robust mix of Elvis and Adele. Not bad, but not appreciated when it cut me off midthought.

Her father, *the* Academy Award–winning Les Morgan, had actually called me, *the* nobody Sonny Bates, this morning on my way to LAX. *"Bates, teach my kid all you know. Make it happen."* Then he ended the call as abruptly as he'd started it.

I cut my eyes over to Lyrica as she played her air guitar and concluded it *ain't* happening. What had to happen, however, was for the perfect island location to magically appear within the next few days. Today, preferably.

The art director's description came to mind as I tapped my fingers against the steering wheel. *Think Lowcountry charm meets island affairs.* The moment I sat down in the production meeting in our LA office and heard the words "coastal South Carolina" and "barrier islands," I had a foreboding sense that this location could very well lead to a day of reckoning. Maybe not right away, but it was coming. The dread to face it all was thicker than the pluff mud I smelled from the nearby marshland as the car crossed the second mile of the cable-stayed bridge.

Knowing there was a line of location manager wannabes behind me who would jump at the chance to take my job, I had no other choice but to agree to go to Charleston and find a last-minute replacement location for the one that had fallen through with filming scheduled to begin in only two weeks. Of course, that meant putting up with Whit in close proximity for at least eight weeks, but I had no choice in that matter either. Funny how I ran away a little over fifteen years ago to spread my wings and fly, yet I'd never felt so caged as I did currently.

Fifteen minutes later, I'd snagged a parking spot and bought Lyrica a Gatorade just before she wilted completely under the Southern June sky. *Bless her heart.*

"This marina would be ideal for some charming B-roll footage," I mumbled to myself while taking it all in. Quaint shops and restaurants lined the congested area, and an assortment of boats bobbled languidly by the docks. Tourists in every shape and color carried cooler bags and cameras.

I raised my camera and captured a few photos. "Let's make a note of this spot. I could see it being a part of a montage after the rescue scene."

"M'kay." Lyrica sighed. "This is taking forever. Are we ever going to get to the islands?"

"There's a whole lot more to this than an island." A rant began bubbling to the surface, which would be a total waste of my time, so I took a deep inhale, catching whiffs of frying seafood and salt air. Those familiar scents mixed together and summoned childhood memories before I could stop it. I didn't have time to let any of that loose today, so I slid my sunglasses over my eyes and joined the ebb and flow of foot traffic, hoping it would eventually wash me and my lagging assistant up on the shore of a certain boat tour shop.

Shop was being generous, I discovered, as we sidled up to a structure that looked more like a ticket booth. No matter, they had my reservation and that was all that mattered.

Our guide, Tom, who was also the owner, brought us around the chain of barrier islands that were separated by meandering inlets and backed by salt marshes. The water wasn't aggressive but not quite calm either. I feared Lyrica's next dilemma would be seasickness, but a glance in her direction only found her sprawled across the bench seat at the stern, sunbathing. She lived in Malibu and probably owned her own yacht, so she was definitely in her element. Seriously, her hair remained in perfectly glossy teal-and-purple waves, and whatever makeup brand she used had to be made of fairy dust. Even after a day of flights, car rides, and the Southern humidity, Lyrica remained looking fresh as a rainbow-colored daisy. Me? I didn't have a gazillion-dollar budget for beauty products, so I resembled a wilted rose that had been stepped on and then deep-fried.

"You good over there, Lyrica?" I asked, just to be sure.

She gave me a thumbs-up and then readjusted her rose-gold Cartier sunglasses.

Relieved that she was pacified for the time being, I pulled out a map of the barrier islands and scooted closer to Tom to discuss where we needed to visit.

Being a visual thinker and having a good sense of place came in handy when needing to take words on a page and find those images in real life. But there were also practical requirements for this film location. Something I had to remind Lyrica about when she insisted we pick the island with the luxury resort.

I motioned for Tom to keep going while shaking my head. "We need a property with very little development and a large, secluded beach." We would also need certain necessities such as easily accessed bathroom facilities and dependable power sources, but I didn't waste my breath trying to explain that to my *assistant*.

After visiting a few potential islands and taking hundreds of pictures, Lyrica hit a wall. Not literally, but if one had been near, I'd have found a corner in it to put her nose.

"My sugar is low. I gotta eat!" A fat tear rolled down her plump cheek in perfect sync with her hissy fit.

Deciding to cut the excursion short, I instructed Tom to head back to the marina, but something in the distance on the next island caught my eye.

"Can we stop at that small island for just a quick look?" I asked as Lyrica let out a groan of protest. I really wanted to pinch her.

Tom shook his head but slowed the boat. "Indigo Isle is private property."

"Indigo Isle? What an intriguing name." I pointed toward the small beach. "I'll only be a minute or two."

"But, ma'am, it's off-limits. Some even say it's haunted. You don't want to go foolin' with that place."

With no patience for a debate, I nipped it in the bud by pulling out a hundred-dollar bill, and that's all it took for the boat to find its way onto shore.

At first glance, Indigo Isle looked forsaken. The beach was more like a graveyard of petrified tree limbs that had become casualties of weather and time. Just past the beach, a fortress of salt-incrusted trees stood shoulder to shoulder, each adorned heavily with strings of oyster and clamshells that sounded like the tinkling applause of a million fairies in the breeze.

"Now that would be a unique backdrop for a scene." I pointed toward the shell-dressed trees.

Lyrica shrugged, not even trying to see the vision of it.

Well, I certainly had vision and wanted to explore this peculiar island a little closer, so I hopped out and started toward the forest.

"Hold up!" Lyrica hollered, staggering from the boat and stumbling onto the sand.

I held up my palms to ward her off. "Just wait in the boat. I'll hurry."

Seemingly over the low-sugar meltdown, she kept stomping up the small beach, dodging chunks of driftwood. "No. I want to see too."

A sigh pushed past my frowning lips. "Fine."

We ventured through the dimly lit canopy of centuries-old oaks and skinny palmetto trees. The alluring perfume from yellow blossoms of jasmine, entwined throughout the underbrush, beckoned us along a well-worn path. Before long, the landscape opened up to a hidden homestead that looked more fitting for a Lowcountry farm than an island.

"Whoa," Lyrica whispered as we craned our necks in every direction to take it all in.

In the center of the clearing stood an aging manor. Redbrick, three stories, and fronted with graying white columns, the Georgian-style house reminded me of an elderly man worn heavily around the edges from hard living. I veered around a bountiful vegetable garden, taking note of another field to the right filled with unfamiliar plants that resembled weeds.

The entire time we explored the homestead, checking out an old building filled with farming equipment and such, I had an eerie feeling of being watched. When no one appeared, I headed to the house, climbed the wide porch steps, and knocked on the dark-blue front door. After several failed attempts to produce an answer, I gave up and looked around for a bit longer, taking note of the solar panels, an outdoor shower, and rain barrels.

"I'm digging the wild beauty of this place, but there's no way it could accommodate a fairly large movie production."

"It's a movie about a group of shipwrecked teens." Lyrica turned in a circle. "This place is too country for that."

"Yep." I held my damp hair off my neck, relishing the slight breeze that fanned my hot skin. Dropping my hair, I pulled out my phone and read aloud the small movie description that I'd saved in my notes. "'A group of runaway teens set off in a stolen boat only to end up shipwrecked on an island somewhere off the eastern coast. At first, all is well and the group basks in their newfound freedom on the island, but soon the tides change when their food supply runs out and tempers flare. As the situation becomes harrowing, survival of the fittest and smartest will be tested. Alliances will form with jealousy tearing them apart. The group will battle the elements, themselves, and each other.'"

"Welp. That settles it. Let's bounce." Lyrica took a pronounced step as if coercing me to agree.

"You should have just stayed in the boat." I wandered toward the garden. Ripe tomatoes gave off a sweet aroma and vines hung heavy with vibrant green cucumbers. I tried appreciating the feast for the eyes, but the grumbling behind me ruined it. "Why are you in such a hurry?"

"Because it's spookier than the cemetery." She faked a shiver.

I didn't find the cemetery spooky but peaceful. This place, though? Yeah. There was an undeniable eeriness about it, and I suspected we were being spied on. I gazed up at the looming house, but there were no signs of humans or ghosts staring out of any of the windows.

A rustling noise drew our attention to a rickety woodshed and then suddenly a metal bucket clattered to the ground. We both screamed as Lyrica wrapped her arms around me, knocking me off-balance and nearly to the ground.

"It's a chicken! Let go! You're choking me!" Wrestling out of her grasp, I shook a finger in the direction of the reddish-brown hen where she pecked the ground beside the overturned bucket. "See? A chicken!"

"I about peed myself. Like, seriously, I really need to go." She did a little dance to emphasize her need.

"Fine. Let's go."

"Yes. *Let's*." Lyrica turned on a dime and hurried through the thicket of trees, making enough racket to stir up several birds overhead. Surprisingly, she could move quite fast when the situation provoked it.

Before following after her, I scanned the front of the house one more time and could have sworn a curtain fluttered from a second floor window. Blinking and then squinting, I concentrated on the window but didn't catch the curtain move again.

"Sonny!" Lyrica's screeching echoed through the trees. "Come on!"

I lifted my hand and waved goodbye at the sad, lonely house. Reluctantly I left my curiosity in the secluded yard, but I had a foreboding feeling I'd be back to collect it soon enough.

CHAPTER TWO

THERE WERE DAYS where every detail fell into place without provocation and then there were those days that were so dang stubborn I couldn't even take a step without it blowing up in my face. Today? It had been a mixed bag with me being stuck babysitting a grown woman while fixing a mess caused by another grown woman, but this woman let all that go when my phone began ringing with some good news once we reached the marina.

Relieved, I promised, "Thank you so much. I'll deliver the contracts by tomorrow." I ended the call and slid my phone into my messenger bag. "That was the manager of Moise Island. We have our island."

Lyrica perked up. "Is that the one with the small resort?"

"Yes. The resort is far enough away from the private beach we have permission to use that nosy guests shouldn't be an issue."

"Ooh, that's on fleek." She bobbed her head as we crossed the street to where we'd parked.

Sunbaked and parched, Lyrica and I grabbed a late lunch at a

13

local favorite called Page's Okra Grill. She thought the name was simply fabulous and I had to agree with her. While chowing down on crab cake sandwiches, we discovered they catered, which was also on my list of to-dos for the filming schedule. To celebrate the accomplishments, we split a giant piece of coconut cake and declared it the best cake we'd ever put in our mouths. I decided maybe Lyrica was tolerable after all.

"We need to head over to Shem Creek Inn," I told her, studying the handwritten scribbles from Delaney that Whit passed along to me. Luckily, she'd handed over the research file after he fired her.

"Why? Is that where we're staying tonight?" Lyrica scraped the leftover icing off the plate with her spoon, finishing it off before handing the dish over to the waiter.

I shrugged. "It's summertime, so it's doubtful."

"Yeah, that's a popular place," the waiter interjected. Dressed in a black shirt and pants, he was probably around Lyrica's age, but with less color and flair. "Can I get you anything else?"

"Actually . . ." I motioned him a little closer. Even though we had work to get to, I couldn't resist inquiring about that peculiar island. "Do you happen to know anything about Indigo Isle?"

Reserved recognition eased across his young face. "Just that my dad made me promise to never go messing around it."

"Why's that?" I asked.

He looked around, checking his other tables. "Locals say there's a monster who haunts the island."

A lady at the table next to ours called for him, holding up an empty glass.

"That's really all I know." He shrugged, offering a smile along with the check, and went about his business.

"Dude, we were out there with a *monster*," Lyrica said in a hissing whisper, slapping at the table in all her drama queen glory.

"There's no such thing," I assured her with an outright lie. I'd been on my own since seventeen out in LA and had learned the hard way that monsters came with all sorts of facades. While some fit the profile at first glance, wicked eyes and dark sneers, others came dressed in attractive packaging with twinkling eyes and smiles. "That's just local folklore."

Lyrica finished off her soda and stifled a burp behind her hand. "Huh?"

"Made-up tales to grab your attention. We need to get going." I settled the bill and we hit the road once more.

My passenger yawned dramatically. "This day has just taken it out of me. I could use a nap."

I maneuvered the car through heavy traffic along Coleman Boulevard. "Same, but we need to make sure the reservations for the cast and crew are all secure first."

She wiggled her fingers, nails looking sharp enough to draw blood. "Can't you just make a phone call?"

"It's only a few minutes up the road. I'd rather take a look. Plus, it's always good to make some in-person connections to—" I hushed the lesson as Lyrica reached to fiddle with the radio.

We pulled up to the waterfront hotel with a pristine white exterior with giant red letters spelling out *Shem Creek Inn* across the roof's edge.

"Oooh. So cute. Like country coastal chic, yeah? I hope we can stay here tonight." Lyrica launched out of the car before I could put it in park.

I followed her inside, where she oohed and aahed some more.

"The pool is right on the water!" She turned toward me, those bright-blue contact lenses nearly glowing. "Maybe they shouldn't have fired Delaney. Girlfriend hooked us up good."

Lyrica's commotion drew the woman from behind a rustic reception desk made from weathered reclaimed wood.

Smiling timidly, the petite woman joined us by the back windows that showcased a spectacular waterfront view of Shem Creek. "May I help y'all?"

"Aww! She said *y'all*!"

I ignored Lyrica and the receptionist tried not to stare outright at her.

"Hi—" I eyed her name tag—"Abby, I'm here to check on a reservation."

"Sure thing." She returned to the desk and typed something into her computer. "Last name?"

"Kessler," I pronounced slowly and then spelled it out.

Abby tapped away on the keyboard and paused. "Umm . . . we don't have any reservations under Kessler."

"How about Ewol Entertainment? Two weeks from today should be check-in." We rarely booked under Whit's production company's name in order to stay low-key, but Delaney the Dimwit might have screwed that up like she had everything else.

Abby scanned the reservations and slowly shook her head. "I'm sorry."

Going for broke, I asked, "Do you happen to have a large booking for at least fifty rooms that should have been made back in November of last year?"

Abby did another search, pink lips in a firm line. "No ma'am."

My shoulders sagged. "And I'm guessing you don't have fifty rooms available."

"We're booked almost completely through Labor Day."

"So that means no room for tonight either?" Lyrica piped in. "No. Sorry."

We left the beautiful hotel like two dogs with our tails between our legs. After making a few phone calls and leaving Delaney a threatening voice mail to call me back ASAP, we sat in the car, plundering through the research notes.

On a hunch, I fished out the paper with *Shem Creek Inn* written on the top and studied the address. Earlier, I'd just plugged the hotel name in the GPS and not the address. As I suspected, the address didn't match. I typed the one Delaney had written down and then put the car in drive. I hated these hunches sometimes, leading me to truths I didn't want to acknowledge.

Lyrica looked at me while securing her seat belt. "Where are we going *now*?"

I made a left out of the parking lot. "On a wild-goose chase, I'm afraid."

She made a guttural sound. "Ugh. I've never liked the sound of that."

Twenty minutes farther away from the marina than I wanted to be, the navigation lady in my phone said we had arrived at our destination.

Lyrica huffed. "I'm not feeling this destination."

I had to agree with her on that. Heads angled, we stared at the tired motel through the windshield, neither of us making a move to get out.

"The only thing the idiot got right was this one has *Creek* in the name too." Lyrica stabbed a pointy fingernail toward the sherbet-orange sign with white lettering. Creek View Inn. The word *Vacancy* blinked in a red glow at the bottom of the trapezoid-shaped sign.

"You changed your tune about Delaney mighty fast there," I mumbled and then plastered on a fake smile. "But at least you're in luck. They have available rooms for tonight."

She crossed her arms, taking on the air of a petulant toddler again and still not appreciating my sarcasm. "I'm not staying in this dump."

"Try to keep an open mind. We've not even looked around yet." I tipped my chin toward the mint-green stucco exterior. It didn't necessarily need nip-tucks or even a face-lift. Just a superficial makeover to freshen it up a bit. "It's on trend with this retro vibe."

"There's a big difference between retro and run-down," Lyrica griped as we got out and walked over to the tiny office. The grueling hum of window units and traffic from the busy highway almost drowned out her whining.

An elderly lady with pinkish-gray hair sat behind the small counter. No name tag.

"Hello there," I greeted her.

"Afternoon, gals. I'm Erlene."

"I'm Sonny." I hitched a thumb in my sulking sidekick's direction. "And this is Lyrica."

Her light-green eyes lit. "Great names! Can I help ya?"

"Maybe so. I need to confirm a reservation." I examined the laminate countertop. No computer in sight. Just a notebook with round coffee stains on the front.

Erlene slid on a pair of bifocals and opened the notebook. "Let's see . . ."

After about ten minutes' worth of flipping, Erlene found the reservation for all fifty-three rooms under Kessler. An old-school carbon copy of the credit card receipt was stapled to it and held Delaney's signature.

"That little—" Lyrica finished the oath under her breath.

"Lyrica." I pressed my palm against her tense shoulder. "Why don't you check out the amenities while I tour a room with Miss Erlene."

The older lady reached over to a pegboard and plucked a tarnished key off one of the hooks. Yes, an actual key. Not a card. Not a fob, but a key. Lyrica noticed too and clucked her tongue.

"Give me a minute to switch my shoes." Erlene bent down on a grunt and started exchanging her bedroom slippers for a pair of Velcro sneakers.

I ushered Lyrica outside before she said something to offend the poor little lady. "I know, I know!" I sliced a hand through the air. "Just look around and try to find some positives, please." As I urged her on, we rounded the corner and entered a neglected courtyard that was surrounded by the horseshoe-shaped motel.

Pointing at the empty swimming pool, she sassed, "That's not positive."

Before I could come up with something to say, Erlene shuffled into the courtyard using a walker with tennis balls stuck on the ends of the front two legs. "Don't mind that. There's just a tiny crack in it. The pool man said he can have it patched up before y'all get here."

"Great," I said too brightly and trailed Erlene over to one of the doors on the lower level of the two-story building.

It took some finagling to get the key to work. "It's the salt air's fault. Makes everything rust. Even us old folks." She wheezed a laugh at her joke and I managed a small wheeze of my own.

"Do you have a security guard?" I asked, noticing the doors only had the single lock.

"No, hon. It's pretty safe round here." She pushed the door wide and welcomed me inside.

Wood paneling on the walls and rust-orange shag carpet on the floors. A rattan table and chair sat beside a double bed with green-and-orange floral pattern bedding. I crossed the small room and ran my hand over the blanket, finding the texture close to plastic. The only other door led to a beige bathroom, clean with only a faint hint of mildew.

Erlene plopped in the chair, making the wood frame creak. "Well, what do you think?"

What did I think? For starters, I thought calling this place *retro* was an absolute stretch. *Outdated* suited it better, and there was no way the pampered lineup of cast members would agree to staying here.

Keeping all that to myself, I said instead, "It's clean and cool."

"Oh yes. My niece and her daughter take care of the cleaning. They're good people. And all the window units are practically brand-new."

I opened the small rattan armoire that matched the table and chair. A few empty hangers swayed on the clothes rod, stirring the acrid smell of mothballs.

"Is that a permanent?"

The smell? Being stuck with Lyrica? Or the unhealthy situation I found myself stuck in with Whit? *I hope not.* Closing the door, I glanced over my shoulder. "Permanent?"

She patted her hair. "Do you have a perm?"

Repressing a cringe, I peeked at myself in the mirror on the wall. Sure enough, the humidity had had its way with my hair, turning my relaxed curls into a tizzy of ringlets. It had hung a little past my shoulder blades when I left California that morning, but now it had shortened and thickened considerably.

I used my fingers as a comb to tame the knots and twisted it up into a messy bun. "It's all natural, actually. The only perm I've ever had was the straightening type, but it didn't work."

"Gracious, why would you want it straight? All those curls are gorgeous." Erlene gave me a kind smile.

Forever ago, during my ill-fitting preteen years and tired of being so different from my family, I had wanted straight hair so that I would look more like my two older sisters. Caroline and Aubrey had gotten their strawberry-blonde hair with soft waves, a splattering of freckles, and light-blue eyes from our mother. I took after my dad's side of the family with hazel eyes that changed on a whim and golden-brown hair that tended to get darker in the winter and lighter in the summer. Apparently nothing about me was *permanent* except for the curls and maybe the mess I'd made of my life.

Putting a stop to that line of thought, I moved over and inspected the small TV on top of a brass stand. It had tuning knobs and an antenna. "Do the rooms have cable and Wi-Fi?"

"Most folks spend their time out by the pool or exploring Charleston," Erlene answered without answering. "We got a laundry room with a drink and snack machine. Oh, and an ice maker."

"Great," I repeated for the hundredth time, heading for the exit.

With the short tour complete, I figured it was time to hunt Lyrica down, which ended up being the easiest task of my day. We spotted her sprawled out in one of the plastic lounge chairs by the crumbling pool. A rainbow Croc dangled precariously from one foot while the other one lay on the sizzling cement.

"Bless her heart, she must be plumb tuckered out. She snores louder than my late husband." Erlene hummed as she locked the door behind us, but I wanted to growl. "I'll meet y'all in the office."

As the old lady shuffled away, I pulled my phone out and hit Record, capturing the sight and sounds of a sleeping Lyrica.

I sent the video to Whit with a text: **Why me?**

Moments later my phone dinged. **Tell Shamu to get her fat—**

Without bothering to read past the word *fat*, I pocketed the phone and rubbed my forehead.

Body-shaming was something else, besides monsters, I'd discovered in the entertainment industry. I'm talking openly too. Not whispers behind one's back, and certainly no apologies about it. Lyrica had a good hundred pounds on my one-sixty, and we were both considered fat by industry standards. It was one of the reasons my acting career had been so short-lived and only consisted of one cat food commercial.

Well, I ended up showing them that this size ten could find her place in the world of fame. Sure, it had taken an embarrassing video on my YouTube channel going viral to make that happen, but it happened just the same. My channel started out as a behind-the-scenes look at location scouting. I thought it was an interesting concept, but I had no following and so the videos were only receiving twenty or so views. Whit said he could take care of it for me, but as with everything with Whit, there would have been strings attached to his offer. I wanted to accomplish something all on my own, without debts or regrets overshadowing it.

About two years back, I finally got my big break, in more than one sense of the word. During a scouting trip up in the Nevada mountains, I decided to film a segment for my vlog. Not paying attention to where I was walking, I fell right off a cliff and was trapped on a narrow ledge for hours. Even with a broken wrist and scared out of my mind, I managed to keep a grip on my phone and continued filming, adding plenty of my go-to self-deprecating humor. It was a train wreck of a video, and apparently viewers couldn't look away. It went viral and my meager following of fifteen hundred shot up to a little over fifty thousand practically overnight. Soon after, I revamped the channel into a type of game. *Where in the World?* gave clues to viewers to help them figure out where I was scouting. Of course, there were prizes, so that brought in even more followers.

So, yeah, the curvy girl with too-curly hair proved she could, even though Hollywood told her she couldn't. I suppose the appropriate response would be that I didn't need to prove myself to anyone, but isn't that the denial everyone is living out, while trying to do just that? To prove themselves? Their success? Their worthiness? Their individualism?

Me? I'd wanted to prove I didn't need my family's acceptance or support and to prove I hadn't made the biggest mistake of my life by trying to prove it.

Deciding Whit owed us "fat" girls a night of luxury, I left Lyrica to sleep a little longer. His words whispered in my ear as I grabbed my laptop from the car. *"You love the lifestyle too much to walk away from me."* Not to be deterred by my conscience, a conscience that had started screaming at me as of late, I booked two suites at a boutique hotel in downtown Charleston for the night. While I was at it, I went ahead and booked Lyrica a flight for first thing in the morning on Whit's dime too. All of this was his fault in the first place.

A year's worth of work needed to be done in only a few days, and the only way that was going to get done was on my own. Like everything else in my life.

CHAPTER THREE

CHARLESTON WASN'T JUST A PLACE TO VISIT but an experience that engaged all the senses. Sights filled with historic relics and vast waterfront views. The aroma of briny air and an earthy pungency of marshland nearby with hints of fragrant sweetgrass. The savory tastes of Lowcountry cuisine with spicy influences of Gullah culture. The texture of humid days and silky nights. The raucous sounds of seagulls harmonizing with ships passing through the harbor. And that was just scratching the surface of the experience.

Even though I ran away from this part of the world and never looked back, there's no denying its beauty and charm. Truly South Carolina is one of those states that has a little of it all. Islands, beaches, farmland, national forests, and waterfalls. No wonder the rest of the country finally decided the small state was worth a second look, and more and more books and film projects were being produced out here. I was surprised I had been able to dodge the state for as long as I did. It wouldn't even be a hardship to be scouting in the area, had it not been for the pressing storm just up the road from Charleston. Ignoring it the best I could, I set out to get my job done.

After dropping Lyrica off at the airport, I spent the morning lining up all the necessary things for the shoot: portable restrooms, security, tent rentals, catering services. Most importantly, I was able to secure several beach villas for the cast on the other side of Moise Island. A perfect solution in my book. For one, they would have accommodations that suited their pampered lifestyle. Also, the cast would be close to set, which would make keeping them on schedule a heckuva lot easier.

Feeling accomplished, I swung by this funky joint by the side of the road called Jack's Cosmic Dogs and treated myself to a hot dog and vanilla shake. Quick, easy, and delicious—three must-haves for my line of work. Afterwards, I returned to Creek View Inn and caught Erlene in the small office watching *Days of Our Lives* on a television no bigger than my MacBook.

"Hi, Erlene. I—"

"Shh . . ." She held up a hand and shooed me away, so enthralled by the drama on the tiny screen that her eyes never looked over to acknowledge me. This reminded me of my grandmother and how serious she became each day after lunch about watching her stories.

Showing some respect, I pulled up a stool on the other side of the counter and stayed quiet for the next forty minutes. I might or might not have gotten caught up in the drama of the fine folks from Salem.

"I haven't watched this show in years. I can't believe Lucas and Sami are still putting up with each other. And Victor? That man has to be old as dirt by now! How is he still kicking?" I wiped my eyes, a little put out by the show and by myself for remembering so much about it.

Erlene leaned over to the end of the counter and switched off the TV. "I'm surprised you know about this show at all. Ain't most of your generation making your own real-life soap operas these days?" Her teasing smile softened the insult.

"Touché." I huffed a laugh. "I used to spend most every afternoon at my grandmother's during my summer break. I either had to take a nap or watch *Days of Our Lives* with her. I sort of got hooked on it. During the school year, I'd have to bike over to her house so she could fill me in on what I'd missed."

My thoughts wandered further to the past, thinking about how it seemed no one really wanted to put up with me but for this time I spent with my grandmother, bonding over a silly show. Yeah, I might have been to blame for that. Mostly described as a handful, I was the opposite of my two older sisters. Caroline and Aubrey were straight A students who excelled at everything they tried. I was a consistent C student, who excelled at nothing but getting into trouble. I blamed it on boredom, always restless with a knack for being in the wrong place at the wrong time.

The squeaking of Erlene's chair brought my attention back to now. She scooted the rolling chair over to a dorm-size fridge behind the counter and retrieved two mini cans of Coke. Rolling back to me, she handed me one.

"Thank you, ma'am." I saluted her with the can and then took a long sip. The cold soda both pricked and soothed my parched mouth. Smacking my lips, I studied the can. "It has tiny slivers of ice in it."

"Just the way I like it." Erlene knocked back her can, taking a long drink from it. "It took some tweaking and a few can explosions before I got the temperature perfect."

"Well done, ma'am." I finished off the soda and sighed. "So I have some good news, a little bad, and then more good news."

Erlene dropped the can onto the laminate countertop and wiped her mouth with the back of her hand. You'd think we were slinging beers at a saloon. "Lay it on me."

"Good news, the film crew will be arriving on time in two weeks. Bad news, we will only need thirty-one rooms. And the best news is I'd love to rent a room for the night."

The older lady grinned, eyes crinkling and the wrinkles deepening around her smiling lips. She looked so motherly—or grandmotherly. I wondered if my mother looked similar to Erlene nowadays. They had to be about the same age, nearing eighty. Last time I saw Mama, she was still a little above average in height and sturdy from years of working at her family's seafood market. Had she done that thing elderly people do? The thing where they shrink in stature? Had she softened to resemble a pillow, like Erlene? It made me long for a genuine hug.

The squeaking of Erlene's chair drew my attention again. She reached for her coffee-stained, circa-1980s ledger and flipped through several pages. "I'm putting you in the best room of the motel. And don't worry none 'bout the room cancellations. I haven't billed y'all the full amount yet. We can square that away when you return."

"Oh, that's so sweet. Thank you." I gave her the company credit card and watched on in amusement as she ran it through the old-school credit card imprinter. The sliding and clicking sounded loud in the small office. More official somehow.

Erlene handed me the credit card, the transaction slip, and a key with a plastic dolphin on the key chain. "All set. I'll be sure you get this room when y'all come back later this month."

I read the number printed on the dolphin underneath the motel's logo, noticing it was the same room I toured yesterday. "Great!"

After squaring things away with Erlene and putting my bags in the best room at Creek View Inn, I returned to the marina to make arrangements with Tom to ferry the crew members to the island for the next two months.

"I have two water taxis I can keep available." Tom pointed to two large pontoon boats as we stood on the dock, inspecting his inventory.

"There will be a few early morning starts before sunrise and some night shoots. I'll make sure to get you the call sheets as soon as possible, but sometimes the schedule can change without much notice."

Tom waved off my concerns. "No problem. I've got plenty of summer help."

"Oh, good." I turned toward the line of fleet rentals. "I'll be going back and forth a lot more than the crew, so I need to rent one of those for myself. That sixteen-footer should be fine."

Tom popped his Costa sunglasses on top of his balding head, revealing a severe tan line around his eyes. "You know how to operate a boat?"

My hands settled on my hips. "Sir, I grew up in Georgetown on the river. I had my own skiff before I could drive a car."

He laughed, holding up his palms. "Ah, a river rat."

"Yep." I smirked, owning it. No matter how much distance I had put between me and my upbringing, the river and salt life would forever be a part of me.

After signing the paperwork and handing over Whit's credit card, I set off to Moise Island with the contracts and release forms.

By the time I wrapped all that up, the day had begun waning toward evening. Before leaving Moise Island, I decided to get some shots of the beach to see how it photographed in different lighting. Sunset produced breathtaking pictures and that tingling in my throat said this was the perfect location for *Beyond the Waves*. I sent the images in a text to the art director and she replied almost instantly. **You nailed it.**

On the return trip to the marina, I veered the boat to make a pass by Indigo Isle. Something about the mysterious island and the little bit I'd heard about it hit me in a tender spot. It seemed opinions had been formed and there was no changing it. *A monster. Haunted. Stay away. Outcast.* The thing is, if you hear something long enough, you tend to accept it as truth, whether it is or not.

I accepted early on that I had never been a part of my parents' plan. Only a few years shy of becoming empty nesters, my mother found out she was pregnant at age forty-seven. They named me after one of their favorite singers, Sonny Bono. Yep, I was named after a man, but at least it's better than Cher, which was the other choice. My parents said I was an unexpected gift for their twenty-fifth wedding anniversary, a gift they didn't seem to want very much. Never said that outright, but through backhanded remarks and my parents' constant exasperation with me, it was pretty clear retirement held more appeal than having to put up with me. Admittedly, I wasn't an easy child like my two older sisters, but still . . .

As the boat skimmed along just offshore of Indigo Isle, a light through the trees drew my attention. Always too curious for my own good, I circled the island and located a small boat dock on the western side that faced the salt marsh. A boat hung in the boat lift, indicating the place wasn't completely abandoned. A trail went through the copse of trees just beyond the deck. After securing the boat, I started down the path, a carpet of fallen leaves and pebbles underneath my feet.

Stepping into the yard, I spotted the light source, a solar lantern on a rickety table in the side yard. A worn, coverless book and a half-empty mason jar sat next to it. Even though the presence of someone lingered, the place had that air of abandoned melancholy just as it had the day before. I picked up the book and flipped a few pages, surprised and impressed to discover it was a copy of *Gulliver's Travels*. There were scribbles in the margins, but I couldn't make out the words in the dim lighting.

As I flipped through the pages, a muffled noise came from the old building to my right. I grew still and tried to listen closely, giving it a minute or two to see if someone or something would step out and join me in the yard.

Nothing but a breeze joined me.

Replacing the book on the table, I peeped inside the building for any sign of life, but the pitch-dark gave nothing away.

Taking a few steps inside, I called out, "Hello?"

Moments passed with no response. No sound. No movement. Nothing. But the sense of being watched made the back of my neck tickle. Shivering in the dark, I began to turn away.

Then, similar to a rogue wave plowing into me, all heck broke loose.

Someone—or something—rose up out of nowhere, bellowing like a wild animal.

I banged into something so hard on the way out of the building that a searing pain shot straight through me, but I couldn't stop to see if I'd torn a chunk out of my thigh because whoever was yelling began chasing me too. Much faster than I could run, that's for dang sure. I shot through the woods with the rabid man hot on my heels. Low-hanging tree limbs slapped against me and spiderwebs tangled in my hair, but no matter, I kept on trucking it until I made it to the beach.

Pressing my palm against the stitch in my side, I braced myself for the impact but it never came. Gasping for air, I looked over my shoulder to see where he went. The ominous figure had paused at the edge of the trees as if considering what to do with me. Frozen in the sand, I focused on trying to catch my breath and not pass out while watching him watch me. His face was mostly hidden in the hood of a sweatshirt, but I swear his eyes glowed as brightly as the full moon above.

We held each other's stare until I blinked and then he was gone. Like smoke in a windstorm, he disappeared before I could be sure he ever existed.

I cocked my ear, listening for any signs of him moving through the woods, but nothing but the hum of the ocean and the tinkling of the shell chimes could be heard. Had my imagination just conjured up the entire thing? Heart hammering away, I decided not to stick around and find out. I turned to the shore, expecting to see my boat, but froze again when I saw nothing but whitecaps drawing near the shore, resembling ghosts, only to disappear out to the sea as the tide receded.

"Shoot, shoot, shoot!" I chanted, realizing my fool self had run to the beach and not the small dock.

There were two options. Head back through those trees and risk another run-in with that wild thing, or pick my way around the edge of the island in the dark, which would probably take twice as long. Bewildered and more than a little spooked, I chose the latter.

Back at the motel, I checked the damage on my leg and was dumbfounded to find only a large bruise forming. With how bad it hurt, I fully expected half of it to be missing. After washing off the spiderwebs and residual adrenaline, I hid underneath the polyester blanket like a frightened little girl.

The night was filled with dreams of monsters chasing me and lots of tossing and turning.

• • •

When the light of day showed up, it brought with it some clarity. Whoever had chased me was doing just that, chasing me off, which meant he had no intentions of hurting me. Once I convinced myself of this, I shoved the scratchy blanket off and decided to go do what I did best: scout out information.

First stop was the diner across the road from Creek View Inn, which was coincidentally named Creek View Diner. Or was it ironic? Because I'd not laid eyes on any creek yet. Neither establishment was directly on any body of water. I guess it really didn't matter as long as the place had strong coffee and decent grits, which it did.

"I've not had grits in over a decade," I told the waitress at the breakfast counter while stirring a dollop of butter into them.

The middle-aged woman made a face. "A decade? I don't even go a week. How can you live in the South and not have grits on the regular?"

"I haven't lived around here in a long time."

"That's a shame." She gave me a pitying look before heading down the counter to refresh coffee cups.

"Shame indeed." I moaned after taking a bite of the salty,

creamy delight. Not even halfway through the bowl, I could feel the grits expanding in my belly. I wouldn't be any good after such a heavy breakfast, but it would be so worth it. How could I have forgotten how good grits were?

The waitress moved in my direction, holding up a new pot of coffee, but I waved her off.

"I'm so stuffed, there isn't even room for coffee." I placed my napkin over the bowl to make myself stop eating.

She smiled warmly, taking out her order pad from the apron tied around her waist. "Anything else? Maybe a piece of pie for later?"

"Tempting, but no thanks." I retrieved my wallet from my messenger bag. "I do have a question, if you have a minute."

"Sure." Always in motion, she grabbed a cloth and began wiping down the counter.

"I've been out exploring the barrier islands and came across one in particular. You might have heard of it—Indigo Isle." I put it out there and watched her finally still for the first time since I arrived. "Do you know anything about it?"

She shrugged. "Only what I've been told. Sad story."

Before she could elaborate, someone called, "Order up."

I waited like a fish on a hook and unable to do anything about it. After she delivered the plates, I held up the check and a twenty to get her attention back on me. "No change. But . . . what did you mean by *sad story*?"

"The owner, I believe his last name is Renfrow or something Ren." She shooed her uncertainty with a flick of a wrist. "Anyway, from what people have said, he was in a horrific accident and is disfigured. That's why he hides out on the island. Been out there all by himself for ten years or so."

"That is sad." And here I thought I was alone, even while surrounded by people all the time. That tender spot inside my chest for the mysterious island stung again.

I left the diner and located the nearest library to do some digging, which didn't amount to much. Unlike the well-known sea islands such as Kiawah and Edisto, very little could be found about Indigo Isle. A small island, only one and a half miles wide and three miles long, and totally off the grid. Owned by E. H. Renfrow. Those were the only facts available. The rest was hearsay.

I was told various regurgitations of what the waitress had shared. A woman at the bait and tackle store said the owner had lost a leg in an accident, but I didn't believe that one, considering I had witnessed him running as fast as a perfectly healthy track star. Most of my inquiries produced something on the lines of disfigurement and burn scars. That could have very well been true since he was mostly covered last night. More than once, I was advised to stay away from the island altogether. *Cruel, cold, and damaged, the Monster of Indigo Isle is best left undisturbed.*

With work taking precedence, I had to abandon my interest in Indigo Isle and the possible beast living out there alone. I wrapped things up by the end of the day just in time to make my flight.

On my way out of town, I came to a stoplight that ran into Highway 17. Taking a left would lead me to the airport and back to the life I'd created all on my own. But a right turn and then about sixty miles north would bring me to my old life and the family I left behind. It would only take about an hour to arrive back to where my blunder began.

With a burning in my belly but no desire to travel into the past, I chose the left.

CHAPTER FOUR

THE RETURN TO CHARLESTON two weeks later had me feeling ill at ease for so many reasons. Being this close to my skeletons just up the road in Georgetown, the burden of putting up with Whit, and then my ridiculous fixation on Indigo Isle. I blamed this last problem on me trying to distract myself from the first two. To focus on anything besides the real issues. Issues that were entirely my own fault.

I picked up my rental after arriving at Charleston International Airport. This time I ended up with a Chevy Malibu. I searched the radio for a song to get me in the mood for the day's long list of tasks. Instead, the first song I happened upon pressed my back against a wall of regret so fast there was no stopping the deluge of memories.

As "Unwritten" by Natasha Bedingfield played through the speakers, it transported me to the night of high school graduation. As per school tradition, our class song would play after the closing speech, but I hadn't been there to hear it. Knowing my family was tucked in the bleachers awaiting my graduation ceremony, I skipped it to make one of the biggest mistakes of my life.

Rainy day money. That's what my father called the cash tucked in the two old Crisco canisters in the back of the pantry. I remembered watching my mother tuck a few hundred-dollar bills in one of the cans one time.

"Who hides money in Crisco cans?" I had asked her, thinking it was so peculiar.

"Most everyone around these parts has hiding spots for money. My parents always hid their savings in old snuff cans."

"Wouldn't it be safer in the bank?"

"That's debatable."

I didn't think so, especially when it came to putting my plan into action.

I'd heard my parents talk incessantly about using their rainy day money for an RV adventure, but I came up with something better. I figured taking the money was an actual *gift* to them, so swiping the fuller can that had four thousand dollars in it didn't feel that bad. At first, at least. But similar to mildew slowly creeping up on a neglected surface, time had revealed just how wrong that decision had been.

My sisters had called me a drama queen from as far back as I could remember, so Hollywood seemed a fitting place to make my escape to. But that fit ended up coming with a hefty price tag, one that quickly depleted the stolen money and what was left of my integrity.

Slapping at the radio until I managed to turn it off, I sucked in a deep breath and pushed it out on a groan. As the car's tires met the beginning of the Ravenel Bridge, I thought about what had led me to this very point.

It took more than talent to break into the Hollywood industry, and I quickly discovered that I wasn't cut out for it. After several months of auditions and only one small part in a commercial, I gave up on the idea of an acting career and settled on a job as a production assistant and waited tables on the side. By then the stolen money was gone and I was close to folding.

With nowhere to go but up at that low point in my life, I hunkered down and dedicated myself to work until finally securing a job as a location scout and then as a location manager. Whit took credit, and maybe he deserved some since he did open doors in the film world that I couldn't, but I wasn't scared of hard work and that proved beneficial.

Traveling was the best part of my career. I'd traveled to every state and all over Canada before hitting thirty, and just last year Mexico and several parts of South America had been added to the travel list. But there was so much more to it than my impressive frequent-flier mileage.

As a location manager, I served as a liaison between the producer or director and the property owner by taking responsibility for all aspects of a filming location—from securing permits to managing on-site operations. But that only scratched the surface of what was expected of me.

Today's main task had me acting as the one-woman welcome committee for the crew members. After speaking with Erlene to properly prepare her for the cacophony of activity that was about to take over her sleepy motel, I set myself up in a plastic chair by the parking lot to greet the arrivals with a smile and a special business card to help make my case.

Most of the camera crew arrived first, some lanky with long hair and some pudgy with fresh faces. I recognized a lanky one right off the bat with his brown skin and neat dreadlocks.

"Hi, Cade!" I hopped out of the chair and walked over to meet the director of photography and a few of his assistants, handing them the card and a food voucher from the Creek View Diner.

"Hey, sweetness. What's all this?" Cade eyed the pieces of paper.

"That is in case you have a complaint." I pointed to the card I'd had specially printed before returning to Charleston. *Delaney Marx booked this hotel. Please direct all complaints to her.* Delaney's private cell phone number and email address were listed below. Was that petty? Sure, but at this point of her screwing everything up and not returning one of my calls . . . ? Yeah, the girl had earned every ounce of my pettiness and then some.

Cade chuckled, tucking the card into the front pocket of his jeans.

"The food voucher is for the diner just across the road." I hitched a thumb over my shoulder toward the small building. "You guys will be on your own for breakfast and some suppers, but lunch will be provided on set."

Cade adjusted the strap of the duffel bag on his shoulder and studied the motel, a look of hesitancy on his handsome face.

I rushed to sell it to him and the other guys before anyone could comment. "It's clean and there's a pool." Their faces lit up. "It's under repair." Their faces frowned. "But I've been told it should be up and running by the weekend." I reluctantly added that last part. It should have already been fixed, but Erlene said there was a holdup with some part needed.

"Great," Cade said, stealing my one-word response while the others grumbled behind him.

"*Ciao, cara. Ti sono mancato molto?*" A familiar voice in an unfamiliar language practically sang the foreign words. Beautifully, I might add.

I turned in time to see the statuesque woman sashaying around the corner, looking ready for the runway in her trendy black romper and open-toed booties.

"Vee, my Nordic warrior princess. This shoot is looking a whole lot more promising," Cade said in that flirty tone he kept on reserve just for Vee. He strutted over to help her with one of the several suitcases she was dragging behind her.

Ridiculously tall, with an icy-blonde pixie cut and equally icy-blue eyes, Vee fit the bill of his description.

Vee dropped her bag and batted her long eyelashes at a grinning Cade. *"Davvero promettendo."*

"You know none of the rest of us spend our free time with Rosetta Stone," I sassed, even though I'd gladly listen to whatever language my friend wanted to spew out. She'd make these next two months much more bearable.

Vee tossed an arm over my shoulder and gave me a side hug. "I asked if you missed me, darling. And I agree with sweet Cade—" she winked at him—"this shoot is promising indeed." She'd made a game of giving him just enough attention to drive him wild.

"Italian?" I asked.

She directed her attention down to me and smiled before dropping her arm. *"Sì."*

The woman never ceased to impress me. Her main hobby besides watching true crime documentaries was learning other languages. So far that included Spanish, French, Mandarin, and Italian.

"What is this place? My itinerary said we were to check into our hotel and then head to the marina, but I think we're lost, signorina . . ." She wiggled her manicured fingers toward the gaudy motel sign.

I handed her a card as explanation.

Studying the card, she tapped a black lacquered nail against it and arched a blonde eyebrow. "You weren't supposed to be here?"

"No, I wasn't, but the project I was working on got put on the back burner so I could straighten out this idiot's mess." I held up the card in my hand.

"Well, if anyone can handle that task, it's you, love."

"Uh-hum," I agreed half-heartedly, knowing Whit had gotten his way yet again. "Let me introduce you to Erlene. She owns this joint."

I led Vee and the guys into the small office and made introductions. I figured meeting the sweet lady would help to soften them to their less-than-stellar accommodations.

It took a while to get everyone situated in their rooms, and by the time that was complete, I could have used a nap. But the life of a location manager didn't allow for naps. I had to head out to the island to go over logistics with the crew so setup could begin.

At least I had Vee to keep things fun and lively. Vee, just Vee, had a crafted persona like everyone else in the industry. *Enigma* and *charisma*, two words that described her persona perfectly. People often mistook her for one of the stars on set and were always astonished to find out she was the makeup artist instead. Don't get me wrong—she was a genius with hair and makeup, but the woman had the looks and acting chops to take over the spotlight if she ever decided to. I'd made plenty of cheap nail polish friends in the years since moving to LA, the ones who began fading and chipping all too soon when I didn't help advance their careers, but Vee was the only one I considered a true friend.

I brought Vee and a few others out to Moise Island in my boat. We arrived to find work crews hard at it.

"This will be your tent." I motioned to the white tent the

events people were setting up near the tree line of the beach. "They should have it ready to hand over to you within the next hour or so. It's bigger than some of the trailers you've had to use on past shoots, but the floor will be squishy. Will that work?"

Vee looked from underneath the brim of the giant straw hat she'd put on as soon as we reached the shore. "I reckon so, since I ain't got much to fool with on this one. I just gotta bronze 'em up and spray sea salt in their hair." Suddenly the Italian-speaking blonde bombshell had transformed herself into a country hick.

It was another interesting feature that came along with Vee. She was a cultural chameleon. I'd witnessed her transform into a mob boss's Sicilian *nonna* who was threatening to put a hex on anyone who didn't agree to use the moisturizer in her makeup kit. Another time, a French maiden. Today, after meeting Erlene and a few other locals, Vee was Southern and would probably remain mostly in this character throughout the shoot.

"I could use a glass of sweet tea, darlin'." Vee fanned herself with the paper fan she'd pilfered from the stack in Erlene's office. It advertised a church revival that had already passed. "How about y'all?"

I looked around me, finding everyone else down the beach a ways. "Your Southern drawl is spot-on, but you just used *y'all* wrong."

Vee dropped the act and lowered her fan. "Did I?"

"Yep, *y'all* is plural." I pointed to myself with the clipboard in my hand. "There's only one of me."

"Then what does a Southerner say to just one person?"

"You."

"Well, that's just boring." Vee huffed, looking around. "I need plural . . ." Her face lit up and then she waved. "Whit! Sonny says *y'all* got business to discuss!"

I looked over my shoulder and saw Whit making his way over to us with his eyes trained on his cell phone. He wore cargo shorts with numerous pockets and a button-down with the sleeves rolled up at the elbows, but his feet were bare, as were most of ours. He appeared docile but I knew better.

"Thanks a lot, Evelyn." I whispered her real name on a hiss.

She gasped. "That's uncalled for. He was already on his way over." Her voice lowered. "News flash, it's going to be impossible to avoid him for the next two months."

"Ladies." Whit's velvety voice wrapped around the one word. With eyes the color of his favorite bourbon trained on me, he said dismissively, "If you'll excuse us, Vee."

She hesitated for a second before walking away. There was nothing about this movie Whit couldn't say in front of her, so I already knew where this was going but tried to make an interception anyway.

"Les should be here soon so we can do a walk-through. I'll need the call sheets ASAP to give to the boat taxis and—"

"Don't waste my time with PA tasks."

I lowered the clipboard and reduced myself into the submissive role he expected. "Of course. May I help you with something?"

"Yes. There's a problem with my villa." He slid his phone into the side pocket of his shorts and stepped closer, invading my personal space as if it belonged to him.

For a brief time that might have been true. I'd just turned nineteen when I met the thirty-five-year-old Whit on set. Quick to flirt and even quicker to misuse his position of power, Whit was brazen enough to push and I was weak enough to fall for it.

Not knowing any better, I had been flattered in the beginning, but then I got myself stuck in a toxic relationship that I couldn't unstick from. The one time I tried to end it, I was passed by for several film projects at Whit's recommendation. I was close to the point of being evicted from my apartment when I gave in, realizing I had no other choice but to play the industry game by Whit's rules.

"What could possibly be wrong with your villa? I personally toured each one. They're gorgeous."

Not caring who might see us, Whit placed his hand on my hip and spoke into my ear. "It's too big for just me. I'll get lonely." His breath tickled the side of my neck, and I hated myself for being unable to suppress the shudder that moved through my body.

After meeting Whit, I learned quickly that his radar picked up those less-than who were still struggling to make it onto the film scene. Once I had caught his attention, the cat and mouse game began. Thirteen years later, the game continued whether I wanted to play or not.

I stepped back, looking at my notes as an excuse to put some space between us. "The cast members are in the neighboring villas and Les is right next door. I doubt you'll be lonely." He'd never been one to fraternize with the well-established actresses or high-up execs, so it was no surprise that my comment made him scoff.

Whit ran a hand through his salt-and-pepper hair. The gray only added to his overall appeal. A silver fox is what most women called him. "You'd be much better company."

This was where the situation got sticky with this man. I couldn't outright reject him, nor would I be falling into bed with him again. I'd made that promise to myself and planned to keep it this time.

With a coy smile fixed on my face, I handed over my excuse along with a shrug of my shoulder. "That's mighty tempting and sweet of you to offer, but I have to stay at the motel and make sure your crew gets here each day on time. I have to do my job."

"That's why you have an assistant, babe."

"Oh, but my assistant will be staying with her daddy in his villa." I backed up and caught sight of a golf cart with Les in it coming to a stop on the beach. "Director's orders. Speaking of the devil, here he is now." I began walking away before Whit could say anything else.

Heart pounding and palms sweating, I reassured myself I'd dodged him successfully and promised I'd do it again next time too.

● ● ●

Time is money. The popular saying was an absolute fact in the industry, so the goal was always to get as much done as possible in the least amount of time. My day had begun before sunrise in California and hadn't slowed down since arriving in Charleston. Hours had passed at the typical high-speed rate while we worked on setting up near the beach and then dealing with a mosquito issue in the wooded area where the castaways' shelter would be constructed.

By the time I reached the motel, my body and mind were bone-tired and it seemed the crew felt the same. Only a few sat by the empty pool to nurse a beer while unwinding. I waved off the offers to join them, promising another time, and went straight to my room on the first floor. It was two doors down from the laundry room/cantina, making it, in Erlene's opinion, the best room in the place. That didn't matter much to me. I just needed a shower and some peace and quiet.

As soon as I shoved the door open, a heat much the same as outside greeted me. I checked the window unit and found it silent. Whoever cleaned my room must have switched it off, making the room stifling. I cranked it up to high, then without slowing down for fear I'd just pass out in my nastiness, I plugged in my phone and stripped out of my sweaty clothes on the way to the bathroom for what I'd hoped would be a refreshing cold shower.

The shower was neither refreshing nor cold but an unappealing lukewarm. Apparently the high heat index was too powerful for the water system as well. My body remained hot and close to breaking out in another sweat, so I tucked the tiny towel around me and shuffled to stand in front of the window unit while I debated the idea of supper. The rumbling in my belly said *food, please,* but my tired muscles begged for an early bedtime.

A knock on the door startled me before I'd made a choice. It was either one of the guys assigned to lure me out by the pool or Vee. I tiptoed over and checked who it was through the peephole. My stomach recoiled at the sight of Whit standing there, looking down at the phone in his hand. He glanced up as if he sensed me on the other side of the door.

Frowning, I leaned away from the peephole and checked the lock and was relieved to find it secured. Holding my breath, I slowly backed away and lowered myself on the end of the bed as quietly as possible. Whit knocked again and then the doorknob jiggled. My phone chimed where it was charging on the nightstand but I didn't bother looking. It was Whit, I was certain. The man never gave up easily, but I'd made a promise to myself not to give in to him during this project.

"Sonny," he said before knocking again.

"Not this time," I whispered, remembering the first time I did give in.

My fight-or-flight instinct never kicked in that night when he brought me back to his place after a long day on set. I saw stars when I looked at the man, and him showing me attention was flattering, so I agreed. I thought we would hang out and get to know each other better, maybe a kiss. The kiss happened almost before the door shut, and it was aggressive and demanding. It scared me. Instead of defending myself, I just froze. I thought if I didn't respond, he would realize I wasn't into it. But he chose to read my actions as me submitting and thus took what he wanted. I hated myself for it.

My eyes started to sting. Blinking, I clutched the front of the towel in my fist and watched the doorknob jiggle again as if he thought the thing would submit to his whim also.

I brought a lot of it on myself. Being with him opened doors quickly for me, and so he expected my door to always be open to him. A successful career shouldn't have weighed in with my self-worth. It should have been an easy decision to stand up for myself and walk away with my dignity. Even after I ended things, he would advance, and instead of taking up for myself, I'd shut down. For some reason I couldn't explain even to myself, Whit Kessler had the power of rendering me down to nothing more than a frozen block of cowering human. My mind would disconnect with my body, taking my thoughts far, far away from my physical presence. Facing it the next day always revealed all the ugliness. It made it hard to look at myself in the mirror.

Tired of the game with Whit and ashamed of myself for playing it in the first place, I reclined onto the bed. Staring at the water-stained ceiling, I managed to at least allow a few tears their freedom.

CHAPTER FIVE

In MIDDLE SCHOOL, my class went on an overnight field trip to a nature center in the middle of a swamp. The first thing the park ranger did was sit our group down and go over safety procedures. We were too excited about the obstacle course to pay much attention, but everyone's ears perked up when he mentioned black bears and what to do if we encountered one during our trip. Slowly retreat if it doesn't notice you. If it does, don't play dead. Stand your ground. Get loud and aggressive so that you don't appear to be prey. Look dominant.

I stood my ground with a bear last night by not allowing him into my room, but as soon as I arrived to Moise Island and met Whit's cold, calculated stare, I wasn't sure I'd survive the day on set.

Putting on my act of obliviousness, I smiled at him as he waved me over to where the crew was setting up for the first scene.

"For the duration of a project you are to be reachable at all times. I realize you're a little slow on the uptake, but you should at least understand this after a decade and a half of working in the industry."

Out the corner of my eye, I noticed several crew members pause. *Great, we have an audience for my scolding.* "I must have been in the shower," I lied.

"I texted you."

"My phone died. I didn't see your texts until this morning."

Whit mumbled something about me being just as incompetent as Delaney as he stomped away.

I touched the side of my flushed neck and managed to keep my mouth shut when what I really wanted to do was lay into him. Though he carried the actual blame, Whit knew how to delegate that blame to someone else as easily as delegating grunt work to the assistants.

I spent the entire morning in a constant state of humiliation as Whit continuously dressed me down with his passive-aggressive remarks, which had always been his weapon of choice. Pretending all was right in the world, I got to work, but it seemed within a blink I was back to facing off with Whit.

"You want to explain this to me?" He shoved a paper in my direction.

I read over it and handed it back to him. "I forwarded this to you earlier. The warehouse screwed up our order."

The muscle in his jaw flexed. "We need those props today."

"I'll see what I can do," I promised, hurrying off before he could berate me any further.

Whit said loudly before I got out of earshot, "I fired Delaney because of inadequacies such as this."

Pretending I didn't catch his threat, I booked it to Vee's tent and stayed there for as long as I could. While I fired off emails, telling the supplier that we'd pay extra to secure a quicker delivery, I had to keep giving myself pep talks. *Just get through this project. Just get through this summer.*

Later in the day, my walkie-talkie buzzed with an assistant announcing, "They just delivered lunch."

Vee looked up from putting away her makeup kit. "We're hitting the beach, right?"

We'd both worn our swimsuits to the set with the idea of spending the lunch break sunbathing and swimming, but now, after the morning I'd had, I didn't feel up to it.

Whit stormed in before I could respond. "There's no gluten-free options for lunch."

I quickly fumbled with my phone, pulling up the dietary needs of the cast and crew and skimming over the details. "I don't see any notations of anyone needing gluten-free."

"You forget what decade you're living in, Bates? Gluten-free should always be an option." His phone went off in his hand. He looked at it and turned to leave. "How long have we been keeping you employed? Overlooking dietary needs is a rookie mistake. You know better."

After the tent flap fluttered shut, I asked Vee, "Can I pass today? I need to get some gluten-free food ordered and out here ASAP."

She gave me a look and after a few beats nodded her head. "If you need to talk, you know where to find me."

"Thanks." I offered her a small smile and dialed the catering company.

Once I made sure two of the actresses received their lunches, I chose to give myself a time-out and roam the beach instead of eating. No way would my anxious stomach have agreed to that anyway.

Walking the shoreline, I spotted a starfish washed up beside a few seashells. Taking out my phone, I captured several angles of it.

"Is this for your little vlog?" Whit asked, coming up behind me.

"Yep," I muttered, busying myself with taking even more photos just so I wouldn't have to face him directly.

"I don't pay you to photograph shells for your personal use."

I straightened and gave him my sweetest smile. "Well, it's my lunch break, so no Whit Rules have been broken, boss." What irritated me the most was knowing that if I had opened my door to him last night, Whit would have been perfectly fine if I did nothing all day but lie on a lounge chair while everyone else worked. He'd not have said one word to me about it.

"If this is about me and Delaney—"

"Your private life is none of my business. I just want to do my job here." I glanced around the shore, making sure we were alone. "We both know why you gave her a job. One she wasn't qualified for. You brought me here last minute and I've busted my butt to clean up the mess she made."

"You forget so easily how unqualified you were at one time." He moved closer and sharpened his tone. "Don't forget who signs your paychecks."

Properly put in my place even though I was so sick of being his doormat, my throat thickened. Thankfully, Whit walked away so I didn't have to form a response.

I spent the rest of the afternoon giving Whit and most everyone else a wide berth. I kept my head down and tried to be invisible until the director called it a wrap for the day.

I set out toward the forbidden island, for what, I'm not sure. Maybe a distraction? An escape from my reality? I tied off the boat at the dock and took the worn trail up to the homestead. I had no expectations of actually finding the Monster of Indigo Isle. I figured he'd be lurking somewhere in the shadows, watching me snoop until deciding to chase me off again. That I was prepared for. Certainly not what I actually found.

As soon as I stepped into the yard, my eyes landed on what can only be described as a genuine wild man. Dressed in a tattered T-shirt and shorts. Feet bare. Unkempt brown hair that was beyond shaggy and faded a good bit near the ends from the sea and sun. A long, scruffy beard covered half his tanned face.

Akin to that night on the beach, we stood frozen for several beats: him, by the field of weeds, clutching a small ax in his right hand, and me, defenseless by the trees, staring in silence.

I waved at him and cleared my throat. "Oh, uh, hi, uh . . . I'm Sonny."

The man's features managed to grow more severe as several strands of hair fell over his piercing gray eyes. "What do you want?" His voice held rusty hints of damage or pain. Or more likely both.

"I, uh . . . I . . ." I tried to explain why I was there, but I really didn't rightly know myself.

He angled his left side away from me, but I still saw the thick scarring along his neck. More scarring riddled his upper arm where it peeked from the edge of his shirtsleeve. A giant rip in his shirt showed off the smooth tanned skin of his abdomen, answering my curiosity about how far the scar spanned. From what I could tell, the damage was mainly on his upper body. Sure, it was bad and fairly extensive, but nothing as grotesque and disfiguring as the locals had made it out to be. Maybe it was his attitude that made him a monster, rather than his physical attributes.

Abruptly, he turned to completely face me, apparently catching me staring and daring me to keep doing it.

I averted my eyes and wiped my sweaty palms against the back of my shorts, trying to muster the courage to do a better job at introducing myself. "I, uh . . . I'm . . ."

"Spit it out already. Use your words." He looked like a crazed man, waving that ax at me, but he spoke with an educated air.

Unsettled, I continued stuttering around what I wanted to say.

"Just leave." He said the words between gritted teeth. Teeth that were straight and brightly clean, a direct contrast to the rest of him.

I'd already had my fill of being belittled for the day from Whit. No way would I be accepting another serving of it from this jerk. Hands finding my hips, I squared my shoulders. "There's no sense in you being so dang rude. I just wanted to say hey."

"I said leave!" With a quick flick of his wrist, the small ax rotated through the air until it stabbed the ground only a few feet in front of me.

Gasping, I jumped back. "Are you crazy?"

He crossed his arms and tilted his head in a way to show off the deep scars on the side of his neck and gave me a menacing look. A look that left no doubt about his crazy. I'd watched a lot of movies with villains. None of them could hold a candle to this man's sinister sneer. I should have been beyond frightened, but apparently I didn't have better sense.

Ignoring his threatening stance, I glared back at him. "I'm not leaving until you apologize."

"For what?" He spit the two words out with a thick measure of disdain.

I bent down to yank the ax out of the ground, which took more effort than I had anticipated. It was good and stuck. Grunting, I finally dislodged it and waved it at him. "You tried to hurt me!"

"I wouldn't have failed if that were my intention." His gravelly tone didn't hide his intelligence, making his exterior such a contradiction. He stormed over before I could react and swiftly tugged the ax out of my hand. "Get off my island."

He towered over me, so I had to angle my head back to give him a good glare. From the grunginess of him, I expected him to reek of sweat and body odor as foul as his mood, but that wasn't the case. His nearness only brought the clean scent of citrus and herbs. With him this close, I also had a better view of the scarring. A strong urge came over me to test the texture of it with my fingertips, but with him snarling like a wild beast, I decided it was best to keep my hands to myself for fear of losing a limb.

For safety measures, I eased back a few steps and crossed my arms with all the attitude I could muster. "Apologize first."

Exasperated, he shook his head and started toward the porch.

"I'm not leaving," I yelled at his back just before he disappeared into his haunted house and slammed the door.

It had already been an exhausting day. I should have just left, but my stubborn side prevailed. I crossed the yard and plopped down in a chair by his small table. As the warmth of the sun worked into the breeze, my eyes grew heavy. Giving in, I closed them and nodded off almost instantly, nearly falling out of the chair. Righting myself and rubbing my eyes, I looked over my shoulder at the front door. Still no sign of the Monster, so I resettled into the chair and drifted off to sleep.

Deep voices roused me. I blinked awake and scanned the yard before realizing the voices were coming from the trail. Moments later, two uniformed officers emerged from the trees.

"Hi there." I greeted them even though I knew from their apprehensive expressions what was about to go down. I seriously couldn't believe that man had called the cops on me.

"Hi, ma'am. Everything all right?" the taller, dark-skinned officer asked.

"Yes—" I read the name printed on his uniform shirt—"Officer Duffy."

"Well, we received a complaint from Mr. Renfrow. Said he has a trespasser."

"I guess that's me." I smiled sweetly as the officers exchanged a look.

"Look, we don't want any trouble. If you agree to leave, we won't even have to file any charges."

My stomach spasmed and my back stiffened. "Charges?"

"This island is private property," Officer Duffy explained. "How about we leave the man alone."

"The man? What did you say his name was again?" I asked, playing the part of airhead. "I think I may be in the wrong place."

"I think you're right. His name is Hudson Renfrow and he doesn't entertain guests. Ever."

"Yeah. Wrong name for sure. Sorry about this, guys." I rose from the chair and started toward the trail willingly.

"No problem."

The two officers escorted me to my boat and even followed me all the way to the marina, making sure I wouldn't cause any more trouble, I suppose.

Between the growling, the ax throwing, and the two officers, I should have been livid. I guess I was, on some level, but finding out his name felt more like a win than a loss. Hudson Renfrow . . .

• • •

With a demanding work schedule and my pride pretty darn bruised, I stayed away from Indigo Isle. I was there to do a job, not pick fights with a peculiar stranger. Truthfully though, I had reveled in sparring with him in his yard. It was invigorating to stand up to someone and for him to give it right back to me. No holds barred.

Something had to be wrong with me.

I managed to leave the monstrous and mysterious Hudson Renfrow alone for a solid four days before I gave in. After wrapping up on Moise Island by late afternoon, I told myself I just wanted to go by Indigo Isle to look at the shell trees. That I wouldn't actually stop. Surely Hudson wouldn't be around anyway.

But there he was on his small dock, casting out a shrimp net. Seeing him jolted me, and a thrilling energy began pumping through me. It reminded me of how I felt as a child when I used to get my first glimpse of all the gifts under the tree Christmas morning. The anticipation. The not knowing what to expect but burning up to find out.

I got within speaking distance and cut the engine. "Hi, Hudson!"

He looked up, a flash of shock on his face, which gave me immense pleasure. *Yeah, big guy, I know your name.*

"Thought I'd let you know I'm out of jail. Real nice of you to call the cops on me!" I moved to the railing to continue taunting him, but before I could, another boat barreled around the corner, narrowly missing me. The vigorous wake pushed me off-balance and into the ocean. Salt water shot up my nose, setting it on fire. As I breached the surface and coughed as much of the sea out of my airways as possible, a set of strong arms wrapped around me from behind.

"What are you doing?" I sputtered, hardly believing Hudson had jumped in to save me.

"Helping you." Well, he sure didn't sound happy about it. Neither was he doing a good job at helping. We were just too tangled around each other.

"I can help myself, if you'd just let go." A wave crashed into us, and not even that made him release his sturdy grip on me.

"You don't have a life jacket on," he pointed out while we treaded water. The ocean wasn't rough but it had ample life to it to make it challenging.

"I know how to swim." I wiggled around to glare at him and immediately saw the error of this choice. It put me nose to nose with him. My eyes connected with his grayish-blue, nearly colorless, ones. No wonder they'd practically glowed the other night on the beach.

Hudson growled, his breath hot against my salty lips, as I squirmed in his arms. "Stop before you drown us both."

We stopped fighting each other and the ocean, allowing our bodies to sway to the water's rhythm. My hands settled against his chest, right over the rhythm of his heartbeat, which was much more aggressive than the sea surrounding us.

My palms began moving up but before I reached his neck, I caught a glimpse of my boat drifting away from us. "The boat!" I pulled away from him and began swimming with all my might. Reaching the ladder at the stern, I hoisted myself up and turned around to offer Hudson my hand, but he was looking toward the dock that was a good ways off now.

"Don't be stubborn. Just get in and I'll drop you off." I wiggled my offered hand at him.

Giving up much faster than I had expected and ignoring my

offered hand, he dragged himself up and into the boat. Pushing the mess of hair out of his face, his eyes landed on my torso.

I looked down and saw that my white shirt was now transparent, showing off the pink bra underneath. I pulled the material away but it clung right back when my fist released it. Spinning around, I started the boat and moved us to the island.

Before the boat reached the dock, Hudson leapt out and landed as smooth as a panther on the wood planks. Apparently he *was* a former track star, running at breakneck speeds and nailing long jumps. He gathered the shrimp net and started down the dock without so much as a backwards glance.

"Hey, you mind if I tie off here and dry out a little?"

He looked over his shoulder, eyes veering south to my chest for only a second before snapping up.

I crossed my arms to conceal what I could of the peep show. "I don't want to go to the marina like this. I promise to stay no longer than I have to."

"Fine." He beat a path down the trail, leaving me alone.

I tied off the boat and lay across the bench seat to dry out some, wishing the warm wind would get the job done quickly. I replayed the bizarre encounter, wondering if every encounter with Hudson would end up in the bizarre category. I wrapped my arms around myself, thinking about how he held me. There had been care and concern behind that embrace, something I wasn't familiar with. The only time a man had ever put his hands on me like that was to take, certainly not to give.

The slow rocking of the hull began to lull me to sleep. Just as I was about to drift off, a throat cleared. I opened my eyes and found Hudson standing over me with a towel in one hand and a blue button-down shirt in the other. Without a word, he dropped both articles onto my lap and was gone again in a blink.

"Thank you," I yelled, hoping he was close enough to hear me. When he didn't reply after several moments, I peeled off my wet shirt, used the towel to dry off, and then pulled on the soft linen shirt that reached my knees. The blue shade reminded me of worn denim, darker in some spots than others. It had been kind of him to lend the shirt, but I decided right then and there I wouldn't be returning it.

I was a thief, after all. A thief who suddenly had her sights set on something totally off-limits, but the appeal was too great to walk away empty-handed.

CHAPTER SIX

BEYOND THE WAVES CAST:

Teak, the surfer dude hero—played by Kingston Boling
Adella, the princess—played by Valentina Flores
Druther, the surfer dude's sidekick and troublemaker—
    played by Ax Beasley
Nevaeh, the tomboy—played by Tejomai Das
Lark, the emo poet—played by Maura Young
Moss, the sports jock—played by Zayden Ellisor
Carlson, the nerd—played by Blake Rodham

I scanned the list, wondering how the screenwriter had come up with such unusual names. Shoot, the actors' real names were quite unique too. Those were probably just as made-up as the character names, though.

Tucking the script under my arm, I stepped inside the hair and makeup tent. The space was fluttering with activity and anticipation for the first day of filming, which was good because the first day always set the tone for the entire project.

Even in the midst of the chaos, Vee was cool as could be, getting the job done without appearing to be in a hurry. Today's attire looked like a beachwear store threw up on her. A sun visor worn backwards. Myrtle Beach Spring Break 1995 tank top, tie-dyed in vibrant hues. Black booty shorts with white piping, the word *Lifeguard* splashed across the backside in white block letters. She'd even gone the extra mile and accessorized with a beaded shark's-tooth necklace and a white puka shell anklet. Only Vee could pull off such a look and not look absolutely ridiculous.

My ears perked up as Vee began carrying on a lively conversation with Valentina, the leading lady in the movie, while giving the already-bronzed actress a spray tan. Two other actresses stood around them, waiting their turn.

"I won't do youse girls like Stefani did me. I told huh bronze and *glawin'*, but what I got was blotchy and *awrange*." Vee moved the spray gun in a smooth pattern, leaving a thin layer of product as she laid an exaggerated Jersey Shore accent on thick. She was even smacking away on imaginary gum. "Between youse and me, I think she's back awn the *sawce* again. I'm gonna have a tawk wit' Vinny about huh."

The girls followed her lead, clucking their tongues and shaking their heads at the made-up story as if it weren't make-believe.

Vee straightened and gave Valentina's coppery-brown body a close inspection, smacking on that gum all the while. "You look *byoo-tee-ful*. Go look in tha mir-uh." She motioned toward a tri-fold portable mirror set up off to the left beside a stack of trunks. The tent was of good size, but Vee had it packed to the gills.

Vee began prepping the next actress, so I left them to it and went to check a few things with the technicians. Once everyone's walkie-talkies began sounding off the ten-minute warning, I returned to the tent and found Vee putting away the tanning supplies.

"Did you rob a beachwear store and not invite me?"

Vee sniffed a laugh and reached for a plastic bag. "Don't pout. I hooked you up too." She pulled out an identical tank top. "Twinzies!"

I snorted, taking the shirt and bag out of her hand. "Where did you find this stuff?"

Vee pulled out a container of antibacterial cloths and began wiping down her supply table. "Erlene is in the know on where to find the best merchandise. She's my new bestie. We went shopping after dinner last night while you were nowhere to be found." She gave me a sideways glance. "Where'd you disappear to, anyway?"

Suddenly everything in the beachwear bag was fascinating. I pulled the sun visor out and shoved it on my head. "Nowhere."

"Uh-huh." Before Vee could razz me any further, her walkie-talkie went off.

"Teak already smeared his abs. Touch up." The PA's request crackled through the small speaker.

"Ten-four," Vee answered, picking up her kit on the way out.

The remainder of the day was a steady stream of work, so Vee never got the chance to pick up where the awkward conversation left off.

Filming wrapped around six and everyone was dismissed, except for a select few from the production side of things. I hopped onto one of the golf carts to head over to Les Morgan's villa for a meeting. The group consisted of Les, Whit, their assistants, Cade, me, and my "assistant," Lyrica. We gathered around a large dining table as Whit led the meeting.

"The first day went well. Only minor hiccups," Whit began and then went over the schedule for the next several days. When he finished, he glanced around the table and asked, "Any questions, concerns, comments?"

Les tapped his fingers on the tabletop thoughtfully. "So far so good, but I want better. We need to find another location for scene sixteen."

Shuffling of papers followed his words as we all worked to find the scene.

I stifled a groan and began flipping through the script too. Implementing changes the first day of shooting was never a good sign.

"Page forty-eight," the production assistant, Tia, provided. "Beach Kiss."

The group read in silence for a few moments. It would be the first kiss shared between the two leads, Teak and Adella. The scene was to take place at night on a secluded section of the beach. *Easy enough*, I thought.

"The next full moon is July 23. The beach will look spectacular that night," I added, hoping to sell him on nixing the change.

Les dismissed the idea with a swift shake of his bald head. "No. We need more ambience. Something to set it apart from any other beach kissing scene. Lyrica has a great idea."

Lyrica looked up from her phone at the mention of her name, her hot-pink nails pausing midtext. The blank expression on her face indicated she hadn't heard a word of this meeting. "What?"

"Tell us about that island with the shell trees." Les looked down at his notes. "Indigo Isle. You said you could envision scene sixteen being filmed there." Les motioned for her to elaborate.

Lyrica's Caribbean-faux eyes slid my way. "Oh, uh, yeah. Great spot. There's, like, a gazillion oyster and clamshells tied to the trees along the shore. Like Christmas tree ornaments. Sounds like wind chimes too."

I wondered if she could put one more *like* in there somewhere. Whit clapped his hands once. "It's settled."

"Oh, good. So, Lyrica, you've already met with the owner and gotten his permission? Fabulous." I made a show of straightening my papers and slotted them into my messenger bag.

Lyrica's eyes narrowed at me. She knew I'd put her on the spot intentionally. "You're the location manager. I'll leave that part to you." She didn't back down and that made me *like* her just a little.

I wasn't about to back down either. "Rule of thumb, Lyrica: don't come into a meeting wasting the time of our director and producer. Until you have things nailed down, don't bring it up."

Her eyes widened as she sat up straight, letting her phone clatter to the table. "I toured the place. We have pictures."

Before I could lay into her on how things worked around here with Ewol Entertainment, Daddy Les came to his baby girl's rescue.

Les reached over and patted her arm, right above the sugar skull tattoo. "Good work, sweetheart. You're new at this, still learning. We'll give you a pass this time." He winked at her, letting us all know baby girl would always have an unlimited supply of free passes. He dropped the fatherly act as he turned to me. "Bates, make it happen. Let's plan to shoot there on the twenty-third. Keep me updated."

I mustered a faint smile. "Sure."

We were dismissed, Lyrica without a care in the world about the trouble she'd just caused, and me strapped with the nearly impossible task of making it happen. No way would the Monster of Indigo Isle agree to such.

"Good going there, Lyrica," I whispered harshly as I passed her seat.

She followed me outside. "Look, I'm sorry. Daddy was talking about that scene and I just mentioned the shell trees in passing. He got all excited about it and—" She brushed a purple wave of hair off her forehead and huffed. "It felt nice to have his approval for once, okay?"

Dang it, that's all it took for me to soften my attitude toward her. I knew all too well about wanting approval even when it seemed near about impossible to garner it.

"I get it, but you know about the Monster. How on earth am I supposed to get his permission?"

Lyrica scratched her elbow and looked off toward the glittering pool, so I figured I'd lost her attention. She returned her focus on me and snapped her fingers. "Oooh, I know! Go out there and introduce yourself. You're totes pretty. Just, like, loosen up some and flirt a little. Bet he'll agree."

No one was in earshot but I lowered my voice anyway. "I already went back and tried that. The introducing myself part. Not the flirting. Bet you can't guess how that ended."

She shook her head.

"It ended with two officers escorting me off the island."

Her eyes rounded. "No freaking way! The Monster called the cops on you?"

"Yes, so there's no way he's going to give us permission to film out there."

Lyrica muttered a curse under her breath. "Dude, I'm sorry."

I waved off her concerns, knowing if it were possible, I'd jump at the opportunity to impress my father too. "Don't worry about it. I'll figure something out." I glanced over at the pool, remembering I needed to check a social media post off my to-do list. "How about letting me borrow your sunglasses for a minute?"

"Sure." Lyrica plucked the rose-gold sunglasses from the top of her head and handed them over.

I shoved them on, pulled off my shirt, and straightened my bikini top. With my phone in hand, I stood on the second step of the pool, angling around to capture a backdrop of turquoise water and green palms swaying in the breeze. Snapping a selfie, I quickly did a few edits and applied a filter before loading it to Instagram with a list of hashtags: #islandlife, #cartiersunglasses.

I checked over the post one last time, thinking about more suitable hashtags for the caption: #fakelife #notmysunglasses #whyintheworld?

Swallowing with a good bit of difficulty, I hit the Share button.

The pool water felt heavenly on my feet. I just wanted to sink completely in and stay there the rest of the day, but the posh life I portrayed on the Internet wasn't real life, so I climbed out and returned the sunglasses to Lyrica.

"You should stay and hang out for a while. I can order us some drinks."

"Thanks, but I still have a lot of work to get done." I put my shirt on and headed for the golf cart.

"Sonny, I really am sorry!"

I tossed a hand up in acceptance but continued moving. What was done was done.

A plan needed to be sorted out before I even dared to present it to Hudson, so I went straight to the motel to get to work on it.

Not so easy though. My mind kept returning to Lyrica and her father and how I wished I had that chance too.

I left my work on the rattan table and moved over to sit on the bed. Plucking my phone off the nightstand, I stared at the screen, toying with the idea of calling home, but then the last time I did that flashed through my mind.

After only a year of being on my own, I realized my mistake. Down on my luck one night, I called home. I expected my mother or father to pick up and was ready to pour out my heart and beg them to come get me, but Caroline picked up instead. My sister delivered the news that our father had passed away after suffering a massive stroke.

"His funeral was yesterday," she said almost robotically as if it hadn't actually registered yet.

Throat closing and eyes burning, I'd barely gotten the words out. "I would have made a way to get home. Why didn't y'all call me?" I'd broken down a few months before and sent Mama and my sisters my phone number, so I knew they knew how to get in touch with me.

"No one thought you'd show up."

World spinning and my legs close to giving out, I'd plopped down on my rickety futon. "But . . . I didn't get to say goodbye."

"Did you give any of us that choice when you ran off?" Caroline's sharp retort sealed it, so I hung up on her and never called again.

After my bitter exchange with Caroline, the rift between me and my family widened even further. Putting the phone away, I told myself it was for the best to continue leaving them alone. Clearly they were better off that way.

CHAPTER SEVEN

SLY, CLEVER, AND A TAD MANIPULATIVE. These three skills came in handy when piecing together a *Where in the World?* vlog. It took more work than most could imagine, since I was a one-woman show. The process began on set, taking photos and videos of anything and everything that had potential of becoming a clue, which was the easiest part. Then came the hardest part. Editing. Hours of work had to be condensed to less than thirty minutes.

Noticing the time at the top of the screen read 1:14 a.m., I finished one more clip, hit Save, then exited the editing software. It had been a long week on set, and I still hadn't figured out how to go about asking Hudson's permission to film on his beach. Deep down, I knew no matter how I presented the request, his answer would be a hard no.

I clicked on my in-box to make sure no little fires had come in that I needed to put out before getting a few hours of sleep. A new email popped up from one of the production assistants. Bracing myself, I opened it.

Ewol will be hosting an Independence Day celebration
this coming Saturday on Moise Island for the cast and
crew.

Closing all the tabs, I placed the laptop on the table and settled
my tired self under the new blanket I'd picked up from Target a few
days ago when I couldn't take one more night with the polyester
thing pretending to be a comforter. Seriously, it had no comfort
to give. I snuggled into the velvety softness and felt my body begin
to float away to the land of Nod. Before it got too far, though, an
idea had my eyes popping back open.

I could invite Hudson to the party! Surely some fun and getting to know the group would help. Maybe. Probably not, but I
couldn't come up with a better idea. I had two days to work up
enough nerve to ask him. Two days where I went back and forth,
but a one-sentence email from Whit had me pushing past my
doubt and apprehension to at least try.

Scene sixteen has been rewritten to include the shell tree
backdrop, so you better make it happen.

My place in the entertainment industry had been firmly set
into the make-it-happen space. Be the shadow behind the glitz
and glam, making magic where none existed, even though you
don't actually exist in the eyes of Hollywood. Just in the background, springing the mechanisms of creativity where a script line
or an overly dramatized expression fell short. Take the location and
backdrop away from a production piece, and you lose over half the
artistic quality of the film. Yet I'm a nobody here. A puppet. One
with no voice. Replaceable.

Again, you hear something long enough, you tend to accept it as truth.

• • •

The day of the party, I dressed carefully for the occasion. I wore Hudson's blue linen shirt as a dress with the sleeves neatly folded up to my elbows and borrowed Vee's red Tory Burch belt to cinch it at the waist. I hoped to catch his attention for more than just a glaring glance, considering my looks alone hadn't done the trick in previous visits.

As I checked myself in the bathroom mirror, finger-combing a few of my wilder curls, I delivered a pep talk to my reflection. "You got this. Be nice. Be persuasive. Flirt a little. Don't chicken out." Laughing at my absurdity, I headed out before I really did chicken out.

I arrived to Indigo Isle late afternoon and announced myself just before reaching the homestead. "Hey, Hudson! It's me, Sonny! Don't throw any axes, okay?"

Of course my tease was met by silence. No surprise. I made it to the yard and caught sight of him at once. He sat on the front porch steps, reading a book and eating a tomato like it was an apple. His T-shirt was gray but looked to have been black originally. In faded board shorts and bare feet, with his shaggy hair flopping in every direction as if it hadn't seen a comb in ages, not to mention his beard, he resembled a weathered beach bum.

"You heard me calling your name, right?"

If I didn't already know better, I would have assumed the man was deaf. He didn't even look up until I was close enough to cast a shadow on him and his book.

With a frown fixed on his lips, his eyes slowly swept along my body, taking in my attire. "That's my shirt."

I did a slow spin, giving him a chance to really look at me. "Yes. It makes a cute dress, dontcha think?"

His glare settled on the hem just above my knees. "It's too short."

To get a rise out of him, I tugged the shirttails upward in a teasing manner until revealing the white shorts underneath. From his sudden intake of breath, I succeeded.

Hudson's face darkened several shades from the normal grimace. "I want it back."

Biting my lip, I unfastened the top button and moved to the next. Suddenly the man was on his feet, half-eaten tomato and book tossed to the ground.

"What are you doing?" His question came out in a terse growl.

"Giving your shirt back," I answered with artificial innocence. I had no intention of releasing the next button but toyed with it as if I did.

"Stop!" His nose flared. If it were possible, flames would have shot out.

"But you said you wanted it back." I batted my eyelashes, barely holding back a snicker. He looked close to coming unglued.

"No!" Hudson slashed the air with his large hand. "Just keep it on!"

I dropped my hands and the flirty act. "Okay. I'll keep it."

Shaking his head, Hudson bent to gather his abandoned book and snack, placing both down on the porch. "What do you want now?"

"The crew is celebrating the Fourth over on Moise Island." I gauged north and then pointed in that direction.

"What crew?"

Oooh, he's finally asking questions!

"A film crew. I'm a location scout for Ewol Entertainment. We'll be out here filming a movie for the summer." I waited for him to ask another question. He didn't. "So do you want to go to the party with me?"

"No."

"Why not?"

His lips pressed firmly into a thin line. I'd never met someone so stingy with their words as this man.

"We don't have to go right now. It's still early. We can wait to head over once it's dark," I offered, wondering if he was sensitive about his scars.

"No." He returned to the step and opened a worn copy of *The Count of Monte Cristo*. The gold embossing had lost its luster and the corners of the fabric cover were frayed.

"Do you have a social anxiety?" I held my hands up. "No judgment."

"No. I just prefer to be alone." His gravelly voice had dimmed to just over a whisper, as if it pained him to converse with me.

"But isn't that lonely?"

Hudson's eyes moved from the page to meet mine for only a split second before looking away. "Loneliness is just a part of who I am."

I'd come here to soften him enough to ask about filming the movie scene on his beach, but he'd gone and poked at that tender spot deep inside my chest. My throat thickened as I turned his sad confession around in my head.

A few chickens strutted by, clucking a few sentiments, but Hudson ignored them too.

I gazed around the impeccably manicured yard and vegetable garden until landing on the giant field of weeds. I recalled Hudson tending to it that one day with the small ax. "Why do you grow a field full of weeds?"

He turned the page and his eyes began moving over the words.

I nudged his leg with mine. "It's a simple question."

On a long sigh, he finally answered, "It's not weeds."

I looked away from him and studied the stalks with small green leaves that reminded me of fern fronds. "Then what is it?"

"*Indigofera suffruticosa*."

"Indi-what?"

"Indigo," Hudson said sharply, clearly out of patience with me. "You do know what that is, right?"

"Blue?"

"Yep." He reached for the tomato, wiped it off on his faded shirt, and finished eating it in two bites.

"So those green plants produce blue dye?"

He nodded.

"You're an indigo farmer?"

Another nod.

I glanced down at the shirt and smoothed my palm over the sleeve. "You hand-dyed this, didn't you?"

Hudson grumbled a yes.

I peered at him in awe. "Wow, Hudson, you're an artisan."

"Farmer, artisan, same difference." He brushed my compliment off and continued reading.

Knowing this conversation had met a dead end, I returned to the subject of the party. "I've saved my appetite all day for the party. I'm really looking forward to getting my eat on." I laughed quietly, but it did nothing to encourage any response from him. "How about you? Are you getting hungry?"

His eyes darted to me and then back to his book. "I ate a tomato. I'm good."

"Are you a vegetarian?"

"No." Hudson heaved a breath. "Could you cool it with the interrogation?" He lifted his book. "I just want to read in peace."

I showed him my palms and bit my tongue to prevent a tart reply from slipping out.

I eased down onto the step beside him, and we sat in silence for no less than an hour. I waited for him to change his mind about the party and I'm sure he was waiting for me to simply leave. Undoubtedly, neither one of us was going to get our way.

I began reading over his shoulder, getting swept away in Edmond's harrowing prison escape, and didn't register the sun making its exit until a solar night-light blinked on in the yard.

Hudson closed the book and stood.

I did the same, rising to my feet and checking the time on my watch. "I bet the food is ready. The company hired a local barbecue pitmaster to grill up all sorts of yummy stuff right there on the beach. You ready to go?"

His stormy gaze cut to me, thick eyebrows pinching together, as if I'd just suggested skydiving naked or something equally outrageous.

"Is that a no?"

He answered by going inside and closing the door firmly behind him.

Although Hudson had made it clear he wouldn't be going with me, I remained on the dark porch a while longer just in case he changed his mind.

Finally giving up, I left him with his loneliness.

• • •

The party was already in full swing by the time I reached Moise Island. Music loud, drinks flowing, dancing, boisterous laughter, giant smiles. It was great, yet I felt completely out of place and stayed on the outskirts of the festivities to keep an eye on Whit as well as avoid him at the same time. He had an uncanny knack for sneaking up and cornering me. He'd kept a cold shoulder toward me since the motel room debacle, but something told me he'd seek me out with inhibitions in the wind if I didn't stay on my toes.

In a sea of red, white, and blue stood Vee resembling a burlesque Lady Liberty. Mint-green flapper dress, an iridescent-green makeup treatment, and a glittery crown.

She twirled around in Cade's arms and her eyes landed on me. *"Danse avec moi!"*

I cupped my ear and shook my head.

"Dance with me!" Vee translated in a thick French accent. The woman was humorously clever, paying homage to the French, who gave the Statue of Liberty to the US. I wondered if anyone else picked up on it, but from the lazy grins and clumsy motions, most had already allowed their intellectual side to check out for the day.

"Later," I said, laughing off the invitation.

"Menteuse!" Vee pointed a green fingernail toward me. "Liar!"

I stuck out my tongue at her.

The crowd erupted as the DJ began spinning a techno remix of "Born in the USA." I spotted Whit with a young production assistant in his arms, making out right there in front of everyone. The crew called Whit's conquests "boss babes" behind his back. A title that had once been attached to my name. More than likely, it still was.

Bodies moved around them, hands touching, hips gyrating,

free and wanton. It hadn't been too long ago that I would have been right in the middle of the debauchery, needing the validation that I fit in, that I belonged. The whole ordeal grew too tiresome and had only validated how far down the wrong road I had traveled, leaving me worse for wear.

Turning my back to the group and all the cringy emotions it provoked, I moved on to the buffet. I scanned the delectable selection, wondering if Hudson would be eating something besides that tomato. Sure, it was red, a July 4 color, but it couldn't compare to the grilled meats and vegetables, pasta salads, breads, and desserts before me. No way would it be possible to enjoy this meal, knowing he was out there on Indigo Isle all alone.

I was about to just go back to the motel and do the loneliness thing as well, but my eyes landed on a good-size cooler bag peeking out from underneath the table. Promising myself I'd return it to the catering company, I hooked the strap around my fingers and slid it out while glancing over my shoulder. No eyes on me, so I got to work.

Everyone was too busy celebrating to pay me much attention, so in no time, I piled up plates, wrapped them in tinfoil that was conveniently left by the giant grill, tossed in some plastic cups and utensils, and even snatched an unopened bottle of Simply Lemonade from the tiki bar.

With my heart beating in my throat, I kept my head down and hightailed it to the boat. I tucked the loot under a seat and scanned the gathering down the beach. It seemed almost too easy, but I guess a food bandit making a clean getaway was the last concern on anyone's mind. After taking a moment to settle down, I pulled away and started over the inky-black water. Dark and eerie yet so alluring, similar to the lonely monster I was about to go disturb.

Fifteen minutes later, I came to a stop at the now-familiar dock. Retrieving the cooler bag, I trekked up to the house. The hushed melody of the ocean and singing insects followed behind me. There was no sign of Hudson as I reached the yard. Undeterred, I marched right up the porch steps and knocked on the front door. Giving it a moment, I knocked again.

"Hudson! It's me, Sonny! I brought you supper!" I waited. Nothing.

I knocked again. "I even brought chocolate cake . . . and strawberry pie!" I figured if he didn't like chocolate, maybe a fruit dessert would be more to his liking. Knowing the sour man, though, he probably didn't like sugar, period. "I also have corn bread and lemonade! No one can say no to that!"

A grumbled groan came from somewhere behind the house and that alone made me grin. If Hudson didn't want me to discover him, he'd never have made a peep. Past visits proved that. I moved off the porch and rounded the house, finding his shadowed figure in a hammock tied between two oak trees.

"The fireworks will probably start soon. Let's head down to the beach so we can watch while we eat." I lifted the cooler bag to entice him out of the hammock, but he didn't move.

"You should have stayed at your party," Hudson said in a cutting tone. I couldn't see his face but could easily picture the harsh expression on his face.

"I wasn't in the mood for a party. I just want to chill and have a quiet meal."

"Then go home and have at it." The hammock swayed.

"But . . . I want to share this meal with you."

"I don't need your pity visits or your scraps."

"This ain't about you or pity."

"Then what's it about?"

I glanced toward the back of the house with its screened-in porch, focusing on nothing in particular. "I like it out here. There are hardly any noises. My life . . . it's too loud." I squared my shoulders. "So if you wouldn't mind not calling the cops on me, I'm going down to the beach to enjoy some peace and quiet. I won't bother you and I'll only stay until the fireworks end." I knew I had no right to be bargaining a beach picnic on his private property, but I turned and hurried away before he could muster a growl or some other nonverbal response.

A blanket danced with a small gust of wind where it was draped on a clothesline in the side yard. I backtracked a few steps, unpinned it, and placed it over my free shoulder.

I reached the shoreline and chose a spot near the shell trees, loving how their melody harmonized with the ocean's hum. After spreading the blanket over the sand, I unzipped the bag and began arranging things. It would be a picnic for one, but I set out Hudson's plate anyway, mindfully placing it to my left so that his scarred side wouldn't be visible in case that bothered him. I tucked a napkin underneath the edge of the plate and put the utensils on top of it, ready for a guest. My picnic looked less lonely that way.

Waiting a few more minutes before giving in, I peeled the tinfoil off my plate and inhaled the savory aroma before the ocean breeze stole it. The first forkful of tangy barbecue was heavenly. I followed that bite with a pinch of sweet corn bread. As I dove into the macaroni salad, the sky lit up with the first burst of red sparkles.

The food and the show were both spectacular, and I was so caught up enjoying myself that I didn't realize I wasn't the only one on the beach until I turned to grab my cup of lemonade and spotted Hudson's long, lean body standing behind me. A jolt of elation shot through me and it was all I could do to contain the giggle bubbling up from my chest. The fizzy sensation reminded me of drinking soda too fast, slightly uncomfortable but oddly enjoyable as well.

"Your food is getting cold." I motioned toward the plate.

Hudson took his spot, sitting cross-legged beside me, and placed the plate in his lap. "I'm not letting you steal my blanket, too."

"I wasn't planning on it anyway." Holding back a smile, I filled a cup with lemonade and handed it to him.

He accepted it with only a nod of his head, taking a sip while studying his plate of food with a good bit of caution.

"It's all really good." I loaded my fork with more pulled pork and crammed it into my mouth.

Hudson side-eyed me as I chewed. Eventually he stabbed his fork into a slice of brisket, sniffed it, and then took a bite. He went in for another taste, so I assumed it met his approval.

Leaving my skeptical dinner companion alone to enjoy his meal, I brought my attention to the fireworks off in the distance. I loved how the ocean roared in a way to muffle the booms, crackles, and popping sounds.

Our gaze remained on the colorful show in the sky as we worked on cleaning our plates. This had to have been the most peaceful dinner I'd shared with someone in, well, ever.

Eventually the fireworks concluded and our plates emptied, but we remained on the beach. With the sky void of any clouds, the light from the half-moon and stars cast an ethereal glow on everything it touched. The sand, the driftwood, the whitecaps rolling onto shore, my picnic companion.

I chanced a sly look in his direction. Hudson's wild hair danced in the breeze, giving him a softer edge tonight, almost making him seem approachable. His shoulders went from relaxed to stiffened, making me aware I wasn't so sly and had stared too long. He began to shift. I panicked, thinking he was going to end the perfectly nice night by ditching me or demanding I get off his property, so I pulled more plates from the bag.

"Dessert." I unwrapped the two plates and set them between us. "Chocolate cake or strawberry pie. Pick your poison."

He hesitated. *Of course* he hesitated, but perhaps the pie was too tempting. He fished his fork from the dinner plate and started slowly tearing the pie apart, eating the berries first and then the crust.

I was beyond full, so I closed my eyes and placed my palms on the ground behind me to recline slightly. The soft tinkling sounds from the shell trees drew my attention. I did nothing but appreciate the soothing sound for a while.

"I am in love with those shell trees," I whispered, keeping my eyes closed. "I have this app on my phone I use for meditation but it's nowhere near as relaxing as this."

Hudson didn't comment, but I didn't expect him to anyway. Even though he didn't fill the space between us with many words or any other form of communication, Hudson did fill a void I hadn't realized was there, simply by being present.

I hummed a long sigh and slowly opened my eyes. "Did you string all those shells by yourself?"

His eyes regarded me but his lips remained pressed together.

"Seriously, what's the story with the trees?" I twisted around to face said trees. The moonlight glanced off the various silvery-white shells as they swayed languidly from their branches.

Hudson shifted around to look too. Moments passed before he

finally answered on a sigh, "That's the handiwork of my eccentric grandfather, Elson Renfrow. Over thirty years' worth." The gruffness of his voice softened with mentioning his grandfather, revealing a reverence for his loved one.

When he didn't elaborate further, I asked, "Why, though?"

"I asked him if it was to ward off evil spirits, but he said it was to ward off melancholy."

My smile faded at that sad answer. Melancholy could plague me at times as if it were an evil spirit. "I'd love to meet him."

"He would have gotten a kick out of you, stomping around here with no concern of my warnings." Hudson shook his head, his frown deepening. "But he passed away a few years ago."

I reached out but drew my hand away before touching his arm. "I'm so sorry. I bet he was awesome."

"More than awesome. He was this silly old man who always seemed childlike to me." Hudson leaned just a fraction my way as if to share a secret. "I thought he was Peter Pan." Eyes lit up, he almost smiled. Almost. And I almost unraveled at the possibility of it.

"Sounds like he would make for a memorable movie character." I smiled, wishing it would encourage him to return one to me, but his lips remained curved downward.

Hudson redirected his attention to the shell trees and brushed a palm down his dark beard. "That's your thing? Movies?"

I nodded my head enthusiastically, tickled beyond words that this mostly mute man was initiating a conversation with me. "Yes. I've been working in film for almost fifteen years."

The filming request almost slipped out of my mouth, but I swallowed it with a long sip of lemonade. Hudson would think the picnic was just a ploy to get his permission. Earlier in the day, that had been my intention, but now? Now I just wanted to spend the holiday in this comfort and forget all about bothering him with the request. This was Hudson's private home, his place of solace, and the outside world shouldn't be allowed to touch it.

I rubbed my forehead, knowing the only remedy to this was to convince Les Morgan to film somewhere else. The idea of that alone made me want to hide out here with this grumpy man indefinitely.

"Where'd you go?"

Stunned that he even asked something, I dropped my hand and looked over at him. "Huh?"

He motioned toward me. "You were quiet. Not that I'm complaining."

"Ha-ha." I gave him a sardonic smile. "Just thinking about work and all that I need to get done."

It had been a perfect night and I wanted to leave it that way, so I pushed to my feet and began collecting our plates.

Hudson helped me shake the sand from the blanket and then we worked together to fold it. Once it was in a neat folded square, he went to pull it from my hands, but I held it away playfully just long enough for him to give me an icy glare.

"Just kidding." Snickering, I offered it to him.

He snatched the blanket without acknowledging my tease. No surprise there, but it was surprising when he walked me to my boat while carrying the cooler bag like a perfect gentleman. I bit my lip to hide the smile at the thought of him being a gentleman. It wasn't a word that came to mind to describe this man.

As we stood underneath the solar night-light hung on a pole by the dock, I gazed up at him and saw the most intriguing disaster I had ever seen. Not even the scars could diminish his appeal.

Behind the overgrown beard and harsh demeanor, I'd bet my last paycheck that Hudson Renfrow was an attractive man in hiding.

The magnetic pull to explore all aspects of this disastrous man made no sense to me, but then again, I was a disaster myself. Perhaps disasters attracted other disasters.

I was pretty sure that idea would only end in disaster.

CHAPTER EIGHT

FIVE ENCOUNTERS WITH HUDSON RENFROW. Only five. Such a small amount of interaction to have formed such an impact on me. Truly, it made no sense. I found myself drawn to the brooding man, nonetheless, and saw something beyond his rough exterior.

My mind wouldn't shut off last night after leaving the island. I went over the few words he'd shared with me so many times that when I finally did go to sleep, I dreamed about Peter Pan playing hide-and-seek behind the shell trees.

With a late afternoon shoot scheduled for today, there was no rush to get moving this morning, so I rolled over and fluffed the deflated pillow. I'd already been lying here for a good while, thinking I'd doze back off, but my thoughts remained out on Indigo Isle with Hudson. I'd honestly never in my thirty-two years of life ever felt this way about a man.

After indulging a little longer in doing absolutely nothing but moon over a stranger, I tossed off the blanket and got dressed. I gathered my laundry bag and shuffled two doors down to the laundry room. Luckily, both the washer and dryer were empty, so I quickly sorted the darks from the lights and started my first load. During my early days in LA, I'd learned the hard way to never leave your laundry unattended after the misfortune of having my stuff stolen or tossed on the floor still wet. I moved a plastic lawn chair just outside the room and took a seat. I had a perfect view of the courtyard and empty pool. It had been patched and replastered this week, but it still remained barren.

The door to my right opened and Erlene shuffled out with her walker leading the way. She noticed me and paused. "Good morning, hon."

"Good morning." I eyed her rayon dress suit. The periwinkle color brought out the pinkish tinge of her gunmetal-gray hair. She'd paired the suit with beige old-school orthopedic sneakers with Velcro straps. "Don't you look sharp."

"Why, thank you." She preened. "I meant to invite you and your friends to church. It doesn't start for another hour."

"Oh . . ." I patted down my mess of curls. "I haven't even showered yet and . . . I didn't pack any church clothes." My face heated.

Erlene clucked her tongue softly. "God won't care if you show up in shorts as long as you show up."

The sweet old lady made it sound so easy-peasy, but she didn't know the rocky relationship I had with God. After that last phone call with my sister, with my self-worth at an all-time low, I had walked even further away from God. If my own family had no use for me, surely God wouldn't either. I seriously doubted he would want the likes of me anywhere near one of his houses. Truth be told, I didn't even associate Sundays with church services anymore, another something on an extensive list of all the things I wasn't proud of.

My mother and sisters were probably already at church. I wondered if they still sat on the same pew midway on the right side and if Mama still sang in the choir while Caroline played the piano.

Too uncomfortable to even look at Erlene, I stared at the empty pool. "Maybe another time. I need to get my laundry done before heading to work."

"All right, but the invite is always open." She patted my slumped shoulder. The walker scraped against the cement as she hobbled away, leaving me alone with the hum of the washing machine moving through its cycle.

A door opened on the second floor, directly across from me. I looked up just as Vee stepped out of Cade's room, dressed in black yoga pants and an off-the-shoulder tee, with her short blonde hair sticking out in every direction.

I cleared my throat, and as soon as her wide eyes landed on me, I gave her a tiny finger wave and a smug smile.

Something changed in her demeanor; the sleepy-eyed Vee switched into an alert woman. She plastered her back against Cade's closed door and her lips started moving. After a few beats, I picked up on the familiar tune.

Dun, dun, da-da, dun, dun, da-da . . .

As she mimicked the *Mission: Impossible* theme song, she craned her neck, looking to the left and then the right. Finding the coast clear, Miss MI started sidestepping down the walkway in a slight crouch, keeping an eye out for the enemy all the while. Around the corner, the spy disappeared out of sight only to reappear seconds later on the stairway, descending a few steps backwards before spinning around and leaping over the last two steps. Her bare feet landed without sound. The song continued as she cautiously made her way toward her room, looking over her shoulder, stopping a few times to duck in a shadow.

Biting the inside of my cheek, I watched on until the spy slipped inside her room. The door closed but reopened almost immediately to present the performer acknowledging her imaginary audience. As I gave her a slow clap, Vee executed an exaggerated bow, straightening with one arm raised and then doing it again.

One step in reverse, the door closed, and she was gone.

"Only Vee," I whispered and laughed quietly. That had to be the most creative walk of shame I'd ever witnessed.

The woman never turned off her persona, probably not even in her sleep. The only time I'd ever witnessed Hollywood Vee slipping just enough to give me a glimpse of Evelyn Smith from North Dakota was a night we spent hanging out in my apartment. She'd had one too many and entertained me until sunrise talking about her childhood with free-spirited parents, who were beekeepers. She even brought out her Midwestern accent, which only added to the tales.

The washing machine chimed, indicating the cycle was complete. I went inside and rotated the laundry while pondering carefully crafted personas. The entertainment business was famous for them, but I believed most everyone had one at the ready. Even my mother. Ronaka Bates was known as the Shrimp Lady in the Georgetown community. She helped run her family's seafood market and had even written a cookbook dedicated to nothing but shrimp recipes. Mama could give Bubba from *Forrest Gump* a run for his money with all things shrimp, that's for sure. But at home, Shrimp Lady was left at the door, because the truth was Mama hated shrimp and refused to make anything for us that contained the shellfish.

I slid to the floor and propped my back against the dryer. I pulled out my phone and tapped the Instagram icon. Scanning my profile, it was easy to see what persona I presented.

My life is fabulous.

I'm fabulous.

Everything is fabulous.

Aubrey was the only member of my family who followed me on social media. Keeping my image glittery and glam, I'd hoped my sister would share all my fabulousness with the rest of them. To show them I'd made it. That I was a success and totally fabulous while doing it.

I hit the camera icon and angled my phone until the laundry bag and jug of detergent could be seen over my shoulder. Snapping a few selfies, I browsed through them to see what the image captured. Nothing more than a curly-headed woman with faint circles under her hazel eyes. Plain and ordinary. I wondered how my followers would respond to this. If letting my fabricated fabulousness slip some to show a truer side would hurt or hinder.

Deleting the images, I reminded myself of my role. I paraded around as a maven, pretending for the masses that I'd somehow managed to figure out the secret of lucrative success at a young age. I was a fraud.

• • •

I finished up the laundry and made myself presentable enough in a plain heather-gray tee and a pair of boyfriend jeans for the afternoon shoot. That was pretty much my go-to work uniform. The tees were always plain, jeans always baggy, and usually a pair of slide-on Vans on my feet. This time though, flip-flops were more suited since we all went barefoot while filming on the beach. Not wanting to fuss with my frizzy curls, I pulled on a baseball cap and called it done before heading to the marina.

An hour after I arrived to Moise Island, Vee had the cast bronzed, oiled up, and ready to go.

The first scene of the day lasted all of five minutes before Les went to yelling, "Cut!"

All eyes snapped toward our lead actor, Kingston, as he came out of the surf carrying the two halves of his red surfboard.

"How'd you manage that?" Les asked.

Kingston shrugged. "I have no bloody idea."

"Props!" Whit yelled. "We need another board. ASAP!"

An assistant hustled by with the broken board, but I stopped her. "Hey. I'll take one of the pieces."

She gave me an odd look but handed over the half with a white hibiscus decal on it.

"Thanks." Most of the crew knew this was my thing. To collect a memento from each movie I worked on. The mementos were always either in the garbage or heading that way, so I didn't see any harm in swiping them. Needing a background for my YouTube channel, I'd splurged on an IKEA shelving unit and displayed my movie junk. Funny enough, it had caught the eye of some viewers and I'd received several offers for the collection. The money was tempting, but I really didn't want to part with my junk.

After the surf scene, we moved on to a group scene. Vee and I stood in the shade, secluding ourselves from everyone else, and watched as the scene unfolded with the group of teens arguing over who had eaten the last energy bar. Deep stuff, this movie.

"Cut!" Les yelled from his perch behind the main camera and

let loose a string of expletives. "Someone get our girl a script and help her learn the lines!"

One of the PAs rushed over to Valentina with a script in hand while the rest of the crew took a break.

"This is *Movie Reel* with your fabulous hosts Vee, just Vee, and the sunny Sonny." Vee slipped into movie critic character, clucking her tongue and straightening her imaginary glasses. "Today we are reviewing *Beyond the Waves*. A teen rom-com minus the com. Sonny, let's start with the actors, shall we? Why must the entire cast be drop-dead gorgeous? I'm deducting a star for that alone. It's just not realistic."

We'd started this game years ago to help kill time on set. Trying to outdo each other's critiques while keeping our voices down so we didn't draw any attention to ourselves. It hadn't always gone as planned.

I tried mimicking her, lifting my nose in the air and frowning in a way that said something stunk. "Well, I'm deducting a star as well, because this cast is made up of twenty-four- to twenty-nine-year-old actors playing fifteen- and sixteen-year-olds." I waved toward teenage Teak played by Kingston Boling, who would turn thirty before we wrapped this movie.

"Yes, the five-o'clock shadows show up before noon. It's a real pain in the butt for their fabulous makeup artist." Vee clucked her tongue again. "Sonny, dear, please explain to me how these *teens* have an endless supply of booze that seems to wash up onto shore in regular intervals, but no food. So not *plausible*."

"Indeed, Vee." I shook my head in disdain. "But I must say, I'm quite impressed that the director cast a Hispanic woman for the lead role."

"The cast is well-rounded with a variety of ethnicities. Hispanic,

Middle Eastern, African American, Caucasian . . . Seems the director's second wife, who is also Hispanic, has helped him realize the
importance of diversity. I'm adding a star."

"Let's not forget the Brit in the midst also." I motioned toward
Kingston, who was in the middle of a set of push-ups on the shore.
"Our time is almost up, so why don't we discuss the far-fetched
ending to this delightful little flick. Miraculously, the parents show
up and rescue their children just when all seems lost. I don't think
this part is all that plausible either." Admittedly, I had dreamed of
my parents searching for me and not giving up until they rescued
me from myself. Yeah, not plausible, indeed.

"Humph." Vee dropped the act. "That's actually my favorite
part of the story."

I shrugged, choosing not to admit that this was my least favorite part. In all honesty, I was actually jealous of fictitious teens and
their parents. Parents that dropped everything to find them. To
bring them home again.

The back of my throat began to burn. I tried clearing it away
with a cough.

Vee nudged me with her elbow. "Hey, you okay?"

"Yeah . . ." Clearing my throat one more time, I straightened
my posture. "I think we should deduct a point for them all looking
like swimwear models in desperate need of a shower. Seriously, do
their hair and bods need to be so greasy?"

A shadow fell across me as an arm looped around my waist,
my body instantly stiffening at the intrusion of my personal space.
"Babe, you're struggling with your own work duties, yet you think
you could do better with producing?"

I looked up and tried to give Whit a playful smile, but my lips
only twitched at the idea. "We were just goofing off."

Whit's gaze roamed down my body and back up before looking over at Vee. "Vee, go see if anyone needs touch-ups before we begin again. I think they're due more *greasing* up." He chuckled, but the velvety rumble did nothing to soften the cut of his backhanded comment.

Vee's eyes connected with mine. "Sure thing, boss man."

As I watched her slowly walk away, Whit's arm descended until his palm came to rest on my backside. I winced, which should have told him I didn't want his touch, that my body language was not giving his body consent. Instead, it seemed to only make his grip tighten.

"Have you made progress with Indigo Isle?"

I shifted, hoping to remove his hold on me, but it did no good. "The owner is really private. I'm not sure it's—"

"That's never deterred you in the past."

"I know, but—"

Whit moved his hand to my hip and squeezed. "Babe, we need to confirm the Indigo shoot. What's the holdup?"

Babe. Whit called me babe only when he wanted more than what my job description required. The burning in my throat returned.

Using the retrieval of my phone as an excuse to put some space between us, I moved out of his grasp. "Let me check my email." I scrolled through my in-box, knowing good and well no news would be there. It was highly doubtful Hudson Renfrow even had an email address. "Nothing yet. Sorry."

Whit tapped his index finger to his bottom lip while assessing my lie. Vee had commented one time that Whit was the perfect mash-up of McDreamy and McSteamy from one of her favorite shows, *Grey's Anatomy.* Those good looks disguised the darker side of him.

"We wrap around seven, so I'll have dinner delivered to my villa. That way you and I can discuss this further."

"Uh, actually . . ." I stepped out of reach. "I have a meeting with the owner of Indigo Isle as soon as we finish up here."

"Lock it down!" the assistant director shouted, and the chatter on the beach drifted to silence.

Whit leveled me with a glare and lowered his voice. "I want a signed contract by tomorrow." He turned and moved back over to Les and the film crew, leaving me with an impossible task.

CHAPTER NINE

I DREADED THE THOUGHT of even asking Hudson about using his beach, but at a little after seven in the evening, I had no other choice but to see it through. It would be the first time I had made a trip out to Indigo Isle unwillingly. The more I got to know Hudson, which wasn't much, the more I didn't want to disturb his privacy with a film crew. Yet here I was on his dock, about to go do just that.

Tossing my hat in the boat, I quickly finger-combed my hair and twisted it into a knot on top of my head while trying to build enough gumption to step onto the path leading up to the homestead.

A heavenly aroma met up with me well before I made it to the yard. My stomach had been too twisted to eat after my run-in with Whit and his wandering hands, but now the savory, smoky goodness in the air magically released all the twists and switched on a growling beast.

There was no sign of Hudson or food in the front yard, but I noticed a stream of wispy smoke rising from behind the house. I walked to the back and caught sight of him sitting at a wooden table set up beside an outdoor brick oven. A bounty of shrimp, new potatoes, smoked sausage, and corn on the cob was spread on top of newspaper before him.

I approached the table but didn't take a seat. "That smells delicious."

His gray eyes flicked up to meet mine but dropped immediately to the shrimp in his hand.

"You, uh, you made a lot." I shifted my weight from one foot to the other. "You plan on eating all of that by yourself?"

Hudson exhaled a rumbly grunt before popping the shrimp into his mouth.

Getting nowhere, I looked around the yard until stopping on the glowing brick oven. "Did you roast the Frogmore stew instead of boiling it?"

He nodded, answering me with the least amount of effort needed, and then picked up a quart-size mason jar filled with iced tea and took a sip.

I stood awkwardly, still waiting for an invitation to sit that I'd yet to receive. "I bet that really adds to the flavor profile."

He set down the jar and plucked a chunk of sausage from the mix of delectable options.

My stomach let out a loud rumble, but Hudson just kept on eating as if I wasn't there with a mean-sounding belly practically begging him for food. "Excuse me, I had a long afternoon on set and didn't get to have lunch or dinner."

After I dropped a few more hints and the rude man completely ignored them, I started fuming. "Would it hurt you to be kind for once?" I deepened my voice to imitate his. "'Welcome, Sonny. You look like you've had a tough day. Why don't you have a seat and join me for supper?'"

"You notice those signs posted on the dock and near the trail at the beach?" Hudson asked before taking a long sip of tea. "They say No Trespassing. You know what the word *trespassing* means?"

"What's that have to do with you being such an awful host?" I flicked a hand toward him.

He leaned back in his chair and met my glare. "It means you entered an owner's property without permission. Trespassing in the state of South Carolina is a misdemeanor and is punishable by fine and up to thirty days in jail. You'd do well to heed to the warnings on those signs."

I scoffed at his threat. "You didn't seem to have an issue with me visiting on the Fourth, when I brought you that dang feast and happily shared it with your crotchety butt."

He grumbled something under his breath, then swept a hand through the air. "Eat if you want to."

A thick scar covering most of the palm of his hand caught my eye, but I decided not to call any attention to it. Doing so would most likely cause him to rescind his invitation to eat, but I filed it away for another day.

"Now was that so hard?" I plopped in the chair opposite him, swiped a plump shrimp from the pile, and began peeling it with all the attitude I could put into the action. "Still, you could've acted a little nicer about it. You're so rude." Baring my teeth, I bit into the shrimp but lost my ire as an explosion of flavors hit my taste buds.

We ate in silence, making a considerable dent in the bounty before us. It was slightly spicy, but in a good way. Needing to cool my palate, I swiped his tea and guzzled it. "Wow, man. You know how to make tea. It's lemony and not overly sweet."

With a lifted eyebrow, Hudson rose from the table and went inside, only to return moments later with another jar filled with ice and a pitcher of tea. He plunked the glass on the table and filled both before sitting down and returning to his meal.

"Thank you," I managed to say around a mouthful of perfectly roasted potato.

He grunted again, the closest I'd get to a reply.

"I wonder why it's called Frogmore stew." I made a face, wrinkling my nose. "It sounds like there's frog in the recipe."

Without looking up from the shrimp he was peeling, Hudson explained, "It's named after the community of Frogmore, a tiny place on St. Helena Island that claims to have invented the recipe. Around here it's called a Lowcountry boil."

"You looked it up?" I popped a piece of sausage in my mouth, unable to slow down my feasting. The stomachache would be worth it though.

"Better to know all the facts. If you don't know something, simply investigate."

"Good advice." I licked my finger and reached for another shrimp.

Done conversating, we tucked into the meal and ate our fill of the spicy goodness until throwing in the towel. Taking Hudson's lead, I gathered the shrimp hulls and corn cobs in the newspaper sheets. Then I followed him to his compost pile behind the shed and dumped the scraps on top.

He returned to the table, picked up our half-filled jars, and started toward the screened-in back porch that ran the length of the house. I figured I was being dismissed until he opened the door and held it for me. I scooted past him and surveyed the large space. It was more like a Carolina room than a porch, with sliding-glass panels that were folded open to let the breeze through. Two seating areas were grouped together to my right, an arrangement of sturdy wicker chairs and a love seat and then a set of wooden rocking chairs, but the sight toward my left was unexpected. A queen-size bed and a nightstand stacked with worn books.

"Why's there a bedroom out here?"

Placing the jars on a small table between two rocking chairs, Hudson sat down and slowly began to rock. "I don't like confined spaces."

My eyes flicked to him, then back to the neatly made bed. I found it odd that a recluse had an aversion to being enclosed. Didn't they favor hiding places over open areas?

Keeping those comments to myself, I settled in the rocking chair beside him and asked, "How long have you called Indigo Isle home?"

"Since I was thirteen."

"You've lived out here for, what, twenty or thirty years then?"

Hudson cocked a single eyebrow and twisted his lips, seemingly both annoyed and amused by my question.

I held my breath, worried he wouldn't answer, but released it when he actually began talking.

"I'm thirty-eight," he answered on a sigh. "I spent every summer out here after I turned thirteen, but I've been living here full-time for about a decade now. Any more questions?"

"Only about a million, but I'll hush for now." Even though he didn't ask, I told him, "I'm thirty-two. Moved out to California right after graduating high school, but I'm originally from Georgetown."

"Close to home, then."

I bit my lip and nodded instead of admitting I really didn't belong to a home. My apartment in LA was just a place to land between film projects. And a home is somewhere you're welcomed. That would not be the case in Georgetown.

I didn't want to talk about myself any more than Hudson did, so I buttoned my lips and set my rocker in a matching pace with his, focusing on the comforting creak of the chairs and the distant sounds of night slowly descending just past the porch.

As we rocked for a leisurely spell, I noticed he kept stealing glances in my direction. As soon as I looked over, he averted his eyes. Apparently against his will, his gaze returned to me.

I turned in my chair and openly stared. "You're aware of me and it infuriates you, doesn't it?"

Hudson crossed his arms and gave me a bored look. "A stranger has encroached on my privacy, so yes, I'm aware of you."

"I think you like me."

"I *like* to be left alone."

"So you've said." I picked up my jar and took a sip while studying his face. Sharp angles precariously hidden underneath a burly beard, harsh eyes barely containing the storm within them. I'd heard my mother say something once about people having ghosts in their eyes. Until now I never understood. But clear as day, Hudson Renfrow had ghosts in his eyes. The man was haunted, but by what? I highly doubted he'd ever tell me.

And for that very reason, it pained me to ask what I came out here to ask. It brought on a stomachache faster than the ton of food I'd just consumed.

"Are you feeling sick?"

"Huh?"

He pointed toward me. "You just made a face." The man was impressively observant.

"Oh, uh . . . I'm just a little too full, but I'll be fine." I patted my stomach sheepishly.

"I have mint growing in the garden. It helps. I can go grab some." Hudson began to rise, but I placed a hand on his forearm.

"That's okay." I moved my hand away when I felt him tense from my touch.

"You sure?"

"Yes." I smiled weakly. Not only was Hudson observant but also attentive. A natural caregiver, even though he'd been doing his darndest to hide it from me.

He settled back into his chair, but his gaze remained in my direction.

Unable to figure out how to go about it, I blurted, "So, funny thing . . . my director heard about your shell trees. His name is Les Morgan. You've probably heard of him."

The concern slipped from his expression and suspicion took its place. "I don't own a TV."

"Oh, well, uh . . ." I laughed, too nervous to do much else. "Les has won several Academy Awards. Great director. He would love to shoot a small scene on your beach near the shell trees. It would only take a few hours one night."

Hudson's mood darkened abruptly, brows drawn together, lips in a harsh line as he shook his head. "Now this all makes perfect sense. You coming out here."

"No. That's not why—"

"Time for you to go, Miss Location Scout." Hudson stood at once, yanking me to my feet, not harsh enough to hurt anything but my feelings. With a slight shove, he moved me along at a clipped pace.

As I stumbled down the steps and through the yard, my mind

whirled in chaos, trying to come up with a way to fix the mess I'd just made. "No worries. I'll tell them your answer is no."

"You're darn right it's no." Hudson snorted a derisive laugh and kept marching close behind me, right on my heels. "No worries. Yeah, no worries, Sonny." It was the first time he'd said my name, but he pronounced it more like a swear word.

Sick to my stomach, I knew whatever progress I'd made with him had vanished in one fell swoop. "I'm sorry. I didn't mean to upset you." I peered over my shoulder at him. "Hudson, please."

He shook his head and continued marching me through the woods until we reached the dock. Eyes glowering, he jabbed a finger toward my boat. "Get out of here and don't come back. This time I mean it." He spun around and started back toward the house.

"Hudson! Wait!" Slapping at the angry tears plopping down my cheeks, I watched him disappear into the night.

• • •

Rest didn't visit me that night. Only hot humiliation and frustration. The painfully slow-budding friendship with Hudson had been the only thing I'd felt good about lately, but I'd gone and ruined it. Ruining things seemed to be my MO.

I couldn't find a solution to fixing what I broke with Hudson, so I decided to focus on coming up with a solution for scene sixteen instead. The next morning I arrived at Moise Island a few hours before filming, with a few assistants from the art department in tow. Their droopy eyes watched me demonstrate the solution I had finally come up with around 4 a.m.

"All you have to do is feed a piece of twine through this tiny hole in the shell, then hang it on a tree branch. Just like decorating a Christmas tree. Easy enough. See?" I tied off the twine and hung the oyster shell on the tree. One down, one zillion to go . . .

Two hours in and all of our hard work was barely noticeable from a few yards away.

Les showed up and frowned at the meager display. "This isn't going to be the same."

"It's not finished yet, but shouldn't we also be able to work some computer magic and maybe CGI more shells into the shot?" My tired fingers fumbled to tie off a clamshell.

Les glanced briefly at me and then at the poor attempt to recreate the magic Hudson's grandfather had worked over on Indigo Isle. Shaking his head, the director marched off the beach.

Moments later, Whit arrived with the same annoyed expression Les had left with. Apparently the director had handed it off to him in passing.

"Is this job too much for you to handle?"

I flinched, dropping the shell I'd been working on. "What? No."

"Then what's the problem with Indigo Isle?"

I picked the shell up and wiped off the gritty sand from its smooth surface. "The owner said no, Whit."

He huffed a wry laugh. "No isn't acceptable. In this industry, we make things happen. We don't take no for an answer." He moved closer, plucked the shell out of my hand, and tossed it into the surf. "There's enough assistants around here to take care of things today. Head over there to that island and do your job."

"Seriously, I don't—"

"If you can't do that, then don't expect to get the contract for the movie in New Orleans."

Whit Kessler never delivered empty threats. What he said, he meant, so if I couldn't get Hudson on board with the shoot, then I'd be out of a job.

Nobodies are easily replaced.

CHAPTER TEN

In the South, you don't have a tantrum. No, *having a tantrum* sounds too civilized. In these parts, you pitch a hissy fit. After Whit delivered his demands, the need to pitch a fit crawled all over me like an army of ants. Riled up and looking for a target, I stomped down the path on Indigo Isle and happened upon one waiting for me at the edge of the trees.

Arm raised, finger pointing in my direction, Hudson ordered, "Back to your boat. Now!"

Not even the vicious growl from the Monster of Indigo Isle would deter me today. I continued walking until we were only inches apart. "How you treated me last night was uncalled for. I've been nothing but nice to you!"

He moved closer, towering over me. "Of course you were nice. You had an ulterior motive."

I placed my hands on my hips. "I was nice because I'm a nice person. And I like you, hard as that is to believe. I just want to hang out with you."

His eyes narrowed. "So you don't want to use my beach any longer?"

Not wanting to lie to him, I didn't answer right away.

"That's what I thought." Huffing, he shook his head. From the way he was acting, you would have thought I'd tricked him into giving over one of his kidneys.

And I thought I could be a drama queen.

I tossed my arms in the air. "Look, buddy, you're blowing this way out of proportion. Seriously, what's the big deal? A few hours is all it would take, and they wouldn't go any farther than the beach." Calming the hostility in my voice and replacing it with enthusiasm, I continued, "And just think, your island will be on the big screen."

Hudson slapped a hand against his chest. "Do I look like someone looking for fame?"

"No." I flicked my wrist toward him. "You look like a man getting all in a tizzy for no blame reason."

"There's no need for your little visits anymore. I'm not changing my mind." He pointed toward the trail again.

We stood toe-to-toe, huffing and puffing, both wearing our best scowls. It would probably be comical had we both not been so livid.

"Well, I'm not leaving." I sidestepped his wall of indignation and made a beeline up to the porch, claiming a chair as if it were my right. I wiped the sweat off my brow and looked up to see what he was doing. I expected him to follow me, but I caught sight of him going in the opposite direction.

Moments passed, and then I heard the gurgling sound of my boat, followed by the distinct whine of it zooming away. "What the heck?" I jumped to my feet and raced to the dock, hardly believing my eyes.

I didn't think Hudson ventured beyond the security of his island. Apparently someone decided he wanted a joyride. A wake in the water showed the signs of his getaway track.

I rubbed at the pain forming in the middle of my forehead and tried catching my breath while listening to the water lap underneath my feet. Taking a deep breath and slowly releasing it, I dropped my hand and watched the morning sun paint the surface of the water in streaks of orange and gold. I waited. Then I waited a little longer.

I debated calling Tom at the marina, but that would only land me in some form of trouble for losing his boat. I swiveled around and eyed Hudson's boat nicely secured in the boat lift, having no idea how to get it down or find the key to it. I sat on the edge of the dock and waited some more.

Twenty minutes trudged by, then thirty, then forty . . .

Growing more frustrated and sweaty by the minute, I decided to go back to his house to get out of the sun. I took a seat on the porch. The heat and all that yelling had left me parched. I craned my neck and studied the front door. If he could steal, then so could I.

Rising from the chair, I stepped over to the door and tested the doorknob and was surprised how easily it granted me access, so unlike its owner.

I assumed ghosts, cobwebs, and a stifling layer of dust would be hovering just past the threshold, but none of that appeared. Only polished wood floors, well-cared-for furnishings, and a refreshingly cool interior. Even though no dust could be found, no life could either. Perfectly preserved yet abandoned.

To the left was a sitting area and to the right was an elegant dining room, both dressed in a tapestry of blue fabrics and dark wood. Taking a few steps past the foyer and the ornate staircase, I checked the first door to the left with hopes of finding the kitchen. Instead, I found a library. One that was well-used, so unlike the rest of the house I'd seen so far.

With overstuffed leather furniture, creased and worn in spots, and mountains of books, the space said to stay a while. And I would have, but my thirst took precedence. I left the library in search of the kitchen and finally located it near the end of the hall on the right. This space also had signs of life. A basket of fragrant peaches on the counter made me want to steal even more, but I decided not to take any of his food.

I walked up to the dining table on the right side and inspected the jigsaw puzzle with pieces scattered around it. *Scattered* was the wrong term. Each piece was laid out precisely, and they were grouped by color. My eyes landed on a purple piece and easily spotted where it would fit in the facade of a mountain landscape. I put it in place and added another piece before remembering my mission for water. I grabbed a jar from the dish rack by the sink and filled it from the tap. I downed the water and refilled the jar and carried it with me to the library.

Walking the perimeter of the room, I scanned the bookcases. Floor to ceiling, they were filled with books with broken spines and tattered covers. One might assume the books weren't cared for, but I thought their conditions spoke a different story. This wasn't a library filled with books displayed like trophies or simply used as decor. No, it was filled with books that had served the purpose they were made for: to be read and enjoyed.

As I moved behind a gorgeous antique desk, my gaze snagged on a line of thin books on the bottom shelf that seemed out of place. They were out of sight unless you walked behind the desk, so maybe they weren't supposed to be discovered. Yet I did. I crouched down to read the spines, but nothing was printed on them. Nothing, that was, except handwritten dates barely visible, going back at least twentysome years.

Dropping onto my backside, I crossed my legs and pulled out the first book, realizing it was a journal. Looking between the journal in my hand and the line of them on the shelf, I knew the right thing to do was to put it back and go park myself on the porch until the Monster returned with my boat. Again, that voice in the back of my head spoke up, reminding me he was a thief, so that gave me a pass to steal a peek into his privacy.

After carefully placing the jar on a rug underneath the desk, I cracked open the journal and read the first entry

March
Age: 13
  It's official. My life sucks, so my therapist says I need to write about how sucky it is. I told him only sissy girls keep diaries, but he said this is a journal. Whatever.
  My parents just split. They were a pair for fourteen years. Now they are singular. Guess that makes me, their only kid, just half a person. I sure don't feel whole.

"Poor Hudson," I whispered, flipping to the next entry.

May
Age: still 13
  My life still sucks. I live with just my mom now, but she says she's lost herself. I guess my dad found himself in his secretary. Yeah, that ticks me off. But my mom, yeah, so she

*says she needs to find herself. Guess she can't do that with me
around. She's shipping me to Indigo Isle for the summer. An
island sounds fancy, but this place ain't. It's just a small beach
and a bunch of trees and stuff. We went there once, a few
years ago, when my grandmother died. My grandfather was
weird then, but maybe he's changed.*

That explained why he began spending his summers here, but
it didn't explain the scars or reclusion. Needing to know more, I
continued reading.

*June
Age: Yep, still 13*
    *I've arrived to hell. Seriously. No TV. No computers. Just
a weird satellite phone, whatever that is. Solar panels provide
crappy electricity, so mostly I'm in the dark. I hate it here.*
    *As for my grandfather, the dude is a certifiable weirdo.
Says if I'm hungry, then go fishing or crabbing. If I'm bored,
which ain't often because he makes me work all the time,
then I should read or go swimming. I hate reading and I
saw shark fins near the coast yesterday, so I guess I'm going
to die in this hell from boredom.*
    *Grandpa's hands are blue all the time. Even after he
showers. Weird. And the shower? Yeah, that's outside and we use
rainwater. Gross. He has this stupid gigantic house with plenty
of bathrooms, so I don't get why I have to shower outside.*
    *I hope my mom hurries up with finding herself and will
come find me before I end up with some weird disease. I
think that's what's wrong with Grandpa and his blue
hands.*

I laughed and it echoed in the quiet room. The irritable tone of his teenage self was quite similar to the grown-up version of Hudson. I flipped the page and sprigs of dried indigo slipped from between the pages near the back of the book and littered my lap. I picked up the delicate plant, cringing when one leaf broke off, and relocated the treasure in its rightful place. I returned to the front and continued reading.

June
Age: 13
  Now the cuckoo old man is making me read books and write a review on them. He says it's not a report, just my opinion, so that's what he'll get.

Peter Pan by J. M. Barrie
  I hated it. It had weird language and weird words like perambulator. Grandpa gave me a dictionary when I complained about it. The only character I liked was Tinker Bell. She cusses.
  I think Grandpa is Peter Pan, even though I'm pretty sure he doesn't have his first teeth. And he doesn't fly, but he walks in such a way that I think he could. He acts like a kid, playful, and is pretty forgetful. He left his glasses in the oven. Why the oven? Weird.
  I'm definitely a Lost Boy. Maybe I'm Nibs.
  Aren't we all lost boys just wanting our mothers?

"Aww . . ." My chest tightened as I reread the book review, recalling how he'd shared a tiny sliver of this memory with me on the beach that night. Reading it in his blunt handwriting added an intriguing layer to the backstory of Hudson Renfrow. So much so that I got lost in his memories, skimming journal after journal, plucking parts every so often to tuck away.

August
Age: 14
    I drove a tractor for the first time today. Five minutes in, I wrecked it. Grandpa wasn't mad like I thought he would be. He just huffed a laugh and asked me what I learned from it.
    I told him I learned trees don't move out of the way.
    He really did laugh after I said that.
    I learned something else too.
    I learned not to fly off the handle when someone or something messes up, like my dad always does. I'm learning how to be a man by watching my grandfather. I like his version of a man better than Dad's version.
    Psalm 103:8 says, "The Lord is compassionate and merciful, slow to get angry and filled with unfailing love."
    This is my grandpa. The old man lives this verse.
    I want to live it too.

I grinned down at the page, just imagining the time those two must have had together. I'm glad Hudson had the quirky old man, but sad that he no longer seemed to have anyone. From what I read, his parents remarried and started new lives and he didn't much fit into either. His confessions made it clear that the only place he fit was on Indigo Isle.

I moved through his teen years quickly until I came to the college

journals. Impressively, he made it into Columbia, graduating top of
his class, and then attended law school. I smiled again, recalling a
book review he'd done on *The Catcher in the Rye*. He'd begun the
review much like all of the ones I read: he said he hated it. Funny
how he said that, but then he listed things he liked or related to in
the story. He'd written about wanting to go to New York one day,
which he eventually did for school. I was impressed by this Hudson
coming to life from the pages. He set goals and made them happen.

I saw this prominently in entries during college after he met a
girl named Reece.

September
Age: 19
I met her today. The woman I'll marry in a few years,
after I pass the bar. We're going to live here in New York.
She doesn't know any of this yet, but she will soon enough.
Her name is Reece, which was made to go with Renfrow.
Reece Renfrow. Mrs. Hudson Renfrow. Both sound right.
She makes me feel right. I'm finally whole again. No more
being just a half person.

Reading about his relationship with Reece felt like I was going
too far with my snooping, so I skimmed over most of their early
dating years. Jealousy sprang up from out of nowhere when an
intimate moment they had shared caught my attention. The way
he described the love and affection he had for this young woman,
it was all-consuming and so, so passionate.

Face flushed, I closed the book on that, replaced it on the
shelf, and picked another book a few years past that new love
period. This one included their wedding in Reece's hometown in

Connecticut. Of course, his grandfather was his best man, which I thought was just the sweetest thing.

Then it detailed them finding the perfect apartment near the law firm he would be working at. It seemed fine, a little boring if I'm honest, but then they took a trip their first Christmas together and things changed after that.

February
Age: 25

We spent Christmas in Aspen with Reece's family. It was fine until it wasn't. Reece had an accident on the slopes, crashed into a tree. Broke her back and had to have surgery. It's been two months and she's still struggling to recover. I don't feel like much of a man if I can't take care of my wife any better than this. She's in pain all the time and it seems like all I do is make it worse.

May
Age: 25

We've turned a corner with Reece's recovery. Grandpa said she's in the short rows now when he came out to visit since I won't be able to make a visit to Indigo Isle this year. But it's a good thing and he agrees. Because Reece is pregnant! She and the baby are fine so far. The doctor just wants to be cautious and has advised no traveling.

I'm going to be a dad . . . Marrying Reece made me whole; creating a child with my wife made us a family.

I'd lost hours sitting on the floor of that library, finding myself wrapped up in the story of Hudson's life. I paused at one point, only long enough to find a bathroom, but quickly returned, knowing the birth of his child had to be soon within the pages.

From the parts of the house I'd checked out, there had been no evidence of a child living here. The unease pressing down on my shoulders warned I wouldn't be finding any either, but I held out hope as I plucked one of the last journals from the shelf.

Age: 26

I thought my parents were full of it when they declared they found love again after their divorce. I believed when I met Reece, I would only find it once and be done. Now I understand it's possible to fall head over heels more than once. Her name is Elsie, after my grandpa Elson. Blonde hair that matches her mom's and blue eyes that match mine. I've never experienced a love like this, like someone has punched me in the gut with sunshine and laughter. I grin like a fool all the time, but I can't help it.

Who knew a heart could fall in love more than once.

My eyes stung with tears. Hudson's life had been filled with joy and love. The proof was right there in his neat penmanship. But during the next year, the shine in his posts dulled.

Age: 26

Reece is hiding something from me. When I ask her what's wrong, she just says she's tired. Says it's because Elsie is such a handful. Elsie is a handful. Aren't all babies?

Age: 27

    The other day when I walked into the bathroom, she jumped and slammed her makeup drawer shut. I remember how my dad got jumpy right before Mom found out he was cheating on her. Only people hiding something act like that, so after she fell asleep, I went back into the bathroom to find out what she's hiding. The Tylenol bottle is filled with mismatched pills, none of which are Tylenol, but I'm pretty sure I know what I'm looking at.

Age: 28

    It's been a long year and now I fully understand why the part in our marriage vows about sickness and health is in there. I've promised to stand by my wife's side, and I did while checking her into rehab earlier this year, even though she didn't see it that way. She's back home now. We don't feel whole yet, but I believe we will get back there eventually.

    I had to cut way back on my billable hours at the firm to take care of my two girls, so it's going to take a lot longer for them to even consider me for junior partner. I know I'm a long way from that, but before this all happened with Reece, I was gaining a lot of notice. No matter, we're going to get through this.

And that's where the journal entries abruptly stopped midway in this book. I returned it to the shelf and grabbed the next one. A year had passed between that last entry and the next one. Gone were the precise strokes and sharp wit of his words, replaced with shaky handwriting and blank emotion. I wasn't even sure it was Hudson's until I read some.

Age: 29

The composition of fire is oxygen, heat, and fuel.

Oxygen sustains combustion.

I gave Reece enough breathing room to sustain her secrets.

Heat raises the material to its ignition temperature.

I allowed my anger to get the best of me. Mad that she couldn't stay clean for Elsie's sake, I gave up on my wife.

Fuel is needed to feed it.

Reece pretended she was clean. And I fueled it by pretending I believed her.

The reaction of oxygen, heat, and fuel is fire. If left unattended, it will consume everything that gets in its way. But take just one of those elements away and the fire will extinguish or never have existed in the first place.

But I didn't do that and the fire got out of control before anyone realized it even existed.

I didn't know what that meant, but no way was it good. The burn scars on Hudson's body attested to that. With tears falling freely down my cheeks, I leaned against the desk and rubbed the ache in my chest. This free pass to snoop had turned out to be much more than I bargained for. I didn't even want to flip the page, but after drying my eyes with my shirtsleeve, I did anyway.

Age: 29

People tell me how lucky I am to have walked away with only third-degree burns. They're wrong. I died in that apartment, right along with my family.

That was the last time Hudson mentioned the fire.

I did the math, roughly guessing his last year in New York, then pulled out my phone and did an Internet search on apartment building fires during that time. There were a few minor fires, but one made a lot of headlines.

Unsure if this was even the right fire, I tapped on the first headline and saw images of pandemonium. A high-rise apartment building with flames licking the frame of every window, smoke rolling from the roof. Rescue workers with soot-covered faces carrying body bags. The article told about an electrical fire starting on the eleventh floor, in a unit that had been undergoing extensive renovation. Thirty-seven injured. Nine dead.

CHAPTER ELEVEN

Shadows began creeping through the library, reaching me where I remained slumped against the side of the desk. Grief-stricken, I couldn't move. I knew in my heart that apartment fire was the one that had forever marred Hudson's life. I looked up *New York fires* and added *Hudson Renfrow* to the search. Several articles filled the phone screen, but before I could tap on one, a noise interrupted me.

Listening closely, I heard the front door open. A shot of panic hit me square in the stomach. I scrambled to my feet and made sure all the journals were put back into place. I hurried over to the leather couch and plopped down, trying to strike a casual pose. I expected heavy stomps but the echoing clack of more than one set of feet shuffling down the hall made me nervous. Had pirates stormed the island, ready to plunder the house?

I braced myself as the door swung open to the library.

"Hudson, dawlin', you in heah?" A little old lady appeared, her eyes rounding as they landed on me. "Oh! Heavens to Betsy!"

A miniature man who looked like he could fit in Hudson's pocket came up beside the lady. He squinted his eyes, peering at me through thin wire-rimmed glasses. "Hello dare, miss. Are ya lost?"

Lost on this tiny island? No, I was sure he actually wanted to know why I was trespassing.

I pulled on a hint of a smile. "I'm a . . . friend of Hudson's." I rose from the couch and crossed over to them. "My name is Sonny Bates."

"I'm Art Lagare." The little man introduced himself and patted the woman on the shoulder. "And dis is my LuAnn."

It was sweet how he referred to her as his. Not in a disrespectful way, but one filled with pride. My dad used to call my mom *his* Ronaka. Mama would call Dad *her* Charlie. Those thoughts alone made my eyes sting again. It was like I'd sprung a leak and couldn't shut it off.

LuAnn glanced around the library. "Where's da boy?"

Dabbing at the tears, I asked, "Hudson?"

"Yes."

"He, uh . . ." I huffed, drying my eyes once again. "To be honest, he caught an attitude with me this morning and took off in my boat."

Art squinted at the grandfather clock in the corner of the room. "It's gettin' on suppa' time."

I looked for myself, finding that it was after six in the evening. "Yes, sir."

LuAnn tsked, cocking a hip and placing her hand on it. "Dat boy."

Art and LuAnn began chatting away, explaining that they were lifelong friends of Hudson's grandfather Elson. And how Elson would have gotten ahold of *da boy* for treating me like this. The couple, tanned and deeply creased from the sun and sea, spoke with a thick accent that I hadn't heard in years. It reminded me of the lazy drawl of my grandmother, who was originally from Johns Island.

There's the South Carolinian accent and then there's the Charleston accent. Two completely different tones and inflections. Surely God formed the tongue and jaw of those in the Lowcountry specifically in such a fashion so as to drawl the consonants lower and the vowels longer. I could have stood there and listened to them talk in that dialect all day long.

"We live in Chawleston dawn by da wuta but come out once a month to see 'bout Hudson."

Simply captivated by the tiny pair, I learned that LuAnn kept the house from being overrun by dust mites and that Art helped out with handling the shipments of the indigo to a textile company in France and delivered monthly supplies of whatever Hudson needed.

"Yeah, we too old to be goferin'," Art answered as if I'd asked, but my brain was too muddled to do much of anything past lingering on Hudson.

LuAnn laughed. "But we made Elson a promise to keep an eye on da boy."

A shadow fell across the couple just before Hudson appeared behind them in the hallway.

"Speakin' of da devil." Art turned and shook Hudson's hand. "See ya got comp'ny. We'll jus' drop off da supplies and be on our way."

It was hard to look at Hudson without recalling his raw and honest words. Blinking against the onslaught of emotion and taking a shaky breath, I willed my hot mess of a self to get it together, going as far as digging my nails into the palms of my hands.

Hudson noticed. Of course he noticed. Brows pinched, he moved into the library, where I dutifully remained beside a wingback chair as if it were home base in a game of tag. "Why have you been crying?"

LuAnn stepped between us and pointed a tiny finger at Hudson. "You left huh out heah all alone. Poor thang has a right to be upset."

Hudson met my eyes over her silver head. A look of remorse and concern settled on his handsome face.

Gripping the top of the chair, I had to physically hold myself back from launching forward to wrap my arms around him. I wanted to hold him and declare how unfair his life had been and how I wanted to be there for him. To help him heal.

But who was I to offer such? A nobody couldn't be somebody worthy of playing a supportive role like that to anyone.

"Sonny?" It was only the second time Hudson had ever said my name, and this time he pronounced it like an apology.

My lips remained on lockdown, keeping my words imprisoned. Not trusting that I could even speak a goodbye without falling to pieces, I moved past him, briefly brushing my fingertips over the back of his hand. Even though he instantly stiffened from my touch, I offered it as a farewell anyway.

As I moved down the hall, I heard LuAnn tsk again. "Da chil' spent one day out heah and ya muteness has already rubbed off on huh."

"I normally can't shut her up," Hudson retorted just before I got out of earshot.

I closed the front door behind me, but it reopened as soon as I stepped off the porch.

"Neither your tears nor LuAnn's scolding will make me change my mind about you using my beach."

Unable to meet his gaze straight on, I gave Hudson a sad smile over my shoulder. "I know."

Arms crossed over his broad chest, he looked at me strangely. I wasn't sure if he was disappointed that I'd finally given up or simply worried about me.

Swallowing past the giant lump in my throat, I whispered, "Take care of yourself, Hudson."

On autopilot, I found my boat right where it should be. No marks, no signs that Hudson had ever messed with it. I could only hope I'd left no marks on him or his island. He deserved to be left in peace with the likes of me and Hollywood leaving him the heck alone.

But I would miss the surly man, as hard as that was to fathom.

I was such a distracted mess, I didn't have any recollection of making it to the marina or arriving at the motel. Standing at my room door, I finally snapped out of it when I couldn't find my room key in the side pocket of my messenger bag. I dug around until running out of patience. Then I squatted down and dumped everything out on the concrete. Still no key. I shoved everything back into the bag and made my way to the office.

"Hey, Erlene."

She looked up from a magazine spread on the counter and smiled. "Hey, suga'." Eyeing me over the top of her bifocals, she asked, "You doin' all right?"

"Yes, ma'am." I heaved a sigh. "But I've misplaced my room key."

Erlene reached behind her and plucked a key off the pegboard. "It'll turn up, but in the meantime you're welcome to this spare."

I accepted the key. "Thank you."

"You sure you're okay? If you want to talk about it, I'm a really good listener."

Waving off her concerns, I moved toward the exit. "Just a long day. Nothing a good night's sleep won't fix."

"Well, I'm going to pray for you."

With my hand on the doorknob, I paused. The pressure began to build behind my eyes as my nose started running. "Would you mind adding my friend to your prayers too?"

"Not at all. What's your friend's name?"

Sniffing, I replied, "Hudson. He's . . . he's endured more tragedy than one person should."

"Poor dear." She watched me carefully, drumming her fingers on top of the magazine. "You know . . . even if you don't want to talk with me, maybe you should talk to God. I like that verse from Philippians. 'Don't worry about anything; instead, pray about everything. Tell God what you need.'"

God probably didn't want to hear a thing I had to say, but I nodded my head, thanking her once again before returning to my room.

I gathered a fresh change of clothes and shuffled into the bathroom. Making the mistake of looking in the mirror, I grimaced at my reflection. Blotchy face, red nose, swollen eyes. No wonder Erlene was concerned. Hudson and his friends as well.

Unsettled and exhausted, I dropped the set of clothes on the counter and stumbled to the bed. Perching on the edge, I sat in silence for a good long while and did a self-evaluation. It wasn't pretty. Embarrassing to say the least. Everything in my life seemed to be painted in flat tones of insignificance and pettiness when compared to Hudson's. The tragedies of my life were also self-inflicted. My fault.

I needed to get over myself and work on rectifying some things, but it was all too overwhelming. Where would I even begin?

With no clear direction—the story of my life—I reclined on the bed and stared at the ceiling until it disappeared with the last rays of daylight.

• • •

After another night of elusive sleep, I managed to get my act together enough to make it to Moise Island on time the next morning. Melancholy followed me around the beach like a thick blanket of fog, but it evaporated the minute Whit approached me.

He gestured toward me. "Well?"

"The owner had to go out of town for a family emergency." I delivered the lie smoothly enough to pass as the truth. "He could be gone for a few weeks."

Whit frowned. "You couldn't get a signature first?"

"No. Sorry. The guy is a lawyer. He's not signing something without reviewing it thoroughly first."

Whit surveyed the beach where the crew was setting up a scene. "That puts us past the full moon."

I made a cringey face, hoping he was buying my apologetic act. "I've thought about that already. Maybe we should go ahead with the original plan. I have the number for a temp agency. I can have extra help out here within a few hours to work on making our own shell trees." I pulled out my phone and brought up an image from a props supply company. "I've even found strands of prestrung shells and can have them delivered overnight."

He took my phone and zoomed in on the image for a beat, then handed it back. "Looks like we don't have any other choice since you dropped the ball on this one."

My stomach pinched as he inflicted the tiny cut. "I tried everything, Whit. Sometimes it's out of our control."

"I know this, but it's not going to be easy to make our famous director understand. The man doesn't take no for an answer." He tipped his head in the direction of Les and his assistant sitting underneath a giant umbrella while going over the call sheet. "You've made my job really difficult today, Sonny."

Another minuscule cut, but I knew it was leading to bigger ones. And I would have to accept it this time without resistance. No hiding behind a locked door.

Whit lowered his voice. "You're having dinner with me tonight."

"Tonight's not good—"

"Yeah? Well, it's not good for me to have to go fix your mistake, either."

I wanted to find my voice and scream, "Enough!" I wanted to refuse. I wanted to demand he leave me the heck alone. But none of that happened. Instead, I asked in a tired voice, "What time is dinner?"

"Be at my villa by seven. We have a lot to work out with this blunder of yours." He walked away.

Rooted in the sand, I watched Whit approach Les. Even though the director's face and bald head colored a deep red in the next passing minutes, I knew I did right by Hudson. And I couldn't even feel good about that right choice, because in only a few short hours I would be driven to make a bad one to pay the consequences of it.

I busied myself by securing extra help from the temp agency and ordering every last string of shells the supply company had in stock. No matter, the night loomed ahead like the bogeyman biding his time until dark.

● ● ●

Well after midnight and Whit finally spent to the point of deep sleep, I left him in bed and locked myself in the guest bathroom. The long, hot shower did very little in washing away another mistake, but I gave it my best effort, scrubbing my skin until it stung.

After getting dressed, I moved to the living room and sat in the dark. My body remained in lockdown mode, but a war raged within me. *I want my mama! She would be so ashamed of me. I'm a rotten human. I don't deserve a family. I really want my family . . .*

I could almost hear Caroline say in her disapproving voice, "You made your bed; now you have to lie in it." Fashioned from thorny mistakes and itchy shame, I knew I deserved the discomfort.

Women like my sister had a lot to say about women like me. We brought it on ourselves. We could easily get out of it if that's what we really wanted. Users, not victims. Trash. Whores. And it was mostly true, I suppose. I did get myself into this lifestyle, but it certainly wasn't what I signed up for.

I had wanted to prove I could make it on my own. Sure, I'd succeeded—on paper. I was keeping my head above water financially while simultaneously drowning in an abyss of the poor choices it took to make that happen.

I choked back a sob as my trembling body broke out in a cold sweat. Hugging my knees to my chest, I rocked back and forth to try soothing myself, wishing it were my mom's arms around me.

Eventually the sky began picking up the edges of light to reveal the new day. Knowing my role, I slipped into the bed with Whit. He pulled me underneath him and began undressing me. It was a steep price tag, but I knew once Whit collected payment and I walked out of here, he would never bring up Indigo Isle again and I would have job security for a little longer.

CHAPTER TWELVE

THERE WASN'T MUCH IN MY LIFE I FELT PROUD OF at the moment, but one thing. Leaving Hudson alone over the next couple of weeks. I even deleted my search history in an effort to exorcise myself of him. So yeah, I was proud of finally practicing some self-control. Every time I thought about just giving in and going out to Indigo Isle, I gave myself the speech.

Hudson is better off without you. He deserves his peace and you'll only ruin it. This is what he wanted, so do something honorable for once in your life and respect his wishes.

I also changed my daily route, zigzagging through the salt marshes, to avoid going by Indigo Isle. The effort it took to leave Hudson alone and to stay several steps out of Whit's reach was exhausting.

So exhausting, in fact, that I couldn't even find the energy to climb out of my car once I arrived to the motel after another long day. Instead, I rested my forehead on the steering wheel long enough to start dozing until loud banging jolted me awake.

"Sonny!" Vee yanked the door open and gripped my shoulders. "Mercy! I thought you had been murdered right here in the parking lot!"

"Stop yelling." I wiggled out of her hold and rubbed my forehead. "And for land's sake, stop watching so many true crime documentaries." I went to move her out of the way so I could exit the car but halted when I got a good look at her. "Why are you roaming around the parking lot in a bikini?" She also had on a full face of makeup, but that wasn't unusual for Vee.

"I saw you pull up, so I came out here to tell you the pool is fixed!" She jumped up and down in place, showing off all her assets in the tiny red bikini for all the world to see. The gold bangle bracelets on her wrist sounded like tiny cymbals cheering her on.

"You're yelling again. And the pool's been fixed for a while already." I collected my bag from the passenger seat, slung it on my shoulder, and locked the car.

"Yes, but now it also has water. Lots of it." Vee did a little dance as we walked across the parking lot. "Girl, we have the Caribbean in our backyard! The crew is having a pool party. Erlene is joining us, so go change into your suit."

"I'll have to take a rain check."

"What? No. Why?"

"Cramps." Rounding the corner, I came upon the rowdy group of people frolicking in the newly filled pool, Erlene in the midst of them on a floating lounge chair, grinning ear to ear.

"Seriously?" Vee's voice rose above the music coming from someone's portable speaker as we scooted around the partygoers.

"You're a woman. You know cramps really do exist." I reached into the side pocket of my bag and pulled out the spare room key.

Mine still hadn't turned up and I was beginning to fear it had ended up on the bottom of the Atlantic somehow.

"Yes, but . . . you've been working nonstop and something's off with you. Darling, you need some fun."

"I need some sleep." I waved at the crowd and left Vee with her cherry-red lips pouted out. "Next time, Vee. Promise."

"Next time," Vee repeated. She didn't believe me, but it didn't slow my retreat.

I unlocked the door and shoved it open with my hip. After relocking it, I turned around and flipped on the lights.

"Eek!" Yelping like a wounded dog, I cleared the floor like a spastic cat. Clutching my chest, I fell back against the door and gawked at the intruder.

He sat unmoving in the rattan chair, looking way too big for it. In a faded-black sweatshirt with the hood up and a pair of tattered jeans, almost every inch of him was concealed, except for those stormy eyes.

Surely my fatigue had formed this hallucination, so I rubbed my eyes and looked again. Nope. Still there. "How'd you get in here?"

"Your key." His eyes left me and zeroed in on the table beside him, where my elusive room key sat.

I gasped. "You stole it from the boat, didn't you?"

Hudson lifted a shoulder.

"Why would you do that?"

"What's the matter? You don't like your privacy being invaded?"

"Look, I get it. That's why I've left you alone." I pushed off the door and sat on the end of the bed. I breathed in a deep inhale, catching hints of that clean scent of citrus and herbs he carried everywhere he went. "I thought you'd be thrilled to finally be rid of me."

The frown on his face deepened.

This situation was almost too bizarre to comprehend, really. It totally blew my mind that the Monster of Indigo Isle could actually exist somewhere besides the island.

Hudson leaned forward and braced his arms on top of his knees, bringing his face closer to mine. Close enough I could have easily reached over and removed the hood from his head, but I didn't dare. He was keeping a respectable distance and so would I.

"Is it my turn to call the cops on you?" I asked, mustering up some attitude while crossing my arms. This man was nothing like Whit. Whit thought of himself as a god, but Hudson treated me like his equal—an aggravating equal, but still an equal. And for that reason, I felt brave enough to put him in his place. "You stole my boat."

After a pronounced pause, Hudson huffed something under his breath and then said, "It wasn't my finest moment of maturity, all right?"

"We're finally in total agreement about something."

His eyes narrowed a bit. "My grandfather . . . he always told me to remove myself from a situation that was getting out of control before I did something I'd regret."

We held each other's stares as I thought about how the situation had gotten out of control. I could respect his decision to leave, to a point, but chose not to acknowledge that out loud. Instead, I said in an accusatory tone, "And what about breaking into my room?"

"Same. This was wrong of me." He started to stand. "I'll go."

I held up a hand. "Wait." Now it was my turn to pause and

then huff. "And I shouldn't have gone into your house without your permission. That was wrong of me."

Hudson gave me his best blank stare. He could make money teaching actors how to pull that off. We did nothing but hold each other's gaze for such a long, quiet spell that when he finally spoke, it confused me.

"You messed with my puzzle."

Rearing back, I blinked a few times. "Huh?"

"The puzzle in my kitchen. You messed with it."

I snorted out a snicker and rolled my eyes. "Putting two pieces into place is hardly messing."

"You also left your glass on the library floor," Hudson added.

"I figured you'd have preferred my quick exit over me sticking around to tidy things up," I retorted.

"I would have preferred you not plundering through my privacy, but that's a moot point now, isn't it?" It sounded like he was leading me to confess something. When my lips remained in a tight frown, he flipped the hood off and scrubbed both hands down his face. Brown locks of hair flaring in every direction, he looked as unkempt as ever. Dropping his hands, he pinned me with a stern look. "You didn't put the journals back in order."

Busted.

"Books in a library are meant to be read. If you didn't want your journals read, then you shouldn't have them out in the open like that."

Leaning back in the chair, Hudson crossed his arms and peered past my shoulder. After a moment, he refocused on me and asked, "How much did you read?"

"Enough."

On a heavy sigh, he hung his head and stared at the floor.

"Hudson, I'm so, so sorry."

"For what?" His raspy voice barely formed those two words.

"Everything." His difficult childhood, the struggles in his marriage, losing his family, the physical and emotional scars he carried as permanent parts of himself. Without voicing it out loud, that all hung in the air as clear as a banner behind an airplane.

"It doesn't change anything."

"I know."

"But . . . also . . ." He muttered something under his breath and tugged on the side of his beard. "I'm sorry."

I squinted at him. "For what?"

"For leaving you out on the island . . . and for making you cry."

I shook my head. "Those tears weren't for me. They were for you, Hudson." My admission had a tightness forming in my chest and working its way up my throat. "So you have nothing to apologize for."

We sat slumped in our spots, neither having the energy to say or do anything for a punctuated pause. Had there ever been two more sorry sorts than me and this battered man?

The insomnia and stress began sitting heavily on me. I kneaded the knot between my shoulders and rolled my neck.

Tilting his head to the side, Hudson scrutinized me with narrowed eyes. "Are you unwell?"

"Just tired and I'm hungry, and it's that time of the month." I shrugged like it was no big deal to overshare. "Do you eat anything besides tomatoes and seafood?" I knew he did, but I needed to lighten the mood in this room before we both smothered from the stifling sorrow we'd poured into it.

Hudson gave it some thought before answering, "Yes."

"How about pizza?" I pulled out my phone and opened the delivery app.

"Yes."

"What kind of toppings?"

He stood. "Look, I'll get out of your way."

I held up a palm, not ready for him to disappear just yet. "I can't eat an entire pizza by myself. You might as well stay and help me out."

Hudson returned to the chair, apparently not wanting to leave any more than I wanted him to. "I'm not picky."

"I could use a balanced meal. How about a supreme with extra vegetables?"

Nodding his head, he added, "Thick crust?"

"That works." I placed the order. "It'll be here in thirty minutes. I'm going to wash up real quick." I gestured toward the TV "You want me to turn that on? Or you could go hang out by the pool with the movie crew."

Hudson glanced at the closed window as if he could see through it. "All those people are with the movie?"

"Oh, that's not even everyone. The actors and bigwigs are staying out on Moise Island. We have this fine establishment all to ourselves, so feel free to join them."

"I'm good right here." He slid off his flip-flops and brushed them over by the TV stand with his bare foot.

"Suit yourself." I grabbed a change of clothes and locked myself in the bathroom. Worried that my trespasser would vanish, I took the quickest shower ever and dressed like my life depended on me getting back out there to him.

I pushed the sticking door open with my shoulder, stumbling slightly into the room, and sighed in relief. "You're still here."

A thick eyebrow arched impressively high. "Yes. Should I have left?"

"No!" Taking a calming breath, I picked up a wide-tooth comb and ran it through my damp hair. "You've been known to disappear, is all. I'm glad you didn't."

Hudson shifted in the chair, looking ready to bolt. Thankfully, we were saved by a knock on the door and a steaming hot pizza.

With only the one chair in the room, we decided to pull the small table over by the bed so I could have a seat too. I grabbed the paper towels I had in the armoire and unrolled several for us to use as plates and napkins. Sitting down, I popped open the box and we both leaned in to take in the aroma of garlic and marinara.

"Great day, that smells good." I wiggled a slice free and oohed over the melting drips of cheese.

Mouth full, Hudson made a noise in the back of his throat, apparently enjoying the meal too.

Halfway through my first slice, I asked, "Can this pizza be my peace offering to you for the whole movie scene thingy?"

He wiped his mouth with a paper towel. "I may have overreacted a bit, so why don't we just call it even."

"I get why you covet your privacy now, so you have my word that there will be no more requests such as that." I plucked a mushroom off a piece and popped it into my mouth.

"Did my refusal cause any issues for you?"

If only you knew. I forced a smile. "We filmed the scene out on Moise Island, so everything is back on track. I think it'll be just as good. Especially after the editing team works some magic into it." I chanced looking up from my pizza and noticed Hudson watching me in a careful way. We both knew I hadn't answered his question, and I had no plans on it.

Time to change the subject.

"Are you a connoisseur of puzzles?"

He grabbed another slice before answering, "No."

"But you acted so offended that I messed with your puzzle."

"You did mess with it." An eyebrow arched, daring me to refute him.

"Two pieces, as we've already established. So puzzles are just a hobby?"

"More like a habit. My grandfather made me put puzzles together after the—" Hudson averted his gaze—"accident. He said it was part of my physical therapy. Guess it worked too, since I'm able to do this now." He held up the scarred palm and began tapping each fingertip to his thumb.

I reached across the table and cradled his hand in mine while smoothing my finger along the scar. Discolored and a bit uneven, yet soft to the touch. "Does it still cause you pain?"

"Not in the physical sense, no." Hudson tugged his hand free and picked up another piece of pizza, making it clear it was time to move on to another topic. When another one didn't appear, we simply ate our meal.

He continued eating at an impressive rate, but I called it quits after two slices. Tossing my greasy paper towels, I retrieved my bag and dug out a medicine bottle. Before I could open it, Hudson snatched it out of my hand.

"What's this?" His gruff voice came out sharper than a knife.

Frowning, I pointed to the blue label. *"Pamprin."*

He dumped the contents out onto the palm of his hand.

"I doubt you need this. It's for cramps and bloating. On second thought, maybe you do. It's also supposed to help with irritability. Go ahead and keep it."

"They're all the same," he muttered to himself while inspecting each pill.

I laughed. "Yep. That's how the company packages—" That's when it occurred to me: Reece's pill addiction. "Oh . . ."

It's wild how circumstances can reshape something common for one person into an entirely different beast for another. A simple over-the-counter medication bottle would never look all that simple from Hudson's perspective.

Similarly I would never be able to accept a favor from a man without expecting strings attached to it. Perhaps that's why I was drawn to Hudson in the first place. He didn't want anything to do with me. Even this unexpected encounter was clearly him getting back at me for trespassing on the island and in his personal life.

Wanting to prove myself to Hudson and to put him at ease, I upended my bag onto the bed, tipping out my wallet, keys, lip balm, a pack of gum, pens, and a notepad. "You're welcome to check my bathroom. My luggage too." I motioned toward the open suitcase in the corner of the room.

Hudson closed his fist, funneled the pills back into the bottle, and handed it to me.

No longer wanting the medicine, I returned it to my bag and tossed everything else in too.

Hudson released a pensive breath and stood. "I can't believe you managed to read so much in only a few hours." He moved the table back into place.

"I have to read a lot of screenplays, so I've perfected speed-reading."

He slid on his flip-flops. "So I should be impressed you were able to speed-read my private journals?"

"Honey, if that's the only way I can impress you, then I'll take it." I smiled sweetly and opened the door, barely registering the few people remaining by the pool.

Flipping his hood up, Hudson looked me straight in the eyes. "Sonny, you impressed me within the first minute of meeting you." He brushed past me and I could hardly believe it when I felt his fingertips graze along the back of my hand. The very same parting gesture I'd given him last time I'd left the island.

Did the man have any idea what that did to me? Thoughtful and tender, his gesture hit me like a freight train and left me momentarily stunned.

Finding my words before he was out of earshot, I asked, "Was it my ability to run through the woods in the dark without smacking into a tree?"

Huffing out a chuckle that sounded sweeter than any shell wind chime, Hudson tossed up a hand and said, "See ya around."

"Hey, wait! Do you need a ride?" It was the first time I'd wondered how he'd gotten there.

His slow gait continued down the breezeway. "I have a truck."

"Wow. You own flip-flops *and* a truck. Wonders never cease."

He chuckled again and I bet that did spectacular things to his stoical face. Too bad his back was toward me.

I closed the door but before I moved away, someone began pounding on it. I reopened it and found a wide-eyed Vee gawking in the direction where Hudson had just vanished.

She barged into the room, pulling on a loudly printed swimsuit cover-up. "Are you okay?"

"Yes. Why are you flipping your lid?"

"Because—" she flicked a hand at me—"I saw you enter your room alone at least two hours ago. And just now a tall, mysterious man came out!"

I snorted.

"It's not funny. Did he rob you or . . . ?" Vee's eyes shot to the bed. "Do we need to call the cops?"

"No. That was the owner of Indigo Isle. He was returning my key that I . . . left out there."

"Say *whaaa*?" Vee's perfectly plucked eyebrows rose way up her forehead. "He looked too creepy, walking around in the dark like a serial killer. Ooh! I bet he dumps dead bodies in the marsh so the crabs will take care of the evidence!"

"For the last time—step away from the true crime docs!" I shook my head.

Vee sniffed the air. "Is that pizza I smell?"

I pointed to the box on the table behind me. "You didn't notice the pizza delivery guy either? Some neighborhood watch guard you are."

Ignoring my sass, Vee helped herself to the last piece of pizza. "So the Monster of Indigo Isle came out of hiding to bring you your key and have dinner with you?"

"It's not like that. I couldn't eat an entire pizza, so I shared it with him."

"Mm-hm . . ." She chewed thoughtfully.

I'd told Vee about Hudson, mainly complaining, so her reservations about him were my fault. I also knew she was smart enough to see past it all to know I'd developed either an unhealthy infatuation with the man or genuine feelings for him. At this point, it felt like a combination of the two.

"What about Whit?"

Just hearing his name made my stomach hurt worse. Reluctantly I asked, "What about him? We're not anything anymore, so I can have dinner with whomever I want."

"Darling, we both know Whit doesn't see it that way." She tossed the crust into the empty box and moved toward the door. "The man is manipulative and if you ever want to have a healthy relationship with someone else, you need to put an end to it."

Vee patted my shoulder and breezed out the door as quickly as she had entered.

I picked up the pizza box and began folding it so it would fit in the garbage. I wished reshaping my life was that easy. Perhaps it could have been at one point, but now? I didn't know.

CHAPTER THIRTEEN

NOTHING GOOD HAPPENS AFTER MIDNIGHT. I couldn't count the times I heard Mama give this lecture. When I was growing up, my parents had one hard-and-fast rule: Never break eleven o'clock curfew. I thought that was the most horrible rule and they were just being silly old geezers.

Well past midnight after another long day of filming, I stared up at the bleary, dark sky with a different view of that rule. Earlier tonight, I had been an accessory to murder, yet that seemed like the least of my crimes in the whole scheme of things. Every time I took a step away from the lifestyle I wanted to escape, I ended up stumbling several steps back into it. Tonight that stumble landed me square on my back.

One celebratory toast to send off Ax Beasley turned into more. It was the actor's last night on set. He played Druther, Teak's sidekick and general troublemaker. Tonight was his character's fated night to meet his end. A freak accident at the hands of his best bro, Teak. A tussle over a girl, where the weaker guy trips and breaks his neck.

It was nothing new to have a send-off party for a castmate, but lately I'd kept a better guard over my sobriety. Ever let that sucker slip, and something like what I found myself in at the moment would happen.

As Whit peeled my shirt over my head, I could hear Mama's voice in my ear: "Nothing good happens after midnight."

"Feels pretty good to me," Whit murmured, making me realize I'd said that out loud.

The damp sand and this man's demanding mouth on my neck felt the furthest from good. Somehow I'd ended up in the edge of the trees along the beach, having no recollection of getting there. Dancing one minute, then laid out in the sand with Whit's body pressing against mine the next. I could have sworn I hadn't had that much to drink—two glasses of champagne, tops—yet my dizzy head and numb body told a different story.

"Stop, Whit. Please," I slurred, my boneless hands pushing against his chest. "No."

Whit chuckled darkly, calling me a tease and lots of other colorful words as he fumbled with the button on my shorts. "You know you like this little game just as much as I do."

"Please, Whit. Not this time, okay?" My begging did nothing to dissuade him. I thought about crying out to God, begging him to get me out of this mess, but I was pretty sure he would ignore me too. Why wouldn't he? I'd done nothing honorable in my life for the sake of my faith, so I had no right expecting a miracle to show up now.

As the music thrummed through the humid night, my hazy thoughts circled around, meeting up with my parents, my sisters, Whit, and then Hudson before making another loop. My parents' scolding, my sisters' judging, Whit taking, Hudson avoiding. It was one messed-up trip and I didn't fit in anywhere. Either a burden or a diversion, never an inclusion.

When it became clear that a physical escape was out of reach, I let my mind escape to Indigo Isle. The sound of the shell trees in the breeze mixing with the clucks of roaming chickens drowned out the deep moans. I pretended the rocking of my body was from the chair on the back porch, and the pressure of Whit's palms holding me down was the tender brush of Hudson's fingers along my hand.

When Whit finally finished taking, I rolled over and vomited into the sand, heaving until nothing was left.

Whit guffawed, swatting my butt. "One too many, babe? Me too . . . me too."

I remained on my side, facing away from him, and quietly wept. *Me too?* I could hardly believe he had enough nerve to put those two words together and use them after what he'd just done to me. As if we were in the same boat, when, in fact, he'd tossed me overboard with no life preserver after stripping me of my dignity once again.

Whit got dressed and then pulled me to my feet and helped me do the same, as if what we'd just done had been perfectly normal.

"I told you no, Whit," I whispered as he straightened my shirt, my throat as raw as other parts of me.

Whit tsked, tapping my nose. "Because you like to tease me, you little minx."

"No." The word was but a breath past my lips as he began leading me back to the party up the beach. As I stumbled along, I wondered if Whit was right, that I was a tease and had brought this on myself.

Whit sat me in a lounge chair off to the side and walked away.

As I blinked in and out of consciousness, homesickness set in stronger than ever before.

Alone and dry heaving in the dark, I knew my parents had been right. Nothing good happened after midnight. I wondered what else they had been right about that I'd gotten absolutely wrong.

• • •

The sun showed up a few hours later. Instead of finding myself still in the lounge chair on the beach, I was in my hotel bed with a concerned Vee hovering over me.

"You're much too pretty to be frowning," I whispered hoarsely. Clearing my throat, I winced from the jolt of pain slicing through my head. I rubbed the right side of my scalp, finding my hair in sandy tangles.

Vee continued frowning. "How can you lie there in this shape and try making light of it? You need to file a report."

I licked my dry lips, repulsed by the sour tang in my mouth. I needed a shower and toothbrush, but a weightiness kept my body on the bed.

"Did you hear me, Sonny?"

"For what?"

"For what Whit did to you last night."

I pinched my eyes shut, not wanting to acknowledge last night.

The bed jostled as Vee sat beside me. "Seriously, Sonny. Your inner thighs are covered in bruises and I think Whit slipped something in your drink. You were so out of it that I had to ask Cade to help me get you here."

I massaged my forehead. "You've been watching too many true cri—"

"This isn't a joke, Sonny!"

I flinched as a wave of nausea rolled over me. Pressing the back of my hand over my mouth, I took several cautious breaths. When the wave died down, I whispered, "It's my fault. I got myself into this with him."

Vee placed her cool palm to my flushed cheek. "We're not done talking about this, but I have to head out to Moise Island. I've already texted Whit from your phone and told him you wouldn't be on set today."

I peeled my eyes open. "You say more than that?"

Glossed lips pressed into a severe line, Vee shook her head. "No, but *you* should." She stood and moved toward the door.

"Thank you, Vee."

She flicked a wrist in the air, not wanting to hear it. "Think about what I said. If you decide to file a report, I'll go with you. And call me if you need me today."

"Okay."

After Vee left, I remained in bed for the better part of the day, sleeping off whatever Whit had given me. Much later, unable to stand the mess of my hair and clothing any longer, I managed taking a shower and got dressed in a baggy T-shirt and jogging pants.

I stood by the bed, regarding the sandy sheets, and wondered if a firm shake would rid them of most of the grit. That was as doubtful as giving myself a firm enough shake to rid me of the ugliness from last night.

A squeaking of the door next to my room caught my attention. Wrestling a smile onto my face, I moved over and opened my door to find Erlene shuffling by.

"Good morning, Erlene." I shielded my eyes from the harsh sunlight.

She paused and glanced over her shoulder. "Oh, my . . . Honey, you look like you've been rode hard and put up wet."

"Umm . . . I just got out the shower."

"You know what I mean, missy. Are you okay?"

I shooed her worries with a flick of the wrist. "We filmed late last night, is all, and didn't finish until early this morning. I, uh . . . I was wondering if I could bother you for a fresh set of sheets?"

Erlene maneuvered her walker around to face me straight on. Her motherly scrutiny reminded me of some looks I'd received from my own mother while growing up. The look said she didn't quite believe me but was going to let it go. For now. "I'll have Jill bring a set over."

"Jill?"

"My great-niece. She helps her mama clean the rooms here, remember?"

Vaguely. "Oh, that's right."

"She's going to beauty school. Gonna open her own salon soon." Erlene smiled with pride but suddenly grew serious. She scooted closer and whispered, "You ain't got to tell me what's going on, but I just want you to know I'm praying for you."

When most people say that, it feels like a hollow sentiment tossed out there for the sake of saying it. But when this lady said it, I believed her.

I cleared the lump from my throat and managed to say, "Thank you. I need it."

Nodding once, Erlene scooted down the walkway.

Moments later, a set of clean sheets and a mini can of Coke arrived at my door. Jill tried handing both over.

"I just asked for sheets. Thanks."

"Aunt Erlene said you need the Coke, too." Jill pushed the cold can into my hand and I couldn't even thank her because I was on the verge of crying from the old lady's thoughtfulness.

I closed the door and shook my head. "It's just a soda, Sonny. Get a grip." Unable to get that grip, I sipped the icy cold beverage with tears streaming down my face. Once the can was empty and the tears dried, I actually felt a little better. Knowing someone cared did that, I supposed.

After changing my sheets, I sat on the edge of the bed and pulled up Whit's text on my phone to read what Vee had said to him.

Hey. Not sure what you put in my drink, but I'm too sick to make it to set today.

I groaned and rolled my neck. "Thanks, Vee."

I expected something more from Whit than a thumbs-up emoji but that's all he'd sent. No explanation or excuse for what he did last night. Fuming, I fired off another text.

May need to see a doctor. Won't be on set tomorrow either. Maybe longer.

Bubbles popped up and then another thumbs-up.

Tossing my phone to the side, I climbed under the clean sheets. Had Whit ever cared for me? Listening to the window unit drone on, I mentally flipped through the last decade, needing to find some evidence that he hadn't always been so cruel. But even the favors and lavish gifts had come at a hefty cost, leaving my bank account of dignity in the red.

Pulling the blanket up to my chin, I tried forgetting Whit altogether and bringing up a happier memory from my BC—before California—life. Surely they were there. But the harder I tried to find the happy times, the more the harsher parts popped into my head.

Stealing dime candy from the store after Mama told me I couldn't have any on account of biting Caroline the day before.

Tearing a page out of the hymnal at church by accident, but then having to apologize to the pastor at Dad's insistence. Backing into my grandmother's mailbox because I was being a careless driver, and then having to buy her a new one out of my allowance.

Seemed I spent my entire childhood in some sort of trouble and kept my family upset with me. Could that really be right? That's the problem with memories. They can make you a liar, and figuring out who holds the truer version is an absolute mystery.

Time crept by, the sun shifting from one side of the room to the other. And sometime in there, my memories shifted as well, from bad times to better ones with my family. Buried behind a thick wall of resentment, the good finally resurfaced after some digging.

Fishing with Dad.

Making strawberry preserves with Mama.

Both of them belting out "I Got You Babe" when I entered a room. Mama deepening her voice to match Cher's while Dad bent down to appear shorter than her.

I pulled up the song on my music app and put it on repeat, using the memory like a security blanket to help me fall asleep.

CHAPTER FOURTEEN

ONCE WHILE ON LOCATION in the Mojave Desert, I came across the gruesome sight of a carcass being torn apart by several vultures. Peck after peck, the birds meticulously erased the identity of the poor animal, making it unrecognizable. Within mere days, I walked past the same spot, astounded that only bones remained.

Lying in bed for the second morning in a row, I couldn't get those images out of my head. The vultures pecking away, reminding me of how my dumb choices had done a meticulous job of stripping away the innocent girl from South Carolina. I flipped the blanket aside and gave myself a quick inspection. Apart from the dark bruises on my thighs, everything remained intact. Perfectly healthy, fairly toned and tanned. The wrapping didn't show any evidence of the riddled wounds just below the surface.

I replaced the blanket and rolled to my side, trying to pinpoint why exactly I ever thought life in Georgetown was so unbearable. My parents had raised me right with simple teachings: Be kind. Be honest. Be faithful to God and your family. Be compassionate to those less fortunate. Sure, they were strict and I spent most of my childhood on some sort of restriction, but they never, not once, did anything to cause me harm. I'd done a fairly good job of doing that all on my own.

My phone began vibrating on the nightstand again, as it had been doing at constant intervals since yesterday morning, delivering texts and calls. The only ones I had responded to were Vee's, letting her know I was still breathing but wanted to be left alone.

After a few minutes of quiet, the vibrating started up again. Knowing there were responsibilities I couldn't keep skipping out on, I reached for the phone. Whit's assistant's name flashed across the screen, along with the time, 7:18 a.m.

I accepted the call. "Hi, Tia."

"Hi. Your voice sounds rough. Heard you have a summer cold."

"Yeah." I cleared my throat and mumbled, "You're up early."

"We had a sunrise scene today."

"That's right. How'd it go?"

"Good. We just wrapped, so I'm doing some paperwork before the next scene. I hate to bother you, but I need an update on the marina scene."

"Hang on . . ." I leaned over the side of the bed, plucked my laptop from the floor, and pulled up my emails. "The permits have been approved, so it's all set for next Thursday. I'll forward the information to you."

"That'll be great."

Buying myself another few days away from Whit, I told Tia, "I just have a few things to take care of off set, so I won't be out to Moise Island until Monday."

"Sure thing. I'll let production know. Do you want me to send Lyrica your way?"

I massaged my temples. "I thought she already went back to LA."

"Yeah, but she changed her mind again, so she's back. Les still wants her glued to you."

Not happening. That girl being glued to me was like having concrete shackles. The title of location manager was too, for that matter. My eyes moved to the door as an overwhelming desire to run away came over me. I'd done it once; perhaps it was time to do it again. Could I reverse it, though? Run in the right direction this time?

"Sonny?"

Sighing, I leaned my head against the pillow. "Just have her help the set crew with any staging that needs to be done. I should be able to make the late shoot on Saturday"—aka be there to babysit the director's daughter.

"Okay. See you Saturday."

After ending the call, I shoved the phone and computer to the other side of the bed and tried going back to sleep, but hunger overruled that idea. I pressed a palm against the beast in my belly, feeling the hollowness from several skipped meals and the mess I couldn't get out of with Whit.

Releasing a long groan, I hauled my sorry self out of bed and scrounged up just enough energy to wash and get dressed. Pulling on a hat and shoving on a pair of Vans, I grabbed a printed map of the marina to at least do some work and trekked across the street to the diner.

I opened the door and a delicious scent of fried breakfast meats and coffee wafted by me. A new level of hunger propelled me toward the counter to the only available stool.

"Mornin'."

I glanced to my right at the older gentleman sitting beside me, barely making eye contact before my eyes skittered away. "Mornin'." I pulled the brim of the hat lower and rounded my shoulders.

"You from around here?"

I shook my head and unfolded the map to start outlining the approved zones for the shoot.

"You lost?"

In more than one sense of the word, but I didn't nod or shake my head, hoping he would take a hint.

"I can help if you are." His voice was friendly, but I didn't trust it.

I shook my head again and reached for the laminated menu, placing it on top of the map to keep it away from the chatty man's sight.

The waitress came over. "Good mornin', hon. You know whatcha want or do you need another minute?"

I ordered something called Big Ben's Breakfast Special, which was delivered in a procession of several bowls and plates.

The man chuckled. "Little lady, if you eat all that, breakfast's on me." He moved his coffee cup over to make more room for me.

"If you're going to do it wrong, do it right, right?" I afforded him a guarded smile while freeing my silverware from the napkin.

He chuckled again. "I suppose."

I dug into the first plate my fork came upon, biscuits and gravy. My eyes slid in the man's direction while I took a generous bite. He looked about the age my dad would have been if he were still alive. That thought alone nearly derailed my breakfast binge, tightening the muscles in my throat and making it difficult to swallow.

"Food's gonna get cold." The man's thick Southern drawl sounded like my dad's too. He nodded his head toward the feast. "The pecan pie pancakes are my favorite."

I blinked away from his crinkly kind eyes and located the pancakes, sliding that plate closer.

"They don't even need syrup," he added.

Taking his word for it, I sliced off a forkful and shoved it into my mouth. Nutty and maple sweet with hints of spice. I could have sworn I had just taken a bite from a piece of my mother's pecan pie.

"Well?"

"Might be my favorite too." I shrugged, taking a sip of coffee.

The man grinned and I worried he would take me answering him as an invitation for conversation, so I swiveled the stool slightly toward the left and placed my elbow on the counter to form a wall. Thankfully, he turned back to his own meal and left me in peace.

Blocking out the clanking of dishes and conversation around me and ignoring the ache in my chest from missing my dad, I tucked into the pancakes and then the grits. By the time I put the fork down, the food had a good dint in it, but I left more than not. Too full to even finish off my coffee, I waved the waitress over and asked for the check.

"It's already taken care of, hon." She winked and motioned to the vacant spot beside me. "He said to give you this." She handed over a business card, or so I thought until reading it.

I will search for my lost ones who strayed away, and I will bring them safely home again.
EZEKIEL 34:16

Clutching the card in the palm of my hand, I looked over both shoulders. With no sign of the man anywhere, I flipped the card and found it blank. Just the Bible verse. Maybe not just a verse, but the right one I needed at the moment. My mother used to tell me all the time that God would give us what we needed when we needed it, as long as we were looking toward him. I'd been giving God sidelong glances lately. Apparently that was enough.

I reread the verse and something my dad used to say rose to the surface of my thoughts. *"Even when you can't trust the world, you can trust the Word of God."* I had no trust in anything anymore, but that one sentence from Ezekiel sparked a glimmer of hope that perhaps I could, one day soon.

A group of teenagers crowded the counter, so I vacated my spot and moved outside into the bright morning light. The briny air already held a promise for a hot day.

Crossing the busy street, I debated going back to bed, but the food gave me a burst of energy instead of making me lethargic. With a hall pass from work, I had the entire day before me and could go explore downtown Charleston or do some shopping, but both options would be too people-y for my current mood.

I stood beside the car, toying with the key ring while listening to traffic whirl past the motel. A splash caught my attention and gave me the fleeting idea of hanging out by the pool, but then I remembered the bruises hiding underneath my jeans.

"Nap it is . . ." Resigned, I went to move away from the car but my feet seemed stuck to the asphalt. There was one place I could show up in broken pieces and one man who'd accept me as is. Probably because he didn't care, but still.

Over a week had passed by since my motel room encounter with Hudson. Even though he'd sought me out, I still planned on leaving him alone. Standing in the parking lot, I went a few rounds with the rights and wrongs of it—*Leave Hudson alone . . . But I miss him and his surly attitude.* I felt my resolve slipping. I knew darn well I was a hazard to Hudson, but making the wrong choice, the selfish choice, always came natural to me, so I finally gave in and got into the car and drove over to the marina. After making sure the coast was clear of any Ewol Entertainment peeps, I hopped into my boat and navigated the salt marsh channels, which were fairly clear of other boats.

The island came into view and then the dock. Nothing looked different but nothing felt the same since the last time I had been here.

I took my time walking the sandy path, appreciating the exotic beauty of the island while giving Hudson a moment to prepare himself for my visit. No doubt he knew trouble had just shown up. Birds sang somewhere overhead in the canopy of tree branches and vines, their melody soothing enough to relax my shoulders. Gradually, the dimness faded and opened up to the homestead. I expected the formidable owner to be waiting at the end of the path, but only a few black-and-white speckled chickens greeted me, clucking and strutting past.

"Hello, ladies." I started toward the porch but before reaching it, I heard a throat being cleared from beside the shed. Biting my lip to hold back a grin, I rounded the corner and came upon Hudson hitching a trailer to an ancient-looking tractor with more rust than red paint.

"Good morning, stranger," I said, tucking my hands into the back pockets of my jeans.

Hudson continued fiddling with the hitch, leaning over and banging the pin into place with the heel of his hand as if it were a hammer. Just like the island, he appeared exactly the same, dressed in tattered clothes and silence. Well, I noticed one small change.

"I see you've found a pair of real shoes." I motioned toward the beat-up sneakers on his feet, which he wore with no socks.

He straightened, casting a shadow over me. "What do you want?"

I opened my mouth to sass him about his impeccable Southern hospitality, but a fragment of my brokenness fell out instead. "I need a time-out."

His brow pinched. "A what?"

I thought about it for a minute before answering, "I spent a lot of my childhood in time-outs. Bet you'd never guess I used to be a handful." I laughed.

Hudson didn't. He just stood there towering over me with his arms crossed.

"That was my mother's go-to punishment. She said that way I could reflect on my poor choices and figure out how not to make the same mistake again." I dropped my gaze to the ground, tracking a grasshopper. "I just need a time-out today. Please don't make me leave."

"Something wrong with you?"

My eyes began to sting, but I blinked several times to halt the tears. "No. Just . . . I'm not feeling the greatest."

Hudson placed a finger underneath my chin and angled my face toward him, waiting until I met his eyes before letting go. "You seem to feel bad a lot. Do you have some type of health issue?"

I waved a hand through the air to scatter his assumption before it formed completely. "No. I just have a sick of life issue." My attempt to laugh sounded more like a strangled hiccup.

His frown deepened.

Needing to sidestep the pile of mess I just dropped on us, I made a crack about his hair. "You ever brush that rat's nest?"

Giving me his signature stone face, he lifted his hand and combed through his hair with ease. Surprisingly, his fingers didn't get trapped in snares of tangles. "Done."

I clutched my chest and gawked at him. "You actually just made a joke?"

"Don't go expecting any more." Sighing, Hudson rubbed the back of his neck and stared off toward the shed. "I was more of a hothead than a handful as a kid. Extra chore duty was my grandpa's punishment of choice. Said that gave me time to work it out of my system."

I looked around, mostly finding farming equipment and gardening tools scattered about. "Does that mean you're putting me to work while I'm in time-out?"

"Might as well, if I have to put up with you. Meet me at the indigo field." He turned to the tractor and climbed on, flipping a switch that brought it to life in a spitting and sputtering tempo.

I waited for the tractor to pass with its glowering driver and then followed behind. Truthfully, Hudson wasn't nice. Even in this subtropical climate, the man was cold, but slowly he'd begun letting the frigidness slip just a bit. Allowing me to spend the day with him was proof of it.

After lining the tractor up on the edge of the field, he climbed down and reached in the bed of the trailer, coming back with a machete.

I stopped in my tracks. "Oh, shoot!"

Hudson glanced at the giant knife in his grasp and then at me. "What?"

"My friend Vee . . ." I laughed nervously. "She, uh, suspects you're a, uh, serial killer." I gestured toward him. "She'd keel over if she saw you right now."

Keeping his eyes pinned on me, he lowered his head as his expression morphed into something menacing, while running his thumb over the blade of the machete. "How'd she find out?" The rasp of his voice made the scene before me even more alarming.

A high-pitched squeak came out of me as I scrambled a few steps backwards.

He held the machete above his head and looked ready to pounce. I turned on a dime and started to run, but a roar of unadulterated laughter made me freeze. Turning back around, I watched on in pure amazement as the Monster of Indigo Isle doubled over laughing.

"Your . . . face!" The grown man giggled like a mischievous little boy, holding his midsection and pointing at me with that dang machete. "I got you so good!"

Darned if I couldn't even be mad at him for it, either. Struck by the transformative power of laughter before my very eyes, I walked right up to him and placed my palm on his smiling cheek. "Wow. Laughter looks good on you, sir."

The smile vanished as Hudson retreated a step, causing my hand to drop away. "We're wasting time."

Knowing the moment was over, I asked, "If you're not going to kill me with that thing, then what are you going to do with it?"

"It's time to harvest this field." He moved over to the first row of green plants, which were at least a foot or two taller than him, and demonstrated what to do, gathering the branches in one hand and then slicing through them with the machete near the base.

I accepted the stalk he offered and noticed a hint of sweetness in the air. I stuck my nose close to the indigo and sniffed it. "This smells sort of like sweet peas."

"Indigo is from the legume family." Hudson sliced through another plant and tossed the bundle into the trailer. "Think you can manage?"

"Sure." I took the machete from him and gave it a try, but it wasn't nearly as easy as he'd made it look. I fumbled with gathering the branches all at once, so I had to do it in sections.

"We'll be here all day," Hudson grumbled.

"I can't help it my hands aren't giant-ogre-size like yours," I grouched, tossing the bundle and then watching as half of the stems bounced off the side of the trailer and onto the ground. Mumbling a few sentiments under my breath, I hurried over to pick up the pieces. After tossing them in, I moved to the next plant.

"Would knitting a blanket be better for your baby-size hands? You'd probably have it finished a lot faster." He made a move to take the machete, but I dodged him.

"No! I'll get the hang of it. Just stay out of my way." I expected him to complain some more. When he didn't, I looked over and caught him fighting a smile. Rolling my eyes, I went back to work.

A quarter of the way down the row, I found my rhythm. *Strangle, chop, toss. Strangle, chop, toss.* "Man, I kinda feel like a serial killer, butchering these poor unsuspecting plants."

Hudson huffed a chuckle and left me in the field, returning several minutes later with another machete. He started on the row beside mine and passed me in no time flat.

Not to be outdone, I sped up.

Hudson grumbled something under his breath. "Knock it off before you slice your leg open or something."

I heard what he said, but I also noticed him speeding up too. Next thing I knew we were racing. Of course, I had no chance. The man had years of experience and a whole lot more muscle than me, but I liked the challenge all the same.

Halfway through the field, I gave up on the race and settled into a more reasonable pace. Hudson also slowed a bit to stay near me, which I appreciated.

"My arms are a little itchy." My right shoulder also ached from slinging the increasingly heavy machete, but I decided not to mention it—or the blisters forming on my hand.

"Indigo itch. The plant has a built-in insect repellent." Hudson tossed his bundle into the rapidly filling trailer.

"Okay, but how to make it stop?" I rubbed my forearm on the side of my jeans. The itch was mild, just there enough to make me aware of it.

"Scratching only makes it worse." He delivered the warning, catching me in the act. "You'll get used to it."

As the day wore on, I eventually did get used to it. Or maybe the growing ache in my shoulder stole all the attention. Either way, I stubbornly plowed on, only stopping for a drink of water every so often.

Once we had the trailer overflowing with indigo, I gladly handed over the machete.

"Something's wrong with my arm." I let it dangle limply for effect.

Hudson's brows pinched together as he focused on my puny arm. "What do you mean?"

"I think it's out of socket. Seriously, it's not working right." I dropped my shoulder to add to the pitiful picture.

He snorted. "Are you so wimpy that after only one morning of physical labor, you're in need of a medic?" He picked up my arm and wiggled it every which way. "Seems fine to me."

I rolled my lips inward, trying not to smile but too pleased about his sudden playfulness.

"Is your left one not working properly either?" He moved behind me and picked it up, but suddenly stopped. "How'd you get those bruises?"

I angled my head, trying to look at the back of my arm. "Probably bumped into something." I turned around and asked, "What's next?"

Eyes narrowed, Hudson regarded me suspiciously. After a weighty pause, he pointed to a narrow platform behind the tractor, "Think you can stand there without falling off?"

I wasn't a hundred percent sure, but I shrugged and climbed up while he settled onto the seat and cranked the tractor. I held on to the back of his seat, but when the tractor lurched forward, I wrapped my arms around his neck.

"You're choking me!" He patted my arm and I loosened my hold, but only enough so he could breathe.

As Hudson maneuvered through the thin patch of trees behind the homestead, I could feel his muscles bunching and relaxing underneath his shirt. I rested my chin on his shoulder and felt his beard brush against my cheek. I was surprised at how soft it was, but more surprised that he seemed okay with me touching him.

Soon, we came to another clearing with a small cabin and more farming equipment.

"I had no idea all this was back here," I said near his ear, satisfied by the tiny tremor that moved through him.

We came to a stop beside two offset rectangle forms that resembled swimming pools. Hudson shut the tractor off, unraveled my arms from around him, and leaned forward to put even more space between us. "The plants go in the top vat." He pointed to the one raised behind the other.

Following his lead, I jumped down and began tossing armfuls of indigo into the vat. This part of the process had its own rhythm. *Twist, scoop, twist, toss. Twist, scoop, twist, toss.* A new ache in my back joined the one in my shoulder and a few new scratches joined the others.

By the time we had the trailer cleared, my body was worn slap out and it was glorious, because nothing but indigo had taken up space in my mind for several hours. No regrets about the past. No worries about the future. Nothing but good honest work.

I used the collar of my shirt to dry the sweat from my face. "Now what?"

"We fill the vat with water." Hudson turned on a faucet connected to a rain barrel behind the taller vat that had a hose leading from it. Slowly the vat began filling.

I moved to the lip of the vat and saw nothing but green. "Shouldn't it be turning blue?"

"Not yet." He lowered a metal-and-mesh grate on top of the full vat.

I kept my eyes trained on the submerged plants. "How much longer?"

Hudson placed a few clamps along the lid. "Should be done steeping by Saturday morning."

I whipped around and asked with more whine than necessary, "Two days?"

"Yep." He wiped his hands on the front of his threadbare shirt.

"Ugh. This takes too long." My bottom lip poked out.

"Come back Saturday. It'll be worth the wait." He motioned for me to climb in the back of the empty trailer.

I could hardly believe he'd just extended such an invitation to me. Smiles and invites . . . surely the world was about to end. I scanned the sky but nothing appeared amiss.

"Let's go," Hudson ordered.

Lowering my gaze, I shuffled toward him. "I don't mind standing on the back of the tractor."

"But I mind not being able to breathe." He helped me get in and I reluctantly let him. "Stop pouting or I won't make you supper."

Smiles, invites, and supper. Yep, I was done for. A giant grin spread across my face. Hudson's eyes dropped to my lips briefly before he stepped away, muttering something under his breath Feeling all sorts of warm and fuzzy, I stretched out, smiling up at the sky, and enjoyed the bumpy ride.

The Monster of Indigo Isle proved he knew how to be a proper host. After we washed up at an outdoor sink, he doctored my blisters with aloe and settled me on the back porch with a glass of tea while he prepared supper. I offered to help, but he insisted he had it under control.

Later, we moved to the outdoor table and Hudson presented me with the prettiest salad I'd ever seen, a mix of greens, cucumbers, tomatoes, peas, and blueberries.

"It looks like a rainbow," I complimented.

He handed me a jar filled with dressing.

I dipped my clean fork in and gave it a taste, surprised at the sweet and tangy flavor. "You make this?"

"Yes. Blueberry vinaigrette."

I dressed my salad and offered the jar to him. "I noticed the blueberry bushes on our tractor ride. What else do you grow out here?"

"There's a small peach and apple orchard on the western side of the island. And several pecan trees." He angled his head in thought. "A few lemon and orange trees too."

"You really are self-contained out here."

"Pretty much. With Art and LuAnn's help, I really never have a reason to leave the island." Hudson began eating.

The appeal of his solitary lifestyle grew on me the more time I spent out here. I loaded a fork with as many colors of the rainbow as it would hold and crammed it into my mouth. "Oh, wow. I can taste the sunshine. It's delicious."

Hudson grunted before taking another bite. The man communicated like a caveman, but I didn't mind those deep rumbling answers.

No further words joined our meal, as we tucked into the richly flavored salad. The amicable silence was the perfect accompaniment, so I don't know why Hudson chose to ruin it before we even finished eating.

"What's going on with you, Sonny?"

A wedge of tomato escaped my fork and plopped onto the front of my shirt, leaving a violet smear of vinaigrette. "Making a mess obviously." I laughed, trying to clean my shirt but only making it worse. Giving up, I placed the napkin by my plate.

"You know that's not what I'm talking about. You don't look well."

"I'm starving and exhausted. You worked me to the bone today." I speared a slice of cucumber with my fork and stuffed it into my mouth.

Hudson's gaze lingered as he mindlessly moved his fork around the salad. "You showed up with those dark rings around your eyes. That's not on me." His head tilted to the side.

I shrugged, staring at the beautiful salad he'd prepared until my eyes blurred. "Everything seems to be catching up with me lately."

"Vague much?" His condescending tone had me looking up at him.

"Excuse me?"

Hudson leaned over his plate and leveled me with a look. "You don't come with journals open at the ready to spill all your secrets as I did. You've been nothing but vague from day one. And those bruises on the back of your arm? Did you happen to bump into someone's hand? Because they're suspiciously shaped like fingers. So either be honest with me or get off my island."

Taken aback by his bluntness, I crossed my arms and glared to prevent myself from crying, but a tear mutinied and plopped down my cheek anyway. I was so sick of crying.

"Are you in some kind of trouble?" The sharp edges of his voice softened, which made another tear escape.

I shook my head. "Just caught up in some dumb choices. Nothing illegal," I clarified. He wouldn't think twice about kicking me off the island if he thought otherwise.

"What about the bruises?"

I shrugged. "My ex . . . he's not clear on us being over, and . . . he got a little handsy the other night. That's all." Gosh, how I wished that was the extent of it. Another tear tracked down my face. I batted it away with the back of my hand.

"This ex? You two work together?"

I nodded.

"Want to tell me about him?"

I shook my head.

Hudson pushed out a deep sigh. "Keeping things bottled up, it's unhealthy."

I snorted a derisive laugh. "Hypocritical much?"

Grumbling about me being stubborn as a mule, Hudson shoved away from the table and stormed into the house.

The night appeared to be thoroughly ruined, so I stood to leave, but Hudson came barreling back outside.

"Here." He forced a brown leather book into my hands. "If you can't talk about it, at least maybe write it down."

I fanned through the crisp blank pages, catching a whiff of brand-new paper. "But . . . 'only sissy girls keep diaries,'" I said, quoting his very first journal entry.

It took a minute for him to catch that. When he did, he played along. "Good thing this is a journal for grown-ups and not a diary for sissies." He tapped a blank page. "Journaling helps me make sense of things when nothing else does. Give it a try and see if it works for you too."

"Okay. Thank you."

"You're welcome. Now can we eat this sunshiny rainbow meal I worked so hard to prepare for you?" His flat tone did nothing to hide the underlying tease. If the man only knew how therapeutic that alone was for me. He kept giving what he noticed I needed, whether it be food, a journal, or a joke to lighten the heavy. And what was the biggest gift in all that? Hudson required nothing in return. Not once.

CHAPTER FIFTEEN

I THOUGHT SATURDAY WOULD NEVER COME, but when it finally did, I beat the sun up. Such a wild idea of actually being excited about something again. It had been quite a while. To kill some time while waiting to head out, I decided to check my emails. There were several messages from fans, wanting to know when new content would be arriving on my YouTube channel. I'd always been that person to answer each email, because if a fan took the time to watch my stuff and then email me, then I should respect them enough to reply. Looking at the in-box, I felt frozen with no idea how to respond. I just didn't want to pretend anymore.

Leaving the task of figuring that out for later, I picked up the journal and reread my first entry.

It's official. My life sucks, so my friend—that's what Hudson is, even though he would deny it—says I need to write about how sucky it is. I told him only sissy girls keep diaries, but he said this is a journal. Whatever.

I'd made a joke with the first entry, but then something unleashed inside, maybe from some well that I'd kept the lid on for far too long. Soon the pages had begun filling from the depth of that well. I glanced over several pages, my eyes snagging on poignant points.

> *I ran away from home instead of going to my graduation. Looking at that choice fifteen years later, I consider it one of my deepest regrets . . .*

> *Whit Kessler is known as a production king in Hollywood and my 22-year-old self quickly fell on my knees and worshiped him. A decade has gone by with me bending to his will. I'm exhausted, but I cannot figure out how to stand up . . .*

> *I love location scouting and hate being a location manager, but when Whit dangled the position in my face, I only saw the prestige that would come with it. More recognition in the industry. A better paycheck. Another door opening. I want to close the door . . .*

> *I'm homesick . . .*

> *I love Indigo Isle . . .*

> *I like Hudson Renfrow more than I should . . .*

Closing the journal, I stuffed it into my suitcase for safekeeping and got ready for the day. I packed a change of clothes in my beach bag before getting dressed. I put on a bikini underneath my white T-shirt and jean shorts. The shorts reached my knees, which meant the bruises on my thighs were out of sight. After grabbing breakfast sandwiches and two bottles of orange juice from Creek View Diner, I took off to Indigo Isle.

As the boat glided around the corner and approached the island, I saw Hudson sitting on the dock, staring at a book in his lap. Was he there waiting for me to arrive? Surely not, but my stomach fluttered at the idea of it anyway.

As soon as I cut the engine, Hudson sprang to his feet and tied off the boat.

"Thanks. I brought breakfast." I held up the greasy white bag. "Hope you haven't eaten yet."

Hudson swiped it and peeped inside before handing it back to me. "I could make room for something else. What is it?"

"Sausage and egg biscuits. That okay?" We sat cross-legged on the dock and I divvied out the food and juice.

"I'm not opposed." Hudson unwrapped his biscuit and sniffed it before taking a bite.

"You always smell your food." I placed a napkin on his knee and grabbed another from the bag for myself.

The wind lifted his long hair away from his face as he met my gaze. "Just appreciating it."

"I thought maybe you were checking it for poison or something," I teased and decided to sniff my own biscuit, finding the appealing aroma of sage and butter.

He didn't bother with a response. That was okay. I didn't expect one anyway.

As I bit into the biscuit, my eyes wandered to the book on the plank between us. *1984* by George Orwell. "Is this book any good?"

Hudson looked at the red cover with the giant blue eye staring up at us. *1984* was written in the black pupil. "No."

I snickered, loving his matter-of-fact truth. "Why not?"

He gave the book a repulsed sneer and flipped it over so that the eye no longer looked at us, only to reveal another eye on the back cover. Grumbling, he wedged it underneath his thigh to hide it from view. "Gives me the creeps."

"Then why read it?"

"I can't not finish it."

"Oh . . . you're one of those readers. I'm opposite—if I ever get the chance to actually read. I give a book three chapters. If it hasn't grabbed me by that point, I move to something else."

He wiped his mouth and took a sip of juice. "That would drive me crazy. Leaving something incomplete."

"Well, is there anything you like about the book?"

"It's short."

I really liked that the Hudson in his journals was the same guy as the Hudson sitting beside me eating breakfast. I wished I could be the same all the time too. Keeping the mask of *everything is fabulous* in place had become pretty burdensome lately. Out here on Indigo Isle, there was no pressure to wear such false pretenses.

Staring at the water rippling by the dock, I wondered if I could pull it off as Hudson had. Just walk away from everything and hermit away. Maybe nothing that extreme, but after the movie wrapped in three weeks, I wouldn't mind taking a break from the public.

Leaving that issue for another time, I turned my attention to my silent breakfast companion. "I wore my swimsuit, so if you don't mind, I may grab some beach time later before I have to head to work." I tore off a piece of biscuit and nibbled on it.

Hudson finished the last of his biscuit and shrugged. I guess that meant he didn't care one way or the other. A major improvement from his normal answer of no.

"What is it you actually do?" He balled up his wrapper and dropped it into the bag. "I thought you travel all over, looking for places to film, but you've been here most of the summer."

"I scout locations for films, but I'm also a location manager. Once I secure a site, my main duties consist of preparing the area for the crew and coordinating any logistics. I'm here for the duration to keep all that in check, amongst other responsibilities." *Such as the tedious job of Whit Kessler.* Barely containing a shudder, I finished off my juice and tried banishing those thoughts.

Hudson rose to his feet and actually held his hand out to help me up. "Time to get to work."

I glanced at his bare feet. "No work shoes today?"

"No sharp tools needed today, so no shoes needed either." He started down the path with me following beside him.

I plucked a yellow blossom from a thick bush and brought it to my nose. "Mm . . . this smells like honeysuckle. I used to suck the nectar out of them when I was a kid."

"Well, I wouldn't suck on that one. It's poisonous."

I dropped the flower and wiped my hand on my shorts.

Hudson gave me a wry smirk. "It's okay to touch jasmine, just don't ingest it." He reached past me and picked another delicate bloom. After considering me for a moment, he brushed a wayward curl behind my shoulder and tucked the flower behind my ear.

Heat climbed my cheeks and my neck tingled where his fingers had grazed my skin. Stunned that he had done such a sweet thing, I stood staring up at him for several beats.

Clearing his throat, Hudson averted his gaze and began

strolling down the path again like he didn't just wreak havoc on my equilibrium.

Steadying myself, I adjusted the flower behind my ear and hurried to catch up to him.

We walked along, passing the homestead and through the trees before coming up on the vats. The tractor and trailer were already parked beside the top vat. All of a sudden, a foul stench overpowered the sweet scent and moment we'd just had with the flower. The closer we got to the vats, the more pronounced the odor became.

"Hate to tell you this, but I think your indigo went bad." I tried breathing through my mouth, but that only made me gag.

Hudson sniffed. "No. It smells just right."

My nose wrinkled. "Seriously? Like rotten fish?"

"Fermentation." He removed the clamps and then slid the grate off the top.

Holding my breath, I peeked over the side. A greenish sheen that reminded me of antifreeze swirled around the floating remains of indigo. "Looks like toxic waste."

"That's how it's supposed to look." Hudson twisted a faucet on the front of the top vat that sent the stinky water pouring into the bottom vat.

"Well, it's nothing like I pictured." I stepped out of the way to avoid getting splattered.

While it drained, he grabbed a pitchfork, shoved it into the top vat, and began scooping out zombified stalks. The poor things looked drained of all life.

"Can I help?"

"Not with this part." He continued until the vat was empty and the trailer held the plant remains.

"What do you do with the plants now?"

"They've done their job here and given up the pigment. Now they go into the compost pile and will help fertilize next year's plants." Hudson motioned for me to follow him to the small cabin, its roof lined with solar panels.

"Is the entire island off the grid?"

"Yep." He opened the door and held it for me.

I stepped inside and could see where a kitchen used to be, but the rest of the space had been transformed into a type of workroom. To the right were rows of shelves filled with plastic storage containers and whatnot. Hudson went to the left, where various pieces of equipment were housed. He handed me a rolled-up hose and picked up some sort of pump system.

"What's that?"

"Aerator."

Knowing that was all the explanation I was going to get, I trotted behind him to the vats and remained quiet while he set up the aerator. Once the thingy on the end of the hose had been submerged in the vat, Hudson returned to the cabin. I assumed the role of his shadow and went too.

"Will you grab that measuring cup?" He pointed to a large tin canister on a shelf.

I stood on my tiptoes and hooked a finger through the handle to snatch it down, barely escaping it hitting me straight on the nose. Fortunately, Hudson was too busy lifting a fifty-pound bag of something to notice. "This is the biggest measuring cup I've ever seen."

He settled the bag on his shoulder and then we were off again.

"I'm trying not to be a nag, but all this is truly fascinating, so I'd really appreciate it if you'd explain what we're doing. Pretty please."

Hudson dropped the bag on the ground beside the vat and placed his hands on his lean hips for a moment, considering the murky water and then me. Finally he tipped his head. "Come here."

I skipped over eagerly and waited.

"Do you see anything in the water?"

"Not really." I shrugged.

"That's because the indigo is hiding. We need to do a few things to talk it into revealing itself."

"Oh yeah? Are you going to read poetry to it?" I grasped his arm. "Please don't read *1984*. That'll make it hide even more."

Finally he gave me a half smirk. "To talk indigo out of hiding, we need to breathe some life into it." He flipped the switch on the aerator. Seconds later, the water began to bubble vigorously, almost producing a fountain. "Oxygen activates the indigo so it will turn blue."

"Well, ain't that nifty." I also thought it was rather nifty how this man seemed to be a natural storyteller.

"Nifty indeed." He hunched over and opened the big bag. "This is lime. We add it to turn the indigo liquid into a solid."

I surveyed the vat. It was the size of a roomy hot tub. "Really? All that will solidify?"

"No. Just the indigo." He shoved the metal measuring cup into the bag, grabbed a scoop of the white powder, and then sprinkled it into the vat. I still didn't understand the entire process, but it started making some sense. "It'll take about an hour for the oxygen and lime to work their magic." He added another measure of lime and by the time he had the correct amount added, the water had begun frothing a purplish-blue foam.

"Oooh, it's so pretty." The wind shifted, blowing over the vat and hitting me with a whiff of that funky odor. "But it still smells awful."

Hudson gathered the bag and cup, returning both inside the cabin. He was definitely a tidy person. Just like the big house, the small cabin had no signs of dust and everything was neatly in its place.

He sat in one of the chairs on the narrow porch and pulled out his book.

I placed my hand on the cover to stop him from opening it. "No, sir. You might as well put that book away. I need to hear the story about how this indigo dye making came to be."

"Didn't you read about me learning how to do this from my grandfather?" Hudson didn't even sound mad about me reading his journals anymore.

"Yes, but how did Grandpa Elson get into it? Was it a family trade or something?" I sat in the chair beside Hudson and crossed my legs, not missing when his eyes landed on them briefly before returning to the unopened book in his hand. I gave them a good inspection myself, making sure no bruises were peeping out. None were, so I guessed he was looking just to look.

"Grandpa inherited this island from his grandfather sometime in the sixties. Back then it was an unnamed barrier island no one had ever done anything with, so my grandparents decided to build this fishing cabin and use the island as a little retreat. Pretty primitive, but that's what they wanted. While Grandpa was out here doing some clearing, he discovered a substantial amount of indigo plants growing wild."

"How'd he know it was indigo?"

"At first, he assumed it was a type of weed. But there was so much of it, he decided to do some research and figured it out. After that, he was so intrigued that he educated himself on everything indigo. In the eighteenth century, indigo was a major export crop for the Lowcountry."

"Oh, wow. You think the indigo out here was from way back then?"

"Grandpa thought so. He was passionate about it. Even took trips to India and Japan to learn the art of indigo dye and shibori." The wind picked up and made his wild hair dance around. He didn't seem to notice, just let it hang in his face.

"What's shibori?"

"It's a Japanese tie-dyeing technique. Sort of the same as what you see here, but the patterns are more intricate. Grandpa made my grandmother a scarf using nui shibori technique, where he threaded it before dyeing and then pulled the thread out afterwards to reveal the resist pattern. She had it framed. It's hanging in their bedroom upstairs. It looks like ocean waves."

"I'd love to see it," I said but he didn't reply. "What did your grandmother think of him getting into indigo?"

"She was right there with him on the trips and when they got back here, Grandpa managed the growing and extraction part and Grandma handled the business side of it. In no time, they were selling exclusively to a high-end textile company in France. It's the same company I sell to now."

"So they celebrated their success by building that big ole Southern manor?" I pointed at the roof in the distance where it peeked over the treetops.

"They celebrated their success by officially naming the island Indigo Isle. The 'Southern manor' was my grandmother's dream home. Grandpa built it for her the year she was diagnosed with cancer for the first time."

The chair creaked as I shifted to face him. "The first time?"

"She went to battle three times, as Grandpa used to say." Hudson combed the side of his beard with his fingers, staring off. "She passed away a few years before I started spending my summers out here."

I placed my hand on his forearm and gently squeezed before returning my hand to my lap. "I'm sorry."

"Thanks. Me too. Back then I didn't appreciate my grandparents properly. Thought they were old and weird and didn't know anything."

"Yeah. I know all about that. My parents were old enough to be my grandparents when my mom had me. I thought the same thing about them." Swallowing past the lump in my throat, I added, "But it seems you figured it out and had a good relationship with your grandfather."

"I did. He was a man like no other. Indigo is his legacy. Out of respect for him, I want to preserve it." Hudson stood and started across the small yard. "Sit tight. I'm just going to adjust the aerator."

While Hudson fiddled with the equipment, I couldn't help but think about my family and their legacies and how I'd done nothing to preserve or respect them. I wondered if Mama still helped at the seafood market, if she'd written any more cookbooks. If my sisters were preserving her legacy. The tightening in my stomach rose to my chest. Rubbing my palm over the pain, I wondered if it was too late for me to go home and do my part.

"What's with that face?"

I lifted my eyes to find Hudson standing before me. "Oh, I was, uh . . . just thinking."

He tilted his head to the side. "Care to talk about it?"

I considered his question, my lips pressed into a firm line.

"Are you at least writing about it?"

"Yes. Thank you for the journal. It really is therapeutic."

"Good." Hudson returned to his chair and opened the book. This time I didn't stop him.

I drew my knees up and rested my cheek on them, listening to the sounds of nature mingling with the hum of the aerator pump while I watched Hudson read in peace. Well, *peace* was a stretch. Judging from his pinched expression, the book was causing anything but peace. I made a study of him while he glared at the book, noting how expressive he could be, even with so much of his features hidden behind all that hair and wild beard.

Eventually Hudson snapped it shut and declared it was time to shut off the aerator. He handed me something that looked similar to a pool net. "Skim the foam off the top and dump it in that barrel." He pointed at a plastic drum about as tall as me.

As I got busy doing that, Hudson pulled the hose out of the vat and put it away.

"What now?" I asked once all the foam had been removed.

"Take your shirt off and I'll show you some more magic."

I crossed my arms and rolled my eyes. "That's like the lamest pickup line ever."

Hudson shook his head and made a gruff sound in the back of his throat. "Not even close to what I was going for." Fisting the back of his faded-gray shirt, he yanked it off and tossed it into the dye vat. He angled away, but I could still see the scars. The intricate pattern veined out from his neck and along his broad shoulder, uneven texture meeting smooth tanned skin.

A few minutes later, he scooped the shirt out with a dip net.

"Ah, man! Did we mess up the dye? It's neon green. Not blue."

"Wait for the magic." Hudson wrung out the shirt, and with a snap of his wrists, he held it up for my inspection.

And right before my very eyes, I witnessed magic. The green darkened and then suddenly a brilliant blue spread over the material until the green vanished completely. I gasped. "Oh, my word! You are a magician!"

Hudson chuckled, showing off another form of magic when his lips actually curved upward.

"That smile looks dang good on you. I wish you'd wear it more often." I knew my comment would probably send up his walls, so I scooted closer to the vat and pulled off my shirt and tossed it in. Taking a page out of Hudson's book, I kept the back of my arm out of sight, even though only yellowy remnants of the bruises remained.

Soon he fished my shirt from the dark water and I grabbed it, wringing out the dye and watching the magic happen once again. "This is the most amazing thing I have ever witnessed." The breeze picked up. "But shoo wee, it's a smelly one. How on earth did someone way back in history figure out how to make this happen from a green plant?"

"Most likely by accident." Hudson lowered another grate on top of the lower vat. "This is it for today. The dye has to settle to the bottom for a day or so."

"What happens after a day or so?"

He peered down at me, curiously or just in confusion. "You really want to know?"

I hitched a shoulder. "Why wouldn't I? It's fascinating."

Hudson held a finger up and strode into the cabin, returning moments later with something in his fist. "Once the dye settles to the bottom of the vat, I'll drain the water off until only the mud is left. I'll score it into bricks and then leave it to dry." He opened his hand and showed me a blue brick in clear cellophane wrap.

"Looks like a bar of soap," I commented.

"You wouldn't want to wash with this." He pocketed the brick and took the shirts from me and draped both over his shoulder, concealing most of the scarring behind the indigo fabric. No cares about the dye discoloring his skin.

I looked away from him and checked my hands. Sure enough, they were stained the color of a twilight sky. "How am I ever going to get this dye off?"

"Go take a dip in the ocean and scrub them with sand."

I had planned on stealing some beach time anyway, so I headed that way after grabbing my bag from the boat. Making sure I was alone, I shimmied out of my jean shorts. The bruises on my thighs were also yellowing but still remained. After wading in the surf to hip-deep, I soaked a while and used the sand as a hand scrub. A good bit of blue washed off, except for around my fingernails. Giving up, I moved to the shore, spread out my beach towel, and lay on top of it.

A comfortable hush swept over the beach as the heat of the sun kissed my skin. Like a weighted blanket, relaxation settled around me for the first time in months. My thoughts tapered off as I drifted to sleep.

Sometime later, a shadow came over me. I shielded a hand over my eyes and caught Hudson scrutinizing my legs.

"Sonny . . ."

I lifted the edges of the towel and wrapped it around me. "It's nothing."

"It's abuse. Don't try prettying that ugly up." He used what I thought was probably his lawyer tone, seeing right through me.

He plopped down beside me and peeled the towel away from my legs and just as quick, he started to return to his feet. "I'm calling the cops."

Sitting up, I grabbed his wrist before he could stand. "No. Please don't."

"But—"

"I'm figuring it out, okay?"

"Hiding out on my island while covered in bruises is not figuring it out." He rolled his wrist until I let go, but before my hand dropped completely, he linked our fingers.

And just like that, tears formed at his tenderness. Sniffing them away, I whispered, "I want to. Figure it out, that is."

Hudson stared out at the ocean like maybe an answer to my stupidity was about to roll in with the next wave. If only it would. His eyes cut briefly to me before returning to the water. "Will you tell me who did this to you?"

I brushed a patch of sand off my shin. "No."

"Why not?"

Running my thumb along the scarred terrain of his palm, I asked, "Will you tell me about this?"

"No," he answered quietly, moving his hand away from mine.

Shaking my head, I stood and began gathering my belongings. "We're a fine mess, my friend."

"You can stay." His offer came as a surprise, almost a plea, and I almost sat back down.

"I'd love to, but I need to head in to work."

With a prickly stab of reluctance, I left Hudson and the visceral need to stay.

CHAPTER SIXTEEN

The barrier islands were only separated by veiny inlets, so traveling from Indigo Isle to Moise Island didn't take much time. I hopped out of the boat and braced myself as Lyrica beelined toward me, her mermaid curls bouncing with each step.

"Sonny, girl, you ghosted me."

Concealed behind my sunglasses, I rolled my eyes and looped my messenger bag around my neck.

"I had to talk to the island manager about letting us use another spot for a scene last night. All. By. My. Self." Lyrica jabbed a purple-tipped fingernail in the air to express her point.

"Looks like you survived." I sidestepped her and started up the beach with her hot on my heels. She continued whining but I tuned her out and made my way to Vee's tent.

"'Sup." Zayden Ellisor gave us a chin-jerk as he exited the tent with a fresh new sheen to his dark skin. A tall brick house of muscle and swagger, he definitely fit the description of his sports jock character.

Lyrica and I craned our necks to watch him walk past.

Snapping out of the gawking trance, I moved inside the tent as Lyrica followed after Zayden. The girl was like an easily distracted toddler.

"Hey, girl, *hey*," I sang, putting on my happy face.

Vee glanced my way before refocusing on spraying something on Maura Young's back. "Hello, my dear."

"Do you have any blue nail polish?"

"In the pink case." She motioned toward a fuchsia container.

I crossed over to it and easily found about ten different shades of blue. I grabbed one with *fast-drying* on the label. Reading the bottom, I huffed a quiet laugh. *Indigo Sky*. "Can I buy this off you?"

Vee squinted at the bottle through a pair of red-framed glasses that held no prescription but matched her strapless romper perfectly. "No, but you can have it."

"You sure?"

"Of course, darlin'." Vee winked at me as she refilled her airbrush.

"Thanks." I dropped into her chair and quickly painted over my blue-stained nails with more blue. "Are you spraying her back with red?"

"Yes, the pasty emo poet needs a sunburn for today's scene." Vee shaded a spot on the actress's shoulder. By the time she was done, Maura's artificial sunburn looked so severely real, I wanted to douse her in lidocaine and aloe.

Maura checked her scorched reflection in the trifold mirror and cringed. "You're an artist, Vee."

"You gave me a perfect canvas, mademoiselle." Vee returned the compliment in a French accent and then sent the actress on her way. "Au revoir."

I twisted the lid back on the polish and blew on my nails.

Vee stretched her arms over her head, bending to the left and then the right, and released a long sigh. "How are you feeling?"

Before I could answer, Whit entered the tent.

"Ladies." He tipped his head, debonair as ever. "Vee, I need a word with Sonny."

I started to stand, but Vee pretty much blocked me in her chair. "Go ahead then, suga'. Little ole me won't be a botha'."

His eyes narrowed, not buying her genteel lady act. "Alone."

Vee placed a palm on her chest and fanned herself. "Why, my mama raised me to neva' leave a single young lady unaccompanied." She tsked, batting her eyelashes. "Folks would talk and we can't have her reputation jeopardized."

Whit huffed, spearing a hand through his hair. "I don't have time for this."

Vee motioned toward him. "You best be on with it then, suga'." As tall as Whit, she met him nose to nose, and I could have sworn Vee intimidated him.

Whit proved the assumption as he slid his attention to me instead of making her leave. "You and I have a meeting at my place after the shoot to go over the marina scene and some B-roll Les has added last minute."

Again, before I could react, Vee spoke, minus her Southern accent. "Actually, we have plans after the shoot. And anyway, all that can be handled via text. Seriously, boss man, isn't that why you have an assistant?"

They had a silent standoff and my heart gave out a few times while suspended in it.

Finally Whit reversed a step, eyes sweeping to me, then returning to Vee. "You've become a bit too big for your hot pants, *Evelyn*.

I think maybe I'll give you time to cool off and pull another hairdresser for my next film."

Vee shrugged with enough attitude that I expected her thug-life character to emerge and throat-punch the man. "Do whatever you gotta do. Other producers know the importance of using their assistants to handle booking *hairdressers* such as myself instead of using them for sexual perversion. My email is full of job offers."

If I hadn't been sitting down, I'd have fell out from the impact of her curt reply.

Whit's angular face darkened several shades of red as he retreated another step away from Vee's venom. *Who in the heck is this woman? And why can't I be more like her?*

"Sonny will not be meeting you alone again, so don't bother." Vee held up a hand when his sneering lips parted. "I took pictures of the bruises on her thighs, so don't even."

Whit's eyes bounced to me, but I averted mine and kept them pinned to the sandy floor until he was gone.

Taking several breaths to stop from hyperventilating, I asked Vee, "What's gotten into you?"

"What's gotten into me?" Vee straightened her posture, pulling on another persona, and held up an invisible microphone. "Good afternoon, ladies and gentlemen. I'm reporting live breaking news. I officially feel like the world's biggest fool. For years I was led to believe Sonny Bates was in an on-again, off-again relationship with the infamous Whit Kessler when, in fact, he's assaulting her."

Face rising in heat, I crossed my arms. "Why are you so upset over this?"

Vee held up a finger. "*Upset* is too tame for this. I'm furious with you." She waved that finger around, emphasizing the point. "And more importantly, I thought we were friends."

"We are friends."

Humming haughtily, she fluffed the front of her messy pixie cut and then smoothed the sides around her ears, her tell for frustration. "I've worked with Academy Award–winning performers, but they have nothing on you, Sonny Bates. You could outact anyone in Hollywood any day."

"Vee—"

"You led me to believe whatever was going on between you and that man was consensual."

I pressed my lips firmly. Truly, nothing could be said to make this right.

Vee began a slow clap. "I bought it hook, line, and sinker. Bravo, my dear, bravo. Take a bow."

Eyes stinging, I brushed past her.

"Exit stage left." Vee's parting words reiterated just how wrong I had been to lie to her.

The next two hours moved on without much needed from me. The only task I managed was setting up some B-roll filming with Cade per the director's request while Lyrica stood close, smacking gum the entire time.

As soon as Les called wrap, I hurried off before anyone could catch sight of me. The boat seemed to have a mind of its own, and minutes later I was tethered to the dock at Indigo Isle. I cut the engine and sat still.

The waves gently rocked the boat as I reclined in the seat and stared at the bright moon and stars. This was a sight that wasn't afforded to me in LA. The only views from my studio apartment came from the closed Chinese restaurant and a run-down tattoo parlor across the street.

Skimming my index finger along my bottom lip in a slow

pattern back and forth, I mulled over the turbulent day on set. Who knew Vee was that invested in me and our friendship? It felt criminal, the way I'd let her down with not trusting enough.

"Are you planning on just sitting out here?"

Jolting, I sat up and scanned the dock, catching sight of Hudson's tall figure standing out of reach of the night-light's glow.

"I didn't feel like going back to the motel just yet." I shrugged. "But I didn't want to bother you either. I'll leave soon. Promise."

Hudson walked over and boarded the boat, taking the seat beside me. "You want to tell me what's going on?"

No, I didn't, but I needed someone to talk to. Someone who would accept my truths, no matter how debauched they were. "I'm not a good person."

"Well, you're in the right company, so you might as well tell me about it." His response came without hesitation and it opened the gate for me to talk about Vee. He inclined his ear my way and listened as I shared how the day went down.

"I don't have any close relationships, so I didn't realize Vee had invested more into our friendship than I had. Now I feel like such a jerk."

Hudson crossed his ankles and combed the side of his beard in repetitions.

I didn't know why I'd expected him to suddenly become chatty. He didn't, so I zoned out and watched the whitecaps perform within the inky water.

"You could bring Vee out here to try to make it up to her."

Blinking away from the ocean, I focused on him. "Did the Monster of Indigo Isle actually just offer to host me and my friend?"

His hand stilled against his chin. "I didn't say I'd make an appearance."

"You don't mind the nickname the locals have given you?"

"No. It makes people keep their distance." He cut me a look. "Well, most anyway."

"How'd you end up with that nickname, anyway?"

Hudson gave me a sidelong glance, an eyebrow edging upward.

I held up my palm. "Don't even blame it on the scars. You're not hideous."

"You're not the first I've had to run off my island in the middle of the night. A good chasing and some mean growling can strike enough fear in nosy kids to spark their imagination to the point of creating monsters in the dark."

"You might be a tad bit grumpy, but you're no monster, sir."

He shrugged. "My offer still stands if you want to invite Vee. If you'd like, I could set up some dye and you could show her our magic."

I couldn't believe he'd included me in his magic, as if I were a part of this, more so than just as an unwanted trespasser. I also couldn't believe he'd actually suggested inviting Vee, but I knew she would love it. "I'll talk to her tomorrow and let you know. You should meet Vee though. I think you'd get a kick out of her."

"I believe I may have already met her."

"When?"

"A tall blonde woman hissed at me that night I left your motel room. Said something about having eyes on me and then started banging on your door. That was Vee, right?"

I snickered. "Yes. Sounds like something she'd do. I think you two should be properly introduced."

"No thanks."

"Why not?"

"I prefer my own company."

"Yes, but why is that? You're not all that entertaining," I joked, completely lying. Even in his silence, Hudson was the most fascinating person I'd ever met.

"Because I'm the only person I can trust."

"I understand that more than you know." I laughed without a trace of humor and tugged down the legs of my shorts.

Hudson uncrossed his ankles and angled toward me, his sigh morphing into a frustrated growl. "What your ex did to you . . . I'd like to put some bruises on him. What's his name?"

"I'm handling it," I lied. I wasn't handling anything very well lately.

He propped his elbows on his knees and leaned closer. "What can I do?"

"Just be my friend."

Straightening, he scooted away from my request. "I'm not friend material."

"You sell yourself way too short. Besides Vee, I think you're my only other true friend."

"Don't, Sonny." Hudson rose to his feet, causing the boat to sway. "You left your shirt earlier. Let's go see how it turned out." He stepped onto the planks and held out a hand for me to join him.

We walked through the dark woods as a hooting followed behind. I glanced over my shoulder. "Is that an owl?"

"Yes."

"All the way out here?"

"It's not that far from the mainland. He's probably been here longer than me." Sensing my unease, he placed a hand on my lower back. "There are at least fifteen different species of birds on this island." He gave me a nature talk as we moved along the path, his raspy voice soothing, until we made it to the clothesline where our shirts swayed in the breeze.

Hudson removed the clothespins and handed the shirt to me.

Without thought, I stripped off my shirt and pulled the indigo one over my bikini top. The texture felt rough on my skin. It needed to be washed, but I couldn't wait. Smoothing it in place, I looked up and caught a heat in Hudson's shadowy eyes, one that I'd seen in many men's gazes. It spoke of desire, of attraction, yet in a blink he had his under control, so unlike my norm.

"Do you find me attractive?"

Clearing his throat on a small cough, Hudson glanced away briefly before meeting my eyes. "Why do you ask that?"

"You seem to like me okay, but you haven't made any move." I shrugged. "Most men would have taken something from me by now."

His brows dipped together. "Most?"

I dropped my eyes, not wanting to elaborate and knowing he understood without it.

"No one should ever take anything from you without permission. I promise I won't."

I focused on my shoes. "Not even a kiss?"

Hudson edged closer until we were toe to toe. "A kiss should never *take*. Well, maybe your breath. But never your dignity. Or your freedom." He tilted my chin until our eyes connected. His lips a hairbreadth away from my trembling ones, Hudson hovered the choice before me.

Considering his words, I knew what I wanted to do but knew

I had to pick the right choice this time for my own self-respect. So I walked away.

As I reached the trail, Hudson spoke. "Sonny, I'm proud of you."

All that talk about not taking, but this dang man did take something from me that made my chest hurt with its departure.

I nodded but didn't turn back, knowing if I did, it would be only to rescind my choice. And that wasn't an option.

Returning to the motel room, I went to the suitcase and retrieved the journal. I sat at the table and flipped to the next blank page. The pen didn't poise idle for very long. Soon it moved over the crisp paper, filling it with thoughts I could never find the voice to openly share with someone.

CHAPTER SEVENTEEN

MY FATHER HAD A PECULIAR OUTLOOK ON STORMS. He actually appreciated how they came in uninvited and shook things up.

"*Life gets too mundane sometimes, Sonny girl. Shakin' things up ain't so bad. Besides, storms show up and there ain't a thing we can do to stop them. They gonna do what they gonna do and it's best we stay out of the way until they're done doin' it.*"

I'd heard various versions of those sentiments throughout my childhood every time the sea spawned a tropical storm or hurricane. Dad would often sit out on our porch during storms, as if he were the official storm greeter. And I'd normally find my way out there too. From our spot on the porch, Dad would talk about how the shake-up from storms did a service in getting us out of life's ruts, helping us to refocus on what truly mattered.

As the tropical storm alert flashed across my phone screen for the second time this morning, those memories of my dad caused a sharp sensation to poke me between the ribs. Grunting in discomfort, I pocketed the phone and rubbed my side. I exited the car and made my way to the nearly deserted marina.

"I shouldn't be out there too long," I reassured Tom while boarding my boat.

"I ain't worried. It's insured." He used his foot to move the boat away from the dock. "But you be careful out on the water. It's gettin' rough already."

Dark clouds hung heavily over the grayish-blue water. The Atlantic Ocean seemed to be churning up something rather un-favorable, which was the reason I'd had to call an emergency crew meeting.

"Will do." I waved before reversing out of the slip, feeling the more pronounced rocking of the boat from the choppy water.

I met the crew on the beach and went over a game plan. "They're evacuating the island, so let's secure what we can within an hour and get the heck out of Dodge."

We went to work, taking down the makeup and crafts services tents and moving the supplies to a storage shed. Two hours slipped by instead of one before I called it quits.

"That's as good as it's going to get. Let's head to the marina."

I followed the water taxi over the choppy water until we neared Indigo Isle. I caught sight of Hudson's boat still at the dock, so I veered that way to go check on him.

The island's pulse appeared to be at a quickened pace today, as if it sensed the storm's approach. I hurried down the path with the trees and vegetation quivering around. I found Hudson by the clotheslines.

He glanced at me while unfastening a shirt from the line. "You shouldn't be out on the water."

"I'm not on the water." I raised my arms and gave him a *duh* expression, twisting my lips and widening my eyes. "I'm on land."

Shaking his head, Hudson muttered, "Smart aleck." He tossed some shirts into a wicker basket, picked it up, and started toward the house.

"I wanted to check on you. See if you needed help doing anything before heading inland."

He held the screen door for me. "I'm not heading anywhere."

I walked past him and paused. "But there's a storm."

Hudson set the basket on top of his bed and moved around the screened-in back porch, securing the latches on the windows as he went. "If this place can withstand cat 4s like Hurricane Hugo, then I think I'll be fine during a tropical storm." He returned to the bed and began folding laundry.

I plucked a threadbare T-shirt from the basket and folded it. "You could use a serious shopping trip. One more washing and I fear most of your wardrobe will disintegrate." I swiped another shirt out of the basket and held it up for his inspection. This one had a giant hole in the armpit.

Hudson stacked a pair of shorts and scowled at me as if my suggestion was the most preposterous suggestion ever suggested.

"You do realize you're not actually shipwrecked, right?" I grabbed the last pair of shorts. The entire hem was unraveled and frayed. "You can leave this island and go clothes shopping."

He snatched the shorts out of my hand and tossed them on top of the folded pile. "You should probably head on to the marina before things get worse." He glanced out the window. "It's coming in fast."

I moved out of the way so he could put away the stack of holey rags in the small dresser by the back door. "I thought you said the storm's no big deal." My phone chimed again. I pulled it from my pocket and read the alert. "Hurricane Watch. Shoot, it's picked up speed too. They're expecting landfall in the next hour or so."

He shoved the drawer closed with enough force to rattle the lamp sitting on top.

"What's wrong?"

Hudson muttered something about being stuck with me, but I chose to ignore it. He headed outside.

I trailed behind him. "Where are you going?"

"Just going to put some things away."

I fell in and helped with whatever I could, figuring it was the least I could do since he was stuck with me. I toted a lawn chair inside the shed, where the chickens were clucking up a debate. I turned and caught sight of Hudson jogging past the door. Before I could decide on chasing after him, a roar whooshed over the island and dumped a thick sheet of rain. It rang piercingly against the metal roof of the shed.

Ears popping, I chanced going outside. The cool rain felt good after dealing with such a humid morning, so I remained in the yard until Hudson reappeared.

He tipped his chin toward the house. "Let's get inside before the bottom finishes falling out."

Spinning in a circle with my arms spread, I tilted my face to the angry sky and blinked away the raindrops. "Go ahead. I want to feel the storm first." A deep rumble of thunder moved across the island, vibrating the ground beneath my feet.

In a flash, Hudson lunged and lifted me into a fireman hold and barreled across the yard. "You're gonna feel something smack into you and it ain't gonna be rain."

Laughing, I playfully popped him on his drenched back. "You just went all country on me!" Then I had another thought. "Oh, shoot. I need to check on my boat!"

He stomped up the steps. "I already took care of it."

On the back porch, Hudson placed me on my feet and shoved his wet hair out of his face. Rivulets of water dripped from his beard.

I straightened my shirt and grinned up at him. "You always speak so proper or in that authoritative lawyer tone. I didn't even know you had country in you. I like it."

His full lips parted as if to enlighten me, but a bright flash followed by a sharp clap of thunder stole his attention. He moved us inside. "Let me grab some towels."

I stood dripping onto the hardwood floors in the back hallway while listening to the echoing calamity outside. It reminded me of the last time I went bowling with my dad. I was twelve and he was already really old. But it didn't matter. For a brief two hours we were equals. He and I. Competitively chasing ten pins with a bowling ball. The loud crashing of the sport. Our laughter when I managed to knock down a few pins. Dad mussing my hair and calling me *pal*.

I'm not sure I ever thanked him for that day. I wished I could turn back time and tell him that . . . and how much I loved and missed him. But I forfeited all that when I ran away.

Hudson strode down the hall, towels in hand.

I accepted the one he offered and began drying myself, wishing the towel could wipe away my thoughts as easily.

"Here."

Lowering the towel from my face, I saw the bundle of clothes in Hudson's outstretched hands.

"They'll be too big, but at least you'll be dry. The bathroom is before the library on the left."

"Thanks." I toed off my shoes and padded down the hall, wet feet slapping against the floor. I checked my phone and was glad to see it had survived. I took my time drying off and hanging my wet clothes over the shower rod, then slipped on Hudson's buttery soft shirt and sweatpants. Both well-worn but hole-free. After tightening the drawstring on the pants and pocketing my phone, I finger-combed my curly hair. I left the bathroom and went to search for my quiet host, finding him hunched over a jigsaw puzzle in the kitchen. He'd changed into another shirt and a pair of sweatpants with a giant hole in the knee.

I picked up the collar of the shirt and sniffed it. "What do you use to wash your clothes? It smells so good." I sniffed again, picking up hints of sweet citrus and refreshing herbal notes.

He answered without looking away from the puzzle. "Something LuAnn makes. She's into homemade soaps and such. Sells the stuff in the markets around Charleston."

"I'd love to purchase some of her products."

Hudson grunted. Who knew if in agreement or not, so I dropped the subject.

I sat across from him and began searching the pieces that were forming a field of sunflowers, but I didn't dare touch any of them.

Hudson flicked his hand toward the puzzle. "You can help."

We worked on the puzzle as the storm howled in aggressive gusts, but it did nothing to sway the strength of the house.

"You said your grandfather passed away a few years ago. What happened?"

"Natural causes. I found him in bed with a big smile on his face." Hudson's lips twitched without forming one himself.

"Grandpa always went about a new task with a giddy childlike outlook. I guess going to heaven was no different."

I returned to the puzzle, wishing I had closure with my dad's death as Hudson seemed to have with his grandfather.

The first hour went well enough, but by the second hour, hunger pangs hit me more severely than the storm outside and my stomach started growling.

Fitting another piece into place, I released a long sigh.

"What?"

I looked up and met Hudson's pale eyes. "What?"

"You keep huffing." Waving a hand toward me, he let out a huff himself.

"It's just . . ." I scanned the tidy kitchen, nothing edible in sight. "I had to meet the crew over on Moise Island fairly early." I checked the time on my phone. Two in the afternoon. "I haven't eaten since supper last night."

Hudson sighed, getting in on my huffing action. "I guess that means you're hungry."

My stomach growled and I pressed both hands against it. "Sorry."

Sighing once more, he dropped the puzzle piece and shoved away from the table.

I remained in my chair while he plundered the fridge. Placing a jar of Duke's mayo and a bottle of Heinz ketchup on the counter, he went to the pantry. Moments later, he returned with a loaf of bread and an oddly shaped can.

"Need any help?" I asked but I doubted any help could be found for what he was about to have me eat.

Hudson met my question with a grunt and nothing more. After filling a small pot with water and putting it on the stove to heat, he turned to the counter. His broad frame blocked my view, but I knew what that hissing sound was all about—the seal breaking on the can and then the metallic ping of the lid peeling back.

"That's canned ham, isn't it?"

"I'm surprised you know what that even is." Briefly eyeing me over his shoulder, he grabbed a knife and began slicing it.

"I'm from Georgetown, so of course I know all about potted meats." I joined Hudson by the stove. "I can't believe they still make such," I mumbled as he dropped a thick slab of congealed ham into the boiling water.

"Look, I'm not fishing in this mess, so it's either ham or nothing at all." Hudson glanced in my direction as he dumped a scoop of mayonnaise into a bowl and topped it with a generous squirt of ketchup. He mixed the two until the concoction turned a piggy pink. Just as unappealing as the suspicious ham.

Trying not to grimace, I shrugged. "Beggars can't be choosers."

He grumbled something under his breath while building the sandwiches with the pink goo, slabs of the ham, and pickle chips.

We returned to the table and Hudson chowed down on his sandwich while I stared at mine. Even though my stomach rumbled with hunger, I didn't make a move.

"Just try it," Hudson said around a mouthful.

A loud banging announced another interval of the storm colliding with the island. Our eyes darted to the window, but not much could be seen past the thick curtain of rain.

Knowing I wouldn't be getting off this island anytime soon, I gave in and took a bite and chewed and chewed and chewed . . .

"Well?"

"It's . . . chewy." I made a face before gnawing off another rubbery chunk, overdramatizing the chewing.

Hudson frowned. "I don't think I like you all that much."

"Fibber." I peeled the lid off the sandwich and started popping pickles in my mouth. They were crisp and the sweet brine had a hint of heat to it. "Now, these have to be the best pickles I've ever eaten."

Hudson retrieved the jar and planted it beside my plate. "They're easy to make."

"You made these?"

He shrugged and went back to eating as if a giant beast of a man canning pickles was no big deal.

I dug a pickle out with a fork, trying to imagine him doing something as domestic as canning pickles.

Hudson finished off his sandwich and then mine as I snacked on the pickles. He put our dishes in the sink and made another trip to the pantry, returning to the table with a jar of marshmallow fluff and a bar of dark chocolate.

"Oh, sir, this totally redeems the canned ham sandwich." I followed his lead, dunking a square of chocolate right into the jar of fluff, coming back with ribbons of sugary goodness. I popped it into my mouth and hummed in absolute pleasure. I swiped another piece of chocolate and caught Hudson looking at me. Instead of the typical annoyance, there were flickers of interest as he zeroed in on my lips. "What?"

"You have some chocolate . . ." He lifted his hand and I waited for his thumb to swoop in, but he surprised me by simply pointing his index finger at my lips. "Right there."

"Oh, thank goodness, you didn't just go all cliché swoony and wipe my lip." I laughed at the absurdity of Hudson Renfrow doing anything romance-hero worthy.

From my experience in the past, most men would have had

me cornered somewhere in this house by now with my clothes at my feet. Not this man. No, he seemed rather uncomfortable being trapped with me.

"You made the mess, you should clean it up. Messy thing." Even though he tried to suppress it, a smile peeked through his tightly pressed lips.

His response made me crack up all over again. I licked my lips with exaggeration to emphasize I could handle cleaning up my mess, but the playfulness of the moment slipped away as his eyes zeroed in on my lips once again. We paused there in the tension until he cleared his throat and chugged his entire glass of tea.

Not long after that, we were back in puzzle mode with our mute buttons on.

• • •

As the rainy day began a sluggish procession toward night, I had exceeded my limit of silence and puzzle pieces. I eased away from the table and stretched my sore back. "Let's go sit on the porch."

Hudson glanced up from the puzzle, his eyebrows rising and disappearing underneath his tousled hair. "Right now?"

"Yes." I stood, twisting one way and then the other to alleviate a few more kinks. I gestured for him to get up and was surprised when he did.

"What's with you and storms?" Hudson followed me to the front porch even though his tone suggested he didn't approve.

"Porch sitting during storms was my dad's thing. It sort of became my thing too when I could sneak out there without my mom catching me." We located a dry spot on the right end of the porch and I sat with Hudson to my left as always.

"Your parents still live in Georgetown?"

I leaned against the house. "My mom still does. My dad died when I was eighteen."

"I'm sorry."

I lifted a shoulder and dropped it as if it weighed a ton. "Me too." Sorry for so much more than he knew about. "What about your parents?"

Hudson grumbled under his breath, something he did quite often. "Don't you already know enough about them from snooping through my journals?"

I held my hands up. "I'm not asking for in-depth details. Just where are they, if they're still alive. Sheesh."

He scrubbed his face and then stared out into the darkness. "Dad still lives in Raleigh. Mom is living overseas with her third husband."

I thought about how different his dad and grandfather seemed to be, from what I read in the journals. "Did your dad and Grandpa Elson get along?"

Hudson cut me a sharp look. "That's getting in-depth."

"Sorry." I watched the trees dance with the wind. *Sway to the right. Dip to the left. Shimmy forward. Writhe back.*

Hudson shifted beside me. "Grandpa Elson was my mother's father. Not Dad's."

"Then why do you have the same last name as him?" I studied his profile.

"Mom refused to take Dad's last name, so he agreed to taking on hers." Hudson finally turned his head to look at me with a hint of a smile on his face. "Dad's last name is *P-e-n-t-t-i*, pronounced *panty*."

I snorted before I could stop myself. "Oh, my. That's unfortunate."

"Yeah. At least Mom did me right by keeping her maiden name."

"Truly." I listened to the lively croaks of frogs for a while, but I really wanted to hear more from Hudson. I nudged his arm. "Tell me something."

Hudson looked at me out the corner of his eye, lips pulling downward in apprehension. "Like what?"

"Anything." I drew my knees up and wrapped my arms around them. "Something nonsensical. Random. Or . . . a secret." My eyes flashed at that idea, but his dimmed. "I'll start us off. Random fact, no number from one to nine hundred ninety-nine has the letter *a* in its word form. Not until the thousands is an *a* used."

Hudson turned toward me, brows pinched. "Why do you even know that?"

"I read it somewhere on the Internet."

"That's such a useless fact."

"That's the point. Now it's your turn." I rested my chin on top of my knees.

He combed the side of his beard. "Stop signs used to be yellow."

"Really?"

"Yeah. Whoever was in charge at the time thought yellow would grab drivers' attention. Plus, yellow paint was readily available. But clearly yellow didn't stick for very long before they changed it to red."

"You know what I have a hard time seeing?"

Hudson shook his head.

"Green street signs. They blend in with the trees and grass."

"What color would you suggest?" Hudson appeared genuinely invested in this oddball conversation and it made me pure giddy.

I pondered different colors, and Lyrica's brightly colored hair came to mind. "Purple would stand out better, for sure."

"Humph. Guess you have a good point. Did you know red and green are the most difficult colors to distinguish for people who are color-blind?"

"I did not. Wow, sir, you're decent fact competition." I gave my next random fact some thought. "It's impossible to hum while holding your nose."

Of course, we tested and confirmed the random fact to be true while pinching our noses and giving it our best shot. Hudson snorted while trying to prove it wrong with great effort, causing me to also snort.

He wiped his nose with the back of his hand. "That tickled."

"Ooh! Did you know it's impossible to tickle yourself?"

He scoffed and tapped the tip of his straight nose. "I believe I just proved that one wrong."

"Not like that. Like this." I fluttered my fingers against my side where I was most ticklish and wildly enough I barely felt anything, as if my own touch was muted. "See. Didn't tickle."

Hudson's hand shot out and replaced mine, playfully digging into my side. The annoying sensations jolted through me, making me yelp and giggle until I could hardly breathe.

"Stop!" I slapped his hand away and tried catching my breath. "Your turn. Try tickling yourself."

With a lofty smirk, he shook his head. "I'm not ticklish."

I pinched near his hip bone and he flinched. "Liar."

With narrowed eyes, Hudson pinched his side and frowned. "That's so weird."

I loved this game and how it had easily drawn the stoic man out of his shell, making me greedy for more. "Tell me something else."

Tilting his head side to side, he raked his teeth along his bottom lip and I couldn't help but wonder what kissing him would be like. "Riding roller coasters can help you pass kidney stones."

Talk about random. "Nuh-uh."

"It's the truth. Studies have proved it. Plus I've seen it firsthand."

"You had kidney stones?"

"Not me. Grandpa Elson. He didn't want to have surgery since it was summer and I was his responsibility. Someone at the urologist's office told him about the roller-coaster trick, so he drove us three hours to Carowinds and we rode roller coasters all day long." Hudson shrugged. "It worked. Grandpa went to the restroom grimacing and came out grinning. He bought us funnel cakes and cherry slushies to celebrate."

"Sounds like you two had a day of it."

"You want to know something else?"

"Sure." I wanted to know anything and everything this man wanted to share with me.

"Even though Grandpa was in pain most of the day, it will always be one of my favorite memories."

I smiled, enjoying Hudson's memory with his grandfather. It made me think about my father once again, and the smile vanished. If I could just have a redo . . .

Hudson tapped my knee. "You went quiet. I should like it, but it makes me nervous."

I leaned back and stretched my legs out in front of me. The bulky sweatpants gave me plenty of cushion against the porch floorboards.

He tapped my knee again. "If you've run out of random facts, then share a secret."

"I have plenty of those."

Our eyes connected in the dim light, but he didn't ask for me to share. Just simply waited.

I turned my attention away from him and focused on the shimmery raindrops catching the beams of the night-light. "Solar power comes in handy during coastal storms. No power lines to tangle up. We always lost power when a storm rolled through Georgetown."

"That's your secret?"

I considered agreeing with him, but I whispered, "I want a *take two.*"

"A what?"

"A take is one recorded performance. In film, every time they have to reshoot a scene, they'll say *take two, take three, take four* . . . One time I remember it took over sixty takes for one thirty-second scene. It was the longest day on set, for sure." I crossed my arms around my middle. "But the audience only sees the one perfect take, not all the mess-ups. I wish I could have the chance for a *take two* on life. I've made a lot of stupid choices. Ones I really wish I could take back." Eyes stinging, I sniffed the tears away, and for once, they receded. "The road to hell is paved with good intentions. I never set out to make so many mistakes, but that's all I seem to do."

A lengthy pause passed, only the echoes of the storm interrupting the quiet.

"You and I, we have the same secret," Hudson said, his voice raspier than normal.

I looked over to meet his gaze, but he was staring off into the night, perhaps contemplating his choices and mistakes. I shifted a little closer to his side as gusts of wind swept through the porch. Something clanged against the side of the shed and sent the chickens into a tizzy.

Wanting to veer us back into the lane of random, I said, "Chickens are the closest living relative to the Tyrannosaurus rex."

Hudson's lips twitched. "They also have excellent color vision, contrary to what most people think."

I didn't fight the smile like he did, letting it stretch along my lips.

Leaving the secrets alone, we returned to the safety of non-sensical until I couldn't stop yawning and my head drifted to his shoulder.

"Okay, Miss Random Facts, it's time to call it a night." Hudson stood and then helped me to my feet. He led me inside and stopped at the bottom of the staircase. "There are four bedrooms on the second floor. Take your pick."

"Thank you for letting me weather this storm with you." I brushed the back of my hand against his as I started up the stairs.

After scoping out the bedrooms, I settled on the last one on the right. Dressed in blue like much of the house, this room held a few personal touches that gave away who it belonged to. The first clue had been the photo on a low-standing dresser. A picture of a teenage Hudson and his grandfather holding up their blue hands with wide grins on their faces. I sat on the bed and scanned the bookcase. Most of the books were the ones he'd written book reviews on in his journal.

Even though this room felt right, I considered picking another one. Hudson did say I had my pick of any room, so that was on him. Surely he knew by now to make boundaries clear when it came to me.

CHAPTER EIGHTEEN

No MATTER HOW LONG a storm extended its stay, the sun always showed up to bid it adieu at the door. Tucked underneath the soft quilt, I knew this was the case once again. Taking a deep inhale of the familiar clean scent of citrus and herbs, I rolled over in the bed and winced against the onslaught of daylight.

After my eyes adjusted to the brightness, I grabbed my phone and checked my email, confirming what I had already assumed. The shoot would be delayed until a safety inspection of the island could be completed. I exited out of the email app and hovered a thumb over my contacts. Giving in, I pulled up my sister Aubrey's contact and sent her a quick text. **Y'all fare okay in the storm?**

Before long, she replied with a smiley face and a thumbs-up. That had been the extent of our communication over the years. Short check-ins and emojis. At least I knew they were okay. I tossed the phone on the pillow beside me and gazed around the bedroom.

Golden sparkles of sunshine drew me from the bed. I shuffled over to the window and peered out and gasped. From this room,

I had a perfect bird's-eye view into the outdoor shower and the very naked man washing inside it with his back toward me. I suddenly understood exactly what King David wrestled with when he stood on his roof and spied Bathsheba bathing.

With his hands busy scrubbing his bubbly hair, Hudson began to turn around. Face scalding hot, I jumped away from the window and squeezed my eyes shut, but there was no unseeing that.

After taking a few calming breaths and willing my pulse to settle down, I busied myself with making the bed. That only made me picture Hudson under the sheets. Needing to get away from that idea, I darted down the staircase to check on my clothes. Thankfully, they were dry, so I put them on.

I peeked inside the library and spotted two books open on the desk. Curious, I crossed the room and saw that they were a Bible and journal. I closed the journal to stop myself from reading it. Thinking the Bible would perhaps be a good distraction from what I'd just witnessed, I skimmed over the page to find out what Hudson had been studying. The sixth chapter of Joshua—the walls of Jericho. I was vaguely familiar with the story, so I sat down and read from the Bible for the first time in more years than I cared to admit. I had never been a fan of the complicated language, but the words seemed to make sense today.

I stopped on verse 20, pondering those walls and how they fell. I figured most folks had some form of Jericho walls that needed tearing down. My walls consisted of stones of shame, cemented with fear.

"Hey."

I jumped at the sound of his voice and looked up, finding Hudson leaning on the doorframe with his arms crossed. His damp hair had already settled into complete disarray with thick strands hanging in his eyes. My cheeks instantly heated right back to scorching as images of him in the shower flashed through my mind.

I held my palms up. "I didn't look in your journal. I swear."

He glanced at the journal, but his guarded stance didn't let up. Something else was wrong.

Oh no! Oh no! Oh no! Did he see me peeping out the window upstairs? Must have.

"Look, I didn't mean to see you in the shower . . ."

The tops of his cheeks instantly colored and his posture stiffened. Dang it, he hadn't known. But now he couldn't unknow. Never had I wished to suck words back into my big mouth so badly as I did right then. Instead of shutting up, I kept on, making it even more awkward.

"I looked out the window to see if the storm caused much damage, not to watch you wash . . . I turned away as soon as I realized—"

"It figures you'd pick my room." Tension rippled through the space between us. Hudson pushed off the doorframe and stared down the hallway. "There's hardly any debris on the beach and none near the dock." He nodded in the direction of the front door. "I already lowered your boat, so you can head out." Apparently I'd worn out my welcome.

Confused, I searched his face, but none of the openness from last night remained. It should have come as no surprise though. Since meeting him, one minute we would be getting along and then the next, Hudson's wall would go up and totally shut me out.

I rounded the desk and joined him by the door. "I received an email saying we aren't allowed on Moise Island, so I thought I'd stick around and help you clean up."

"There's not much to do. I can handle it on my own." Hudson started down the hall with me lagging behind him.

"I didn't mean to offend you. Truthfully, I had no idea the shower—"

"Goodbye." Hudson opened the door and stood back.

I stared up at him but he refused to make eye contact. Sensing something was wrong, I reached for him, but he recoiled.

"Please go," Hudson begged, his voice strained with something besides anger.

Reluctant to leave him like this, I paused on the porch, but the door slammed behind me and left me with no other choice. Walking on the unsteady ground that seemed to be ever-present around this pensive man, I left as he wished and spent the entire trip back to the motel stewing on his demeanor. As soon as I rounded the corner to enter the courtyard, those thoughts scattered away.

"Erlene!" Dropping my bag, I ran over and caught her just before she and her walker tumbled into the pool. I righted her and took the pool net out of her hand. "What are you doing?"

"Whoa. That first step was almost a doozy." She dabbed at her forehead, then pointed a shaky hand toward the pool. "The storm tossed this mess in and I need to get it cleaned up. My nephew said he'd be here over an hour ago to help, but he ain't showed up yet."

I inspected the pool, finding palm fronds and a deck chair floating in the deep end. "I'm sure this can wait until he gets here."

Erlene tsked. "But this is bad for business."

I glanced around the courtyard, taking in the faded paint and cracks in the sidewalks. A dirty pool was the least of her concerns in the business department, but I kept that to myself. "Well, we can't have that." I toed off my shoes and waded in. The water was cooler than I expected it to be, sending a shock up my spine.

"Oh, honey, you don't have to do that."

"It's no problem." I dog-paddled to the clump of palm fronds and slung them out first. Then I grabbed the chair by the arm and wrangled it over to the shallow end, but the darn thing didn't come willingly. By the time I pulled it onto the cement, I was winded so bad I had to sit in it to catch my breath. "It must have gotten rough here," I said, wheezing.

"I think the storm spat a tornado at us sometime in the middle of the night. It took part of the diner's roof, so they ain't open today."

"Oh, man. I hate to hear that."

"They're putting a tarp over it and said the doors will open in the morning." Erlene looked me up and down. "Where'd you stay during the storm?"

Even though I was dripping wet and a little chilled from the pool water, my cheeks heated. "Oh, uh, with a friend."

"Humph. The same friend I saw coming out of your room the night of that pool party?"

Little ole Erlene didn't miss much. "It's not like that." I wrung the water from the hem of my shirt.

"If it ain't like that, then it should be." She clucked her tongue and winked at me. "He looked like one of those mountain men from the Discovery Channel. All brawny and self-sufficient."

I chuckled. "He's definitely brawny and self-sufficient." A sigh pushed past my lips. "But he can be so closed off. One minute he seems sort of like my friend and the next he's pretty much running me off, like this morning."

"We talking about Hudson?"

My eyes darted up to meet hers. "You remember him?"

"Honey, he's on my prayer list. Of course I remember him. What's going on with Hudson today?"

I slumped in the chair and took a deep inhale, catching a strong whiff of chlorine. "I'm not exactly sure." I suspected something else had been bothering Hudson other than my Peeping Tom mishap. I just wished I could figure out how to make him open up to me. "He's not one to discuss what's bothering him. It's like pulling teeth with that man."

"Sometimes people like Hudson need to be nudged into talking."

I laughed. "More like *knocked* into it. The man is a fortress."

"Then you need to figure out a way to get past his walls." Erlene nodded her head.

Her words had me sitting up a little straighter. They reminded me of the walls I'd read about earlier. "What do you think about the walls of Jericho in the Bible?"

"It took a lot of faith to do what those Israelites did. People probably thought they'd lost their minds, but God showed them."

"I think . . . maybe we all have Jericho walls that need coming down."

"I believe you're right." Erlene reached over and patted my knee. "You need me to walk some circles around you to get you to open up to me?" She grinned, softening her tease.

My cheeks heated again. "I wouldn't if I were you. It ain't pretty behind my walls."

"I bet your friend Hudson feels the same way." She slowly stood, joints popping out a tune as she did. "It's time for my stories. You want to watch them with me?"

"Tempting, but I better not. I'm going to finish drying off and then catch up on some email. Another time?"

"Sure. And thank you for helping me clean the pool."

"No problem." I watched her shuffle out of sight and then sat there stewing on what to do about Hudson.

• • •

Early the next morning, I was still stewing. On Moise Island, I helped clean debris off the beach, reset the castaways' campsite, and made sure the crew redid the makeup tent to Vee's likings. All the while, Hudson remained heavy on my mind. We finished up by noon but wouldn't resume filming until the following day, so I headed over to Indigo Isle. While tying off the boat, an idea sprang to mind. Maybe if I marched around Indigo Isle seven times, God would take down the walls of Hudson. Or at least irritate the man to the point of letting me know what had been wrong with him yesterday.

One glimpse around the eerily quiet island, and I knew I had my work cut out for me. When the second sweep didn't unearth the recluse, I stopped at the front of the house and peered up at the brick facade. Sturdy yet vulnerable, much like its owner.

After checking and finding the door locked, I backed into the yard and glared up at the windows, hoping to catch sight of my ghost. "I know you're here! I'm not leaving, so you might as well come out." Crossing my arms, I waited. Even though the idea of reenacting a Jericho march had fizzled out on the way here, I vowed to stay until getting some answers. "And don't even think about calling the police. They're too busy inland with flooding issues to be bothered."

A bird flew overhead and the wind rustled through the surrounding woods as I waited some more. Still nothing.

"Why are you so stubborn?" I yelled. Throwing my hands up, I stomped around the homestead as planned. If for nothing else but to blow off some steam.

On the second lap, Hudson appeared in the front yard, a hooded sweatshirt covering his head. The sight of that hood concealing his face broke my heart. He was back to hiding from me.

Straightening my shoulders, I walked swiftly past the cloaked figure without acknowledging him.

"What are you doing?" His words pressed against my back in a flat tone void of emotion. He sounded as defeated as his hunched posture suggested.

I chose to take a page out of Hudson's playbook and not answer. On the fourth lap, I noticed his arms were crossed, his dejected manner now a formidable wall of annoyance.

"You're being ridiculous!" his raspy voice roared.

"Who, me?" I spun around and walked a few steps backwards. "No. I'll tell you who's ridiculous. You!"

"Me?"

"Yes, you. Something's bothering you and instead of confiding in me, you kicked me off the island yesterday!" I faced forward and continued stomping along. "Why can't you just trust me?"

"I'm a lawyer. Trust is against my nature!" His voice faded as I rounded the corner.

As soon as I returned to the front yard, I continued the argument. "That's just an excuse to keep me beyond the walls of Hudson!"

He muttered an oath. "This isn't Jericho!"

As I marched, Hudson remained in the yard arguing with me.

"You're a fine one to be talking about walls, Sonny. What's in Georgetown that you're hiding from?"

I twisted around to glare at him but my foot snagged on something and sent me down. My palms slapped against the ground. The impact stung but I barely registered it.

Before I could get my bearings, Hudson rushed over and scooped me into his arms. My mouth opened to protest, but then he cradled me to his chest. Thinking better of it, I shut my mouth and tucked my face into the crook of his neck. His shoulders stiffened but I didn't let it deter me.

Hudson carried me to the porch and sat me down. He took a step back, his face remaining cloaked by the hoodie. "You're not crying."

"No."

He motioned toward my legs. "But I thought you twisted your ankle."

"I just tripped. That's all."

Unconvinced, Hudson sat down close beside me, placing my legs in his lap and smoothing his hand over each ankle. His gentle inspection found no injuries, but his touch lingered in a way that said he didn't want to let go. And I wished he wouldn't.

I placed my hand over his and laced our fingers together before he could move away. "You're drawn to me, Hudson Renfrow. You might as well admit it."

He shook his head and released a grave sigh while studying the ground. "I've been drawn to you since the day you waved at me from the front yard, Sonny Bates."

My lips popped open on a gasp. "I knew someone was watching me that day!" I reached over and brushed the hood off his head and had to hold back another gasp at the sight of his haggard face. "Hudson, what's wrong?"

He lifted a shoulder slightly. "Same old same old. You won't leave me alone." The rust in his voice ruined his attempt at humor.

"Besides that?" I inched closer and traced the deep shadows underneath his stormy eyes with my fingertips. "You look exhausted."

"Because I am." His lips quivered and suddenly a fat tear rolled down his cheek, disappearing into his beard. Another tear followed; then the dam broke altogether.

I recalled a passage from one of his earlier journals about a book review for *Old Yeller*. He'd stated that he hated it. Of course he hated it. I hadn't read one of his reviews that didn't start with that negative sentiment. He had complained to his grandfather, wanting to know why the old man made him read such a sad story. His grandfather said it was because Hudson needed to know how to cry for what mattered.

Unable to take it anymore, I placed my arms around his broad trembling shoulders and held on—and continued holding on, to make sure he knew he mattered to me.

Hudson rotated in my embrace, wrapping his arms around my torso. He clung to me tightly, just shy of being painful. I'd take that pain if it meant relieving some of his.

Violent sobs turned to exhausted whimpers after a while before completely tapering off. I would have thought Hudson had fallen asleep had it not been for him winding and unwinding the same curl over and over around his index finger. I'm not sure he even realized he was playing with my hair.

I returned the gesture, combing his hair away from his face. "Why don't you come back to the motel? Erlene has extra rooms. We could swim. Go out to eat. Or just take a long drive."

Hudson lifted his head from my chest and shook it. With red

swollen eyes and blotchy skin, the poor guy looked completely wrung out.

"I don't want to leave you out here alone. It's not healthy, being this cut off from the world." I touched my palm to his cheek. "It's like this is some self-imposed punishment for no reason."

He moved away from my touch and scrubbed his palms down his face. "My carelessness cost me my daughter's life. There isn't a punishment harsh enough for that crime."

Understanding began to dawn on me. "Today . . . Is today the anniversary of Reece and Elsie's deaths? Or was it yesterday?"

My question shuttered his expression and it seemed like we were right back to where we started. Hudson shoved off the porch and walked away.

Granting him space, I remained on the porch and tried recalling more details from his journal. I couldn't remember anything that would have put him at fault for the fire, but he certainly blamed himself.

Eventually Hudson returned. Shoulders rounded, face downcast, the very definition of a broken man. His chest expanded with a deep inhale and then deflated as he released it. "The anniversary of Elsie's death was yesterday. As for Reece, she lives in Connecticut with her new husband."

"I'm sorry. I assumed Reece died too."

Hudson sat beside me, keeping his eyes to the ground. "My office was only two blocks from our apartment building. As soon as I got word about the fire, I took off . . . Reece was on the sidewalk, face covered in soot with a blanket on her shoulders." He huffed. "It was summer in New York City. Why would she have needed a blanket?"

I didn't think he actually wanted an answer to his question, so

I remained a silent form of support and waited for whatever he wanted to share.

Hudson cleared his throat. "When I asked where Elsie was, no one knew. I went into a blind rage and charged past the fire crew. All the door handles were molten, but it didn't slow me." He flexed his hand with the thick scarring on his palm as more tears streaked his face. "Elsie was in her crib, holding a stuffed animal . . . Looked like she was just taking a nap . . . But I knew from all the smoke . . ."

I scooted closer and laced our hands together. His hold shook, so I held it tighter.

Hudson sucked in a jagged breath and blew it out. "I grabbed her up and we made it to the living room before a part of the ceiling caved in. That's all I remember until waking up in a burn unit."

"What about Reece?"

"She was too high to remember anything. Rescue workers found her in the hallway, disoriented, and led her outside with everyone else." He sniffed, wiping his cheeks. "It's all my fault."

"You didn't start that fire, Hudson."

"No, but if I'd made Reece get help, Elsie would still be alive." He lifted his chin and stared straight ahead, possibly seeing that awful day and those that led up to it instead of the trees just past the yard. "I knew Reece was spiraling again, but I was too busy trying to carve out a place in my firm. Truthfully, I was so sick of dealing with her and her episodes. And the lies. The marriage was over before the fire. After losing Elsie, I couldn't stand to look at Reece. There's no coming back from that."

"I'm so sorry, Hudson," I whispered, aware of how protective I felt over him. Here I'd come to the island intending to tear down his walls, and now all I wanted to do was construct one to shield him from any more pain.

He sat beside me and placed his head on my shoulder. As I held him, I finally admitted something to myself. I wasn't *in* love with Hudson. *In love* implied I could get out of it, but my love for him had grown from the broken pieces of me and had formed deep roots. There was no getting out of that. I loved this man.

After the Jericho march and Hudson's breakdown, something shifted between us. With him finally opening up to me, it put his frailty on full display, and it looked a whole heck of a lot like my own.

We had both made choices.

Choices that led to heavy consequences.

We carried the blame.

And neither of us planned on forgiving ourselves anytime soon.

CHAPTER NINETEEN

WANDERLUST AND ADVENTURE were as much a part of my identity as my crazy, curly hair. That's why location scouting fit me so well. It was the same reason why location managing had not. Being cooped up in meetings made me stir-crazy. I didn't have the patience for it, like this stupid meeting today. We were only a week shy of wrapping, so it made very little sense to me to sit around the director's villa and rehash scene after scene for no good reason.

An hour in, Les continued droning on about the bonfire scene that probably wouldn't even make it into the final cut. Rubbing my temples, I had the sudden urge to stand on top of the table and yell, "Enough!"

Tamping that down, I let my mind wander out to Indigo Isle. I loved it out there. The wide-open space. Surrounded by nature. I especially loved that there were no expectations strapped to me while there. I could just be—

"Did you hear me, Sonny?"

I snapped out of the daydream and focused on Whit. "Sorry. What?"

"I need to discuss some things with you."

I looked around the room and realized people were gathering their belongings and beelining for the door at breakneck speed. "I can't. I'm attending a funeral." I stood and smoothed the skirt of my black wrap dress to reinforce my excuse, but that only had Whit giving me that wolfish look.

"I'm sorry for your loss." Whit's PA spoke with sincerity, which made me feel like the awful liar that I was.

"Uh, thank you." I shoved my laptop inside my bag and slung it over my arm.

"Were you close?" Tia asked.

I couldn't even remember the first name of the deceased, that's how close we were. "Felt that way."

Tia patted my arm as she passed by me.

"We can make it quick," Whit said as soon as she was gone. He had enough nerve to wink.

I made a show of checking the time on my phone. "Shoot. I'm about to be late."

Whit's dark expression shifted to annoyance. "Email Tia with a time you can meet."

"Sure." I breezed past him and spotted Lyrica standing by the door. She gave me a knowing look, her glittery pink lips forming a droll smile. I pretended not to notice.

She followed me outside. "Whose funeral?"

I didn't slow. "A friend."

"Friend got a name?"

"Of course." When I didn't supply a name, Lyrica laughed.

"I so knew it. You're, like, crashing a funeral!"

"Shh!" I looked over my shoulder to see if anyone had heard her.

"It's at Magnolia Cemetery, isn't it?"

I picked up speed, weaving through the resort grounds. "The art director wants some specs on a chapel near the cemetery and how many it can hold for a service. I figured the best way to get a visual of all that is to attend an actual service."

"Hold up. I want to go."

I rolled my eyes. "No, you don't. You hated it last time. Whined like a baby the entire time."

"But I'm *so* bored. Please let me go."

I regarded her multicolored jumpsuit. "You can't go looking like Rainbow Brite."

"I have something black." She spun around and hurried back in the direction of her father's villa. "Wait for me!"

Like I had any other choice but to wait on the boss's daughter. "You have five minutes!"

Ten minutes later, Lyrica came flouncing up to the boat. Gone was the rainbow couture. In its place was a sequin tube top and shiny leather leggings. The black outfit left a lot of skin and tattoos on display.

I groaned, knowing we didn't have time for another wardrobe change. I also knew she would be just as distracting in that getup as the bright colors, the complete opposite of my plan to blend in at the funeral. "We're going to a funeral. Not the club."

Lyrica ignored my comment and handed me a small bottle of fancy-looking hair product. "Put some of this serum in your hair. It'll tame the frizz. A little goes a long way, so one pump will do ya."

I should have probably been offended, but my hair was giving me a fit today, so I applied it as Lyrica had directed. "Wow. This stuff is good. My hair feels like silk." I worked it through the curls and couldn't stop touching it.

"You can keep it. My assistant sent me the wrong one for my hair type."

My fingers stilled in my hair. "You have an assistant? For what?"

"For coffee runs and stuff like that." Lyrica slid on her designer sunglasses and settled her shimmery self on the seat.

I dropped the bottle into my bag, not caring that the high-end product probably had a hundred-dollar price tag. The spoiled brat could afford it.

As I started the boat, a voice rang out just above the gurgling of the motor, but I pulled away like I didn't hear him. I didn't let up on the throttle until reaching the marshes.

"Are you and Whit, like, a thing?" Lyrica asked, obviously having been stewing on the question since we left the island. Perhaps longer than that. Who knew what people saw that night of the party?

"Whit and I are a *no-thing*," I replied in a sharp tone.

Lyrica fluttered her neon-orange nails around, her head doing that attitude bob. "I wasn't throwing any shade about it. Just asking."

"I know, but I just want to make it clear Whit and I are nothing but colleagues." Glaring straight ahead, I navigated the boat through the channel and slowed a little more.

The neon claws fluttered about again. "I totes get it."

I seriously doubted she did.

"And who cares what people think, right?"

Her comment landed hard against my conscience. I rotated my shoulders a few times but it wouldn't let up. That had always been

---

T. I. LOWE

one of my problems. Worrying what others thought and morphing myself into a version more pleasing to them. I think the whole morphing thing was a lot like a cat with nine lives, and I'd finally reached my limit.

Lyrica actually took the hint and didn't say anything else about Whit and me, praise be, and we made it to the funeral just in time to snag a spot in the back row of the chapel. Shoulder to shoulder, we barely squeezed into the pew.

"This dude must have been popular," Lyrica whispered, scanning the packed sanctuary and then the service program we'd received at the door.

"He's a 'the third,'" I whispered back, pointing to the Roman numeral at the end of the seventy-seven year-old's name. "Old money, I'd bet."

"Probably." Lyrica tsked like she didn't sprout from the same background herself.

The organ music concluded as a man dressed in a robe moved behind the podium, drawing all eyes to the front. He began the service with prayer and then went right into his eulogy. There were too many on our pew to pull out the notepad I had intended to use, so I settled in to take mental notes.

As the service droned on, I pictured my home church and wondered if they had set my father's casket up at the front in the same fashion as this one.

Had my family made sure cattails were included in his casket spray? The man had such a fondness for those tall things, always pointing them out on the riverbanks as our boat slid past them.

Did Caroline sing his favorite hymn? He loved belting out "Royal Telephone" and it always cracked me up, picturing Jesus

231

picking up a telephone while in the middle of a meeting with the angels.

Had Aubrey held my mother together while she fell apart? I had no doubt about that part, feeling the sharp pinch in my stomach, knowing my mother had to have taken it hard. My parents were absolutely crazy about each other. In public and behind closed doors, their love remained on a steady rhythm no matter what life threw at them.

Lyrica poked me in the side, thrusting a tissue into my hand. "I didn't think you knew the man."

I shook my head and blotted my cheeks, embarrassed at how easily the tears came. I wondered if this would have been my experience at my father's funeral. I'd never know though, because I all but spit in his face and ran off.

Growing flustered, I dried my cheeks again and made myself focus on something else. Limited on choices, I settled on studying the artwork decorating Lyrica's arm. Running along her inner forearm, the tattoo appeared to be intricate lines and filigree at first glance, but the more I studied it, the more an image began to emerge. I squinted and looked again to make sure I was seeing it right.

I snorted before I could stop myself.

Lyrica cut her eyes at me, the artificial purple contacts putting a damper on her glare. "Are you, like, losing it?"

A lady in front of us shushed us, so I just shrugged. Truthfully, me losing it might have been the case, but at least I wasn't crying anymore.

Sniffing away the last vestiges of grief, my gaze drifted to Lyrica's arm again, and I wondered what on earth had possessed her to permanently ink such a thing on her body. I did give her credit for being clever enough to hide it in plain sight with the stunning black-and-gray line work.

The service finally concluded, but before we could get completely out the door, a small group of animal print–wearing women joined us. It was like *Wild Kingdom*. They were probably in their forties or fifties, but it was hard to tell.

"Y'all one of Huey's girls too?" the blonde one with an orange spray tan asked while tugging at the hem of her leopard-spotted micromini.

The women leaned close to catch our answer as we descended the steps as one unit.

I cleared my throat. "Umm . . . no ma'am. He wasn't our father."

The women clucked and cackled.

"Not that kinda girl," said a redhead with a voice rougher than sandpaper. She lit a cigarette she'd pulled from her zebra-print purse that matched her dress.

I was still confused, but Lyrica seemed to catch their drift. "Oh, so Huey was your sugar daddy?"

They all whipped their heads around to see if anyone had heard Lyrica, as if it mattered. Clearly this group didn't belong here anymore than Lyrica and I. I'd seen the man's widow up front earlier, resembling the queen of England and nothing like this bunch.

The darker blonde sucked her teeth, her cheeks matching the pink background of her cheetah-print pantsuit. "We were more than that to our Huey. He put all four of us in his will."

"Well, good for you." Lyrica patted the blonde on the back in a condescending way and walked off.

I followed her and kept quiet until we reached the car. "I guess ole Huey liked his sides a little on the wild side." I laughed at my own joke and put on my seat belt.

"Eww . . ." Lyrica's face scrunched up. "After all those nice things the preacher man said about him, and that weasel had *four* mistresses. That's just nasty."

I tried to maneuver through the congested funeral procession with little progress.

"Argh. This is going to take forever." Lyrica shifted in her seat, jostling the entire car, and peered out the back window. "There's a break after this white car."

I cut in line and the driver of a silver Mercedes began blaring his horn. I waved and Lyrica, well, she shared another gesture.

"I think the chapel will be perfect for the scene. The gothic architecture is gorgeous."

Lyrica reached over and changed the radio station. "You were so spastic back there I'm surprised you noticed. What was up with that?"

No way was I answering, so I turned it on her. "I also noticed you have a freaking toilet brush tattooed on your arm. What's up with that?"

She studied her forearm and smoothed those long orange nails over the tattoo as if she'd forgotten it even existed. "It's a reminder of how crappy life can get."

I turned the blinker on and changed lanes. "And you know something about that?"

"As a matter of fact, I do." Lyrica didn't say anything else for a moment or two, making me think she didn't have a clue. "When I was eight, I learned my dad knocked up the maid."

I shot her a quick glance. "I thought you were an only child."

"I am. The maid's my mother. He paid her a nice chunk of change to disappear, but she forgot to bring me with her."

I looked her way again, seeing the socialite through a much different lens. "Dang. That really is crappy."

She huffed a bout of laughter. "Tell me about it. My dad's wife at the time wasn't going to get what she demanded in the divorce, so she decided to take me to Chateau Marmont for lunch. While there, she broke it to me that she wasn't really my mother, that I was the illegitimate child of a maid they once employed."

"Man, Lyrica, that's really awful." I exited at the base of the bridge to head toward the marina.

"Yeah, but—" Lyrica tapped her forearm—"just like the pretty hiding the ugly, life can be beautiful after the ugly. My dad loves me. Takes good care of me. And was wise enough to get a vasectomy right after I was born."

This young woman was more clever than I thought. The two fold symbolism of the toilet brush was almost genius. "You know, you're pretty all right, Lyrica."

"I'm fabulous, babe!" Shoulders gyrating and fingers snapping, she shook off the somberness caused by the tattoo story in her own flamboyant way, and that made me like her a little more.

"You're so fabulous that I think we need to grab ice cream and go let Erlene be in the presence of your *fabulous* for a while."

"Hello from the ice cream cone!" Lyrica belted out, sounding a heckuva lot like Adele. "I must have licked a thousand times! But I'm not sorry for the mess that I made anymore."

I parked at the ice cream parlor and gave the Adele impersonator a slow clap.

• • •

After dropping Lyrica off, the boat seemed to navigate over to Indigo Isle all on its own. I emerged from the forest and rounded the house, noticing the hammock swaying in the backyard. I walked over, stood beside it, and peered down at the man who was beginning to feel like home base in my life of chase. In the usual holey attire with his ankles crossed, Hudson held a book in one hand with the other crooked behind his head. He appeared relaxed and in a better state of mind.

"Whatcha reading?"

He held the book up so I could read the title. *The Book Thief.*

"Besides not liking it, what do you think so far?"

"It's way too long."

"And . . . ?"

"Yet every time I get to the end of a chapter, I tell myself just one more." He grumbled. "Been doing that since this morning. Wasted almost the entire day."

I pushed the hammock into another sway. "Well, that's a good sign."

Hudson lowered the book. His mouth parted to say something but it snapped shut as he took in my outfit. Opposite of Whit's ogling, Hudson gave it an appreciative once-over and then met my gaze. "What's with the dress?"

"I just got back from a funeral."

He closed the book and gave me his full attention. "Who died?"

"Not sure. Some old dude."

Hudson's brows bunched together. "Then why'd you go?"

I took a step back to give him space as he climbed out of the hammock. "Location research."

"You went by yourself to a stranger's funeral for research?" He placed the book in the hammock and stretched his arms over his head.

"You'd be surprised at what all I'm willing to do for research." I fanned a fly away. "My assistant went with me."

His arms dropped to his sides. "You have an assistant?"

It was funny that I'd asked my assistant the very same question earlier that day.

"Lyrica is the director's daughter, so it's a nepotism situation. 'Assistant' is a loose term when applied to her. She's more like my annoying sidekick." I scanned the yard and it sparked a memory. "Oh, you know what? You probably saw her out here that first visit."

"The loud one with colorful hair."

I chuckled. "That's the one. She wasn't so annoying today, though. I'm glad she went with me."

He grimaced. "I hate funerals."

"It wasn't that bad." I shrugged. "Would you believe I've never been to a funeral until today?"

"What about your father's?"

My chest tightened. "I was already out in California when he passed away."

Hudson's eyes narrowed as he combed his fingers through the side of his beard. "What business did you have in California at only eighteen?"

"Actually, I moved there at seventeen, right after graduating high school. You already know what business I've been in since then."

Hudson seemed about to say something that wouldn't be pleasant, but he blew out a breath and asked, "You want to stay for supper?"

His question caught me so off guard that it took me a moment to respond. "You don't plan on boiling up some canned ham, do ya?"

"I was planning on boiling up some blue crab." A gleam of lightheartedness made his gray eyes appear silvery.

"Well then, I'd love to stay for supper." I followed him to the dock and stayed out of the way while he hauled in a crab trap. The metal-and-mesh cube breached the water, showing off a bounty of blue crabs clinging to one another.

Hudson placed the trap over a bucket and began shaking the creatures into it. A few were stubborn, holding on to the mesh, so he had to reach in and pry their claws loose.

"Be careful," I warned, moving closer to peer inside the bucket. "Those things can deliver a mean pinch."

"You don't say." His tone was flat but not terse. He plucked a fairly large crab from the bucket and held it up for me to see.

"He's a giant."

"She."

I glanced at him and then back at the crab. "How do you know?"

"Her nails are painted red." Hudson pinched the claws shut and showed off the red tips.

Feeling brave, I asked, "Can I hold it?"

He passed the crab to me, making sure it was secure in my hands before letting go. The hard shell felt slightly slippery, but I managed to keep a hold of it.

"She looks hand-painted," I mumbled, inspecting the vibrant-blue claws with red tips and the greenish-gray body. "Hey, will you take a picture of me holding this?"

Hudson didn't seem too keen on the idea, but he grabbed my

phone and did as I instructed, opening the camera app and taking several pictures.

While he finished gathering the crabs, I edited and applied a filter to the image. After loading it to my account and adding several hashtags, I turned the phone screen in his direction. "What do you think?"

Frowning, he leaned close and studied the screen. "It doesn't look right. The colors are off."

"No. It's just the filter I used. I think it makes the blue really pop."

"I don't know. Even your face looks wrong in it." His nose wrinkled. "You look like you're glowing or something."

I laughed. "It's the filter."

Hudson wasn't amused. "But it's fake."

"Everyone knows it's fake." A notification flashed on the screen, letting me know the post already had several likes. "Look—"

"Whoa." Hudson held a palm up, ignoring the phone altogether. "Wait. Repeat that last bit to yourself. The part about everyone knowing you're fake." Shaking his head, he grabbed the bucket and brushed past me.

I shoved the phone into my skirt pocket and debated on whether to stick around for more of his reproachful comments or just leave. By the time I decided to stay, Hudson already had the black kettle pot filled with water and seasoning. Garlic, herbs, and cinnamon perfumed the humid air. The combination of savory and sweet set my mouth to watering.

"It's just part of social media and entertainment. Everyone does it." I tried explaining but he kept his attention on starting a fire underneath the hanging pot.

Once the fire was going, Hudson straightened and dusted his palms together. "So that's why your channel seems fake too?"

I crossed my arms. "What are you talking about?"

He moved the bucket over by the pot but didn't dump the crabs in. "I have a computer with Internet access and know how to use it. I looked you up."

"Okay, but . . . my channel isn't fake."

"Sure seems like a bunch of pretending to me. Your voice is different and you keep this fake smile plastered to your face the entire video. It was painful to watch."

"Then, please, for your sake, don't watch anymore!" Feeling like a scolded child, I spun on my heels to get away from the mortification. Before I could take a step to leave, Hudson spun me back around.

"No ma'am. If I can't kick you off the island when things get uncomfortable, then you can't run off when it happens either." His grip on my wrist tightened as he drew me closer. The gentle brush of his thumb over my pulse somehow lessened his blunt comment.

I lowered my voice, letting the edge of anger go as vulnerability crept in. "Why are you calling me out so much today?"

Hudson dropped his hold on me and ran his fingers through his wild hair. "I don't know . . . I saw those videos last night and they're nothing like the Sonny Bates I know. Honestly, I didn't like that version. It doesn't even look like you enjoy doing it, so why have a channel?"

My eyes lowered to his bare feet, noticing a blue stain on top of the left one. "I started the channel and the social media stuff as a way to show my family—" I stalled on the embarrassing truth.

Hudson bent slightly, trying to catch my downturned gaze. "To show them you're all right?"

I sputtered a haughty laugh and finally lifted my head to look him straight in the eye. "No. To show them I didn't need them.

That I was perfectly fine on my own." I let that hang between us for a moment before adding, "You're smart not to like me, Hudson. I'm not a nice person."

Without breaking from my glare, he declared with conviction, "Neither am I."

"What a sorry state we are."

We stood inches apart, silently watching each other, until Hudson retreated a few steps. I wanted to reach for him. To remain connected in our bubble of raw honesty. But it seemed we'd reached our limit for the day, so my arms remained drooped by my sides in defeat.

"Then we should celebrate our sorry state with a feast." He began preparing the meal and then spent the next few hours contradicting his declaration on not being a nice person.

It made me want to be wrong about myself too.

CHAPTER TWENTY

A DAY ON THE RIVER IN MY OLD SKIFF used to be my favorite way to spend a day during my teen years. Seemed to be the only way to keep out of trouble too. This one time I took the boat out on the river, this dang horsefly worried me incessantly the entire time I tried to fish. No matter how many times I moved the boat down the river to another fishing spot or how many times I batted the air to shoo it away, the thing kept right on until I picked up my oar and beat the water like a deranged lunatic.

Staring at Lyrica as she launched into yet another whiny rant, I wondered if I could get away with taking an oar to her. No, probably not. She'd spent the morning complaining about every little thing while following me around like that irritating fly.

Now, as we sat leaning against the trunk of a palm tree, I dropped my stack of papers to the sand between my feet. "You need to tell your father you don't even like this job."

"He says I need to work or he'll cut me off." She stood and began brushing sand off her backside.

"Then find something you like doing and do it." It should be clear to her, but I decided to spell it out. "Your makeup is always impeccable, even in this overbearing humidity. And, girl, you rock a winged liner. You have that artist's flair, much like Vee. You should talk with her."

Lyrica bit her vibrant-pink lip. "You really think so?"

"Absolutely. I'll mention it to Vee first if you want me to."

Her eyes widened. Today's shade was lavender. "Yeah, then will you help me spill the tea to my dad?"

I gathered the papers and stood. "We're in the South, honey. Spilling tea is a sin. Speaking of, I'm thirsty. There's tea on the crafts table. Let's go share some of that."

Lyrica snorted, walking beside me. "You know what I meant."

After we took a tea break, I snuck away from Lyrica and went over to Vee's tent. I sat in a vacant seat beside her workstation and watched her give Kingston his midday shave to help keep up his youthful appearance.

Vee wiped the last remnants of shaving cream from his chiseled jaw and applied some bronzer. Wiping her hands on a towel, she finally spared me a glance. "You need a shave too, love?" Her voice lilted into a British accent.

Kingston smirked, giving her a wink, and then strutted out in all his leading man glory.

I rubbed my cheeks and tipped my head side to side. "I think I'm good."

"Suit yourself." She cleaned up and put away the shaving supplies.

"Hudson has invited you to Indigo Isle."

"The serial killer?"

"Yep. He's chosen you as his next victim."

"I'm so honored. Whatever did I do to earn such a prestigious invite?"

"Your friend was truly rotten with not confiding in you about something really important. Hudson said she owed you an apology and a girls' day on a secluded island would be a good start."

Vee twisted her lips, looking at me thoughtfully. "He's quite an astute man. I'm really starting to like your serial killer."

"Yeah. I think I really like him too. So you want to skip the crew stuff tomorrow and go to Indigo Isle with me?"

"Skipping out on dreadful meetings and another cold-cuts lunch? Count me in."

"Good deal." I turned to leave but paused. "What's the name of that beachwear store you raided?"

"Umm I can't remember off the top of my head, but I'll text it to you when it comes to me."

"Can we stop by there before heading to Indigo Isle in the morning?"

"Honey, you don't even have to ask. I'm always game for shopping. You looking for anything in particular?"

"The serial killer is in need of some new gear."

"I doubt the beachwear place has gloves and ski masks," Vee quipped.

• • •

The next day we wasted no time slipping away from the motel. We stopped off at the beachwear store and loaded a bag full of new clothes before heading to Indigo Isle. After a quick sweep of the homestead and then the indigo cabin, we found no sign of Hudson anywhere.

"You think he's left the island?" Vee asked.

"No. His boat is still here." I hitched my beach bag higher on my shoulder. "The thing with Hudson is you won't see him unless he wants to be seen. I guess today is a ghost day."

"You sure we're welcome?" Vee eyed me skeptically.

"Yes. He wouldn't have set up this indigo dyeing station if he didn't want us here." I gestured toward the table on the cabin's porch with several jars of premixed dye. Rubber bands and a roll of twine sat next to them. "Did you remember to bring a shirt?"

"I brought two." She tugged a plain white T-shirt and a tank top from her bag and moved closer to the table. "I watched some shibori demos on YouTube last night, so this girl is, *like*, totes pro now."

"You sounded just like Lyrica." Chuckling, I pulled my T-shirt dress from my bag and started prepping it. I'd watched a few videos myself and had decided to go with an accordion fold. Once the fabric resembled a sloppy triangle, nothing like the instructor's on the video, I twisted a few rubber bands around it.

"This is fun," Vee mumbled, concentrating on snugly wrapping one of her shirts with the twine. "It's like we're at summer camp."

I scanned the secluded yard just past the porch, wishing Hudson would emerge from the thicket of trees and be our camp counselor. He'd make an interesting one, for sure.

We took our time, enjoying the process, and were amazed at the results.

Vee held her shirt up after unwinding the twine, turning it one way and then the other. "It's wild how unique each piece is."

My shirt dress had abstract white circles peeping through

various shades of blue, whereas Vee's shirt had squiggly white lines veining from the blue. "Let's see the tank top."

She unraveled it and showed off the tie-dyed pattern.

"Nice."

"I like it, but how are we supposed to get this dye off our skin?" Vee held up her blue hands.

"Let's hang these on Hudson's clothesline and then we'll head down to the beach. The ocean helps to get it off."

We cleaned up the mess we'd made on the table and started our trek over to the beach. Still no sign of the recluse.

I heard the whimsical chimes of the shells before we stepped past the line of trees. "You hear that?"

"I do. It's the shell trees?" Vee hurried onto the beach and then turned to take in the beautiful display. "Oh, wow. It's so much more, up close. It's . . . breathtaking."

Vee snapped several pictures with her phone and then we set up near the water before wading in. The waves pushed and pulled, tugging us around until we grew tired.

"My beach towel is calling my name," I said over the roar of the swells.

With the sun already happy to keep us nice and warm and the breeze keeping it in check, it didn't take long for me to start dozing off.

"We wrap next week," Vee murmured, pulling me out of my stupor.

"Mm-hmm."

"What's next for you besides playing YouTube catch-up?"

I rolled over and sat up, riffling through my bag for a bottle of water. After taking a long pull, I answered her. "I'm not sure. I'm thinking of stepping away from my channel."

"You've basically already done that all summer. Your fans aren't chomping at the bit?" Vee reapplied her sunblock and I spotted a smear of blue on the back of her forearm. Neither one of us had done a good job getting the dye off.

"I've uploaded a few times, but I've been busy." I'd toyed with an idea recently and decided to share it with her. "Would you be interested in collaborating with me?"

"How so?"

"Taking the same concept but through the lens of a makeup artist. YouTube world would fall in love with you and your many personas."

Vee handed me the bottle and then finished rubbing in the sunblock on her long legs. "I've thought about starting a channel but it felt too daunting."

"Exactly." I squirted a white blob into my hand and passed the bottle back to her. "If you collaborate with me, you won't have to start from scratch with finding followers and sponsors. And it would really help me out. I'm in burnout mode, so it's either do this with you or I'm going to take the channel down altogether."

"Now that would be a cryin' shame, chil'." Country-twang Vee clucked her tongue. "Explain how we go 'bout this, pray tell."

I laughed, loving all the little sayings she'd picked up from Erlene and other locals this summer. "You'd be your fabulous self in front of the camera and I'd handle all the editing and behind-the-scenes stuff."

"I'm not sure you'll be able to get away with that. Your viewers are used to their curly-headed host."

"I could make some appearances, but you'd be the star." My plan was to eventually phase myself out of the channel and give her the reins completely, but Vee didn't need to know that part for now. The only reason I'd started the channel in the first place was to prove something to my family. The only thing I ended up proving was that I could pretend like a pro. All that pretending had become exhausting.

We spent some time volleying ideas back and forth while sunning and playing in the surf. And it seemed a done deal by the time we waded out of the water for the second time.

"About Whit," Vee said abruptly as we moved up the beach. "What are you going to do?"

I didn't have an answer and wasn't in the mood to lie, so I busied myself gathering my damp hair into a ponytail. Maybe I could pretend I didn't hear her and she'd drop it.

"Seriously, Sonny."

No such luck.

I let go of my hair and huffed. "I know I can't work with Ewol Entertainment anymore. I guess I'm going to put out a few feelers when I get back to LA. See if any other studio will give me some work. I've looked at some smaller production companies around here. Surprisingly, both Georgia and South Carolina have a good many."

Vee's lips pulled into a deep frown. "You're just going to let Whit off the hook, then?"

"You know how this sort of thing plays out in the entertainment industry. I'll look like the scorned lover wanting to cash in on my famous ex. The nobody trying to ruin the somebody because I'm jealous."

Vee shook her head and glared at the ocean.

"It's easy for you to sit there and say that when it's not your career at stake."

"So a career is more important than standing up for what's right?"

I looked heavenward and groaned. "Come on, Vee. I didn't want to spend the day arguing."

"Sometimes an argument is called for. You can't just keep avoiding it. It's like you're scared to death of confrontation."

"I argue rather well with Hudson."

"Good. Keep doing that and maybe it'll help you grow a backbone."

"Vee!"

She held up her hands. "Fine. I'm letting it go. For now." Her attention snagged on something down the beach. She pointed. "Look at that giant piece of driftwood."

I angled around to check it out. "It's an entire tree."

"Ooh! Selfie time."

We walked over and took a ridiculous amount of photos until settling on one with several branches rising behind us in the background. After working the image through the edit app, I loaded it to Instagram and tagged Vee to it. @vee_fabulous #driftwood-dreaming #girlsday.

We returned to our belongings and started gathering everything.

"So I have a favor," I blurted after working up enough nerve.

Vee stopped folding her towel. "What?"

"Lyrica hates location management and scouting."

Vee clucked her tongue. "That's old news."

"She's passionate about hair and makeup, though."

Vee tossed her towel, smacking me in the chest with it. "No! You are not dumping that whiny brat off on me."

"She's a whiny brat because she hates her job. She won't hate it with you." I tossed the towel back. "And don't think I didn't see her helping you bronze and oil up the cast a few days ago."

"Because she has the hots for Zayden Ellisor. She was just using that as an excuse to touch him."

I shrugged, knowing Vee's assessment was on point. "Yeah, but didn't she do a good job?"

"I guess. She does have an eye for detail that most of my assistants lack." Vee groaned. "Fine. If Daddy Director says yes, then his little girl can help me the remainder of the shoot schedule."

"Thanks, Vee."

"Sure." She put on a cover-up and picked up her bag. "Now let's go on a ghost hunt."

"Okay. But don't get your hopes up on finding him."

We checked around the homestead one more time. The front porch and hammock in the back came up empty.

Giving up, I asked Vee, "You wanna go find something to eat? I'm starving."

"Ahem."

We both turned toward the sunporch, catching a glimpse of the shadowed figure sitting in one of the rocking chairs.

Smiling, I motioned for Vee to follow me. "The ghost has decided to grace us with his presence. Finally." I opened the screen door and shook my head at him. Wearing another tattered hoodie, he had a book lifted in front of his face.

"*Jack the Ripper*? Really?" Vee asked, her voice rising in suspicion.

I rolled my lips inward to hold back a laugh, knowing Hudson had deliberately picked that book to goad Vee. I wanted to high-five him. Instead, I stepped aside to enjoy the show I knew these two were about to put on.

He flipped the page.

"Are you going to grace us with conversation or only the silent treatment?" I asked him, crossing my arms.

Sighing as if my request caused him pain, Hudson closed the book. His eyes slid my way briefly, just long enough for me to catch a glint of mischief, before settling on Vee. "You live out in LA too?"

"Yes."

He motioned for Vee to have a seat to his right. Always to his right, the action deliberate. It was the first time I'd seen him do this with someone else besides me. "And you like living there?"

She sat down, looking at him suspiciously. "Of course."

"Don't you know California is the murder mecca for serial killers?"

Excited to see where this banter was headed, I lowered myself onto the side of his bed and placed my beach bag by my feet.

Vee tsked. "South Carolina has had serial killers too. One of the most notorious, in fact." She waved a hand in the air. "Crazies are everywhere."

Hudson dipped his chin in agreement. "Yep. Even on barrier islands."

Vee returned his unyielding look. "If you're trying to freak me out, it won't work."

"We'll see about that." Hudson flipped the hood off his head, revealing a disheveled mess of brown hair. Angling his body slightly away from us, he gave Vee a sidelong look. "I haven't let my crazy out yet."

Shooing his threat with a flick of her wrist, Vee snorted a terse laugh. "My friend, you're not the only one with crazy at the ready."

They went back and forth for a while, Vee quite animated and Hudson as subdued as ever. I hadn't been so thoroughly entertained in years. What struck me the most in all their banter was the fact that Vee didn't pull on a persona, not once, and Hudson slowly quit hiding.

"I'm a professional stylist. Would you like for me to give you a haircut?" Vee offered in the midst of their serial killer debate.

Without missing a beat, Hudson answered, "I wouldn't."

"How about a beard trim?" Vee tapped her bare chin.

"No."

"Well, you do you. But a comb and some beard balm could work wonders." Vee pointed a long bright-pink fingernail at him. "I have a question."

Hudson's frown deepened. "I fear answering will only encourage you to ask more."

"Well, sure. That's how conversations work."

He shook his head. "We're done talking now."

"Fine. I'm getting hungry anyway." She turned to look at me. "Let's take the boat over to that redneck taco joint by the marina."

I rose to my feet and retrieved my bag. "Sounds good to me. You and Cade have talked about that place enough that I need to try a pulled pork taco. Want to come, Hudson?"

"No thanks." He opened his book, looked at a random page, then handed it to Vee. "You can have this."

"Then you need to let me treat you to dinner as a thank-you for this and for letting us girls spend the day on your island." She motioned for him to stand. He didn't comply. No surprise there. "Everybody eats on their boats, so you don't even have to socialize."

"I heard they put mac and cheese on tacos. How can you resist that?" I boldly picked up his hand and was relieved he didn't instantly push off my touch, but he didn't budge from the chair either.

Hudson did his typical grunt-grumble. "I'll manage."

"Fine. We'll just bring it back here." Vee scooped up her bag and left.

I really didn't want to let go of his hand, especially when his fingers curled around mine, but I gave it one last squeeze and took several steps backwards. "We'll be back."

"You don't have to."

"I know. I want to. Think my friend does too."

"Then get some guacamole if they have it."

"You got it." Grinning, I spun around and hurried to catch up with Vee on the path.

"His scars don't look too bad," she said as if it were heavy on her mind. "He's good about keeping his body angled away though. I wonder how extensive it is."

"It's just mostly on his neck and here." I moved my hand along my left shoulder. "Not much extends to his back."

She lowered her giant sunglasses and squinted at me. "And just how would you know that?"

Images from the outdoor shower incident flashed through my head. That view had shown off lots and lots of skin with no scarring.

Vee edged into my line of sight and asked, "Why's your face so red?"

I pressed a palm to my scalding hot cheek. "Sunburn."

"Mm-hmm. You gonna tell me how you happen to know where the scar ends?"

Silently vowing to keep the shower incident to myself, I told Vee about another. "He took his shirt off once while we were processing the indigo."

I could tell she wanted to tease me about that, but it seemed her curiosity about Hudson was more pressing.

Vee slid the shades back up her nose. "What's he said about his injuries?"

Feeling protective over him, I said, "He doesn't talk about it."

She glanced over her shoulder as we reached the dock. "What do you do out here all the time then?"

"For one thing, I've helped with the indigo. We packaged up the last batch and have it ready for shipment. They look like blue bars of soap." I hopped into the boat and placed my bag underneath the seat. "I looked up the website for the company he ships to and it's fancy. They have the exclusive Indigo Isle collection. Crazy expensive though. I can't even afford a set of linen napkins. How can people pay that much for such?"

Vee shrugged as she settled into the seat beside me. "I can see someone who has an eye for textiles and the pocketbook to support it investing in something like that. I saw that linen shirt you swiped from him." She elbowed me. "It's gorgeous. And let's not forget about our works of art on the clothesline."

I backed the boat away from the dock. "I suppose."

"Hudson has to be making a small fortune each summer."

I snickered, thinking about his wardrobe of rags. The shopping bag in the storage chest on the back of the boat would remedy that some, if the stubborn man would accept it. "You wouldn't be able to tell it by looking at him."

"That's for sure. He could be a model for vagabond couture." Vee slid off her flip-flops and crossed her legs. "I get good vibes from him. I believe he's one of the good ones."

"Yeah. Me too."

• • •

I returned alone with tacos and found Hudson where I'd left him over an hour ago, but now he had his journal open with a pen moving across a page.

He glanced behind me as I opened the screen door. "You lose your friend?"

"More like she ditched me. Cade met us at the restaurant and she took off with him." I plopped the greasy bag and tray of drinks on the small table between the rocking chairs. "I got us cherry limeade. Hope that's okay with you."

"That's fine." Hudson placed the journal underneath his chair and freed the cups from the tray. "Is Cade her boyfriend?"

"Sometimes, I guess." I rummaged through the bag and divvied out the food, handing Hudson the container of guacamole and a straw for his drink. "Movie production life doesn't allow you to stay in one spot for very long, so relationships don't usually stick. But Vee and Cade always seem to pick up where they left off from one project to the next."

"So you don't always work with the same crew?"

"Not always. No." I unwrapped a taco and took a crunchy bite. "This is good stuff."

Hudson dunked a corner of his taco into the guacamole before taking his own noisy bite. He nodded in agreement. "What about you?"

"What about me?"

"Do you have a 'sometimes' boyfriend?" He averted his eyes and took another bite.

I fished napkins from the bag and handed him one before wiping my mouth with another. "Would you believe I've never officially had a boyfriend?"

His eyes returned to me in a flash, disbelief clear in the clouds of his irises. "Never?"

I shrugged, swiping a scoop of guacamole with my last bite of taco. Instead of popping it into my mouth, I stared at it. "I thought so one time, but that ended up being the biggest mistake of my life. A mistake that just keeps on giving." I finished the taco even though I'd lost my appetite.

"I haven't seen any more bruises, so it better not still be giving."

"No. Ever since Vee laid into him, he's left me alone." I didn't say how Whit had been extra hard on me on set, belittling and demanding, but I could handle that better than the alternative.

"Good." Hudson fisted the back of the sweatshirt and pulled it off, revealing a ridiculously holey shirt underneath. He tossed the hoodie aside with a frustrated huff. "He better keep leaving you alone if he knows what's best for him."

I decided to veer away from the subject of Whit. "Oh, I almost forgot." I took a sip of cherry limeade, placed it back on the table, and stood. "I'll be right back."

I heard him grumble something like "Now what?" but I kept walking away.

I retrieved the shopping bag from the boat and hurried back, lickety-split.

Hudson looked at the bag suspiciously as I set it in his lap.

"It's nothing much," I rushed to explain. "So don't make this weird."

Hudson glanced at me and then peeped inside. Somehow he managed to laugh while maintaining his frown. "You bought me clothes?"

"Yep." I picked up my cup and took another long pull from the straw.

"I'm good. I have plenty already."

He tried handing me the bag but I shoved it away. "Honey, the only thing you have plenty of are rags. When most of your torso is on display, that means the shirt is no longer doing its job." I poked his firm stomach through the large rip in the shirt, causing Mr. Not Ticklish to flinch.

Hudson gave in and started taking the stack of new T-shirts and shorts out of the bag. His fingers moved over the surf logos. "You didn't have to do this. How much do I owe you?"

"I know I didn't have to. I wanted to. It's a gift for putting up with me. I probably still owe you more for that."

Replacing everything in the bag, Hudson rose from his rocking chair and stood before mine. He leaned over until our eyes were level. "Putting up with you has never been a hardship. I take back what I said about not liking you."

"No need. I already know you like me." Smiling, I winked at him.

A huff of laughter escaped his lips and brushed against mine. It tickled, but that sensation quickly vanished as another took over when he pressed a kiss to my lips. Before I could even register his actions, he'd disappeared inside the house.

Did he?

Did the Monster of Indigo Isle really just kiss me?

Snapping out of the shock of it, I shot to my feet and went after him, finding him only a few steps inside, frozen in place. Hands on his hips, head bowed toward the floor.

"Don't go ruining what just happened," I demanded, watching his back stiffen. "It happened and it was perfect and you will not take that away from us."

Hudson turned around. "But I took something I promised I wouldn't."

"You took nothing. You gave me that kiss." As we held each other's gaze, I considered him, the scar on his neck, the scruffy beard, his severe scowl. Adding up the imperfections equaled a darkly handsome man. Even his sadness added a certain depth to his attraction. "You're the first to give, Hudson. Don't you understand how important that is to me?"

Hudson blinked several times and cleared his throat. He moved closer and pulled me into his arms. His bearded cheek rested against my temple as he held me. This man knew how to hug properly. Firmly yet not too tight, reassuring me I could get out of the embrace at any time.

Sighing contently, I wrapped my arms around his tapered waist and held on to the moment for as long as I could.

I thought the acknowledgment and the embrace would be the end of this and I expected him to begin pulling away, but Hudson surprised me for the second time in the span of mere minutes.

Weaving his long fingers through my hair, his lips brushed along my cheek before settling against my mouth. He pressed closer but kept the kiss nonaggressive. Instead of freezing and giving myself over to another situation that left me sick and ashamed, I relaxed into something that finally felt right.

CHAPTER TWENTY-ONE

COULD A KISS REALLY CHANGE THINGS? Perhaps not, but Hudson's kiss did put things in perspective for me. Weird as it might sound, his kiss reminded me of my parents. The respect they had for each other, more specifically. I'd spent the last two days since our kiss contemplating that and thinking about how I could implement being a more respectful person, to others and to myself. I knew it had to start by cutting ties with Whit, and then I'd have to make things right with my mother and sisters. Those thoughts followed me as I eased down Highway 17. We'd finished up a predawn shoot and now I had the entire day ahead of me, so this spur-of-the-moment road trip felt right.

The road between Charleston and Georgetown reminded me of one of the strangest and most challenging films I'd ever worked on. A dark trope with a lot of Quentin Tarantino vibes, the entire movie took place within the confines of a car. The director wanted the viewer to feel like they'd traveled thousands upon thousands of miles with the characters in the car, so the landscape had to continuously change. Traveling thousands of miles wasn't practical, so I had to find a location within a tight radius that had enough variables to pull off the director's vision. Mountains, deserts, coastlines. Northern California and Nevada fit the bill, and I'd never worked so hard on a set in all my years of working in the film industry.

Much like the characters from that movie, I didn't plan on getting out of the car today. This trip to Georgetown would be a dry run. Hopefully, when I came back the next time to finally admit to the egg on my face, I'd be brave enough to see it through.

With a ball cap pulled low on my head and palms slick with sweat, I crossed the bridge into Georgetown. I bumped up the air and held my hand to the vent, only to be slapped in the face by the overwhelming odor known as the Georgetown smell. Distinct and downright rancid, some said it smelled like rotten cabbage, others said rotten eggs, yet the locals called it the smell of money. As a dedicated employee of the paper mill, that's what my dad always called it too.

Hitting the Recirculate button, even though it was too late to keep the stench outside the car, I took a right on Front Street to check out the historic downtown area. Tired facades had recently had face-lifts, and the sidewalks were spruced up with bountiful planters and quaint seating areas. As I took in shop after shop and restaurant after restaurant with patrons coming and going, a puff of pride worked its way up my chest. Happy for the town's revitalization yet put off a bit by how well life had gone on without me.

I turned around at the marina and made my way out of the downtown area and toward the more rural part of town. Taking a back road along the river—one that was paved with only dirt and memories—I made it to the turnoff to my parents' place in no time at all. Funny how it had taken me fifteen years to decide to revisit my mistakes, but the trip itself took only minutes.

Tires crunching against the gravel, I slowed to a stop at the mouth of their driveway, deciding that was far enough. My gaze settled on the white mailbox with Bates spelled out on the side in black block-lettered stickers. The sight of the raised red flag kicked my heart, a sure sign someone had been here recently. I wondered how close I'd been to running into possibly my mother. I also wondered if her White Diamonds perfume was still lingering by the mailbox. The woman loved wearing one too many spritzes of the strong fragrance, but it smelled good on her.

The deep rumble of a truck jolted me. I tugged the brim of my hat lower and scooted down in the seat. I peered over the steering wheel and watched until the truck disappeared around a curve in the road.

Too chicken to step out of the protective bubble of the car, I lingered a few more minutes. The long drive leading to the riverfront homestead didn't give any glimpse of it, but my mind easily conjured images of the stilted home. I wondered who gave it the yearly coat of pale-yellow paint now that Dad was no longer here to do it. Or who raked underneath the house after the flooded banks receded. Or who shooed the gators out of the yard when they got a wild hair to pay a visit.

Blinking against the onslaught of memories and concerns hovering just beyond the car, I wiped away a stray tear. "I'll be back soon." I whispered the promise before driving away.

I made it all the way to Awendaw, just north of Mount Pleasant, before making a pit stop at the popular Sewee Outpost. I topped off the tank of gas and then went inside to explore the bounty of treasures inside. The briny scent of boiled peanuts greeted me, along with the young lady at the register. I smiled in her direction and began a slow circle around the rustic store that carried a wide selection of offerings. Fishing bait and tackle, outdoor apparel, fresh produce, a wide range of food choices . . .

I grabbed a Diet Dr Pepper to soothe my parched throat and a giant homemade chocolate chip cookie to feed my feelings. Then I backtracked to the food section and did a little more shopping. I settled on a frozen pack of their famous cheese biscuits for Hudson. Thinking about him and his tender kiss had my lips upturning in a private smile. I hadn't had a free moment since in which to try talking him into giving me another, but I planned on changing that this afternoon.

With my mind on Hudson, I mindlessly shopped until reaching the front register with two armloads. After settling the bill for the gas and my retail therapy splurge on mostly junk food, I lugged it all to the car and decided to move to a parking space to enjoy my cookie and soda before hitting the road again.

Chewing on the soft, buttery cookie, I considered ways to scrape up the money I owed Mama. No way could I go back to apologize without it. Contrary to what most thought, I didn't make a fortune from my work in the movie industry. And the astronomical cost of living in California ate up most of that, so I'd never been able to put any away in savings. The only thing I had of any value was my collection of movie memorabilia.

I brushed the cookie crumbs from my lap and plucked my phone from the empty cup holder. Even though it was trash, each piece meant something to me and I'd never planned to give any of it up, but perhaps now was the time. I searched through a folder in my email app until finding one labeled Big Texas. This guy had been persistent, contacting me several times in the last year or so, and had sent me an email just two weeks ago inquiring about it again.

Not giving myself time to second-guess, I fired off an email with my counteroffer. With a mix of anticipation and anxiety whirling around with the cookie in my stomach, I put the phone aside and reversed out of the parking space.

Once I reached the marina, I checked my email and was surprised he'd already responded. Surprised but then instantly disappointed. The punk lowballed me as if sensing my desperation. I did a quick search of GIFs, finding one of an old man laughing hysterically, and sent it as my reply. If this guy was serious about owning the collection, he'd come back with a decent offer. I needed it closer to what I owed. If I could just pay it back, plus some, would my mother forgive me? Would Caroline and Aubrey?

Leaving it be for now, I gathered the bags and made my way to the boat and to the one bright spot in my life at the moment.

That bright spot glowed even brighter when I spotted Hudson sitting on the dock. As soon as I pulled alongside the dock and shut off the boat, he rose to his feet.

I gave him a slow once-over, appreciating that he was wearing the new T-shirt and shorts I'd gotten him. "Nice outfit."

Paying my comment no attention, Hudson crouched down and made quick work of securing the boat to the dock. He straightened and met my eyes. "You get lost?"

I smiled, loving the idea that he really was waiting for me. Maybe even missing me. "It's only been two days."

"Yeah, but you normally bother me daily." Hudson's comeback held no bite, only tease. He offered his hand to help me step out, but before I could pass, his lips descended to mine. Soft yet firm.

With the waves rocking the boat and this man kissing me, my world tilted, messing with my equilibrium.

"What's all this?" Hudson tugged a bag from my grip.

Feet planted on the dock, I tried to balance my dizzy mind. "Huh?"

He held up the bag, raising an eyebrow.

"Oh, I stopped by Sewee Outpost, and—" I shrugged—"I couldn't help myself. There's frozen cheese biscuits in one of them."

"Mmm. I think I have just what we need to go with that." He gathered my hand in his and led me toward the house.

We stood in the kitchen as Hudson plundered the bags, slowing just long enough to crack open a boiled peanut and pop it into his mouth. Once he found the biscuits, he left everything on the counter and started heating the oven. Then he rummaged around the pantry and came out with a mason jar filled with a pinkish-orange mixture.

"What's that?"

"Peach preserves LuAnn and I put up this summer." He dumped the entire jar into a small pot and set it on a burner.

I made a face, wrinkling my nose. "Jelly on cheese biscuits?"

"Absolutely. Just you wait." He said it with such conviction that I had to laugh.

"I'm not sure I can trust your taste buds. You did feed me canned ham."

Hudson cut me a look over his shoulder and went back to stirring the jam. "You act like that's the only thing I've fed you all summer." For such a wild-looking man with his disheveled hair and long beard, he moved around the kitchen with fluid confidence. It made me want to wrap my arms around him and rest my head against his back.

Uncertain on how he'd receive such affection, I decided to keep my hands to myself and lean against the counter instead. "You have fed me well. I'm really going to miss it."

Another glance over his shoulder. This time his expression seemed a bit sad, but he blinked and it disappeared. "Do you know how to cook?"

"I can do the basics. It's just me and I'm on the road a lot, so it makes more sense to just eat out." I reached into the damp bag of boiled peanuts and snacked on some while watching him load the biscuits into a well-loved cast-iron skillet.

Hudson skimmed the instructions on the clear package, head tilted in concentration. "The biscuits only need to be heated, so maybe ten minutes, tops."

Once the biscuits were in the oven, he stood beside me, close enough to indicate my touch would be welcomed, so I passed him the bag of peanuts and leaned my head against his shoulder. He didn't flinch or move away, simply enjoyed the peanuts while I enjoyed his closeness.

Soon, a tangy sweetness wafted through the kitchen, setting my mouth to watering.

Hudson pulled the skillet from the oven and picked up the pot of warmed peach preserves. "Grab the butter and we'll be in business."

I stacked the butter dish on top of two dessert plates and followed him and the delicious scent out to the table in the yard. We settled in our chairs and Hudson went to work preparing a biscuit, splitting it open and smearing butter on one half and spooning a generous dollop of preserves on the other. Sandwiching it back together, he dropped the biscuit on a plate and handed it to me before making himself one.

We ate in peaceful silence. I'd finally gotten the hang of not wasting words and simply appreciating being still. One of the many things this man had taught me by showing instead of telling.

"Well?" He motioned to my empty plate, save for a few crumbs.

"Not bad." I pinched the crumbs and sprinkled them on the ground for the patiently waiting chickens.

"Not bad?"

"Fine. It was delicious. I'm stealing a jar of those peach preserves. Did you add cinnamon?"

"And nutmeg." He began assembling another biscuit.

"You like cooking," I stated.

Before I could protest, he plopped it onto my plate and began making his own. "I like to eat."

"Clearly I do too." I took a bite of the flaky biscuit. I made myself stop halfway through and gave the rest to the chickens.

"Stop spoiling my chickens."

I rolled my eyes and flicked the last piece of biscuit a bit farther from the table, sending the hens waddling after it. "They're already spoiled and it's not my fault. Don't think I haven't noticed the oyster crackers you slip out of your pocket every time you pass them in the yard."

He grumbled without forming any words to go with it, knowing I was right.

Neither of us seemed in a hurry to leave the table, so we stayed put while watching the sun wrap up its daily visit.

"Tell me something," Hudson said after a nice long stretch of no words.

I almost smiled at the memory of our tropical storm night but tamped it down to play along. "Like what?" I asked, mimicking his irritated tone from that night.

He settled his elbows on the table. "How about something useful this time?"

Twisting my lips, I gave it some thought. "The law states that you are supposed to post No Trespassing signs in at least four conspicuous places." I swept a hand through the air. "I've only seen two on this island."

He took a sip of his water to hide the smile forming on his lips, but I saw it anyway. "I believe you've been verbally warned not to trespass, which could also result in charges."

"Yes, but you also verbally invited me, so no takebacks."

"So I guess that means there's no getting rid of you." He released a long-suffering sigh, acting put out by the idea.

"Have no fear, my friend. You're almost done putting up with me." I tried to inflect tease in my tone, but it seemed stuck to the roof of my mouth. "The movie wraps tomorrow night."

Hudson grew still, his brow furrowed. "Already?"

"Yeah. Feels like I just got here yesterday." I shook my head. "That's the problem with time. It's like smoke. There's no way of grasping it."

"Yeah," he muttered, eyes cast toward his empty plate. I wondered if the realization of me leaving saddened him as much as it did me.

"I'd love for you to come to the set and see a movie production in action."

With a shake of his head, the stubborn man turned down the suggestion automatically.

Taking a deep breath, I prepared to make my case. "It's at night. You can easily see the action from the trees lining the beach. That's where I mainly hang out at during the shoot. No one will even see you. Please."

After a minute or two with no answer, I braved rounding the table and plopping down in his lap. I wrapped my arms around his neck, rested my forehead against his, and tried again. "Please."

His chest heaved and then a long sigh pushed past his lips to meet mine. I closed the space and pressed a gentle kiss to his frown until he softened and returned the kiss.

"Okay," he finally said, resigned.

I couldn't help but reflect on how often I'd gotten my way with this stubborn man since I met him. I also wondered if getting my way with him would end up coming back to haunt me.

CHAPTER TWENTY-TWO

Night shoots were always my favorite. With the darkness beyond the scene, it gave off the illusion of us being in our own little world. Today, only hours away from the night shoot, the normal excitement hadn't shown up. Instead, a nagging sensation did. I folded a shirt and tucked it into my suitcase, blaming that nagging on leaving Hudson soon. Or perhaps the fact that I dreaded the return trip to LA tomorrow.

Brushing off the unsettling sensation about as successfully as brushing off wet sand, I glanced out the window and noted that dusk had finally arrived. I left the rest of the packing for later and set out for Indigo Island.

Hudson sat on the porch steps with a book in hand. Nothing new there, nor in his unseasonable attire.

I stopped just shy of bumping his jean-clad knees with mine and planted my hands on my hips. "A hoodie? Why?"

Closing the book with a brisk snap, Hudson offered me his signature blank look. A look that I'd learned over the last couple of months said a whole heckuva lot, if you were paying attention. Today it said, *"You know why."*

"The scar isn't that bad." I waved a hand toward his concealed neck. "Gives you character."

With a grim expression, he retorted, "Gives daft people the insolent notion that they have the right to ask questions about it."

"*I've* never asked you about it," I reminded him instead of poking fun at his wordy declaration.

Hudson dropped the book beside him and pulled me closer. "I never thought you were daft or insolent either, Sunshine."

I bit my lip, but the grin broke through anyway. The grouch just called me sunshine. No way could I not beam at that. "Sunshine?"

The only answer he gave me was another stare, but this time the harsh creases around his eyes softened. This look told me he kinda liked me.

"So if you never thought I was daft or insolent, then what have you thought of me?" I settled my hands on his shoulders.

Hudson tilted his head to the side, those stormy eyes never leaving me. "I've thought . . . much more than I should." His lips pressed against mine, confirming we thought the same of each other.

After kissing him thoroughly, I leaned away and playfully asked, "You need a ride, hot stuff?"

Hudson gripped my waist and gently moved me back a bit so he could stand. "We already went over this last night, so knock it off." Planting a kiss on my frown, he stepped around me and shoved his feet into a pair of flip-flops.

"Fine." I huffed, recalling the conversation we had. Well, he spoke and I listened for once.

He'd given me a lecture for the stunt I pulled with sitting on his lap, saying it was inappropriate to use my womanly prowess to get my way. Then he laid out the ground rules for tonight, only agreeing to go if he took his own boat so he could leave whenever he was good and ready.

"Let's go get this over with." Hudson held my hand and led me toward the dock.

"You'll have fun if you let yourself." My comment only earned me a glare, so I hushed and enjoyed the walk through the island. I took in the canopy of trees and the sweet smell of jasmine. With a tightening in my chest and throat, I wondered if this would be the last time I ever walked this path. The big, imposing man holding my hand hadn't said a word about ever wanting to see me past this summer. How silly was I to even expect such? But I did, and that was probably the reason why I'd struggled to breathe with ease the entire day.

We took off across the dark water, the boats' lights sending out sparkles across the ripples to lead the way. In no time, we arrived at Moise Island. I hopped out immediately but my guest stayed put.

"I've got some things to check on." I pointed to the thick line of palmetto trees. "I'll end up there when they begin shooting the scene, if you want hang out there."

Hudson nodded, making no move to get out of his boat.

I left him and went to work. Fifteen minutes passed with me keeping an eye on the tree line. I was relieved when I caught a glimpse of him. He hovered nearby, observing everything going on while staying in the shadows of the trees. He thought he could blend in, but the man needed to realize the impossibility of that.

Vee zeroed in on him rather quickly, sashaying over while twirling a long comb like a baton, with Lyrica hot on her heels. Vee held the comb up and asked him something. His head shook immediately, making her laugh loud enough that it reached me over the roar of the ocean. Lyrica stepped closer, taking her turn to talk. He crossed his arms and scooted a bit more behind the tree while both women yammered on and on.

I warred between amusement that he was being forced to socialize and terror that he'd bolt because of it. I'd just taken a step to go rescue him when Whit blocked my path.

"We have a stray." He tipped his head toward Hudson. "Get security on it."

I stifled a laugh and waved off his concern. "No. He's with me."

"Since when did you start befriending the homeless? Is this some kind of service project? Because if it is, I don't have time for—"

"Nothing like that. He's actually the owner of Indigo Isle."

Whit straightened, his face transforming from bored irritation to something stonier. "Oh? So we aren't allowed on his precious island but he's welcomed on *my* set?" He grabbed my hip and tugged me closer, laying some kind of claim he had no right laying.

"Lock it down!" The assistant director's command had the chatter on the beach instantly falling silent.

Whit gave my hip a final squeeze, bringing me close and then pushing me away, before walking away. The touch delivered a warning. One disparaging look, one domineering touch. That's all it took to put me in my place.

I pivoted around to face the scene being filmed on the beach. The actors were huddled around a bonfire, guessing about what had happened to a missing member of the group.

Blake Rodham started his lines. He was supposed to give a snooty assessment of the situation, speculating on the probability

274

of Lark falling victim to malaria. I inclined my head, trying to listen more closely, because I could have sworn he'd just said *malarkey* instead.

"Cut!" Les practically growled the word. "The wrap party isn't until we wrap, correct?"

Murmurs of agreement wafted around the cast and crew.

"So someone explain to me why Rodham is already too sloshed to deliver his lines?"

No murmurs, just a lot of looks of confusion and shrugging.

Rodham hiccuped an apology, nearly toppling off the driftwood stump. Zayden's giant hand shot out and righted Rodham before he fell. Instead of looking like a professional movie shoot, it more closely resembled a circus.

I rubbed my forehead and sighed. No way would Hudson find any respect for me or my profession after this. I should have never asked him to come here.

Les heaved a loud groan. "Someone get Rodham coffee and something to eat!"

Several assistants scampered toward crafts services. Whit moved over by the fire and crouched beside a swaying Rodham, delivering a speech, I supposed. The actor played Carlson, the highly intelligent nerd. It was kinda funny, him slurring while butchering his prim lines.

With the unexpected break, I joined Hudson and the two women by the trees. "Well, this is a first. Seriously, Hudson, this isn't the norm."

He glanced at me briefly, clearly not believing it for a second.

"I better go get some eyedrops." Vee twirled the comb, blew on the end like it was a smoking gun, and then shoved it into her pocket. "I'll see ya later, pardner." She winked at Hudson before strutting off with a pronounced gait. Lyrica sashayed behind her like nothing was amiss.

"What was that cowgirl act about?" I asked Hudson while watching the cowgirl mosey away.

"Not sure. She approached me like that, saying something about a showdown with my hair and her comb."

I snorted, turning toward him, but the laughter died instantly when I caught a glimpse of his harsh scowl underneath the hoodie. "Vee's just kidding around."

Hudson's glower stayed pinned somewhere past my shoulder. "That's him, isn't it?"

I knew who he was talking about but looked anyway. "Oh, that's one of the producers."

Hudson's brow knit as his overcast eyes studied me.

I squirmed under his scrutiny, but now wasn't the time to get into it with him. I hitched a thumb over my shoulder. "I better go see if I can do anything to help the crew reset." Swiveling around, I got back to work, half-expecting Hudson to disappear. Pretty much hoping for it. But he remained by the trees, taking it all in. I had a bad feeling he was building a case on a hard truth I didn't want exposed.

Due to Rodham's drunken stunt, we didn't wrap until after one in the morning. In between sobering up the actor enough to finish the scenes and doing countless retakes, Whit made it his mission to grope me, to leer, to make crass remarks. He made sure to deliver all of this in view and earshot of the ghost hovering nearby.

"That's a wrap!"

As soon as those freeing sentiments were yelled, I turned to make a break for it, but Whit was on me in a blink. Backing me up into the darkness by the makeup tent, his hands took, took, took.

"Get rid of the weirdo, babe."

Huffing a weak laugh, I tried wiggling out of his hold. "He didn't get in the way or anything."

"He saw the mess with Rodham. If that makes it to the Internet, I'll—"

"You have nothing like that to worry about." I attempted to brush his palms off my backside. "Come on now. Please let go."

"Don't be like this. I know I got a little rough last time, but I thought you were into it." Whit kissed along my neck, making my throat burn.

I just wanted to walk away quietly tonight. To never find myself in this situation again. Seemed I never got what I wanted.

I pushed against his chest and swallowed past the tightness. "Please don't do this, Whit."

"But we need to celebrate tonight." He clung to me, making it impossible to break free.

"You need to get your hands off her."

Whit's head snapped up as my entire body flinched. The demand sounded like two boulders colliding.

Instead of listening, Whit pulled me closer. "This is none of your business."

Hudson's gaze iced over. "Clearly she's not into whatever you're offering. Maybe it should be the cops' business."

"It would be the cops' business to know you're trespassing on a private movie set." Whit sneered, never one to back down.

Posturing up like he was about to deliver Whit the beating of his life, Hudson took a step closer.

I jumped between them. "No cops need to be called. Whit, go celebrate your success with the crew. I'll be there shortly." I gave him a smile of encouragement over my shoulder and then turned my sights on Hudson.

Just as quickly as he'd puffed out his chest, Hudson backed off with a sharp shake of his head.

"Kessler!" Les yelled out from somewhere on the other side of the tent.

I turned to encourage Whit to go, but he was already moving away. He mumbled something about handling this with me later, but I wouldn't be here to take part in it. Not this time.

The tension at my back made it painful for me to turn around to face Hudson. His disappointed frown hit me hard, my knees close to buckling. It was the same look my parents had worn all too often when it came to dealing with me. And it had the same effect too, making my stomach roil forcefully with shame.

"Hudson—"

He held a palm up to me and shook his head. Even though his lips remained pressed firmly together, I could barely stand the blaring condemnation. He stormed past me and disappeared into the night.

Mortified and disoriented, I stayed behind the tent until finally gathering enough strength to head over to Indigo Isle.

My insecurities about being not good enough and nothing but a screwup followed me down the trail leading to the homestead, not letting up even when I found Hudson pacing his front yard.

He whirled around and gestured behind me. "Who was that back there?"

I stopped several feet short of him. "Whit."

"No." Hudson yanked off the sweatshirt and threw it to the ground. "Who was that woman?"

His accusation made me flinch and retreat a few steps. "You know me. Out here, you've seen me."

"How am I supposed to know if the woman I've spent the summer with is the real you? Or is it the one past the shores of this place? That coward I witnessed tonight?"

"I was planning on handling it. I—"

"Him touching you— that was you handling it?" Hudson shoved his hair out of his eyes and growled. "I don't want to even think about what would have happened had I not put a stop to it!"

Hot with humiliation, I blinked the tears away and swallowed forcefully. "I don't need you to be my hero."

"Good. Trust me. I'm not one." He jabbed a finger at me. "You need to be your own hero. Stand up yourself. And stop this act!"

I crossed my arms as anger began mixing with my shame. "You're a fine one to talk, Monster of Indigo Isle. Hiding out here instead of facing what happened with your daughter and refusing to forgive your ex-wife. You're just as much a coward as me!"

Visibly stunned, he clutched his stomach. "That's where you're wrong. I refuse to forgive myself."

I pitied him but refused to back down. "Yeah, and you're holed up out here in some self-imposed imprisonment. You ever think about how that affects Reece? How this imprisons her too?"

"You have no right." He spoke his raspy words through clenched teeth as his broad shoulders heaved up and down, resembling the monster he'd been accused of being.

"Truly, I know. Just like you have no right calling someone out on their problems when all you do is hide from your own."

I watched as the walls of Hudson went up in a flash. He stared right through me and pointed toward the boat dock. "You need to leave."

Heart hammering and throat burning, I did as he said, leaving for the first time without having to be told twice.

• • •

I somehow made it back to the motel, dead on my feet yet too wired to settle down. I stood at the foot of the bed, scanning the open suitcase and the stacks of clothing beside it. Instead of clearing it away, I eased onto the floor and leaned against the foot of the bed. After staring at the wood-paneled wall for a while, I took my phone out and stared at it for a while too.

Hudson had accused me of being fake. Needing to face the evidence of that, I pulled up my channel and skimmed through the three hundred videos, clicking on random ones as I scrolled. Video after video confirmed it. Even though she had my curly brown hair, the woman on the screen wasn't the real me at all.

With so many thoughts whirling around in my head, I exited out of YouTube and opened the video app. Taking a deep breath, I hit Record.

"Hi from my glamorous motel room," I spoke, sounding too loud. My reflection looked too loud as well, curls frizzy and windblown, eyes red and swollen, lips wobbling with barely contained emotion.

My thumb hovered over the End button, but then I thought better of it. What if I dropped the facade, stepped from behind that wall of glitz and glam, and showed them the real me?

I gave the camera a small smile. "I did something this summer. I harvested indigo plants and then processed them into vivid-blue dye. Made me think about what it had taken to make that happen. It began with bruised and battered leaves. Although it was a lengthy endeavor that really wasn't all that fun or glamorous, in the end, the damage was transformed into something rare and beautiful. Never could you have convinced me this weedy-looking plant could become something so unique."

I reached behind me and grabbed a shirt, using it to dry my cheeks. "I had sort of given in and accepted that I was nothing but a weed. A nobody pretending to be somebody." I let out a flat laugh. "I think I'm ready to take the weeds I've been growing and see what beauty can come out of them. But that's not going to happen if I don't let this fake version of me go."

Sniffing, I scanned the motel room. "I need to step away from all this for a while, maybe permanently, I don't know. I'm sorry for not being real with y'all. As they say in the movies, that's a wrap." I hit Upload before I could second-guess it or edit or filter. Real and raw, that's what I would leave as my farewell to an audience I'd been completely fake with from the very start.

More wrung out and homesick than ever before, it took great effort to get myself up off the floor. I changed into my pajamas and after brushing my teeth, I chugged a bottle of water. Still feeling parched, I grabbed another bottle of water but just stared at it. I needed more than water to quench the drought inside me.

Dry bones. This term came to mind as I sat down on the edge of the bed, realizing every last part of me ached with a tiredness nothing seemed to be able to cure. On the nightstand, where it had been ignored my entire stay, sat a Gideon Bible. I recalled when speakers from the Gideons International association used to come to our church and share about how those Bibles changed lives. Always so inspiring. I'd take their testimonies in and just be in awe of God's loving power. How he would take someone with a near-death soul and breathe new life into them.

With tears blurring my vision, I picked up the Bible and simply held it to my chest. I knew what was inside. The words, the only true promises anyone could depend on. Words that I desperately needed to breathe life into me again.

Nothing more than a sack of dry bones, rattled and desperate, I slid off the bed with the Bible clutched over my heart and laid every failure, every regret, everything . . . I laid it all out and could do nothing but weep.

My words weren't needed. God heard them as they seeped through each tear and whimper. He took those broken shards of my dry bones that were scattered all over the rust-orange carpet and began a mending. Fifteen years overdue.

CHAPTER TWENTY-THREE

SLEEP NEVER FOUND ME THAT NIGHT, but I finally found some bravado to face what needed facing by the time the alarm went off. I leaned forward in the chair and grabbed my phone off the table and silenced it. I gathered my suitcase, leaving some metaphoric baggage behind, and headed for the motel office.

Erlene sat behind the desk in her normal spot, flipping through an Avon cosmetics brochure with a pen in hand.

"I didn't realize Avon was still a thing." I leaned close and watched her circle a tube of pink lipstick.

"Oh yes. It's better than ever." She flipped a few pages and started scanning eye shadow options.

"My mother was a huge fan. She used to swear by the Skin So Soft bath oil. The one in the pink bottle."

Erlene circled a purple eye shadow and glanced up. *"Used to?* She doesn't anymore?"

I shifted from one foot to the other. "I'm not sure."

Closing the brochure, Erlene gave me her full attention. "You look plumb tired, sweetie. You okay?"

I tugged my hat a little lower over my eyes. "Just a long night shoot, is all." I handed over my room key. "I'm here to check out and to make sure everyone else did too."

Erlene accepted the key with a sad smile. "I sure am gonna miss y'all. This place hasn't seen so much liveliness in decades." She gathered my hand with both of hers and sighed. "Sonny, I'm worried about you."

I gave her a half-hearted laugh. "No worries. I plan on sleeping at least a week straight once I get back to LA."

"No amount of sleep is going to solve whatever it is you're running from."

My eyes stung but I was too wrung out to cry anymore. "Pardon me?"

"Don't act offended. I'm an old lady with nothing better to do than people-watch. You're an easy read."

I stared at the Avon brochure on the counter. "I'm just homesick."

"Then I'd say it's time to go home." She squeezed my hand, then let go.

"I have some things to fix first." I adjusted the strap of the messenger bag on my shoulder.

"Then you'll never make it back home. Just go, and worry about fixin' things later."

I wished it were that easy, but I nodded my head in agreement. After signing a few papers and promising to keep in touch, I loaded up my bags and headed to the marina. I had one last production meeting and then this chapter would be closing, as long as I didn't chicken out.

• • •

The meeting droned on for over an hour, but I didn't hear a word of it. Light-headed, the only thing I could focus on was trying not to vomit. I was about to commit career suicide, but I knew it was the only way I could live with myself. I had to do this. No way around it.

"Any last thoughts before we put this shoot to bed?" Les studied the tanned yet tired group slumped in chairs before him.

Clearing my throat, I pushed to my feet and clasped my hands together to hide the trembling. "I have a few thoughts I'd like to share."

"Let's hear it." Les motioned for me to get on with it.

After a wave of dizziness passed, I chanced a glance at Whit, making sure I had his attention. Our eyes briefly connected. He was listening, but that look on his face said I better not have much to say. *Not today, sir. Not today.* I was sick of being his puppet. Sick of being shamed into doing things that caused me more shame. So sick of the person I'd become. Just so sick of it all.

"We don't have time for this," Whit said.

He made a move to stand, but Lyrica spoke up. "I want to hear what she has to say." She looked at her father and he nodded, so Whit sat back down on a huff.

I dared to meet Whit's eyes again, the whooshing in my ears reaching a crescendo. *If looks could kill.* Averting my gaze away from his glare, I settled on looking at one of the new assistants who had found herself in the same predicament as I did with Whit. She needed to hear this, perhaps more so than anyone.

"Today, Bates. I have a plane to catch," Les spoke, causing me to flinch.

"Sorry." Wiping my damp palms on the sides of my pants,

I refocused on the young woman sitting off to the side by herself. "Power and clout does not give a person a pass to take whatever he wants without permission. And just because a victim doesn't respond with a flight-or-fight instinct certainly doesn't mean the victim is granting her attacker permission." Feeling defeated yet brave, I turned and stared directly at a red-faced Whit. "You've taken a lot from me, most importantly my dignity. The last thing you're going to get away with taking from me might be my career, but that's okay. I'm leaving this island today, finally respecting myself for the first time since I met you."

The room resembled a frozen frame of a movie. I'm not sure how I managed to unfreeze and not pass out, but I found myself moving toward the door somehow. I heard someone clapping. Most likely Lyrica, but I didn't slow to see who. This wasn't about accolades. This was about finally standing up for what was right. This was about me being my own hero and hopefully the hero for others who didn't think they had a voice to do the same.

• • •

I had one last stop to make before heading to the airport. Even with the No Trespassing signs posted on the dock, the small island had become my refuge this summer. I started up the path, paying attention to the fragments of shells and tiny rocks that speckled the sandy floor. I made sure to listen to the birds singing somewhere above me in the tree canopy and to appreciate the sweet perfume of the jasmine vines. Even though Indigo Isle wasn't my home, it looked, sounded, and smelled like home.

I knew the Monster of Indigo Isle wouldn't be making an appearance. The plan wasn't to go on a ghost hunt for him anyway.

Stepping onto the porch, I pulled my journal from my messenger bag and stared at it through a sheen of tears. I'd taken Hudson's truths without his permission that day in his library, so I owed him some of mine. Amongst those truths were my regrets about stealing that money and then running away from my family and how I'd feared Whit could potentially sabotage my job if I didn't play nice with him. I decided to leave every page, even the confessions of how I felt about Hudson. That I'd developed deep feelings for him over the summer. And how those feelings had grown into love.

This morning before sunrise, I'd written one last entry.

Today, I'm changing the lens on how I view my life. My friend—I hope he's still my friend—told me I needed to be my own hero. So here goes nothing. It starts with me confronting some hard truths and Whit Kessler. I have a voice. It's time to use it. This is just the start. It's also time to go home. To ask my mother to forgive me. To reconcile with her and my sisters. I may not be able to go back and start over, but I will turn this page and start fresh. And no matter where that lands me, I will forever be grateful for my friend for making me face all this.

Thank you, Hudson.

Love,

Sonny

I added my phone number to the end, telling him to call if he ever found it in his heart to forgive me.

I placed the slim book on the table by the front door and made my way off the porch. As I reached the edge of the yard, I turned and waved at the house. I would miss it too.

CHAPTER TWENTY-FOUR

Whit didn't disappoint, keeping true to character by taking the one last thing he could from me. The email was delivered to my in-box even before the plane delivered me to LAX. Ewol Entertainment had terminated my work contract.

Hollywood was like a fickle girlfriend. Quick to drop you as soon as the next shiny thing came along and grabbed her attention. But she could also turn a cold shoulder on you if she didn't get her way. Ewol Entertainment hadn't gotten their way, so hello, cold shoulder.

The Uber driver pulled up in front of my apartment building. Between LA and San Bernardino, this area wasn't considered all that great, but it worked for me. A place I'd hung my hat for fifteen years. Pretty much a pit stop between projects. Even silk plants didn't stand a chance.

I made a detour to the landlord's ground floor apartment to pick up my mail and the surfboard I had shipped from South Carolina. It took two trips up the stairs to lug everything, dumping the surfboard by the door before sprinting back down to grab more. I always seemed to return from trips with way more than I left with.

Sweaty and out of breath, I shoved my suitcase to the side, opened the three locks, and shoved the flimsy door open. Stale, dusty air was the only thing to greet me. I stood by the entrance for a moment. After drying my face with the collar of my shirt, I looked around the one-room studio. A twin bed in one corner, a burgundy futon in another, and a kitchenette between the other two corners. A right past my bed led to the world's tiniest bathroom. When no critters scampered across the cracked linoleum floor, I walked the surfboard over and propped it by the shelving unit housing my hodgepodge collection of movie memorabilia. Well, it wasn't mine anymore. I gave the collection a long, appreciative look while contemplating how to pack it all up to ship to Mr. Big Texas. The check had hit my account last night, giving me two days to send my part of the bargain on its way. The decision to sell hadn't come easily. Looking around this small studio apartment, I realized my memorabilia backdrop was the only personal thing in the space.

I studied the shelves, spotting the one thing I'd swiped that wouldn't be included in the sale. I picked up the Crisco can and peeled open the dusty lid, releasing the faint scent of paper money and grease. Two objects remained inside, a one-dollar bill and the magnet my dad had used to add weight to the can. I replaced the lid, deciding I would return it soon to its rightful owner.

• • •

Life after leaving the vivid setting of Indigo Isle was bleak. No job. No family. No word from Hudson. Just bleak. As bleak as my dingy beige walls. I waded through the next two days, going through my belongings, tossing a good bit of them. The hardest part was packing the movie memorabilia, but it had to be done. I rolled each piece in bubble wrap and then nestled it inside one of the three boxes that it would take to ship it all.

After returning from the post office—it took more time to get there than to actually mail the boxes—I plopped onto the futon and a spring poked me in protest. Scooting over a bit to avoid it, I opened my laptop to work on my résumé. So far, my queries to a few studios had been met with silence, just as I had feared.

After a couple weeks, when I had begun to settle into the idea of walking away from Hollywood for good, I received a call requesting a meeting with the HR representatives from Ewol Entertainment. Turned out, they wanted my statement on Whit Kessler's misconduct.

With nothing to lose, I gave it, and within days a big blowup happened in the production company. The ball rolled rather quickly after that. Not surprising, considering everything had a way of happening faster in the entertainment industry than anywhere else. Whit was fired, while I and three other women who'd been harassed by him were offered substantial settlements. I felt weird about taking the money at first, but then I changed my mind. If a crime is committed, the criminal should pay for it in some way. So many victims didn't get any type of compensation. Thankful for myself and the others in this case, I decided to keep the money with the plans of giving it to my mother for what I stole from her and my father. I was also a criminal with a debt to pay off.

With nothing standing in my way, I started wrapping things up so I could return to South Carolina permanently, whether my family welcomed me or not. The only time I slowed was to check my emails once a day. Of course, each day produced only disappointment, but then I received one that made my insides twist.

It took a while to work up enough nerve to click on the email from Ewol Entertainment. I opened it, finding a request from Jocelyn Richards to schedule a meeting with her. She was the new owner—and Whit's sister. I owed nothing to the company, and certainly not to someone I'd never met, but curiosity had always been a weak part of my character.

Two days later, I walked into a place I'd hoped to never lay eyes on again. An unfamiliar face greeted me at the reception area.

"I'm Kim, Jocelyn's assistant," she introduced herself after I told her my name. "Nice shirt."

"Thanks." I touched the collar of the blue linen shirt I'd never returned to Hudson. Today I'd paired it with leggings. If I had to go into an uncomfortable meeting, at least I'd be comfortably dressed.

Kim led me to Jocelyn's office, which used to be Whit's, and that was enough to make my skin itch underneath the comfortable shirt.

"Come on in," Jocelyn called out as soon as Kim knocked on the frosted glass door. I'd always hated the industrial vibe of the studio offices. The atmosphere felt cold and impersonal.

With a phone to her ear, Jocelyn held up a finger and then pointed it at a black leather chair in front of her glass-topped desk. I sat down and waited.

"Just handle it." Without saying goodbye, Jocelyn hung up the phone and sat back in her chair. "Thank you for agreeing to meet with me, Sonny. I don't believe we've met before." She resembled her brother quite a bit, but it seemed she'd invested in high-end hair color treatments to keep the silver out of her black bobbed hair.

"Only in passing." I remembered seeing her at a few events in the past, but I'd never actually spoken with her.

"As of last week, I'm the sole owner of Ewol Entertainment. I allowed the debt Whit owed from the settlement to be his buy-out. Before now I've been a silent partner." She leaned forward and rested her forearms on the desk. "I want you to understand I had no idea how he was treating you and the others. I'm ashamed for not knowing. For that I am truly sorry. I know no amount of money can make that right."

"Thank you." Thinking that was the gist of it, I began to rise.

"Wait. I also asked you here today—well, to beg you to not walk. Please consider staying on. You're good at what you do. The best, I've been told."

I glanced out the windows at the high-rise view of nothing but the cement and steel of the hard-edged city beyond. Not even the sun seemed to want to shine on it. "I'm getting out of LA, so I'm not sure it'll be possible to continue working with you. And to be honest, I never enjoyed location management. Whit sort of pushed me into that role."

Jocelyn grimaced. "I promise I'll never force you to do anything. The production assistants said I wouldn't find anyone better than you for location scouting. Would you consider keeping that role?"

I sat up straighter, willing my newfound backbone to remain sturdy. "I've always loved that part. I plan on looking into continuing that, but independently, with some smaller production groups in the southeastern region."

"Sonny, I could really use your help on the New Orleans project. You've already done a lot of preliminary legwork. Won't you consider staying on for this one at least?"

"I don't know. I need some time off."

"We've pushed it back until the beginning of the year, so you'd have a month or two off before getting the rest of the locations secured. Will that give you enough of a break?"

This woman was a tough cookie, not taking no for an answer.

"Tell you what. You do this favor for me and I'll be a reference for your résumé." She smiled just then, and a memory of that exact smile on a masculine face flashed through my mind, repulsing me.

My jaw tightened, but I managed to push my words out. "I've been forced to do enough things with strings attached. If that's the only way you'll give me a positive reference, then no thank—"

"Wait!" Jocelyn rose to her feet as I did, cutting me off. "Wow, that made me sound just like my brother. Sonny, I am so sorry. That wasn't my intention." She shook her head and smoothed the front of her charcoal suit jacket. "Look, you'll have the reference in your in-box by the end of the day. Take a week or so to think about finishing the New Orleans project. If your answer is no, then I'll respect that and you'll never hear from me again. Promise."

Still uncertain but ready to bolt, I picked up my bag from beside the chair.

"You women went through enough. Again, I apologize for that."

It was like my jaw finally sealed with a layer of cement, clinching it to the point of pain. *You women.* I hated that I'd been labeled as a sexual assault victim. It ranked up there pretty high as one of the main reasons I wanted out of LA. I didn't want this to be my perpetual badge to wear. I wanted to move on, so I knew this would be the last time I ever walked into this building.

"Like I said, just think about it," Jocelyn spoke as I reached the door. "Take all the time you need." That was sweet of her to say, but this was the entertainment industry, so I knew better. Say one thing, mean another.

I left her office, promising to be in touch in a few weeks at most. The answer would be no.

Later that night, I checked my emails, finding a glowing reference from Jocelyn. Deciding to sever all ties with Ewol Entertainment, I deleted it. As I moved the mouse to exit, another email hit my in-box. I had to read the address twice to make sure I'd seen it correctly. Les Morgan.

Bates,

When I think about what happened to you, I can't help but think about my own daughter and how I'd want to kill the man who dared to lay a finger on her. I'm sorry Whit got away with this for so long. You've been good to Lyrica, and don't think I take that lightly. She needed a female role model and I'm glad she now has you. For what it's worth, I'm proud of you for standing up to that scumbag at our meeting

I'm not sure what your plans are, moving forward with your career, but know I'll always have a spot on my production team for you. Just say the word.

Les

I reread the email several times, actually touched by him taking the time to reach out to me like this. It also made me realize that I didn't have to associate myself with the production company but could reference the numerous directors I'd worked with over the years. Most people paid attention to director names and not the production company anyway. I pulled up my résumé and got to work, adding my employment history. I had plenty of experience to speak for me without having to rely on favors from anyone. I had talent all on my own. Les wouldn't have offered me a job if that hadn't been the case. For the first time since I'd left that last production meeting back on Moise Island, I felt like I had a chance to get back on my feet by my own strength alone. Dang, that felt good. Felt honest and respectful too.

Putting that to the side for the time being, I shifted my main priority to preparing to make my LA exodus. ASAP. Fifteen years of my life only took a few days to pack up. How was that even possible? Sure, it made the task easy, yet it showed just how insignificant I had been in this world. I had no job or home, but as I handed the keys to my landlord, I felt a sense of finally finding my way. The right way.

CHAPTER TWENTY-FIVE

Roller coasters never bothered me much, nor did the curvy terrain of the mountains. So it made no sense that the flat road of Highway 17 was doing such a number on me. The return trip to Georgetown was nauseating at best, so I made sure to breathe through my mouth as I crossed into the smelly city.

I'd traveled down a lot of memories and regrets in the past month, realizing my running away had been fueled by childishness, pigheadedness, selfishness, and pettiness. Honestly, I'd figured that part out a long time ago, about the same time the stolen money ran out, but pride kept me rooted in those mistakes. Too proud to crawl home with my tail tucked between my legs. So even though this would be the most difficult trip I'd ever made, I allowed myself no other choice but to face it head-on. No more running.

I barely slowed when the tires hit the gravel driveway and kept moving forward until the yellow house on stilts came into view around that last bend. I parked my newly purchased Chevy Blazer beside a Chevy Tahoe and couldn't help but smile at seeing some traditions still held.

Gathering my wits, I got out of the SUV and made my way up the porch steps. A fall wreath decorated the cedar door, which seemed a little early to me since it was only late September. It felt strange to knock, but until I knew for certain I'd be welcomed, I decided to play it safe.

Moments later, the door opened and there stood a gray-headed woman with a severe scowl on her face. Her blue eyes widened slightly with recognition.

I squinted, trying to refocus this image to make it match the strawberry-blonde girl I remembered. Sure, she was close to fifty, but she'd aged beyond that. Like something had sucked the life out of her. "Caroline?"

"Yes, Sonny." Her reply held enough chill to trigger a first frost, even though we were still a ways off from that. On a tired sigh, she asked, "What do you want?"

I wanted to apologize. To beg for forgiveness. To be accepted. "May I speak with Mama?"

Her face hardened even more. "She's no longer here."

"Oh no, no, no . . . I'm too late." The world started spinning violently. I held on to the porch railing and pressed a palm to my stomach. "Wh-when did she pass away?"

Caroline checked her watch and laughed coldly. "Not even a full minute and you've already brought out the theatrics."

My head swam as I started hyperventilating. "What are you talking about?"

Caroline huffed, making no move to invite me inside. She had to see I was close to collapsing. "Calm down, Sonny. Mama's not dead."

My face heated. "But you said—"

"I meant she doesn't live here." Caroline sucked her teeth. "For crying out loud, you are such a dra—"

"Where is she, Caroline?" I demanded. My sister's appearance might have changed, but her bitterness toward me was as strong as ever.

Her glare connected with mine. "I think you've caused enough damage. It's best you leave her alone."

"Where?"

"In an assisted-living facility."

I balked. "You put our mother in a nursing home and then moved into her house?"

"You don't even know what you're talking about. And you have no right. After you ran away and Dad died, Mama fell apart. I had no other choice but to move in here and take care of her."

"So when did you stick her in a home?"

"You're not owed an explanation. Now, my youngest will be home from school soon. I want you gone before he gets here." She jabbed a finger toward my vehicle. "Leave."

I forced myself to see through her vinegar, to focus on the hurt and sadness etched along the deep lines around her mouth and forehead. My older sister had made sacrifices and I made nothing but selfish mistakes.

Respecting her wishes, I left without saying another word for fear I'd speak them in anger, which would only be added to my long list of regrets. I was sick of that list.

I checked the time and decided to try a different approach with Aubrey. Coming to a stop at the end of the driveway, I put the Blazer in park and sent her a text.

I'm in town. Can I see you?

I sat tight for a few minutes, but when no response came through, I placed the phone in the cup holder and drove on. Heaven forbid Caroline come along and catch me lingering in *her* driveway. Antsy, I drove back to town and checked the phone at the first red light.

Give me two hours to get home. Aubrey included her address.

With two hours to kill and unable to locate one parent, I made the uneasy decision to go visit the one I knew where to find. The brick church had no vehicles in the parking lot, so at least I had the small graveyard off to the side all to myself.

I exited the SUV and began meandering around the gravestones, reading names until finding Bates. A simple granite stone. Square-shaped, with my father's name and dates of birth and death below it. I plucked a few weeds so I could read the Bible verse inscribed along the bottom.

I will search for my lost ones who strayed away, and I will bring them safely home again.

EZEKIEL 34:16

Flabbergasted and covered in goose bumps, I fell flat on my bottom and stared at that verse through a veil of tears. Ever since that last night at Erlene's motel, each of my days had started by reciting this verse with each night concluding in the same manner.

"I strayed. I'm so sorry, Daddy. So sorry." Voice cracking, I cleared my throat. "But I'm home now. God brought me home."

Underneath the shade of giant oak trees dressed heavily in Spanish moss, I settled in to have a good long chat. I said all the things I should have said a long time ago when I'd had a chance.

I thanked him for being a darn good father. I told him how much I loved him.

By the time I left the graveyard, exhaustion had set in, but going back to the hotel to crash couldn't happen just yet. I had more to face before that. I headed over to Aubrey's house on Front Street to get the answers Caroline had denied me.

I parked at the curb and craned my neck to check out the house through the windshield. A two-story colonial with white siding and a wraparound porch, the Sampit River peeking from the sides. It gave me a sense of pride and relief that my sister had done well. I gathered my phone and the little bit of courage I had in reserves and started toward the house.

Aubrey opened the door before I even knocked and actually invited me in, albeit hesitantly. After a stiff side hug, she offered me a glass of lemonade. We took our drinks outside and sat on her back porch that had a gorgeous view of the wharf.

"You have a lovely home," I commented, hoping to ease out from underneath some of the awkwardness.

"Thank you. It's been in my husband's family since the early 1800s. We just finished restoring it last year."

"It's lovely," I repeated and then cleared my throat, but the lump seemed to be growing, making it hard to speak. "I know I don't deserve to know, but would you please tell me where Mama is and what's going on with her?"

Aubrey tucked her shoulder-length blonde hair behind her ear. Sure, she'd aged some, but she'd done it much more gracefully than Caroline. "Mama was diagnosed with macular degeneration about three years ago."

"What's that?"

"She's slowly losing her eyesight. At first it was only in one eye, but now it's both."

"That's why Caroline put her in a nursing home?"

"No. That was Mama's doings. She took care of it without telling me or Caroline. And don't think for a minute that didn't devastate Caroline. Our sister has dedicated most of her adult life to caring for Mama." Aubrey took a sip of lemonade, and when she spoke again, her tone had lost its edge. "And you can rest easy. Mama found a pretty unique place to live. It used to be a resort and spa near the coast. It was close to completion when the recession hit and investors backed out. The company ended up filing for bankruptcy and the resort sat abandoned for seven years until a restoration company came in and renovated it, turning the vacation resort into an assisted-living resort."

"Humph. That's pretty cool."

"Yeah. When we took the tour before Mama moved in, the director gave us the history spiel. That restoration company travels all over the place, looking for ghost towns and abandoned buildings to renovate."

That was quite interesting and something I'd want to know more about, but that was for another day. Today I needed to find my mother. "So where exactly is the resort located?"

"The Palms Estate is just north of Awendaw. You remember where that's at?"

My heart kicked hard against my ribs. My mother had only been about fifteen minutes from me all summer. "Yeah. Near Sewee Outpost."

"Yes." Aubrey finished off her lemonade, the ice clinking against the glass. "So our mother basically lives in a resort. She even has her own apartment." Aubrey snickered. "And don't get me started on her social calendar. She's requested we only visit on Sundays or Mondays because those are her slow days. That woman has a more active social life than even you."

I was in the middle of rolling my neck to release some tension. Halting, I looked over and found Aubrey smirking at me. I'd forgotten for a moment that she kept up with me via social media.

"I saw your last video." Aubrey gave me a sad smile. "That was so brave."

"I've made such a mess. I need to fix things with Mama. With you and Caroline."

"Grandma Bates used to have this saying. 'Some things ain't fixable, so it's best to let that mess go.'"

"I still want to try. Please go with me to see Mama today."

"I would, but . . ." Aubrey blew out a sigh. "It's Tuesday, which is afternoon pool aerobics followed by taco night and karaoke."

We both laughed and it felt so good.

"We can go tomorrow morning. She'll have an opening in her schedule around ten. That work for you?" Aubrey rose from her chair.

I stood too and nodded. "Okay, but it's mighty tempting to go spy on her during karaoke tonight."

"Girl, she still has it too." Aubrey winked, looking so much like Mama that I didn't think before reaching in for a real hug. She pulled back and seemed uncomfortable again. "I'd invite you to stay here, but—"

"That's okay. I've already booked a hotel room. Thanks, though." What I was thanking her for, I hadn't a clue. "And I don't want to bother you, so I can go by myself tomorrow."

"No. I want to go." She tipped her head quickly, up and down. One part of me wanted to tell her I'd be fine on my own and didn't need her. But another part of me pointed out that that other part of me had a tendency of being wrong.

"Okay. I'd like that." I followed her inside to put away my glass and to head out.

The day hadn't gone exactly how I'd hoped, but I'd gone into it with my expectations too high. I hadn't run away for a day, but for fifteen years, so the split that needed mending would take several rounds to close back up. I'd just have to remember that going into tomorrow.

CHAPTER TWENTY-SIX

ONE OF THE MOST IMPORTANT TALENTS to have as a location scout is the ability to take words on a page and find those words in three-dimensional forms somewhere in the world. So when my sisters said my mother was living in an assisted-living resort, I expected to find a high-end hospital vibe with geriatric folks mostly in wheelchairs with aides helping to keep the drool cleaned off their chins.

As I followed Aubrey inside the airy clubhouse at the Palms Estate, I had to admit my imagination had gotten it completely wrong.

"This place is breathtaking," I mumbled, trying to take in the tranquil space all at once. With rich woodwork, lush tropical plants, and giant ceiling fans with bamboo woven blades rotating languidly overhead from the vaulted ceilings, it looked like it had bloomed from a tropical island.

"Yeah. It's a secret paradise in the middle of the Lowcountry." Aubrey motioned for me to take a left down a breezy hallway that led us into a community room. Some were playing card games, some watching a movie on a gigantic flat screen, while others were stretched out on plush chaise lounges with books or electronic devices in hand.

My eyes swept the room, looking for any sign of Mama, skipping from one woman to another. Finally one sitting in a rocking chair by the wall of windows caught my attention. Her hair and posture seemed familiar, yet she was a good bit thinner than the last time I'd seen my mother. Her frailness shouldn't have caught me so off guard, but it did.

I moved toward her slowly on numb legs, my nose and eyes beginning to sting.

Aubrey caught my arm. "Where are you going?"

"Mama," I explained, but my sister began pulling me inside an art room with easels set up, about a dozen in total, and each one had an elderly person sitting behind it, painting away.

I hovered by the door while Aubrey pointed to a woman with red hair that had pink undertones. Pixie cut and styled in a pompadour. Even in the paint-stained smock I could tell she was thinner than I remembered, but in a healthy way. Nothing frail about this one.

"No. Way."

Aubrey grinned. "Yes. Way."

"When did our mother get cool?"

"Guess she has always been cool, just started letting it show once she moved in here." Aubrey giggled. "Caroline 'bout had a duck on our first visit. We moved Mama in with long gray hair and found her as a brunette the next time. There's a cosmetology school nearby and the students come out and practice on the residents. Mama is one of their favorites. She says it's just hair and lets them do whatever they please."

"Dang. She's a rock star." I chewed my lip, watching her move the paintbrush over her canvas. "Can Mama see to paint?"

"She still has her peripheral vision. Watch how she looks at the canvas sideways. It's not easy, but she calls herself an abstract artist."

I studied the canvas. It was covered with layers of colors in no apparent pattern, yet they formed an interesting work of art. The Mama from my childhood never seemed interested in arts and crafts, or perhaps she never had time back then. "An abstract artist. Who is this woman?"

"Oh, she's a hoot. How about I introduce you to her?" Aubrey motioned for me to go over to our mother, but a sudden case of nerves hit. Palms sweating and heart racing, I couldn't move.

Sensing this, Aubrey squeezed my shoulder before walking over and placing a kiss on our mother's bronzed cheek. "Hey, Mama."

"Hey, sweetie. This is a surprise." Mama's Southern drawl sounded like home.

"I have a special guest with me today." Aubrey looked up and winked at me.

I shuffled forward and whispered, "Hi, Mama."

Mama gasped, whirling in my direction as her paintbrush hit the floor. She reached for me and wrapped her arms around me so fiercely it had me gasping too.

From an awkward stoop, I went to my knees and returned her embrace.

Mama rained kisses on one cheek while patting the other. "My baby has come home. My baby . . ." She quietly wept and I joined in, unable to say anything at all.

Right in the middle of this art studio, we didn't rush our reunion. After my sisters' cold reception, Mama's was pure sunshine, and I wanted to bask in the unexpected comfort for as long as I could, no cares to give that we had an audience.

"Y'all want to take a walk?" Aubrey asked eventually.

Reluctantly I let go to stand up and Mama started laughing. "Oh, Sonny girl, I got paint all over you! I'm sorry!"

I looked down and saw smudges of reds and purples on the front of my white T-shirt. "It's now my favorite shirt."

Mama grinned, pleased by my reaction. She stood nimbly, grabbed my hand, and practically pulled me along. I noticed she kept angling her head, the only indicator she had any issue with her eyesight.

It wasn't until we settled on a love seat glider outside that I realized Aubrey had disappeared, and I was grateful she'd given us some time alone. We were in a relatively secluded spot underneath the shade of two fat palmetto trees.

"Mama . . ." My voice broke. "I am so sorry. What I did to you and Daddy was so awful and disrespectful."

She wiped the tears streaking my cheeks and brushed a curl behind my ear, her touch soothing. "No need for apologies. You needed to find your way. And from what Aubrey has told me, you've done just that. I'm proud of you."

I shook my head, wishing she'd treat me more like Caroline did. My mother's compassion was harder to accept than my sister's resentment. "Please don't. Don't be kind. That's not what I deserve."

"I learned something important a long time ago about grace and mercy. Grace is God giving us what we don't deserve, and mercy is him *not* giving us what we *do* deserve." Mama dried my cheeks again. "I think we could all use a little more grace and mercy. We could also give more of both too."

I nodded, overwhelmed by how easily my mother had forgiven me. I leaned my head on her shoulder and just savored her grace and mercy for a good long while. She seemed just as content to stay right there with me, too.

I lifted my head and pushed my foot against the ground to set the glider in motion. "I'd like to be a daughter again. I think I could be better at it this time."

"You've never stopped being my daughter." She patted my knee. "Why don't we try being friends this time?"

"Friends. I think I'd like that very much." After we sat in silence for a spell, I asked, "So what should we do to kick off this friendship?"

Mama smiled, and the slyness of it raised my guard. "How about telling me about your love life?"

I laughed. "Seriously?"

Mama scoffed. "What? Friends share that sort of stuff."

I patted her arm and she caught my hand before I pulled away. I really liked holding my mother's hand, something I wouldn't have been caught doing growing up. "You're right. But there's not much to share in that department."

She lifted her shoulders nonchalantly. "Share what you have."

An image of Hudson flickered through my mind, his penetrating clear gaze, the unruly hair and beard, his indigo-stained hands as they reached for mine, his gentle kisses, his frown of disappointment. His journals, the constant book in his hands, him cooking in that cheery kitchen, his bare feet.

Before I knew it, I'd spilled the tea, as Lyrica liked to say, telling Mama all about my summer on Indigo Isle and the grumpy recluse living out there.

Mama cackled. "He called the cops on you?"

"It's not funny." Unable to stop it, I cracked a smile.

"So he lives out there all by himself?"

"Yes, ma'am." I gave her the CliffsNotes version of Hudson's life.

"Oh. That poor man. No parent should lose a child."

We grew quiet and gazed at the ocean. I thought a child shouldn't ever lose a parent either.

"I saw Dad's headstone. That Bible verse . . ."

"Ah. Ezekiel 34:16. After you left, that became our verse. Every time I started in about wanting to go get you, your father reminded me of that verse. We knew you were safe and doing well, so we figured it was best to leave you alone." Mama wore a sad yet thoughtful smile on her lips while twisting her wedding band around her finger.

"How'd you know I was safe and doing well?"

"You didn't think we'd let you take off and not find you, did you?" She patted my knee again. "We hired a private investigator. You made it fairly easy for him to find you, using your debit card and stuff. We had him follow you for about a month and then check in on you every other month after that."

Dumbfounded, I stared at the ocean waves with the sun making them glitter. "I had no idea. I wish y'all would have made me come home."

"Honey, I was married at age seventeen. Who was I to make you do anything?"

I felt close to tears again while coming to terms with what Mama had just shared about them knowing all along where I was at. That they had really cared.

Mama chuckled. "I'll never forget the first time we saw you in that cat commercial."

I dropped my head against the back of the seat and groaned. "You saw that?"

"We were so proud of you. Your father recorded it, and he showed it to everyone who came over. He'd point at the TV and say, 'That's my girl! She's famous.'"

Mama's words were such gifts and she had no idea. Had my vision been that distorted before about my parents? Perhaps the truly blind person sitting on this glider was actually me.

Aubrey appeared before I could figure out a way to apologize once again. "I don't know about y'all, but I'm hungry."

"Then let's go out to eat," Mama suggested.

We decided to drive to Mount Pleasant for a late lunch. When it was time for us to leave, I didn't want to, and I wondered aloud if I could hide out in Mama's room.

"Come back tomorrow. We still have a lot of catching up to do."

• • •

For the next few weeks, I showed up every day not wanting to leave and Mama would invite me to return the next day. We fell into a routine of getting to know each other again, and I discovered that I not only loved my mother but truly liked her as well. It made me realize how idiotic I had been to give myself that self-imposed sentence of staying away.

Mama might have been open-armed, but my sisters remained standoffish, so I decided to move back into Creek View Inn with Erlene. That way I was close to Mama and could give my sisters some space to adjust to my return.

I showed up with a case of mini Coke cans and asked Erlene if she rented rooms by the month. She shuffled over and hugged me. "Honey, for you, I'd rent by the year." That little old lady's hug told me I had landed in the spot where I was meant to land.

I helped out around the motel where I could, and I even started going to church services with Erlene. I had a long way to go, but for the first time I knew I was on the right track.

There was still the matter of paying my debt, and I figured that needed to be squared away with Caroline. Swallowing another measure of humble pie, I made a trip out to see her, making sure to knock again. And again, she didn't invite me inside the very house I'd been raised in. I wondered if she'd thrown out all my childhood belongings. That possibility seemed pretty likely.

"You handle Mama's finances, right?" I asked Caroline, getting straight to the point.

She crossed her arms. "Why? You scoping out who to rob this time?"

Holding back my own dose of bitter, I shook my head. "No. I need to know who to fill the check out to."

"We don't need your money." Caroline's back straightened as she lifted her nose slightly, casting her eyes downward at me. "We've been perfectly fine without you."

"You realize that's the same attitude I took when I ran off." I swatted the space between us, the tension carving out a chasm. "It did nothing but land me in a world of hurt. I owe Mama the money I stole from her and Dad. I need to pay off my debt to her." I spun around and started down the steps. "You know what? Never mind."

My sister did nothing to stop me. No surprise there.

I loaded up and went straight out to the Palms Estate to speak with someone in the billing department. They happily accepted my check to cover my mother's stay for the next year. The sum went way beyond the money I owed, but I didn't care. It felt good to give this secret gift to my mother.

With that burden gone and a slight giddiness at doing something sneaky but with good intentions, I looked for Mama, finding her by the pool. Even though we'd come to the end of October, the temperatures remained in the mideighties.

"I never pictured you as a beach bum." I plopped onto the lounge chair beside hers. "Looks good on you though."

Mama reached her hand out and gave my wrist a squeeze. "Hey, sweetheart. This is a lovely surprise."

"I know it's not your desired visitation day, but I just couldn't stay away." That had become our little joke, because I showed up every day and it certainly didn't surprise her anymore. I stretched out and closed my eyes, releasing a satisfied sigh. "You think I could secure a room here?"

Mama laughed. "In about thirty more years."

I pouted my lips. "But I'm ready to be in this assisted living now."

She laughed again. "You should be spending time with your boyfriend and sisters, not with a bunch of old folks."

"Ah, see, there's a few issues with that. For one, I don't have a boyfriend. And Caroline would much rather toss me in the swamp. She hates me."

Mama reached over again, taking my hand this time. "Caroline is a hard nut to crack. Don't give up on her. She probably thinks she's defending my honor with that attitude she's giving you. Promise me you'll give her time."

"Yes, ma'am." I agreed, but it looked doubtful either of my sisters would ever come around to the idea of a relationship with me. I didn't blame them one bit.

"And as for not having a boyfriend—" Mama tsked—"I think you need to take your butt on down the road a little ways more and go see your non-boyfriend."

I huffed, feeling frustrated over that stubborn man. "I put the ball in his court before I left." Nearly three months later, I guessed he still wasn't ready and might never be.

"Do you love him?"

My reply took no thought. "With my entire heart."

"Perhaps he needs more time, like your sisters. Don't give up on him either."

"I'll try not to."

Hudson let me go that night, but I could still feel him days, weeks, months afterwards. As if a part of his soul had entwined with mine. It scared me, not wanting that part of us to ever untangle. Scarier still was the small voice telling me, *He let you go regardless.*

CHAPTER TWENTY-SEVEN

CHRISTMAS SHOWED UP OUT OF NOWHERE. Leading up to it, I continued growing closer with my mother while my sisters kept their distance. Sure, they were both cordial when we met up to spend time together with Mama, but I knew it was out of duty more than anything else. Because of this, Mama struck up a plan on how I could work on getting into their good graces. She helped me buy gifts for them as well as their families. Of course, I didn't know anyone well enough to buy for, so I was glad to have her guidance with personalizing the presents.

With three sacks full of neatly wrapped gifts, I joined my family on Christmas Eve at Aubrey's house. The place was gorgeously dressed in evergreen garlands, deep-red and gold ornaments, and glowing twinkle lights on every surface. The sizzling logs in the fireplace added to the ambience of holiday cheer.

After placing my offerings by the giant twenty-foot tree and taking a deep inhale of its woodsy aroma, I moved around the room, taking time to speak to each individual. It was odd how this was my family yet it felt like I was amongst strangers. Only one way to fix that, I supposed.

I approached Caroline's husband, Beau, and their oldest son, Charlie, first, asking Beau how the banking world was going—it wasn't—and then I asked Charlie about graduate school. I found that all I really needed to do was ask a specific question about something going on in their lives and they opened up and spoke quite easily.

Next, I talked to Drake, Caroline's youngest son, who was a high school senior. He played baseball and had signed with Coastal Carolina on a scholarship. Then the middle child, Natalie, joined us, and I found out she was attending Coastal as well, majoring in music education. She'd gotten her musical talent from her mother and happily showed me a video of her latest performance. I was blown away and even more so when she invited me to her next one.

I spent time speaking with Paul, Aubrey's husband, who now ran my mother's seafood market. This conversation was easy. Paul was what you called a good ole boy, and so I found myself feeling welcome just from his kind nature. Paul Junior, "PJ," came in late with his new fiancée on his arm. They were late because he had just proposed before they arrived. After that, my family spent a long time congratulating the couple, who looked like true American sweethearts, both blonde and blue-eyed, with giant grins that wouldn't quit.

After feasting on the traditional dishes I remembered from my childhood—seafood dressing, barbecued turkey, succotash, homemade yeast rolls, and jelly cake—we moved into the den to exchange gifts.

Mama looped her arm around mine and whispered, "Leave your sisters' gifts for last."

"You think?"

"Yes. I think that'll make it more special." She smiled broadly.

"Okay, then."

So that's what I did. After everyone had opened their other gifts, I handed Caroline my gift for her.

She frowned at the gift wrapping as if she really didn't want to accept anything from me. After a short pause, she finally peeled the paper away and gave the gift inside a strange look before sucking her teeth. Eyes shooting up to meet mine, she held up the ABBA album and the framed lyrics to "Dancing Queen" without saying anything.

"You like it? Mama said it's your favorite song." I smiled encouragingly.

Caroline looked at our mother in shock. "Mama!"

"Don't yell at her. She told me so I could buy you something special. She even told me about your favorite lyrics. 'See that girl. Watch that scene. Digging the dancing queen.' That's why I had them highlight those lines in a different color." I pointed to the framed lyrics. All black except for the teal blue for her favorite lines.

The room grew quiet. Dread trickled down my spine. Had I messed up somehow?

First, a small snicker echoed just over the crackling pop from the fireplace. Then a cough that sounded more like a laugh. Apparently it was contagious, the muted laughs. But then a dam broke and everyone began belly laughing. Cackling, really.

"What?" I asked no one in particular.

Aubrey dropped her hand away from her mouth. "Caroline sang that song at the family night karaoke contest last year at the Palms."

"We would have won, too, if she hadn't gotten the lyrics wrong," Mama spoke up between giggles.

"Wrong?" I asked, needing clarity on what I'd accidently just done.

Mama began singing, "'See that girl. Watch her scream. Kicking the dancing queen.'"

The room splintered into raucous laughter.

"Mama!" Caroline and I yelled at the same time.

Mama shrugged. "That's what she sang."

"Now I'm scared to open this." Aubrey held up her gift.

"I'm going to go ahead and apologize to you both. I had no idea!" I placed my palms against my scalding hot cheeks.

Aubrey opened the wrapping with such caution you'd have thought it was a bomb. She didn't open it enough for anyone else to see but herself. After one glance at the book, she quickly smoothed the wrapping paper back into place.

"No way! Y'all saw mine. We get to see yours." Caroline jumped up and snatched it out of her hand. She finished unwrapping the book and held it in the air.

"What's it say?" Paul yelled over the lively chatter.

"*Ultimate Guide to DIY Plumbing*." Caroline's stern expression finally cracked as laughter broke free from her. She laughed until her eyes glassed over.

Aubrey screeched. "Mama!"

I looked around the cozy room at everyone surrounded by crumpled wrapping paper and good humor. "Someone care to explain?"

Paul chuckled. "Aubrey didn't want to wait on me to change out the sink fixture in the guest bathroom, so my impatient wife went about doing it herself and ended up flooding this entire room." He tapped his foot against the polished wood floors. "We had to replace all the flooring."

"Grandma, you had Aunt Sonny buy these gifts without telling her why?" Drake asked.

Mama smirked. "Where would be the fun in that?"

Another wave of laughter hit the room.

I didn't even care that Mama had made me the butt of a joke, unbeknownst to me. I knew this would be my first new good memory with my sisters. One that would be revisited every Christmas from here on out.

After another round of desserts and hot chocolate, Mama and I headed back to the Palms Estate.

I held my tongue until we made it out of Georgetown. "I kinda want to pinch you, but I understand what you did there. You're an evil genius."

"Nah. Just a wise ole bird." Mama batted the air. "It was good to see you and your sisters bonding."

"Funny how gag gifts got 'er done."

Mama reached over and patted my arm. She did that a lot, and it made me wonder if she worried I'd disappear again. "I think you would have managed without the gag gifts. You could have just been present tonight, but you chose to be involved, making it a point to spend time with everyone. That was brave and considerate."

My smile fell as I stared at the highway before me. "I'm not always that woman, but she's who I want to be the most."

"Then you work on that." She gave my forearm one more pat before moving her hand to her lap.

I glanced over and found her smiling with so much contentment that I wanted to discover how to pull that off too.

I drove through the gates at the Palms Estate and parked near the front entrance. I grabbed Mama's bags of gifts and leftovers, with one unopened gift tucked in another bag, and walked her inside. Opposite of Aubrey's traditional Christmas decor, this place was decked out with a tropical flair. Palm trees glowed with twinkling lights and nautical ornaments. And instead of evergreens, banisters were wrapped in seashell garlands.

"They went all out with the decorations," I commented, inclining my head to check out the fishnet hanging from the ceiling with glass ornaments in various shades of blue dangling from it.

"I helped build the snowmen." Mama pointed toward the wall of windows. Just outside, the pool area glittered underneath strings of colored lights, illuminating a trio of sand snowmen wearing sunglasses, colorful leis, and straw hats.

"Very cool." I heard Christmas carols and conversations spilling out from the community room. "Sounds like they're having a party in there."

"I'm sure."

"You want to go join in?"

"I'll stop by later." Mama headed to the right wing, where the apartments were located. "I wish you'd come back tomorrow. I hate the idea of you spending Christmas Day by yourself."

Mama and a few of her friends were getting together tomorrow. A tradition they began two years ago when one of the friends didn't have any loved ones to spend the holiday with. I didn't want to impose on that, so I made excuses. "I'll probably spend the day with Erlene so she won't be alone. She has a few guests checking in, so she'll be stuck at the motel."

"Well, my offer still stands." Mama unlocked her door and I followed her inside the apartment.

After helping to put away the leftovers Aubrey had forced on her, I sat beside Mama on the couch and handed her my gift.

"You shouldn't have," she said before opening it.

"Yes, I should. I should have done it a long time ago, actually." My admittance earned me a curious look, so I waved for her to get on with it. "Open it."

Slowly she fished the gift from the tissue paper. Her lip trembled as she held up the old Crisco can and eyed it from various angles. A tense moment passed and then she tried handing it to me. "Sonny, I don't want the money back."

"Good thing there's no money in here then." I took the can and peeled the lid off. "Hudson showed me how writing your thoughts down can be so healing. I thought maybe filling this can with thoughts I wanted to share with you . . . it could be our new thing, ya know? And well, there's your favorite Dove chocolates too, in case that's lame." I dug a foil-wrapped candy out and handed it to her.

A tear slipped from my mother's blue eyes as she smiled. "It's not lame at all. I love this idea."

"I know reading is a challenge for you, so I can read a few on my visits." I shrugged.

"Will you read a few to me now?"

I pulled a folded strip of paper out and smoothed it. "'The day my mother wrestled a gator out from underneath our house is the day I saw her as more than just a mother. I saw this strong woman who I wanted to be like one day. No fear. Just determination.'"

Mama chuckled. "That's a day I'll never forget. All I could think about was getting it away from you young'uns. Your daddy had a conniption when he found out. I reasoned with him it wasn't all that big, not even four foot." She made a face, making me laugh too. "Read another one."

"Okay." I plucked another paper from the can and unfolded it. "'My parents were strict, and I believe I broke every rule they ever made. Now I see those rules were for my own good. That they made them out of love and concern for my well-being. Wish I would have known then what I know now.'"

Mama wrapped her arm around my shoulders. "Honey, no child understands that until they're older. It's a part of growing up."

"I'm sorry for being such a handful back then."

"You kept us on our toes, that's for sure." She smoothed my hair and patted my cheek. "It kept us young."

I huffed a laugh. "If you say so."

We remained on the couch for a while longer and Mama came up with the idea of adding her own thoughts to the can for us to share on my visits.

I wished her a merry Christmas and started toward the motel. I couldn't wait to get to my room to write all about the craziness of tonight. But just as that thought entered my mind, another one formed. *I wish I could share it with Hudson.*

Patience completely gone, I couldn't stay away any longer, so I gave in and called Tom at the rental company as soon as I made it to my room. I sweet-talked him into letting me rent a boat last minute.

"I'll leave the keys in the lockbox outside the door. The code is 0806."

"Thanks so much, Tom. And merry Christmas."

"Merry Christmas."

After setting the phone down, I stared at my tiny tabletop Christmas tree with only one gift remaining beside it. The thin rectangle box held a silk tie, hand-dyed with Indigo Isle dye I'd swiped that one time I helped him pack up the indigo cakes. I ruined three ties before I managed to get one dyed evenly. The note card I placed in the box stated *I think this represents you perfectly. The dye artisan and the lawyer.* Hudson had pushed me to straighten up my life and I truly hoped he'd been busy the last several months doing the same for himself.

• • •

Once the foggy morning showed up, I had breakfast with Erlene in the motel office.

"Don't chicken out," she demanded, taking a bite of the cranberry Danish I'd picked up for us the day before.

"But . . ." Now that a new day had arrived, my bravado had begun to wane. "It's been months. He hasn't reached out once."

Erlene cackled. "When has that ever stopped you?"

I stared into my cup of coffee and cracked a smile. "I suppose you're right." I took a sip and then reached for the gift I'd brought her. "Merry Christmas."

Grinning ear to ear, Erlene opened the wrapping with the vigor of an excited child. When she saw the book, she giggled and read the title. "*Days of Our Lives 50 Years.* I love it. Where on earth did you find such?"

"You can find anything on the Internet nowadays."

She flipped through a few pages before setting it aside and handing me a gift bag. "I got you a little something, too."

I peeked inside and found enough Avon products to host my own makeup party. "Aww, Erlene. You shouldn't have!"

We spent some time going through all the goodies in my bag, trying on different cosmetics, and flipping through her book like teenagers gawking at a *Teen Beat* magazine. Best. Christmas. Morning. Ever.

Finally Erlene declared that I'd stalled long enough and practically kicked me out of her office. "Go see your friend!"

"Yes, ma'am!" I grabbed Hudson's gift and took off to the marina.

I found the same boat waiting for me that I used last summer. Smiling, I backed out of the boat slip and began the familiar trek. The bite of cold was definitely a new experience. I'd have to beg Hudson to start a fire, but he'd give in after grumbling about it, I was pretty sure. I could already picture it, but those ideas died a quick death when I coasted up to the dock and realized his boat was gone. New No Trespassing signs had been posted since summer. More than four of them now, but it didn't slow me from wandering down the trail to the homestead.

I recalled the first time I laid eyes on the giant brick home, thinking it appeared abandoned. I'd been wrong then, but this time I really did find it abandoned. The only signs of life were the chickens clucking a welcome. I walked over to them and noticed a solar heat lamp on a timer and also a bird feeder. Both indicators he wouldn't be back anytime soon.

Not giving up, I wandered around the property for a while. Maybe Hudson was spending the holiday with LuAnn and Art. I wished I'd gotten to know them better last summer. We only crossed paths that one day in the library and I passed them twice on the way to the marina, so I didn't even know exactly where they lived.

After waiting for another hour or so, I reluctantly left his gift on the porch and returned to the motel.

• • •

Days moved on with no word from Hudson. New Year's came and went, but I remained suspended, waiting for my sisters to come around and for Hudson to do the same. I was also waiting for a local production company to get back with me about a small film they wanted me to scout for them in Savannah, but there hadn't been a green light yet. All this waiting did nothing but make me restless.

The only things to keep me from going stir-crazy were my video chats with Vee and editing her debut video on my old channel. It was scheduled to upload next week and I already knew it would be a hit.

"I'll add the social media tabs and a gag reel at the end. Viewers love bloopers."

Vee's giant smile lit up the screen, showing off just how excited she was about becoming a YouTuber. "That'll be fun. I didn't even think about that."

"That's where I come in handy." Editing her video, I recognized how much I enjoyed being on this side of the camera once again.

"True, darling." Vee finger-combed the sides of her hair.

"And your talent is in front of the camera. I died laughing at that Jennifer Coolidge bit. Your impersonation of her is spot-on."

Vee puckered her lips and squinted, morphing into Coolidge. "I'm a very appealing person. Glad we had this talk."

I laughed again. "Me too."

Just as quickly as Coolidge had appeared, she was gone. "Have you heard anything from my favorite serial killer yet?"

Sighing, I leaned against the headboard and readjusted the computer on my lap. "Nothing."

Vee huffed. "I thought the silk tie would draw him out."

"So did I. I can't believe it's been five months since I've seen him." I massaged the side of my neck and looked around my motel room. It now had a mini fridge and microwave. I had also brought in my own bed linens and towels, making the tiny space much more personalized and homey. "It's probably a good thing though. Right now I need to focus on getting my act together and working on things with my family. Who needs a man, right?"

Vee's smile was small and sad, more pity than I cared for. "Don't give up. Especially on yourself." She glanced over her shoulder as a masculine voice said something.

"Is that Cade?" I craned my neck even though I knew I wouldn't be able to see past her camera angle.

"He's in town." She looked off once again before redirecting her focus on me. Her cheeks warmed to a soft shade of pink. "Think we're giving this relationship thing a real go this time."

"Aww, Vee. That's great!" I was genuinely happy for the both of them.

She grinned, showing off bright-white teeth. "He's taking me out, so I better wrap this up. We'll chat after the video goes live Wednesday, right?"

"Sounds like a plan." I waved goodbye and clicked out of the app. Moving the computer off my lap, I picked up my journal and flipped open to a new page.

Stretched out on my bed, I had just put the pen to the paper when someone began pounding on my door. Closing the journal, I went over and peeked through the crack in the curtain. There stood Caroline and Aubrey. Both had arms crossed and severe frowns dragging their faces downward.

Panicked, I yanked the door open. "Mama? She okay?"

"She is, but we're not," Caroline answered harshly.

I took a step back and they rushed inside.

"First off, why are you living in a run-down motel?" Caroline scanned the small room in disgust.

I closed the door a little too hard, frustration already making my neck stiffen, but I forced my chin up. "It's really none of your business, but I'm good friends with the owner and I like it here. Plus it's close to Mama."

"We just met Erlene. She's nice," Aubrey spoke, her voice much softer than our older sister's. "Sonny, how could you not have told us about what that producer did to you?"

I cringed, the stiffness moving to my shoulders now. "What are you talking about?"

Aubrey pulled something up on her phone and handed it over. The bold font of the headline made my stomach pitch.

Movie Producer Facing Sexual Assault Charges

Not wanting to see any more, I gave her the phone back. "I had to sign a nondisclosure."

Caroline scoffed. "What a crock. They name you in that article."

"I'm sorry if this embarrassed you in any way." I started back to the door, ready to send them on their judgy way.

"Wait!" Aubrey grabbed my arm. "That's not what we mean. You shouldn't have had to keep quiet about being assaulted. You should have told us."

I didn't want to have to discuss what happened with Whit. Just wanted it to go away as easily as dissolving my lease in LA. "This is on me. I got myself in that . . . and, well . . ."

Caroline practically growled. "I don't care if you paraded around naked, that man had no right to touch you. Wake up, Sonny!"

"Stop yelling at me! I've already been lectured enough about

327

this. I know I should have stood up to him long before now, but that's on me too." I laughed with nothing but bitterness. "Trust me, I wear regret like a dang accessory I refuse to take off." Feeling cornered, I hiked up my sagging night pants, then settled my hands on my hips while glaring at my perfect sisters.

They exchanged a look and I hated not being included in that too. I was an outsider, something else I wanted to fix but was beginning to give up on.

I slumped onto the end of the bed. Elbows braced on my knees, I cradled my head in my hands and stared down at the orange carpet. "Please . . . just leave."

No one moved and we lapsed into an uncomfortable silence.

I gathered some steam and started talking. "I've been going to church with Erlene, something I haven't done since I left home. Last Sunday's message was about the Israelites roaming in the wilderness for forty years because they kept turning away from God." I sat up and rubbed my eyes as Aubrey sat beside me and Caroline took a seat at the small table in front of us. "That's all I did from the moment I turned away from y'all and ran away. Roaming, trying to find my own path, but all I managed was to get more lost. Crazy part about that, just like the Israelites, all I had to do was simply turn back. I just wish it hadn't taken me over fifteen years to figure that out. I wish you two would forgive me. I'm so sorry."

Caroline sniffed and then cleared her throat. "I owe you an apology too." She glanced toward the ceiling and blinked several times. "I told Mama and Aubrey I'd call you on the way to the hospital with Dad, but I didn't."

Aubrey grew still beside me, both of us eyeing our oldest sister.

I wasn't so sure I wanted to hear this apology, but she took a deep breath and finished telling it anyway.

"I was so mad at you, Sonny. And so scared about losing Dad." She paused. "You said your accessory is regret. Mine is spite. I didn't think you deserved to be called. He held on for four days before passing away. I shouldn't have taken the choice to come home to say goodbye to him away from you." Her tears finally bubbled over and spilled down her narrow cheeks.

Her confession hurt worse than anything I'd endured at the hands of Whit Kessler. Seemed all three of us were walking around with limps we'd inflicted on each other. In too much pain, we just sat in it for a while. If I wanted forgiveness, I'd have to grant it to Caroline also.

Aubrey sniffled beside me. "My accessory is jealousy."

I gave her a sidelong glance, scared to death where her confession might lead.

She licked her lips and said quietly, "I didn't want a baby sister. I liked being the baby. And then you just showed up and stole not only that but also all the attention. It was *Sonny this* and *Sonny that*. Shoot, Caroline and I were named after great-aunts who were spinsters, but you got the cool name. The one that really meant something to Mama and Daddy. Then you took off to Hollywood." She sniffed a small laugh. "You should have heard how our parents bragged, but I thought you didn't deserve it. You ran away but they never seemed to remember that part. I've spent all my life being jealous of you. I apologize for that."

Realizing just how much my own sisters had despised me sent rivulets of pain throughout my entire body. Had I not known these were symptoms of grief, I would have thought I was coming down with the flu.

Caroline sighed. "We didn't come here for this, but I guess it needed airing."

The thickness in my throat blocked any reply, so I simply nodded in agreement.

"Now back to why we're here. Whit Kessler needs to get what's coming to him." Caroline crossed her arms, looking as hostile as she did that day I showed up on her porch.

"Whit lost his job and had to pay the victims a settlement. Apparently someone else has come forward and is pressing charges. That's getting what's coming to him." I scrubbed my hands down my face and blew out a long breath. "I just want to put that in my past. I want to fix things with y'all and Mama. I want to live an honest life so that I can rest when I lay my head down at night." My vision blurred as tears formed. "Because I'm just so tired." I hunched over.

Before I knew what was happening, Caroline shoved out of the chair and moved to sit on the other side of me. She wrapped her arms around me. "I'm so blame mad. Mad that someone hurt you. Mad that you didn't think you could come to us about it." Her embrace tightened, reminding me a lot of Mama's hugs.

We spent the rest of the day hunkered down in my small room. Moving forward, the three of us agreed to keep communication open and honest, even when it hurt.

The reconciliation was as painful as I had expected, but with the facade finally torn down and all the ugly truths exposed, my family and I began the long arduous task of mending our relationship.

CHAPTER TWENTY-EIGHT

I MIGHT HAVE LOST A LOT IN THE PAST YEAR, but at least work found me. It took nearly six months, but it finally happened, and I already had a year's worth of film projects lined up. My résumé did the selling for me. Not my connections nor my body. For the first time, I could be proud of my work with no shame.

My first project took me to one of my most favorite places in the States: Savannah, Georgia. Rich in history, folklore, and gorgeous landscaping, Savannah became the star in any film graced with its appearance. A serious feast for all the senses, much like Charleston, so I easily felt at home in the sister city.

After a day with a city representative of setting up a shoot schedule in Forsyth Park, all I wanted was a fat piece of pizza from Vinnie Van Go-Go's. I grabbed a slice of pepperoni and chose a spot outside to eat and people-watch. I took my time and then walked back to the Marshall House. It's one of the things I loved most about this city: basically everything was in walking distance. I also loved how most places were rumored to be haunted, such as my hotel.

I pushed through the front entrance, the cool air of the reception area greeting me like an old friend. Gorgeous black-and-white checked marble floors and cheery yellow walls. The set of blue couches in the sitting area off to the left of the staircase made me think of a certain man who had a fondness for the deep shade.

"Miss Bates," someone called out from my right.

I turned to see the young blonde at the reception desk waving at me. "Yes?"

"You have a package, ma'am."

Ma'am. Sure, it was a Southern thing to call even two-year-olds ma'am, but it still seemed a bit jarring when the term was directed toward me.

I accepted the rectangular gift box she held out. No tag or card. "Who left this?"

"A man."

Well, that narrowed it down.

I glanced from the box to her. "Was he . . . ? Did he look like a creeper?"

She laughed. "Not sure what that looks like, but this man looked more like a Tom Ford model."

"Oh. Okay. Thanks."

I waited until I made it to my room before opening the box. Nestled inside a bed of tissue paper was a slim book. The hand-dyed cloth cover in swirling indigo gave it away.

"Hudson," I whispered on a sigh, gliding my fingertips over the silky material. I cracked open the journal, finding the first page dated back to last June. The month I arrived in Charleston.

I picked up the phone on the nightstand and dialed the front desk. When the receptionist answered, I said, "This is Sonny Bates.

Can you tell me if the man who left me that package is staying here at the hotel?"

She hesitated. "I'm not supposed to say one way or the other, but no. He didn't check in."

"About what time did he drop off the gift?"

"Umm . . . about an hour ago."

"Okay. Thank you." I hung up the phone and frowned at Hudson's journal. With no way of tracking him down, I decided to stay put and read what he had to tell me.

The first entry made me laugh.

I had this rash once. It drove me crazy and I scratched at it until my skin was raw. Sonny reminds me of that rash. It's been six days. She still won't go away, but just like that rash, I'm starting to get used to the irritation.

I skimmed through several entries, pausing on poignant lines such as the one after the Fourth of July.

I didn't want to live until she showed up and all but opened a vein and poured life back into me.

Next, I reread the entry after the tropical storm at least three times.

I'm used to weathering storms alone. Been doing it most of my life. Of course Sonny showed up during one, and I'm not talking about the tropical storm. Elsie's death will never get easier. I break each year on the anniversary, but this year

Sonny was there to help me weather it. Yeah, I broke, but she managed to hold me together. She walks around with this way of looking so small and weak, but she's only playing a role of frail. That woman is a force of strength. It makes me want to be stronger.

I placed the journal in my lap and pondered his view of me, wondering if he had seen the real me. The me that I couldn't see when looking in the mirror. I liked his vision much better than mine, that's for sure.

Picking up the book, I turned the page and continued reading, stopping on the night shoot blowup. It was unnerving to read about that awful night from his perspective.

I've never wanted to pick someone up, sling them over my shoulder, and run off with them so badly as I wanted to tonight. Sonny doesn't belong where she's at. It's like watching a timid animal sitting in a cage, not realizing the trapdoor is open. All she has to do is walk away, yet she won't do it.

We blew up at each other. Probably said some things we shouldn't have, but I don't want to baby her. I want to push her to stand up for herself. That's all. Well, that and I want her to be safe. Being around that snake isn't safe. She knows it. I know it. By the looks of it, others on that set knew it too.

The next entry was dated September.

Sonny was right. By not forgiving myself, I've held Reece in a cruel limbo of guilt as well. I went to see her and saw the proof for myself. We spent the day forgiving ourselves

*and each other. Missing Elsie will always have me limping
slightly, but now that I've made peace with Reece, I can
stand straighter.*

Hudson leaving the island like that was a huge step for him
and I was so proud of him for making it. I soaked in his words for
hours until my eyes grew too heavy to continue. I drifted off to
sleep, replaying the one line that had been repeated several times.
I miss Sonny.

• • •

On my final day of scouting before returning home to Charleston,
I sent an email to the production assistant with potential dates
for filming and attached the collection of photos that I thought
showed the best spots. Wrapping that up, I headed out to meet
with a local security company to see about hiring them for the
shoot. Thankfully, that didn't take too long, so I had most of the
day free. Even though it was late February, spring seemed to have
already shown up on a warm breeze. I returned to the hotel to drop
off my laptop and to switch out my sweater for a T-shirt so I could
go spend the afternoon playing tourist.

I entered the hotel lobby and my eyes landed on someone in
the sitting area. Coming to an instant stop, I watched as a man
impeccably dressed in a designer suit rose from one of the blue
couches and began walking toward me. I barely recognized him.
Short hair styled away from his face, much darker than before. A
neatly trimmed beard, so short that it left his scarred neck exposed.
He was stunning, but all that paled in comparison to his confident
posture. The man had presence, with no shadows in sight.

I waited until he stood only inches in front of me. "Well, it's about time."

"Sorry I'm late." Oh, that deep raspy voice did something to my heart, making the pace quicken. "Had some things to take care of, which took longer than I'd anticipated."

"Nice tie."

Hudson smoothed his hand over it. "A thief gave it to me."

My lip twitched. Of course he knew I took the dye. Before I could figure out how to tease him, a tour group came piling into the reception area. My instinct kicked in, thinking about the other version of Hudson, the one who liked to hide from others. I grabbed his hand and started up the staircase. "My room has a balcony. Let's go."

We settled in rocking chairs overlooking the street below. Gorgeous hanging planters dripped with flowers and greenery, giving the balcony ample shade and a sense of privacy. The chairs creaked against the wood decking as we listened to a horse-drawn carriage trot by. For the life of me, I couldn't figure out how to begin this long overdue conversation.

I looked at Hudson out the corner of my eye, still reeling over the drastic change he'd made to his appearance, sitting there in a fine suit. He'd even allowed me to sit to his left, so I had a good view of the scar on his neck. I wondered if this was what took longer than he had anticipated, finding the confidence to stop hiding.

"I'm trying not to stare," I admitted when Hudson caught me looking.

"You can stare, Sonny." He angled in his chair to face me more.

"But you don't like being looked at."

The corners of his mouth lifted slightly, gracing me with a faint smile. "By you I do."

I shook my head, hardly believing my eyes. "This is a pretty drastic change. How'd you go from a recluse to . . . this?" I flicked my wrist toward him and his display of confidence.

"After you called me out that night, I didn't have much choice." Hudson loosened the indigo tie and slipped it from around his neck, hanging it on the back of the chair with his jacket. "I sulked for a few days and read the journal you left on the porch."

"And?" I prompted when he fell silent, gazing past me.

His gray eyes reconnected with mine. "I spent a day at that shopping plaza in Mount Pleasant."

I cringed for his sake. That place had been bustling every time I'd visited last summer. "How'd that go?"

"The stress of it sent me to bed with a migraine for three days. But I went back and tried again the next week. Same results. But then the third week I decided to just sit somewhere and take it in." He chuckled, shaking his head. "I got caught up watching people for hours."

I grinned, getting a kick out of imagining him people-watching, of all things. "Yeah?"

"Yeah." He angled toward me and said out the side of his mouth, "There are some strange individuals out there."

I laughed. "You don't say."

"After that, it got a little easier."

"That's so brave, Hudson. I'm happy for you." I knew clothes shouldn't matter, but this man sure did know how to wear a suit and wear it well. "Did you wear this suit just for me?"

"I put it on for work this morning but with you in mind." He shrugged out of the jacket and began rolling up the sleeves of his dress shirt.

"Work?"

"I'm working part-time with my grandfather's lawyer in Mount Pleasant. Well, he's been my lawyer since Grandpa passed away. He knows about the indigo, so he doesn't expect me there much. It's just a way to get me off the island some."

"That's good, though. A big step." The breeze picked up, sending smoky wafts from a grill nearby, making my mouth water.

"Yeah. It's been a challenge to acclimate to society." He grimaced. "It's too people-y some days."

"Right?" I laughed, totally understanding that. His recluse lifestyle had rubbed off on me. I appreciated time alone more than ever nowadays. "I'm assuming Erlene told you where to find me."

He met my gaze briefly and nodded.

"I can't believe she shared my whereabouts with a stranger." I huffed, crossing my arms. "I'm going to have to have a talk with her."

"Erlene and I aren't strangers."

I sat up straighter and gaped at him. "How so?"

Hudson combed the side of his short beard with his fingers. "I received an email from a certain true crime–obsessed enthusiast back in the fall, letting me know you were living at the motel."

Eyes wide, my mouth popped open on a gasp. "Vee!"

He fought a smile and lost. "We've become email pen pals." He brushed a curl away from my face and then cupped my cheek. "I heard you became your own hero. I'm proud of you too."

"That sneaky woman." I leaned into his touch. "But you said you know Erlene?"

"Yes. I've been taking her out to lunch once a week for a while now. Had to butter her up." He winked.

I snorted. "I can't believe you and those two did this behind my back."

"Erlene and Vee care deeply about you. They want to see you happy."

We lapsed into silence, and it was as comfortable as I remembered with him. We people-watched awhile until Hudson spoke.

"Tell me something."

I gave it some thought but couldn't come up with any random fact, so I told a truth instead. "My mother has macular degeneration. It's an eye disorder where you still have your peripheral vision, but you can't see right in front of you. That's all I've ever wanted was for my mother to see me. Funny enough, she's always seen me, even when I wasn't right in front of her." I grew quiet for a moment. "I have perfect eyesight and still can't see a dang thing clearly most days. Think I'm gonna start paying attention with my peripheral vision. There's a lot more to see there, so it seems."

Hudson gripped the armrest of my chair and scooted it closer to his and then laced our hands together. "I'm sorry to hear that about your mother."

"Thank you. Me too. It isn't slowing her down, though. She beats me at dominoes all the time."

"So you're spending time with her?"

"Yes. And my sisters too. That was slow to begin with but we've been in a better place recently." Caroline and Aubrey had started texting out of the blue about random things, sisterly things, and it didn't seem forced anymore.

"Good." He lifted our entwined hands and kissed the back of mine.

"Your turn. Tell me something."

Hudson dipped his head before looking my way again. "I'd like to be your first boyfriend."

I bit my lip, feeling suddenly giddy and shy. "I think I'd like that too."

"Good. How do you feel about going on our first date before I drive back to Charleston?"

I laugh. "You're not wasting any time, are you?"

"I've wasted enough of that, so no." He leaned toward me, his gaze locking with mine. "I want to do this properly with you, but I'm not sure how patient I can be."

"What do you mean?"

"I want to be your first boyfriend and more than that, I want to be your last."

Grinning like a fool, I rose from the rocking chair and caught another savory whiff of a grill. "Then we better get on with it. I'm in the mood for barbecue."

We walked outside and paused on the sidewalk. "Where are you parked?"

Hudson pointed down the street. "Just up on the next street." He took my hand and we started that way.

As we rounded the corner, he reached into his pocket and brought out a key fob. A shiny new Ford Bronco beeped and flashed.

I halted in the middle of the sidewalk and groaned. "Please tell me that's not yours."

"Yeah. What's wrong with it?"

"It's a *Ford*."

"Why are you whispering?" Hudson whispered back, amusement softening his features.

"Because." I pointed toward the sky. "My dad might be listening up there in heaven."

Hudson looked at the Bronco, then at me. "Oh . . . he was a Chevy man."

"Through and through. He said the only vehicles that should be allowed on the highway were Chevrolets."

Hudson gave me his stern blank stare. "Well, I'm not getting rid of the Bronco. I just got it and I like it."

"Shh! Don't say that so loud." I ducked behind him and heard him chuckle quietly.

He turned to face me, his brow furrowed. "So . . . all I had to do was post Ford emblem posters instead of No Trespassing signs to keep you off the island?"

"Pretty much." *Not a chance.* We both knew not even that would have deterred me. "I'm driving. Come on." I headed back in the other direction, leading him to the parking garage. As soon as I unlocked the Blazer, Hudson chuckled openly. "You bought a Blazer and I bought a Bronco. We're destined to always butt heads, aren't we?"

"Apparently." I waved a hand in a sweeping motion like a game show hostess presenting the Blazer. "I splurged on a custom paint job. Guess what the name of the color is?"

The small smile on his lips said he knew, but he tilted his head and waited for me to answer.

I smoothed my fingertips over the sleek surface of the dark-blue hood, so dark it nearly looked black. "Indigo."

Humming appreciatively, Hudson closed the gap between us and pressed his lips to mine. But just as quickly as he kissed me, his lips were gone. He grumbled something under his breath before saying, "Sorry. We haven't even gone on our first date and I've already stolen a kiss."

I looped my arms around his neck when he tried to move away.

"This sounds like déjà vu, but I'm repeating it anyway. You didn't steal that kiss. You gave it to me, so knock it off."

Hudson rested his forehead against mine. "I can't help it. I love you and want to show you."

"You're doing a fine job." I placed my lips to his, delivering a slow kiss to show him just how much I loved him too. "I love you," I said against his lips, feeling the smile blooming. Not wanting to miss it, I eased back a bit and took him in. "I love you," I repeated and witnessed the smile light him up. Wow, what a stunning sight.

"I really like hearing you say that," Hudson said quietly.

"And I really missed you. Why'd it take you so long to come around?"

He nuzzled the side of my neck. "You know why. We were both a mess when we parted ways in August. It took a lot of work for me to get to this point."

"I know."

"And it was harder than I thought to find someone to come forward about Kessler. That took longer than I expected."

Flinching at that name, I wiggled some room between us to make Hudson look at me. "What are you talking about?"

"With Vee's help, we tracked down a few other women who weren't part of that settlement with Ewol Entertainment. Two of them finally agreed to come forward and press charges."

"But I thought you said I needed to handle that. That I had to be my own hero."

"You did need to, and Vee told me you were your own hero in that meeting and how that started a chain reaction for other women to file complaints with HR." He brushed my hair out of my face and cupped my cheeks. "Don't be mad. He needed to pay for what he did to you and other women too."

"As of this moment, can we please be done with this? I can't move forward while constantly going back to Whit and all that."

"Yes, ma'am."

A car door slammed and then the roar of an engine echoed through the garage.

After placing a feather-soft kiss to my lips, Hudson helped me into the driver's seat, closed my door, and moved to the passenger's side.

"You know if you'd waited one more day, I would have been back in Charleston and could have saved you a trip here," I told him as soon as he was settled into his seat.

He placed his hand on mine where it rested on the center console. "No. I needed to come to you. Wish it would have been a little farther away for effect."

"Why?"

Hudson's thumb brushed along my wrist, slowly, back and forth. "Grandpa Elson always said action is needed for what matters. Whether it's a cause, an argument, or love. If it matters, you need to show how it matters to you. So I'm here to show you how much you matter to me."

If that wasn't the sweetest thing ever. The sincerity of his declarations left me feeling so light and content that I made no move to crank the Blazer. We sat there in the dim parking garage holding hands while holding on to the new truths we'd shared. I couldn't wait to share more with him.

"I'm glad you had your grandfather. He was a wise man."

"He had a good woman by his side too."

"Yeah?"

"Yeah. Grandpa kept journals too. He's the reason why I kept journaling. I took a page out of the Sonny handbook and read through his journals. My grandparents' relationship reminded me a lot of us. They were always challenging each other but supportive." Hudson laughed quietly, looking out the windshield. "He shared some crazy stories about him and my grandmother. Maybe I'll share them with you someday."

"I'd like that." I tightened my grip on his hand. "We certainly have a few stories of our own to tell, don't we?" I began ticking off some of the highlights. "You chasing me through the woods. You calling the cops on me. Wrestling each other in the middle of the ocean . . ."

"I want more stories with you."

"I want more too. Just no more calling the cops, sir!"

Truly I loved this man enough to put up with cops, but I wouldn't dare tell him that.

EPILOGUE

BEING ABLE TO LAY MY HEAD DOWN AT NIGHT and rest with a peaceful conscience was a gift I spent most of my life ignorant of, but the years since discovering this gift had been bountiful in more ways than peace. Waking up each new day reminded me of this.

"Hey." Hudson's gruff whisper pulled back the edge of sleep.

Without opening my eyes, I snuggled closer to him. "Hmm?"

"It's raining." The warmth of his breath touched the side of my neck.

Still suspended between the haze of sleep and awake, I nestled into his arms and listened. A few moments passed before my ears picked up the hushed tapping. Smiling, I repeated his words. "It's raining."

A soft kiss met my shoulder and then another. "I love listening to the rain with you."

I agreed with a lazy hum. "Remember the first time we listened to the rain together?"

"Yes. The tropical storm." He smoothed my hair and kissed my temple. "And I wanted so badly to hold you like this."

His confession had me wide-awake now. "You did?"

"Yes." His quiet chuckle rumbled through his chest and my back. "I believe you have a magnet inside you specifically for me. I had a hard time not reaching for you all the time that first summer."

My eyes scanned our dark bedroom, our bedroom that was once his childhood room, as I remembered that night on his porch and how I too wanted nothing more than to have Hudson hold me. "Well, you can hold me and listen to the rain to your heart's content now, my husband."

His arms tightened, pulling me firmly against his chest as he whispered in my ear, "Yes, and you know what else we can do to our hearts' content, my wife?"

"What's that?"

"We can make love while listening to the rain." He rolled me over and as the rain formed a barrier around us in a muffled drone, my husband showed me once again the beauty of our marriage bed. It's a divine place for a husband and wife to share, never take. To give and accept. Truly such a form of raw beauty that never left shame in its wake. Another gift I had no clue about until after I married this man five years ago.

"You're sunshine even in the rain," Hudson said softly. Then he whispered a few more sweet sentiments for my ears only.

Nothing Hudson Renfrow did ever had a careless air to it. Always mindful and meticulous. And that also applied to these private moments we shared. I never had to question whether my husband of little words loved me. He showed it every chance he got. And this morning, well before the sun would rise behind the clouds, he loved me and I loved him back.

● ● ●

We eventually untangled ourselves from each other to start the day on Indigo Isle, where we continued to spend our summers growing indigo for dye making.

Standing by the stove, I worked on preparing the only meal I was in charge of, breakfast. Hudson handled lunch and dinner. The man could say what he wanted, but he loved cooking and I happily let him do his thing in the kitchen.

Breakfast was a simple task, so I didn't mind. Well, it was usually simple, but this morning the nuisance standing beside me made it a bit more difficult.

"It's too early for this argument," I mumbled while flipping a pancake.

"But, Mama! I'm a desperate man. I'm beggin'!" The little guy tugged on the hem of my night shorts.

A rumpled Hudson entered the kitchen. Grumbling something under his breath, he knelt before Arliss. "Look here, Son, a man never begs."

Arliss lifted a hand, looking as desperate as he claimed to be. "But—"

"No buts. There are better ways to handle things besides begging." Hudson glanced at me. "If you'll excuse us for a moment." He tipped his chin toward the doorway, a quiet order for Arliss to follow him.

I turned to the stove, took the golden pancakes out of the skillet, and then started on the last batch. The room was heavily scented with maple syrup and sizzling bacon, making it a bit hard for me to swallow.

They came back downstairs several minutes later still in their nightclothes, but with the addition of neckties. Hudson carried Arliss while our son clung to his briefcase. "My client has a proposal, ma'am."

I bit my lip, warring with a grin and a grimace. On one hand, they were both so stinking cute. On the other, I knew I was about to get played. No way would I be able to say no to anything they proposed. But that was okay. I had a counteroffer prepared.

Hudson placed Arliss on his feet.

"We need a dog," Arliss began, matter-of-fact. He pulled a paper from the briefcase and handed it to me.

The drawing was a stick figure standing in a yard with a frown on his face.

"Look on the back," Arliss instructed.

I flipped it over and found another stick figure, but this one wore a giant smile and had what I assumed was a brown dog by his feet.

Returning the drawing to him, I leaned against the counter and crossed my arms. "Why do you *need* a dog?"

Arliss glanced at his father and Hudson gave him a supportive nod. "'Cause I need a playmate. I'm lonely out here."

I gestured toward the window over the sink. "You have a dozen chickens."

Arliss gave me a blank stare, a dead ringer for his daddy's steely gaze when he meant business. For a second, I could see Hudson at age four.

"Okay. I get it." I tapped my fingertip against my bottom lip. "You do need a playmate." As soon as I said this, my little boy's face lit up. "What if, say, in about six months I give you a brother or sister instead of a dog?"

Hudson sucked in a breath at my surprise news, but I remained focused on Arliss, wanting to gauge his reaction.

Arliss twisted his lips to the side, contemplating the suggestion. "Hmm . . . I think I'd rather have a brother."

I smiled. "That part is up to God."

Arliss huffed. "Okay." He turned on his heels and started running out of the kitchen.

"Where are you going?"

"Gotta go have a word with God!" Arliss shouted without slowing down. Moments later, a door slammed shut. Probably the library, where we tended to have important conversations.

I pointed the spatula at my husband. "You marked our child by naming him after that wild little boy in *Old Yeller*."

"At least he doesn't run around naked like the kid in the book."

Scooping out the last pancake, I turned off the stove. "There's that."

Hudson approached me, his silvery-blue eyes shimmering in awe. "You're pregnant."

"I'm pregnant."

Slowly his lips curled into a devastating smile. He rested his hand on the curve of my hip, giving it a gentle squeeze. "Have I ever told you how grateful I am that you trespassed on my property?"

Wrapping my arms around his neck, I gazed up at my husband, grateful for so much. "No. I don't believe you did."

"Well, I am. And I'm glad that every time I ran you off, you came back." He pressed his lips to mine, giving. Always giving.

This night not only marked the end to the drought, but also the end to the long-held secret we'd kept hidden under the magnolias.

"What a voice! If you're looking for your next Southern fiction fix, T. I. Lowe delivers. . . . A must-read."

Julie Cantrell, *New York Times* and *USA Today* bestselling author of *Perennials*

In stores and online now

A NOTE FROM THE AUTHOR

THE OLDER I GET, the more I've come to respect opportunities to learn something new. I often reflect on my high school and college years and just shake my head at the missed opportunities to learn even more. If I could go back . . . Well, don't we all say that? Good thing is I'm still alive and kicking, so now I'm taking each opportunity that comes my way and making the best of it. I'm especially thankful for this writing career because it has presented me with so many opportunities to learn something new each time I begin another story.

Indigo Isle gave me a pass to research indigo—its history and the art of processing it into dye. I even participated in an indigo workshop. It was such a fascinating experience, touching the satin-soft leaves that smelled like fresh garden peas, then steeping them to extract the most beautiful blue pigment. We then learned the art of shibori and how to make intricate folds to produce patterns on our silk scarves. I'll never forget it!

If you're interested in learning more about the art of indigo dye, check out CHI Design Indigo at chidesignindigo.com.

But wait! Are there other topics that interest you? Then I say go for it! Learn and experience all that this life affords.

DISCUSSION QUESTIONS

1. As the novel opens, we find Sonny in a graveyard. What do you think is the symbolism of this scene? Did you find reflections of that throughout the story?

2. For much of the story, Sonny feels adrift without a home because "a home is somewhere you're welcomed." In what ways can you relate to her? How do you define home?

3. Both Hudson and Sonny have erected walls around themselves. Hudson sequesters himself on the Island. Sonny hides behind the wall of her social media facade. Compare and contrast their walls. Do you agree with Sonny that most people have some form of walls that need tearing down? What walls might you be hiding behind?

4. Hudson calls Sonny out on the fakeness of her social media posts. She explains that everyone knows social media is fake. Why do you think everyone is so enthralled by it anyway?

5. The prodigal story in *Indigo Isle* is told with a focus on mother and daughters instead of father and sons. How did

this version change or broaden your perspective on the Prodigal Son story we find in the Bible? Why was it harder for Sonny to accept her mother's compassion than her sisters' resentment?

6. This novel addresses hard issues, specifically sexual harassment and abuse. Did Sonny's story alter your view about any of these issues? How so?

7. Hudson is a closed-off man, one of very few words. Was it challenging for you, as a reader, to connect with his character?

8. Sonny lives with several regrets and wishes she could have a "take two" on life. Which one thing do you think she should consider "reshooting"? Since retakes aren't possible in life, how can we cope with regret?

9. "That's the problem with memories. They can make you a liar, and figuring out who holds the truer version is an absolute mystery." Do you agree or disagree with Sonny's thoughts on memories?

10. Taking indigo leaves and processing them into dye is a fascinating art. It's also fascinating how we see this transformative art in the lives of our main characters. Discuss their transformations. Are there weedy or damaged parts of your life that have been transformed into something beautiful?

11. Speaking of indigo, have you ever made any shibori (tie-dye) projects? If not, are you interested in trying it after reading this book?

ACKNOWLEDGMENTS

WRITING IS CONSIDERED A SOLITARY CAREER. Partly it is, when I'm at the computer typing away, but it's so much more than that. Team Lowe—Bernie, Nathan, and Lydia—you have been there every step of the way. Lydia even contributed to some of the story this time. For example, when I was stumped about what Lyrica's strange tattoo should be, Lydia suggested the toilet brush. Genius! She also helped name some of the characters. I seriously could not pursue this writing dream without my family's support. Thank you. Love you more.

Vicki Baty. I so enjoyed our adventure at the indigo workshop and am thankful for our growing friendship. Beyond that, I cannot thank you and your bookstore, Bookends, enough for being so supportive. When I ask you to tag along to a book event, you never say no. You also gave me valuable feedback on this story. Thank you. I'm looking forward to our ghost town adventure next!

Teresa Moise. Some friends have probably grown weary of me and my fictional world by now—I don't blame them—but not you. You never stopped asking me about the story. I look at you and see the type of woman I want to be. One who knows the importance of listening to what people want to say, has an abundance of grace, and knows how to give advice in a way that makes me really want to hear it. I appreciate the advice and suggestions you gave during the writing process of *Indigo Isle*. Your friendship is one of the most valuable gifts I have.

Christina Coryell. You never stop cheering me on. You're the best critique partner I have been blessed to have. I cannot wait to critique your next story. (Gently nudging you to hurry up.)

Lynn Edge. My prayer warrior. Just as Sonny spoke about Erlene being genuine about praying for her, I know how that feels because of you. I need each and every prayer you offer on my behalf. Thank you, my dear sweet friend.

The Mishoe family. Thanks for going graveyard exploring with me. I know Bobby has a new hobby now!

Trina Cooke and Jennifer Strickland, aka Trouble. It's your fault I'm addicted to decadent food and Wordle. At least one is healthy, thank goodness! Y'all make life interesting and I love ya for it.

Caroline Harper, owner of CHI Design Indigo. I truly enjoyed your indigo workshop and hope to attend another one soon. Thank you for answering all of my questions. Such valuable information to learn hands-on for this story.

Danielle Egan-Miller. You're a brilliant agent. Enough said. But I feel like I should write an entire acknowledgment just for you. I had dreams you've made happen, and I have more dreams that I am confident you will make happen. Again, you're brilliant!

Kathryn Olson. The best part about typing *The End* on a book is that I know it is about to be placed in your talented hands. You make me a better writer. I so appreciate your guidance. You have such an eye for finding parts of the story I wanted to tell but somehow didn't yet. Thank you.

Jan Stob, Karen Watson, and Team Tyndale. I am one blessed gal to be a part of this team. It's such an honor to work with you. Thank you for your enthusiasm and commitment to helping me reach the world with my plain-speaking stories.

My reading friends. Thank you to those who have been here since *Lulu's Café*, way back when, and to my new friends who are part of the circle that has grown considerably since the release of *Under the Magnolias*. Y'all make my job so fun!

My heavenly Father. I'm an oddball who makes mistakes daily, but you love me anyway. I have Ezekiel 34:16 handwritten on a card and hanging over my dresser: *"I will search for my lost ones who strayed away, and I will bring them safely home again."* Thank you for bringing me back each time I get bullheaded and stray away.

INDIGO ISLE RECIPES

Lowcountry Broil

Ingredients:
 13 ounces smoked sausage, sliced into ½-inch pieces
 3 cups small red potatoes, halved
 4 ears fresh corn, broken in half
 1 pound jumbo shrimp, unpeeled
 1 tablespoon olive oil
 Old Bay seasoning and/or Tony Chachere's Creole seasoning
 1 bundle of chives, finely chopped

Directions:
Preheat oven to 450 degrees. Boil potatoes in salted water until fork-tender but still fairly firm. On a sheet pan, spread sausage, potatoes, corn, and shrimp. Drizzle with olive oil and season liberally with Old Bay or Tony Chachere's. Don't be shy! Bake 15 minutes, then broil on high for 5 minutes. Sprinkle with chives and serve with homemade cocktail sauce (see next recipe) and lots of napkins!

Homemade Cocktail Sauce

Mix together:
 1 cup ketchup
 1–2 tablespoons prepared horseradish (I prefer 2 tablespoons, 'cause Mama likes it hot!)
 juice of 1 lemon
 2 dashes Worcestershire sauce

INDIGO ISLE PLAYLIST

"No Man Is an Island" by Tenth Avenue North
"I Got You Babe" by Sonny and Cher
"All I Know So Far" by P!NK
"Machine" by Imagine Dragons
"Prodigal" by Sidewalk Prophets
"What If" by Matthew West
"Starting Over" by Chris Stapleton
"Jericho" by Andrew Ripp
"Run" by OneRepublic
"Say I Won't" by MercyMe
"Old Soul" by Finding Favour
"Graves into Gardens" by Elevation Worship
"Rattle" by Elevation Worship

ABOUT THE AUTHOR

 T. I. Lowe is an ordinary country girl who loves to tell extraordinary stories. She is the author of nearly twenty published novels, including her recent bestselling and critically acclaimed novel *Under the Magnolias* and her debut breakout, *Lulu's Café*. She lives with her husband and family in coastal South Carolina. Find her at tilowe.com or on Facebook (T.I.Lowe), Instagram (tilowe), and Twitter (@TiLowe).

CONNECT WITH T. I. LOWE ONLINE AND SIGN UP FOR HER NEWSLETTER AT

tilowe.com

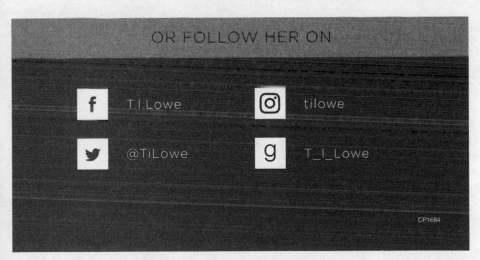

OR FOLLOW HER ON

f T.I.Lowe

⊙ tilowe

𝕏 @TiLowe

g T_I_Lowe

TYNDALE HOUSE PUBLISHERS IS CRAZY4FICTION!

Fiction that entertains and inspires

Get to know us! Become a member of the Crazy4Fiction community. Whether you read our blog, like us on Facebook, follow us on Twitter, or receive our e-newsletter, you're sure to get the latest news on the best in Christian fiction. You might even win something along the way!

JOIN IN THE FUN TODAY.

 crazy4fiction.com

 Crazy4Fiction

 crazy4fiction

 @Crazy4Fiction

By purchasing this book from Tyndale, you have helped us meet the spiritual and physical needs of people all around the world.